RESILIENT LOVE

BANISHED SAGA, BOOK SEVEN

RAMONA FLIGHTNER

Beverly,
The saga continues! I do
hope you enjoy. And thank you for
your enthusiasm for the
saga. Love,
Ramona

GRIZZLY DAMSEL PUBLISHING

Ramona Flightner/Grizzly Damsel Publishing

P.O. Box 1795

Missoula, MT/ 59806

www.ramonaflightner.com

Publisher's Note: This is a work of fiction. Names, characters, places, and incidents are a product of the author's imagination. Locales and public names are sometimes used for atmospheric purposes. Any resemblance to actual people, living or dead, or to businesses, companies, events, institutions, or locales is completely coincidental.

Resilient Love/ Ramona Flightner. -- 1st ed.

ISBN 978-1945609091

Through the years,
from swimming,
To school, to travel,
You've been one of my
Greatest cheerleaders. Thanks
For always believing in
Everything I do,
Champ.

PROLOGUE

"*L*et me see her, dammit," Theodore Goff snapped, grabbing the nearest woman's arm.

She twisted from his grasp, freeing herself and glaring at him as though he were as bad as the men who had jailed the women convalescing upstairs.

"She's my wife." His voice broke on the word *wife*, his eyes roving from one woman to the next, finding none sympathetic to his cause.

"We've already informed you, Mr. Goff. She is well-tended. She simply needs time to rest and recuperate. You will see her soon." She brushed past him with an armful of blankets and headed up the stairs.

He moved to follow her but jerked to a halt as another woman stepped in his way. "Please. I have to see her. To know that she is well." He held out his hands in supplication.

"I'm sorry, sir, but the doctor recommended no visitors, not until at least tomorrow," she said. Her bosom heaved with her deep inhalation as she anticipated further protestations from him.

However, Teddy nodded and walked through the front door, collapsing onto a bench beside it. He rubbed at his temple and the sweat gathering there as he fought nausea. He closed his eyes, unwillingly recalling another sickroom he had been banned from. The whis-

1

pered voices. The nurses scurrying in and out. The pitying glances. He shuddered as he relived hearing the news of his twin brother, Larry's, death. Teddy sat for many moments on the bench, nearly frozen in place.

He stretched as he rose, glancing inside to find the entryway deserted. He eased open the door, shutting it without a sound. He walked on his tiptoes, preventing his heels from sounding on the hardwood floor, and approached the stairs, peering up them. Seeing his way clear, he quickly ascended to the second floor only to halt at the six closed doors that met him. After entering two wrong rooms, he tried a third.

"Zee," he breathed, shutting the door silently behind him. He approached her, ashen and emaciated, curled on her side as she lay on the bed. Sunlight streamed through the window, enhancing the dark circles under her eyes. "My love."

He grasped her hand, earning a startled jerk from her as she noticed his presence. Her eyes widened and then filled with tears. She tried to lift her arm off the bed, but it fell to the mattress after raising it only a few inches. She closed her eyes in defeat.

Kneeling beside her, he leaned over to kiss her eyebrow, her nose, her cheek and finally her lips. "You're alive, my darling." He blinked away tears. "And soon you will be well."

Teddy, she mouthed.

"Can't you speak?" he asked, brushing a hand over her raven hair, its luster lost after her time in jail. He frowned when she shook her head. He felt a slight tugging on his hand and moved it toward her mouth where she kissed his palm.

I love you, she mouthed before closing her eyes and falling asleep again.

"Oh, my Zee. What did they do to you?"

CHAPTER 1

Washington, DC, April 1917

*H*eels clicking on the marble floor echoed off the stone walls as Zylphia McLeod Goff followed her small party through the darkened halls of the Congress of the United States. Shadows filled each corner, creating an eerie sensation as she peered into the dim spaces to see if reporters hid within. They seemed to be ever-present, hoping to earn the latest scoop from the congressmen— or the first-ever congresswoman. Zylphia walked with perfect posture, lest any secreted reporter see her and write further disparaging comments about her. Her steel-gray coat concealed a fashionable purple dress, while a purple hat covered her raven hair pulled back in a tidy bun.

Zylphia forced herself to walk with decorum when she felt like skipping with excitement to see Jeanette Rankin, Montana's Representative, and the only female ever to be elected to congress.

Zylphia grimaced as she recalled a discussion by suffragist leaders at Cameron House about Rankin. Alice Paul, the head of the National Women's Party, had rented Cameron House specifically due to its proximity to the White House as part of her campaign to convince President Wilson to change his view on equal enfranchisement for all.

During those discussions, Zylphia had heard that Carrie Chapman Catt, head of the competing NAWSA, the National American Women Suffrage Association, had commented that she did not believe Rankin to be intellectual enough to be the first congresswoman, especially since she did not have a law degree. Zylphia snickered at Catt's disgust that Rankin was a westerner. "Where else do women have the vote?" Zylphia mumbled to herself. Only eleven states had granted full suffrage to women to date, and all were western states.

Zylphia followed her friends, nodding her agreement when they motioned to be absolutely silent. They slipped into the gallery overlooking the House floor and moved toward the front. Securing seats in the second row, Zylphia sat tall so she could better see what occurred on the floor. She fidgeted with delight when Miss Rankin entered, wearing a blue dress and carrying flowers. All her new congressional colleagues stood and applauded as she made her way to her seat. Zylphia frowned as Miss Rankin seemed uncomfortable with the attention granted her.

Rowena Clement, Zylphia's good friend from Boston, sat next to her and whispered in her ear, "Do you see that man there?" She nodded with her head to a man on the other side of the gallery. "He's from the *Times*. We'll have to see if he writes the correct information when we buy his paper tomorrow." Her brandy-colored eyes shone with distrust.

Zylphia nodded, settled into her chair and waited. "I can't wait to see a woman in congress vote for the first time," Zylphia whispered to Rowena.

"I know. However, I wonder *how* she'll vote." Their voices were low enough that no one overheard them or even realized they were talking with all the loud discussions coming from the House floor. "I know Alice encouraged her to vote no."

"Carrie thinks that will be detrimental to the cause as women need to be seen as strong and capable, like a man," Zylphia murmured, rolling her eyes. "I think Miss Rankin should vote as she believes, as men do."

Rowena's mocking smile met Zylphia's gaze a moment. "If you believe that's how politics works, you are naive. I think beliefs have very little to do with how many of them vote."

Zylphia raised and lowered her eyebrows and shrugged. They turned their attention to the arguments over the prospect of joining the Great War. As the lengthy debates continued, Zylphia saw Rowena nod off. When one of the congressmen wanted to postpone the vote so as not to vote over the Easter weekend, his motion was soundly defeated. There would be a vote tonight, no matter how late.

"Ro," Zylphia whispered, digging her elbow into her friend's side. "I think they're finally going to vote."

"What time is it?" she croaked as she covered her mouth, unable to stifle a yawn. Loose tendrils of auburn hair escaped her once-tidy chignon.

"Just after 3:00 a.m.," Zylphia said. "I hope we have time to collect our bags before returning to Boston for the weekend."

Rowena shrugged, curling into her coat as though going back to sleep. She jumped when Zylphia stomped on a toe. Thankfully she didn't shriek. "I'm awake," she muttered. "Even if we don't have time to collect our bags, we have plenty of clothes still in Boston." She peered around the tall gentleman in front of her. "I think the roll call is about to begin."

They sat through the long alphabetical roll call as the majority said, "Aye," in agreement to a resolution for war. "They thought only ten would dare say no, and there must be over thirty so far, by my count," Zylphia whispered. She sat up straighter as they neared Miss Rankin's name on the alphabetical list.

"Miss Rankin," a man called out in a loud voice.

Zylphia leaned forward as absolute silence fell over the room.

"Miss Rankin," the man repeated, his voice booming.

Zylphia saw Rankin, sitting at her appointed seat, as she shook her head. "No." Although unable to hear the words, Zylphia saw Rankin mouth the word.

5

"Let the record show Miss Rankin voted no," the man said before moving on to the next name.

Zylphia watched Miss Rankin as she sat, composed in her seat.

"That was courageous," Rowena whispered. "No matter what your beliefs, to have your first vote in congress be for something this momentous. I admire her for staying true to what she believes in."

Zylphia grimaced. "I doubt her constituents will think she was courageous. I fear some will question a woman's ability to make difficult decisions."

She and Rowena rose, leaving the gallery to return to their apartment before heading to the train station for their journey to Boston. "More than forty men also voted against the war," Rowena declared.

Zylphia shook her head as she and Rowena shared a long glance after climbing into a cab. "Do you really believe anyone will focus on anything other than how the first woman in congress voted? And find her lacking?"

~

"What are you reading?" Zylphia asked as she entered her husband's office in Boston in the early evening.

Theodore Goff glanced up from the newspaper with a bemused smile. The scar over his right eyebrow was now so faint it was barely discernible. He continued to wear his thick sable hair longer than fashionable to cover the burnt area behind his left ear, although he seemed to forget his injuries at times. He had regained a large portion of his manual dexterity, even missing the tips of his right hand's three middle fingers.

He sat behind his large mahogany desk with two leather chairs before his desk and papers neatly stacked atop it. To the right was a small bow-fronted window with a potted plant, the red velvet curtains pulled to either side of the window facing the darkened front garden. On the wall above his desk hung Zylphia's painting of cherry blossoms. Another of her paintings, of a man and woman so hunched together it was hard to distinguish one from the other, hung from the wall opposite the window within easy view of his seat at his desk, while a fireplace slumbered next to the door.

"You're home," he murmured with a delighted half smile that faded when she remained away from him by the door. He broke his focus on her and tapped one of his injured fingers at an article, lowering his gaze to the paper for a moment. "Boys are rushing to marry, believing that, if they are wed, they will avoid the conscription noose. I wonder when they'll realize that marriage won't prevent their entrance into the armed forces. And that they've bound themselves to women they might otherwise have avoided."

He shook his head. "I always find it fascinating to watch how the fervency for war disappears when one realizes the personal toll it might take. I wonder if those congressmen would have been so eager to enter the war if their sons were destined for the trenches." He rubbed his thumb over his injured fingers and pushed the newspaper away from him.

"I think there are those who believe that an American sacrifice is needed in order to ensure world peace."

"Soon they will know the price of their sacrifice," Teddy said as he fingered the scar on his temple, one of many sustained as a soldier fighting for England during the Great War. "I'm surprised you're here. I thought you were to remain in Washington until tomorrow."

"No, I was up all night at the hearing, and then Rowena and I caught the first train home. We slept the entire way." She sat on a chair across from him. "I was hoping we could have a civil conversation."

He waved at the newspaper and intimated they'd just had one.

She glared at him. "Where we could discuss our differences."

Teddy rose and moved to the front blinds, pulling them closed as cold spring air seeped in and distancing himself from her at the same time. "Zee, I'm thankful you traveled home for Easter. Your parents will be delighted to see you." He pushed aside a potted plant and perched on the windowsill with the curtains forming a cloak around him. "However, nothing's changed."

"How can you say that? I've been away since January. Can you say you haven't missed me?" She watched him with ardent hope.

He looked at her from head to foot, the longing in his entire being evident as he unknowingly canted toward her. "I've missed you, Zee." He paused as his quiet words caused a soft flush in her cheeks. "I haven't missed the constant squabbles." He flinched as she stiffened and glared at him. "Yet I'm not changing my mind."

"How can you be so intransigent? You don't even live in England." Her eyes brightened as she warmed to her argument.

"Enough!" He winced as he shouted louder than he had intended. "I have no desire to rehash this discussion with you. Nothing you have said or done has altered my way of thinking. I refuse to renounce my British citizenship to apply to become an American so that you can regain yours." He glared at her. "I'd hoped by now you would have come to accept how things are."

"How can you be so cavalier about the loss of something so important to me?" She rose. "It's an intrinsic part of who I am. I *am* an American."

"No, you aren't. Not according to your government. You are British, because you married me." Teddy spoke in a calm tone as though soothing a toddler in the midst of a temper tantrum. "It's unfortunate you were unaware of that risk before our wedding. Perhaps you would have made a different choice."

Her nostrils flared at his patronizing tone. "Perhaps I would have." They shared an intense stare before she rose and approached his office door. "I'll remain for Easter, but then I'm uncertain when I'll return again."

Teddy nodded. "I understand. Your cause, unlike other things in your life, is essential to you. I'll endeavor to become a more committed letter-writer." He watched her leave his office, his shoulders stooping once the door slammed behind her.

~

A idan McLeod flung open the front door to find their two visitors, tugging his daughter, Zylphia, into his embrace, while Teddy remained silent. "Oh, Zee, it's wonderful to have you home at last." He pushed her back to gaze into her eyes and smiled. "I can see your time in Washington has been good for you."

"Where is the butler?" Zylphia asked, handing her coat to her father before hugging her mother.

"Oh, he has time off this weekend. It's Easter, and we wanted him to do what he likes." Delia shrugged her shoulders. "Unfortunately, as an orphan, he doesn't have anywhere else to go. He said he'd eat here with the staff and then go to the moving pictures."

Teddy shook Aidan's hand and kissed Delia's cheek. "Hopefully he'll see the latest Charlie Chaplin film. At least his time is his own. You're very kind to your staff."

The two couples moved into the family living room at the back of the house, a gentle fire roaring in the grate. Teddy sat on the settee and watched Zylphia with surprise as she sat next to her mother on a chair near the fire rather than next to him. Her father poured drinks for the men and sat near Teddy in his comfortable chair. "I see you and Zylphia have yet to work out your problems," Aidan murmured as he handed Teddy one of the tumblers of whiskey.

Teddy shook his head, studying Zylphia as she tilted her head closer to her mother's and shared a smile. "I haven't seen her this relaxed in months."

Aidan watched his wife and daughter with pronounced pride. "Having a cause has been essential to her. Feeling she is working toward something worthwhile has also helped her. I imagine it's difficult for you with her so far away."

Teddy shrugged. "I have business to attend to here in Boston, and she needs to be there." He tapped his fingers on the armrest.

Aidan took the hint and dropped the subject. "I can't imagine it's easy on you reading about this country entering the war, especially as you know what is awaiting the soldiers." Aidan watched Teddy closely as he took a sip of his drink.

Teddy's gaze went blank for a moment before he refocused on Aidan. "The newspapers are doing their job by making the war seem heroic and adventurous. The readers have conveniently forgotten the atrocities and horrors they've read about for the past two years. If they even bothered to read those stories." He took a deep sip of his drink. "I want England to win, but, more than anything, I want the killing to end."

Aidan nodded. "Hopefully our entrance into the war will turn the tide." He paused as though waiting for Teddy to say something more. When he remained lost in thought, Aidan turned to include Zylphia and Delia in the conversation. "I thought President Wilson gave a rousing address to congress earlier in the week."

Zylphia rolled her eyes, frowning as she met her father's patient gaze. "He proclaimed that we were to fight for democracy and to fight 'for the right of those who submit to authority to have a voice in their own governments.'"

"I think his reasoning for us to enter this war was well-thought-out and admirable in its idealism." Aidan watched as his daughter flushed with agitation.

"He doesn't promote suffrage for half of the population living in his own country! How can he proclaim that he's a proponent of spreading democracy around the world when he won't even allow it to flourish here? The man's a hypocrite."

Delia stifled a giggle while Aidan smiled. "I see your time in Washington has done little to temper your feelings toward the president." He sobered as he watched his only child. "However, now that we have entered the war, I hope you and your group will change your tactics."

Zylphia's cheeky smile was her answer. "If anything, we'll ratchet up our actions." At her mother's indrawn breath, Zylphia clasped her mother's hand and squeezed it. "It's fine, Mother. We are perfectly safe, and we aren't doing anything illegal."

Aidan grunted his disagreement. "I fear the public's perception of your actions could very well change now that our boys are joining those fighting in the trenches and suffering through gas attacks on the front." His somber gaze sobered Zylphia. "Standing in front of the

White House with banners challenging the president won't be well received now, Zee."

Zylphia raised her chin. "We can't change simply because we might offend a few people. If we did, then we'll never have success, and women will never earn the right to vote." Her gaze became confrontational. "Did you ever consider that, by challenging the way people view the world, we're forcing them to envision a new way to live? A new way to perceive the world around them and those who inhabit it?"

She took a deep breath as she spread her arms wide. "This is 1917. Women should have the same rights as men."

Delia smiled with pride at her daughter. "I fear that belief will be revolutionary for some of our fine citizens even one hundred years from now. Even though you are correct."

"Simply because you want something to be doesn't mean it will come to be," Teddy said. He sighed as Zylphia stiffened as he spoke to her.

"I don't know as it helped your cause to have the only congresswoman in history vote against the war," Aidan said, raising an eyebrow as he met his daughter's indignant glare.

Zylphia faced her father, unable to hide a delighted smile. "I met her. The night before the vote. She was undecided on what she should do. She knew what she believed but was uncertain as to the effect it would have." Zylphia shook her head in disgust. "Fifty voted against the war in the final tally, and the papers focused solely on her."

"What do you expect? She will be scrutinized during her entire term in the House," Delia said. "Besides, this was one of her first votes. Few congressmen, never mind a congresswoman, have had to make such a momentous vote."

"I imagine the outcry would have been greater," her father said, "if Democratic leader Kitchin hadn't also opposed the measure and led to others casting similar votes. I heard, before his vocal opposition, only a handful were considering voting no." Aidan tilted his head as though considering the sway of such a leader. "And then Kitchin speaks, and he has fifty 'no' votes."

"There was never any worry that a sufficient amount of dissents would forestall a Declaration of War," Delia said. "I wonder how things will change now that we are at war."

Zylphia shifted in her chair. "As for Miss Rankin, the newspapers made up lies to sensationalize their readership. She didn't run from the House floor crying. She didn't cry at all." Zylphia sighed with displeasure. "And yet the papers are full of reports of her throwing her head back and sobbing. Or bursting into tears as she whispered, 'No.'"

"One reporter wrote," Teddy said, "that her emotional display was proof of a woman's inability for logical use of reasoning and further demonstrates why women shouldn't be taxed in such a way."

Delia snorted. "Yes, let's keep us all in the kitchen or in the parlor, knitting. It's so much easier for us to know our place that way."

Zylphia snickered at her mother's comment. She sobered after a moment. "I still think it took great courage on her part. I can't imagine having to make such a public declaration."

"And yet you do. Every day you picket," Teddy murmured, earning a startled glance from his wife. "It might not have as profound or as immediate an effect as your Miss Rankin voting in congress, but it has an effect on the conscience of those who make policy."

After an awkward silence, Teddy nodded to his mother-in-law. "I imagine the war will change how we perceive the world, as it always does. We'll see people as threats, whereas the day before they were our friend. We'll give up some of our liberties, in order to feel more secure, even though no threat of attack is on our shores." He ran his thumb back and forth over his wounded fingers. "We'll change ... and not for the better."

"Is that what's happened in England?" Aidan asked.

"Even the suffragettes have given up protesting," Teddy said. "I doubt that would go over well with your Miss Paul."

Zylphia bristled at the thought. "If anything, we're more emboldened."

Teddy raised an eyebrow. "My cousin says that even the Pankhursts believe it's folly to protest against the war movement.

That there are times when the cause must take a backseat to historic events."

"Then I'm afraid they're wrong. Besides, we live in America, and we'll be protected by our laws." Zylphia nodded with confidence.

"I don't want you in jail, Zylphia," Aidan said. "I want your reassurance that you will not do anything foolish that leads to imprisonment."

Zylphia met her father's worried gaze and smiled. "I promise I will be sensible at all times. I have faith in the NWP leaders. They won't want to lose their trusted workers to jail."

Delia hushed Zylphia and clasped her hand. "No more talk of jail or suffering on Easter. We are here to celebrate together." Delia leaned toward Zylphia, their heads bent together once more.

Aidan watched his wife and daughter and murmured to Teddy. "I trust you will ensure Zylphia remains safe even if those in leadership are struck by foolish notions?"

"I will do what I can, Aidan. You know I will." Teddy watched his wife as she spoke with her mother. "However, we both know that she is intrepid enough to elude our care."

Their conversation was interrupted by the arrival of Richard McLeod and his family. Richard entered, shooing his five sons in front of him while his wife, Florence, held back to ensure none of the boys evaded their efforts to corral them in the proper direction. Everyone stood as hugs were exchanged. "We just pushed in. The boys were too excited to wait for anyone to answer the door." Richard gave an apologetic smile to his uncle.

"No need to stand on ceremony. You know you are always welcome here. I couldn't be more delighted that we are together on Easter," Aidan said as he wrapped Richard in a tight hug. He bent down to pick up the youngest of his great-nephews, Calvin. At age seven, he was nearly too big to be picked up.

The other boys swarmed around Delia, speaking over each other in their efforts to tell her about their day and the Easter basket they had found at the front door. She kissed each one on the forehead and listened with rapt attention.

Teddy moved to Zylphia to whisper in her ear, "Seems they've found one of their favorite people."

Zylphia stiffened before forcing a smile. "My mother has always been extremely fond of Richard's children and has been good to them." In an instant, her cold smile to her husband bloomed into genuine joy as Gideon and Thomas grabbed her hands and tugged her to the side of the room, playing marbles with her.

"I'm glad they could visit Zee," Florence murmured to Teddy. "They've missed her." Her sharp gaze roved over Teddy, while he eased the tension from his stance.

He knew he had failed by the concern in her gaze. "She's been quite occupied of late in Washington. I fear she will need to remain there for some time in order to promote her cause." He tapped at his pant leg with his injured hand.

"If that is what you both want, then I can't argue with that decision." At that moment, Aidan called them to dinner, cutting off whatever more she would say.

Teddy exhaled a deep breath in thanksgiving at this conversation being interrupted and followed his extended family into the dining room.

CHAPTER 2

A few weeks later, Rowena walked into the small apartment—more like a suite of rooms in a boarding house—that she shared with Zylphia in DC, and slammed a newspaper onto the table. She tapped an article with her finger as her irate gaze met Zylphia's startled one. "Have you seen this? Have you read the insolence of this man?"

Zylphia shook her head and approached the table. She raised the newspaper, reading aloud the area Rowena pointed at. "*Men, I am convinced that our first duty is to remasculinize America, and that, to this end, we in this state must stand as a wall against the wave of effeminacy which now threatens the semiemasculation of our electorate.*" Zylphia lowered the paper in indignation. "Who is this Henry Wise Wood?"

Rowena shook her head. "We must post a printed response to this nonsense. Such thinking must not be allowed to burgeon. And you can craft your banners today accordingly." She nodded to Zee. "I wanted to ensure you knew of this before I headed to Cameron House to meet with Nina. I hope she'll draw a picture in response to such a horrific quote."

Zylphia smiled. "You'll skewer him with your words either way. I'm rather upset you hid such a talent from me for so long." Zylphia grabbed the newspaper, her hat, gloves and purse. "Come. I'll join you."

She locked their apartment door and walked the short distance to Cameron House with Rowena. "I love spring," she breathed. "Yet it almost feels like summer down here, now that it's the first of May."

They crossed through a square where the trees had already bloomed, and birds flew in and out of the protective canopy, building their nests. Tulip petals carpeted beds as they faded from their previous glory. Zylphia and Rowena left the soothing parklike area and walked along the cobbled streets toward Cameron House.

"Do you picket today?" Rowena asked.

"If they need me to, I will. Otherwise I'll support those who are going and cheer when they return." Zylphia smiled. "I am tired of writing letters and stuffing envelopes, but I'm willing to do whatever is necessary to ensure we are successful."

Rowena looked at her friend with curiosity. "If that's true, why don't you have another showing, like you did a few years ago, with all the proceeds going to the cause?"

Zylphia sighed. "I have considered it, but I haven't painted in months, and, now that we are at war, Sophie has warned me in one of her myriad letters how many will consider an art show a conceited display of ego when our men are in danger abroad. Especially if the proceeds aren't to go to the war effort." She glared at a man she recognized as a reporter. "It's interesting how it was acceptable to have a party when we weren't involved in the war going on across the ocean."

"Everything has changed, Zee. You know that," Rowena said with a squeeze to her friend's arm.

"Have you had any difficulties?"

"People focus on my father. They've mainly forgotten my dead mother." Rowena shrugged. "Unfortunately that's to my benefit at the moment."

"From everything I've learned about her, she was a good woman, Ro," Zylphia murmured. "You shouldn't have to hide the fact you're part German."

"Says the woman who's Irish and English." She sighed as her tone held more bitterness than she intended. "Forgive me. I hate the fact I can be considered suspect or my loyalty to my country questioned, merely because of who my mother was."

"At least you're still a citizen. They haven't taken that away from you yet."

"Yet," they said in unison, before sharing a smile.

"Oh, it's a glorious day, Zee. I wish we didn't have to be cooped up all day long." Rowena shook her head. "And don't even consider advising me that the way to spend time outside is to be on the picket line. You know the one condition my father gave for allowing me to travel here was that I'd never picket."

Zylphia sighed with frustration. "What I'll never understand is why you allow him to dictate what you can and cannot do. You're old enough to be an independent woman with your own money. It makes no sense."

"Unlike you, Zee, I like harmony," Rowena said, before laughing. "Although that may sound strange as I write for the *Suffragist*. But, in my personal life, I do."

Zylphia frowned at her friend. "It's not as though I intentionally bring discord or discontentment into my life."

"Yet it is full of strife at the moment." They shared a long look. "And I wonder what it will take for you to value harmony, to consider compromise." She followed Zylphia into the first floor of Cameron House and was soon too busy writing articles and discussing ideas with Nina Allender and others to think further about Zylphia's problems.

~

"You're quite industrious today," Octavius Hooper said as he perched on the edge of Zylphia's desk. He held himself in such a way as to highlight his attributes. He wore his blond hair cut in the latest fashion and tamed with pomade while his lithe long frame was covered in a perfectly tailored navy-blue suit. His dark blue eyes were filled with mischief as he watched Zylphia and met her disgruntled glare with an affable smile. "Why don't we get some lunch?"

Zylphia shook her head, opening the drawer near his leg, banging into his calf and the side of his shin.

He stood to avoid further injury and moved to sit in the chair across from her.

She pulled out a paper bag and shook it. "I brought my own today."

Massaging his leg, he frowned at her. "I bet that's barely edible. Come out for a real lunch," he coaxed.

"Mr. Hooper, I have work that I must complete today, and I'm uncertain if I'll join the picket this afternoon." She gave him a quelling glare, although a smile flirted on her lips.

He huffed out a sigh. "I'll have to settle for my own company."

Zylphia laughed. "Which we all know is lacking." She sobered. "Thank you for the invitation, but I can't accept today." She signed her name to letters until her fingers cramped, then she stuffed them into envelopes as she spoke with him. "Why do you have so much free time right now? I thought you were a successful lawyer."

"I am. I'm between cases." He shrugged. "I only accept those that interest me and little has lately."

Zylphia smiled. "You're waiting for something truly scandalous before you'll commit yourself."

He grinned and murmured, "Something like that."

His tone provoked a fierce blush from her, and Zylphia cleared her throat as the heat rose to her face. She looked around the bustling room and saw Rowena glance in Zylphia's direction with concern.

"I'm certain Miss Paul could find use of your services." Zylphia frowned when she signed the last letter in this stack and proceeded to sign those in the next stack.

"I find I'd offer my services to only a certain few." He met Zylphia's startled gaze and then laughed. "Come. Let's enjoy the day. I'm certain you are free for a few moments for a walk. You shouldn't be trapped inside all day."

As Zylphia formed a reply, Rowena approached. "Zee, I need your assistance with a project I'm working on. It could take the better part of the afternoon." She sniffed, not looking in Octavius's direction. "Mr. Hooper."

At her chilly welcome, he chuckled. "I believe I've just been dismissed by the termagant. I hope you complete your work today, Mrs. Goff. I'll take a rain check." He sauntered from the room, smiling and calling out greetings to women as he passed them.

"You must discourage him, Zee," Rowena said on a hiss. "He's only interested in you because he sees you as a challenge."

"A little flirtation never harmed anyone," Zylphia whispered. "Besides, it's nice to feel appreciated and attractive in a man's eyes. I haven't felt that way with my own husband in too long." She looked around, ensuring no one was close enough to overhear her whispered conversation with Rowena. Zylphia shook her head, discouraging any further discussion of Mr. Hooper. "Now, what is it that you need help with?"

"Nothing. I wanted him to cease pestering you. He wasn't aiding in the cause and was only harming your reputation." At Zylphia's scoff of laughter, Rowena glared at her. "One day you will regret these actions that you consider harmless."

Zylphia stared at her friend as Rowena strode away. Zylphia leaned back in her desk chair with a huff, her desire to work now absent. She grabbed the paper bag containing her paltry lunch and bolted from the room, desperate for fresh air. As she emerged onto the pavement, she walked toward a nearby park.

After she found a bench underneath a tree, she pulled out an apple and a crumbly meat pasty. She considered her food that sat atop the paper bag on her lap. The sound of a few children laughing and playing in the park lightened her spirit, as did the birds trilling and the soft breeze that provided a respite from the heat. She jumped when someone joined her on the bench.

"I knew you wanted to spend more time with me," Octavius said. He nudged her shoulder, his smile fading as she failed to be pleased at his presence. "Mrs. Goff?"

"Mr. Hooper, you know as well as I do that it is improper for us to have a friendship outside of any working arrangement." She met his gaze, her cheeks tinged with a soft blush. "Although I have enjoyed your company, I cannot continue to associate with you."

"Associate with me? As though I were a disease or a disgrace?" He frowned and moved to sit sideways to better face her. "I'm a respectable lawyer. A successful attorney from a celebrated family. I think you could do much worse than spend time with a man like me."

Zylphia glared at him. "That's the point. I shouldn't be spending time with you, a man. I'm a married woman. I take my vows seriously."

He scoffed. "Even though your husband hasn't seen you in months, except for those few weekends you've traveled to Boston? You always return to Washington as though you've barely survived a tragedy." He grabbed her hand, fighting to keep hold of it when she tugged to loosen his grip. "You deserve happiness. Joy." His blue eyes darkened as he met her gaze. "Passion." He sighed as she jerked her hand free.

"I'd hoped you would understand my desire to remain true to my husband."

"And I'd hoped you'd have the courage to see that your relationship with him has left you miserable." He stroked a hand down her arm, stilling his movement when she flinched. "I know we can bring each other pleasure, Zee."

She stared straight ahead for a few moments. Finally she turned to meet his gaze. "My *friends* call me Zee. You are not a friend, Mr. Hooper. In the future, please only speak with me when we are in Cameron House and when you have reason to discuss a concern about the cause." She rose but came to an abrupt halt when he stood in front of her.

"This isn't over between us, Zee." His blue eyes shone with passionate intent.

"Seeing as nothing is between us and nothing has ever been between us, you couldn't be more incorrect. Good day, Mr. Hooper." She pushed past him, dropping the contents of the paper bag into a trash bin as she marched back to Cameron House.

～

That evening Zylphia sat on her settee, the events of the day flitting through her mind. She jumped as the door to the apartment rattled and then opened. Rowena grunted as she entered, carrying a pitcher of lemonade.

"Why are you so easily startled? Who were you expecting?" Rowena asked. She held up the pitcher in triumph on this muggy evening and smiled as Zylphia walked to their miniscule kitchenette area for two glasses. "I picked up lemons and sugar on my way home so I could prepare us this treat in the communal kitchen. I thought we deserved this on a hot night."

When they sat on the settee, sipping lemonade, Zylphia sighed. "I irrationally feared it was Mr. Hooper. He was at the park today when I went there for lunch." She took a long sip of lemonade. "I've been a fool, and you know how much I hate to admit when I've been wrong."

Rowena smiled for a moment before she became concerned. "What did he do?"

Zylphia's gaze was wild with confusion. "He wants an affair with me. How can that be? I'm a married woman."

Rowena snorted a laugh. "That's exactly why he wants an affair with you. Because you're a married woman with no expectations of marriage." Her brow furrowed as she watched Zylphia. "What did you tell him?"

Zylphia tilted her head in confusion and glared at her friend. "That his offer or thoughts or whatever you want to call them were offensive. That I was married and planned to honor my vows. And that he had no further reason to speak with me unless it related to the cause."

Rowena sighed and settled her head against the back of the settee. "I doubt that will dissuade him. You've just made yourself an even greater prize by thwarting him."

Zylphia rolled her eyes. "I'm not a prize. I'm a woman. I have the right to choose what I want. And I want Teddy!"

"Have you told your husband that lately?" At Zylphia's shake of her head, Rowena rolled her eyes. "You are acting like a child, Zee. I know you don't have much respect for my opinion on these matters as I'm not married, but you must see the damage you are doing. I'm not the only one at Cameron House who has noted Mr. Hooper's marked interest in you."

Zylphia rounded her shoulders in a sulk. "I don't see how that is important."

"What would happen if Teddy were to visit? If he heard the rumors flowing around Cameron House as we find ways to distract ourselves from the next time we have to picket?"

Zylphia paled and quivered subtly. "I simply won't invite Teddy to Cameron House."

Rowena let out a low groan of frustration. "Zee, you're not being sensible. Yes, today in the park you were. You told Mr. Hooper to leave you alone. But you know as well as I do that he won't stop. And you've acted in such a way that no one will believe that you aren't truly interested in him. Your flirting has been embarrassing to witness."

At her friend's fierce glower, Rowena shrugged. "It's true, Zee. You've been acting no better than a silly schoolgirl with her first crush. Although a bit more desperate than a schoolgirl. As though you had something to prove."

Zylphia swiped at her cheeks as her tears poured along them. "Do you know what it is like to tie yourself to a man and then be dreadfully unhappy? To see no way back to happiness?" She let the tears flow now without any intervention. "I love Teddy. At least I think I do. But I don't know that I'll ever be happy with him again."

Rowena patted her friend's hand, concern lighting her eyes. "You say you want Teddy, but everything you do makes it seem as though you don't care to have anything to do with him." She took a deep breath. "Do you regret marrying him?"

"I regret the loss of my citizenship, and that only occurred because we married. I regret that our relationship is one giant argument." She again swiped at her cheeks.

"None of that is new, Zee. Do you regret loving Teddy?"

Zylphia sighed and curled into herself on the settee. "No. Never." She shared a resigned smile with her friend. "Part of the reason I'm so upset with Teddy is that I can't make him bend to my will. But that's also why I admire and respect him. His independent spirit, his belief in what he knows to be true, has always been inspiring to me."

"Until now," Rowena whispered.

Zylphia nodded, wrapping her arms around her waist as she rested her head on the edge of the settee. "I have this irrational love-hate relationship with my husband. How can the very person I love so very much also cause me the worst sort of agony?"

She glanced up at Rowena, not really expecting her to answer. "On one of my recent trips to Boston, I heard Teddy and my father talking. Teddy wondered if I would become more content if I were a mother." She let out a deeply held breath.

"Don't you want children, Zee?" Rowena asked.

"Someday. Not right now. Not when I want to do so much for the cause. If I'm a mother, I won't have the freedoms I have now. And I fear Teddy sees this as a way to control me."

Rowena *tsk*ed her admonishment. "You know Teddy isn't like that. He's upset to see you so discontent."

Zylphia shook her head. "Some days I don't know what I believe anymore. As for my interaction with Mr. Hooper, flirting is freeing and avoids this tangle of emotions." She met Rowena's disapproving stare. "Octavius makes me feel young and alive, Ro. I know that's a weak excuse, but it's the truth." Her closed eyes blinked open at Rowena's snort.

"You just turned thirty. That's far from ancient."

Zylphia waved her hand and sat up, taking a sip of lemonade. "How are you, Ro? I fear I spend so much time thinking about myself that I never ask about you."

Rowena shrugged. "As long as I don't highlight the fact that my mother was German and that I speak German fluently, I'll be fine." At her friend's frown, Rowena fiddled with a coaster on the table. "I was instructed that I had to cease all correspondence with my family last month."

"Oh, Ro." Zylphia clasped Rowena's hand. "Why?"

"My father worries that his business colleagues will remember his

German connection and that his wealth will suffer. He never stops to consider this lack of communication with my grandparents and family there will be difficult for me." She shook her head and let her tears fall. "I've written weekly since my mother died ten years ago."

"Although you haven't visited."

"Of course not. My father couldn't spare me nor did he care for the expense." Rowena's brave smile emerged, tinged with bitterness. "I defied his order and wrote one last letter, explaining my upcoming silence. My only hope is that it reached them."

"I'm sorry, Ro," Zylphia murmured. "I hope you'll hear from them soon."

"The hardest thing about all of it is that I'm now supposed to feel shame for that part of my heritage. As though I no longer should acknowledge that side of my family or where my mother came from."

Zylphia's cynical smile did little to ease her friend's tension. "You know as well as I do that we're supposed to be 'Americans' and that the hyphens after our names that we've used to define ourselves are expected to magically disappear."

"My father doesn't want me in any position where I could end up in trouble with the law. He fears that, if I become embroiled in a legal issue, the fact my mother was from Bavaria could cause many to believe I'm acting on behalf of the Germans."

"I can see his point. But you'd be much better off than the average immigrant." Zylphia stretched out her legs to rise, opening a window to let in the cool night air.

"I hate the stories in the papers talking about the 'vicious Huns.' They're not all cruel. And they forget that the German soldiers are following orders, just as our boys will. It's not their fault."

Zylphia frowned and shook her head. "Never say such things outside our apartment, Ro. Even though you're right, I'd fear for what could happen to you. Too many are infected with war fever."

"It's not a crime to speak the truth. You do it every time you picket."

"I know. And, even though I'm not legally a citizen, I'm at least from an allied nation." She gripped her friend's hand. "It's not right, and it's not fair, but you must be cautious."

Rowena nodded. After a moment's silence, she said, "What about you, Zee? What will you do about Teddy?"

"I'll see him in a few weeks. Hopefully we'll make our peace then."

CHAPTER 3

*T*eddy Goff scribbled at a new business plan, seated in his home office in Boston, stacks of orderly papers on the corners and sides of his large desk. The curtains were pulled back, allowing sunlight to stream in. He looked up at his wife's abrupt entrance. His gaze roved over her, momentarily unable to hide the longing from his gaze. She wore a dark eggplant-colored dress with black lace at the collar and wrists. "Hello, Zee. I wasn't expecting you to return from Washington today." He moved to rise but remained seated when she watched him with an impassive stare. "How are things there?"

"The same as ever. I expect I'll return soon." She stared at the framed cherry tree painting she had given him years ago rather than at him.

"What's the matter, Zee? Not even art is calming you today." He glanced at his papers a moment, the tip of his pen tapping on the top sheet.

"I don't have much use for art anymore."

"You no longer have much use for anything not related to your cause," he muttered, unable to conceal the bitterness in his voice.

"Many admire me for the steadfastness of my commitment," she snapped, before flushing at her rash comment.

His eyes narrowed as he beheld his wife blushing with embarrassment and feigned indignation. "And would your admirers prefer a more intimate relationship with you?" At the flash of guilt in her eyes, he ran a shaking hand through his hair. "I see. I can only hope that you remember what we once were to each other."

"A memory should suffice?" she whispered.

"That's all either of us has had for far too long." He blindly focused again on the papers in front of him, his injured fingers tapping a nervous pattern on the desk. When she slammed her hands to his desk, he bolted backward in his chair, noting the mess she made of the pile of papers on top, smearing her hands and the papers with ink.

"Don't you dare judge me. Not when you are the reason for my discontent." Her breath emerged in a rapid pant, and her cheeks were a bright red from her agitation.

Teddy took a deep, stuttering breath. "I see. Things aren't advancing as you had hoped with your wild antics, and you're looking for a fight to help you feel better. Why must you always turn to me as your punching bag?"

She plucked a handkerchief from her pocket and swiped at her fingers to scrub at the ink stains as she paced in front of his desk. She ignored most of his comments and latched on to what she wanted to discuss. "You read the newspapers with as much interest as I do. You know we're making progress."

Teddy settled into his chair and took a calming breath. "If you call *progress* making a spectacle of yourselves on a daily basis, then I would suppose you are. However, you're losing popular support with your picketing, Zee. Regular citizens do not believe you should act in such a way during a time of war." His voice sounded even more precise and English with his disapproval. "They believe it is unpatriotic to criticize the president and that such actions border on treason."

"Do you know what it is like to picket? To have citizens yell at you, throw things at you and call you un-American because you are speaking your truth?" she demanded as she turned to glare at the maid who entered. Zylphia pointed to a side table near Teddy's desk to deposit the tea tray and then motioned for her to leave. "Do you?"

Teddy watched her, his gaze guarded and passionless, as though he were listening to a discussion of little interest about growing hybrid roses. "Of course I don't. You forbid me from traveling and supporting you. It seems you prefer the company of strangers over that of your husband."

Zylphia's hands fisted atop her hips. "So this is my fault?" She waved one hand around at the space between them.

Teddy rose and moved toward the tea tray. He ran a hand over his slacks and pulled on his waistcoat. He backed away just in time to avoid Zylphia's agitated movement as a half-shriek, half-growl emerged, and she grabbed the tea tray and upended it. The sound of shattering china ricocheted off the wood paneling and through the office.

"Don't ignore me for some godawful tea." She heaved out her breaths as she watched him with tear-glinted eyes. "I'm gone for a month, and this is my reception?"

Teddy fisted his hands as he stepped around the china shards and hot tea pooling on the floor to retreat behind his desk again.

She followed and hit him on his back. "Yes, do what you always do. Retreat. Hide. Evade."

He spun and gripped her raised arm about the wrist, grasping it to the point of bruising. He yanked Zylphia toward him until she stumbled against his chest. His calm facade shattered as effectively as the china, and his irate gaze roved over her face. "What would you have me do? Defy you and accompany you to DC, even against your eloquent request at my absence?" His low, angry voice was more powerful than any shout. "Would you have me jump for joy that you deigned to return to me?" At the tic of his jaw, he clamped his mouth shut until the involuntary tic stilled. "Would you have me beg you to remain here with me?"

He thrust her away, causing her to stumble backward, shards of china splintering under her weight, and he moved to stand on the opposite side of his desk near the window. "Be very careful what you ask for, Zylphia. For, if it is within reason, I will always work to grant it." He met her shattered gaze. "Call me a beast. Call me unfeeling." He raised his chin. "Call me a cold-hearted Englishman." His eyes flashed with pain when her gaze expressed agreement at his self-assessment. "But don't blame the mess our marriage is in on anyone other than yourself."

He took a deep breath and sat. "Now, ... if you will excuse me, I have important matters to attend to." He raised an eyebrow and nodded at the door.

"Teddy," Zylphia whispered as her voice broke.

He watched her implacably, the edge of his pen tapping the papers in front of him. He stared as she sidled from the room, any of her passionate anger long extinguished. When the door *click*ed behind her, he collapsed forward, his head pillowed on his arms.

Later in the afternoon a soft tapping on the door interrupted Teddy. He took a deep breath as he anticipated another altercation with his wife. The maid who'd cleared the floor of the mess had refused to meet his eyes while he had acted as though an accident had occurred. "Yes?" he called out.

He forced a smile as his father-in-law, Aidan McLeod, entered.

Aidan watched Teddy closely before shutting the door behind him. "How are you progressing with our new acquisition plan?"

Teddy laughed. "Good to see you too."

Aidan smiled as he sat in a chair near the windows. "I failed to get the impression you were interested in chatting." He watched as Teddy squirmed in his seat. "I hear Zee has returned."

Teddy stilled and met his father-in-law's gaze. No overt censure was present, although he knew a warning when spoken. "She has. Her time away has not dimmed her animosity toward me."

Aidan nodded. "She is used to receiving what she believes is fair.

However, I think she is unable to see your point of view." Aidan sighed as he relaxed into his chair. "Or the harm her actions are causing."

He shared a sardonic smile with Teddy. "She has always had a singular focus. At times that is a blessing. It has allowed her to become a sought-after painter. It helped her when you were missing during the first part of this horrible war because she concentrated with such fierce intensity on the cause."

"Now it may lead to our ruin," Teddy said. He waved at Aidan as though indicating he should ignore him.

"Is it as bad as that? Do you wish you'd married another?" Aidan asked.

Teddy sighed and leaned forward, his head on his hands. "I know the answer you want to hear is 'Of course not.'" He gripped his head between his palms and pulled at his longish sable hair. "But I can't say that right now. I'm miserable when she's here. I'm in agony when she's away. There is no peace from the torment that is my married life." He closed his eyes in regret. "Forgive me. I shouldn't speak like this with you, her father."

"Of course you should. I consider you my son. You are a part of my family. I can see the damage the discord is provoking between you. I know it isn't all one-sided." Aidan watched him intently. "Have you ever considered granting her what she desires?"

Teddy raised bruised eyes to his father-in-law. "Why can't she understand that what she's asking of me is as hard as what's been taken from her?" he rasped. "I've lived in this country for years, but it's not mine. Not completely. For God's sake, I fought in a war for England." He stroked fingers over his injured hand.

"Have you ever expressed yourself to her as you have to me?" Aidan asked, deep compassion in his eyes.

"Of course. She wasn't receptive. She's never receptive lately." He sat with stooped shoulders. "I fear she finds more camaraderie, more purpose, in her life in Washington than she ever would with a life with me."

Aidan sputtered out a laugh. "I must disagree with you."

Teddy speared her father with an intense glare. "When's the last time she painted? When's the last time she visited her friends here in Boston? She only seems invigorated when talking about Washington or when she's heading out the door to catch her train." He clamped his jaw shut. "No life here would entice her."

Aidan sighed. "If you were to have children …"

"I know you believe that is a viable option, and we've discussed this before. But she'd resent they were American where she wasn't," Teddy snapped. He flushed and ran a hand through his hair. "Forgive me."

"I fear you speak the truth. Zylphia is unable to see anything other than her own disappointments clearly at the moment. My hope is that you continue to reach out to her." Aidan's unwavering gaze held support and an entreaty.

Teddy sighed and nodded. "I have no desire to live my life in a constant state of discord, Aidan. At some point, something will need to change or everything will."

~

"I fail to understand why you must return to Washington so soon," Delia murmured as she watched her daughter pace the back sunroom. Many of the plants had died due to a blight, and she'd yet to replace them. Thus the room appeared more barren and less exotic than in the past.

"There is much work to be done, and I want to continue to be one of the Silent Sentinels." Zylphia roamed the room, only stopping when her mother gripped her hand and pulled her to sit beside her on the wicker settee.

"I know that's hogwash." She speared her daughter with a look, daring her to contradict her. "You've written, most eloquently, of how much you hate being a Sentinel. Of the heat, the rain, the cold, the abuse."

"I should never have written such words during a moment of weakness." Zylphia flushed at having her own words repeated to her.

"There's no shame in not enjoying every task put to us, dearest. You should take pride in the fact you act as a Sentinel even though it's not your favorite activity." Delia tapped her daughter's hand. "And I know you would relish leading by example.

"However, you have to realize that running from Teddy won't help your relationship. You must face what is happening between you and find a way out of this stalemate." She frowned as her daughter's expression became more mutinous.

"He's the one who needs to see my side. He doesn't understand how I feel!" She freed her arm from her mother's gentle grasp and wrapped it around her stomach.

Delia sighed, earning a glare from her daughter. She raised an amused eyebrow as she met Zylphia's disgruntled glare. "I think you are being as narrow-minded as Teddy. Probably more so."

Zylphia's anger faded as she looked at her mother. "Why should I lose my citizenship simply because I fell in love with a man from England and married him? It's unfair!"

Delia grabbed Zylphia by the elbows, preventing her from rising. "Yes, it's patently unfair. You know it. All women know it. But making your husband suffer for it is just as cruel. It's not his fault that he wants to remain a citizen of Britain. Have you ever, even once, truly listened to him about how he feels?"

Zylphia battled tears as she met her mother's irate gaze. "How can you be angry at me when an injustice has been done to me?"

"You're acting like a child. This is your life. Your marriage. Your future. Quit acting as though, if you throw a big-enough tantrum, you'll get your way. You know that's not true. Nor is it fair to you or to Teddy." Delia paused a moment as she emphasized her son-in-law's name. "Quit trying to bully your husband into your way of thinking." She shook her head as she beheld her daughter with frank disappointment. "I thought you more than this, Zee."

Zylphia began to cry. "Don't you understand? I'll never vote here. After all I've done and everything I've worked for, I'll never vote!"

Delia gripped her daughter's chin. "You can't vote now. But you can ruin your marriage now. You'd best decide what you want before it's too late."

~

Sophronia Chickering raised an eyebrow as her rear sitting room door flew open to an unheralded guest. She waved away her beleaguered butler and motioned for Zylphia to sit across from her. "It's about time you decided to visit me," she said in her scratchy voice. She ran one hand over her steel-gray at-home dress, while gripping her cane with the other and frowned as she watched Zylphia.

"I leave in a few hours and wanted to see you before I depart." Zylphia fidgeted with her dangling pearl earring, jolting when Sophie *thunk*ed her cane on the floor.

Sophie *harrumph*ed when Zylphia finally raised her eyes and met her friend and mentor's gaze. "I receive frequent updates from Alice as I am a regular donor. I fear the reality of her picketing is much worse than she has described by the looks of you."

Zylphia flushed and shook her head. "I wish you would journey to Washington to see firsthand all that we are accomplishing. It's invigorating."

"At my age, I have no desire for such travels. They are best left to the young."

Zylphia smiled. "You're not that old, Sophie."

Sophie sniffed but could not hide she was pleased at Zylphia's comment. "I'm near eighty. I constantly harass Alice that she must succeed with greater haste as I'd like to vote before I die." She waved away Zylphia's protestations about her future demise and studied Zylphia to the point she squirmed on the settee. "Therefore, it is your life in Boston that causes you to appear deflated and defeated."

"Teddy and I still have differing opinions." Zylphia looked away at a painting she'd gifted Sophie the previous year of the cliffs near the house Sophie had rented in Newport, Rhode Island. Zylphia's gaze glazed over as though imagining a long distant scene on the Cliff Walk in Newport where she first spoke with Teddy.

Sophie pointed at that painting. "I'd hope you'd recall those memories to help you rediscover why you became enamored of your husband. You've managed to convince yourself he's unworthy of you in some way." Sophie speared Zylphia with a severe glare from her piercing aquamarine-blue eyes. "Which is patently false."

"All we seem to do is fight," she whispered. "I returned home for a visit with the aim of making peace. Instead I fell into our most recent pattern with my goal of causing pain."

Sophie *tsk*ed. "That's not like you, Zee. You've always been passionate and firm in your sense of right and wrong. But you've also been able to listen to another's opinion, even if you didn't like it. I don't understand why you react before there's anything to fault him for."

"There's plenty to fault him for, and you know it!" Zylphia hissed. "He barely tolerates my involvement in the cause. He writes curt letters. He ..." At Sophie's chuckle, she glared at her.

"You can't come up with more than two rather weak excuses for your anger, besides the one you didn't bother to name." Sophie settled into her chair, setting aside her cane. "You have a fine revolutionary spirit, Zee. But not everything or everyone can be converted to your way of thinking by force. Or by sheer will." She gripped Zylphia's clenched hand. "Sometimes you have to accept that those closest to us will never agree with ideals that are precious to us. It doesn't mean that we, or they, are lacking. Or less deserving of love."

Zylphia sniffled. "If your husband hadn't supported you, how would you feel?"

Sophie squinted as though imagining what Zylphia asked. "I don't know. I am a much different woman now than the woman who married many years ago. I imagine I would have felt betrayed at first. Then emboldened to prove him wrong. I hope I'd have loved him enough to search for common ground between us." She smiled at Zylphia. "And I know I would have continued to sway him to my way of thinking."

She sobered as Zylphia sat in a dazed stupor. "However, I like to think I wouldn't have risked my marriage with constant bickering. Or with meaningless flirtations that could be misconstrued."

Zylphia flinched. "Rowena wrote you?" She pinched the bridge of her nose in resignation. "I never meant for anything more than flirtation. He imagined more to it than there was."

"As most men do, darling. I'm sure your mother taught you that."

"And failed," Zylphia said with a humorless chuckle. "I've been miserable. He helped me feel desirable after all the fighting."

Sophie shook her head in disappointment. "Be very careful, darling Zee. For your momentary need to feel attractive could lead you to further estrangement from your husband. No man is above jealousy when even his own wife admits to a flirtation." She sighed. "I'd advise you to remember how you felt when you found his letters from the nurse."

Zylphia bristled. "That is an entirely different matter." When Sophie merely raised an eyebrow at her and waited, Zylphia deflated, her anger seeping out as quickly as it had erupted. "I hadn't thought of it like that."

"I suspected as much. However, now that you're facing a great challenge, rather than turning to the one person you claim to love above all others, you are forsaking that love and acting like a brainless half-wit."

"It's not a claim," Zylphia ground out. She ran a hand over her face. "I don't know how to show him."

"Zee, dearest, you fear looking weak by admitting you need Teddy. By admitting you want him more than you want your citizenship back. All this posturing and prancing about has earned you little except exasperation and heartache. You've backed yourself into a corner, and you must act like the adult you are and accept that you've been a fool."

∾

The tea shop bustled with midafternoon business as Zylphia sat, sipping lemonade on a stifling hot day in late May, having just returned to Washington, DC. She absently massaged her wrist as she perused a newspaper, frowning as she read about the plans for a selective service and the government's use of semantics rather than simply calling it a draft.

"What bothers you, Mrs. Goff?"

Her head jerked up, and she glared at Octavius Hooper as he sat in the unoccupied chair across from her. His tan linen suit was well-suited to the weather, and he appeared a man of leisure.

"I never invited you to join me." She motioned for him to skedaddle, but he laughed.

He smiled at the waitress, ordering sweet iced tea, before focusing on Zylphia again. "You can't imagine that I believe for one moment you aren't interested in me." He smiled indulgently at her. "I enjoyed our conversations at Cameron House and was disappointed when you said they must cease."

"Whether in Cameron House or out, there is no reason for us to speak. Unless you have pressing business for the cause?" She raised an eyebrow as her hands played with the edge of the newspaper.

His eyes focused on her hands, and he frowned. "What happened to your wrist?"

She glowered at him. "It's none of your concern," she sputtered as he traced the light bruising in the shape of fingers along her wrist.

"Did your husband do this?" Octavius asked, but Zylphia remained silent. "You deserve better than that."

"And you have no idea what you are referring to." Zylphia moved her arms so that her hands were under the table where he could no longer touch her. "Why are you here?"

"I saw you sitting here, looking lonely, and wanted to speak with you. I've missed you." When she glared at him, he sighed. "I'd hoped you missed me."

"Mr. Hooper, I have no idea why you believed your presence would aid me if I were lonely." She stared at him impassively. "We are not friends. We are barely acquaintances. I would prefer it if you would cease pestering me."

He took a long sip of his tea and studied her. "There may well come a day when you need my friendship, Mrs. Goff."

"Perhaps. However, you would do well to remember that I am a respectable married woman, and I have no interest in any dalliance." Her blue eyes blazed with annoyance as she glared at him.

"Is that true? Even though your husband leaves marks on you?" His chin jerked down as though to indicate her wrist.

"You barely know me. You have no idea that I have a horrific temper and that I can provoke a saint to near madness. My husband did not hurt me. He prevented me from hurting him." She flushed at her words.

He chuckled and leaned back in his chair. "Ah, you become more intriguing the more I learn about you. I hate that we can't even be friends."

She sighed in frustration, shaking her head. "There is no such thing as friendship between a married woman and a single man. It's unseemly, and I will not shame myself nor cause my husband the worry if he were to hear vicious gossip."

"Which this town seems to thrive on," Octavius murmured. He took the last sip of his iced tea and rose. "In that case, I wish you a good day, Mrs. Goff." He strode from the room, slipping outside.

Zylphia watched as Rowena passed him, her head inching higher with indignation at the sight of him.

Rowena burst into the tea parlor and took the seat just vacated by Octavius. "Was that man here bothering you again?" At Zylphia's resigned shrug, Rowena frowned. "I wish you could do something more, other than tell him you don't want him to speak with you."

"It's my own fault, Ro. I encouraged him by flirting with him. The only one who could set him straight is Teddy. And I don't want him to hear of my foolishness." She flushed as she ducked her head.

Rowena studied her and ordered a lemonade from the waitress. When they were alone again, she leaned forward and whispered, "I have the sense things did not go as you'd hoped in Boston?"

Zylphia shrugged again. "He was guarded when I entered his office, and that made me angry, and then we started fighting." Zylphia folded and unfolded a napkin. "I can't seem to have a conversation with him anymore."

Rowena smiled absently at the waitress as her lemonade was delivered and took a sip. "How sad. You two always seemed to communicate, even when you weren't speaking. I could sense it across a ballroom."

"Why did you write Sophie about Mr. Hooper?"

Rowena flinched. "She wrote me, concerned about you. She'd seen Teddy and was worried by how withdrawn he had become."

Zylphia rubbed at her wrist. "I shouldn't have left Boston before speaking with Teddy again." She sighed. "Sophie helped me see what a fool I've been, but I didn't have the courage to face him after I had acted so horribly."

"You will have to at some point, Zee."

Zylphia shook her head as though to clear it of melancholy thoughts. "What do we have planned for today?"

Rowena opened and closed her mouth as though biting back her words of protest at the abrupt change in conversation. "More picketing. More letter-writing. More of the same." She swiped at moisture on the outside of her drinking glass. "Your leadership among the picketers has been sorely missed. Morale has dropped since you've been away."

Zylphia nodded. "Well, at least I know I'm good at something."

Rowena leaned forward again and whispered, "I fear I may have to curtail my activities soon. I wouldn't want to bring any unwanted notoriety to the *Suffragist* or the cause."

Zylphia laughed. "You bring notoriety? You live a life more boring than that of a church mouse."

"If it's found out that one of the principle writers is half-German, it could be portrayed in a very negative light. You know what the CPI would do with that." She shared a long look with Zylphia as they thought about the Commission for Public Information and their publicity machine.

"Well, I say we should worry about that when it becomes a problem. For now, I hope you continue to write articles that motivate more and more to join the cause."

Rowena's worried gaze met Zylphia's. "You know as well as I do that something drastic has to happen to sway the president and thus congress."

Zylphia nodded and did not bother with a false smile of bravado. "I know. I only hope I'm ready for it when that something occurs."

CHAPTER 4

Butte, Montana, June 8, 1917

*P*atrick Sullivan woke with a start at an insistent banging on his front door. He grabbed his pants from the floor, stumbling down the hallway as he tugged them on. The door flew open as he stifled a curse, his head tangled in his shirt. "What?" he barked, holding up a hand to his wife, Fiona, to keep her behind him.

The messenger had recovered some of his breath from his mad dash across town while waiting for Patrick to dress and answer the door. "You're needed at the Granite Mountain Mine. Fire."

Patrick froze, his hand fisting around his longish locks of chestnut-brown hair shot with gray rather than combing them into place. "How many?"

The man shook his head. "Don't know, sir. But it looks to be a big one."

Patrick nodded. "I'll be on my way within five minutes." The man took off, leaping from the front porch to summon others as Patrick spun to face his wife. "I have to go, Fee. You know I do."

"Of course," she whispered. "I will await word here with Rose."

He took a step toward her before pausing when she instinctively matched his pace backward. "I must go. If there is any way to save the men, I have to help. No man should die in such an inferno."

Fiona bit her quivering lip, blocking the hallway. "Remember that, Patrick. *No man*, including *you*, should suffer such a fate." She met his startled gaze before stepping aside and allowing him to rush to his room to find heavy boots.

When he returned to the hallway, she handed him a light jacket and a glass bottle of water. "'Tis foolish as I'm sure they'll have water for you." She shook her head, chagrined as he stared between her and the bottle a moment.

"Yes, they will, but it won't be from you." His fingers caressed hers a moment as he accepted the bottle before he ran from the house, leaving Fiona on the porch, watching him until he disappeared down the street.

~

When he arrived at the Granite Mountain Mine yard, smoke billowed from the mouth of the shaft. Flames burst over the collar of the mine, heating the immediate area and singeing anyone who ventured too close to the edge. Patrick nodded to the foreman, who stood to one side of the shaft, his eyes filled with a barely discernible panic. "Why aren't we dousing the fire?"

The foreman shook Patrick's hand as Patrick was a low-level mining executive as well as a trained helmet man. "The firemen don't want to cause a downdraft by pouring water onto the burning cable and timbers. They fear the smoke underground could worsen if we take such action, harming even more men."

Patrick scratched at his head. "How are you planning to reverse the draft to create an updraft to get as much smoke from the mine as possible?"

"I've ordered the reversal of the fan's flow at the Spec Mine, hoping the downdraft there will cause an updraft at the Granite, expelling the smoke. They've done the same at the Rainbow and Gem Mines."

"You're doing fine work here, and I hope you're successful. I need to join the helmet men." Patrick slapped the foreman on his shoulder and moved past exam areas set up for doctors, then a row of ambulances and finally the undertakers. The hint of pink on the horizon heralded dawn's impending arrival and the reminder that the men trapped below had been there for over six hours.

Next to one of the mine buildings, the man in charge of Anaconda's Safety Crew gathered the helmet men around him to organize a rescue of the men trapped below. They were fondly called "helmet men" due to the large helmets they wore that carried the oxygen they needed while searching for survivors.

Although this was a North Butte Mining Company fire, all mining companies would work together to save the men clinging to life in the mine shafts below their feet. Most rescuers were miners, although a few were from the community. Patrick was one of a handful of nonminers and nonfiremen in the group. He had earned his place among the gathered men during a grueling training course the previous summer where just such a scenario had been acted out.

Patrick approached the group and nodded as he listened to the plans for trained helmet men to venture into the shafts. "We will use the shafts of adjacent mines, and we will work methodically in groups. You will always be in at least a pair. No one should work alone."

The Anaconda man's voice rose to a bellow. "I want no heroics. We've already lost good men tonight in rescue efforts. Men like Con O'Neill." At the mention of his name, a murmur moved through the crowd as he was the well-respected foreman at the Anaconda-run Bell and Diamond Mines.

The Anaconda man held up the English-made Fluess breathing apparatus with its hoses, helmet and bags. "Remember, these are the best devices we have for now, but they aren't perfect. They leak, and they are delicate. Don't carry anyone. Don't hit your head on the mineshaft. Don't rub your belly on the ground." The Anaconda man's severe gaze pierced them all as he glanced from man to man. "Remember your training and walk slowly. You'll faint if you go too fast. You'll be hot and miserable down in the mine, but think of the men struggling to survive without oxygen." He paused as he looked at the group huddled around him. "If you think your mask is leaking, come up, and we will fix it."

He broke the men into small groups and finally got to Patrick's group. "When you get between the 1800 and 2200 levels, you need to find the drifts that will take you toward the Granite. The Granite shaft has been ruined. We can still use the Spec, Rainbow or Gem cages if you get that far. Be methodical and work from the cage where you are let out. Remember, we are looking for survivors. We'll have the task of recovering the deceased later."

After a few moments where the men grumbled, he bellowed to gain their attention. "When you get to the different drift levels, you'll have to go up and down ladders to find the men who were working on drifts where the cage didn't stop." He frowned fiercely as he looked at the men. "Keep a mental map in your mind how to get back to the cage. It's your only way out." A rough map had been drawn, showing the honeycomb nature of the drifts and mine shafts below them. "Some drifts have been sealed shut, and you'll have to find your own way. Most of you are miners." The man's gaze rested on Patrick and a few others. "For those of you who aren't but are trained to use the new equipment, your partner needs to be a miner."

After a pause the gathered men muttered again. The foreman barked out, "Remember, the mine air is poisoned with smoke from the fire. Don't become another casualty."

Patrick nodded and was paired up with a stocky man with a faint brogue. "Call me Mac," the man muttered. "Seems they want us as the second shift."

He settled the small oxygen tank on his back and pulled the little bag over his front that aided in clearing the carbon dioxide. He carried the forty-pound helmet, waiting until the last moment to put it on. He flicked on and off his Ever Ready flashlight, frowning at the anemic illumination it provided. "How are we supposed to see with this?"

Mac shrugged and made his way to the cage as they were

motioned forward. "I'll lead but don't lose sight of me." They pulled on their helmets, adjusting them to ensure they were on tight, ending all conversation.

The cage lurched into motion, and they sped downward into the bowels of the mine. As they were lowered, the temperature changed from cool to warm to hot. One pair of men got off at the 1800 level; another twosome would get off at the 2600 level. Patrick and Mac got off at the 2200 level—2200 feet underground. A thick greenish-yellow cloud filled the air, and Patrick instinctively checked his mask to ensure it was on correctly. He saw Mac do the same before stepping from the cage. A few feet from the cage, they found three men gasping for air but without the strength to reach the cage. Mac and Patrick heaved them up and returned to the cage area, but it was empty, delivering other rescuers to a lower level. Mac ran to the signal booth next to the cage, pushing buttons that acted like a telegram to the surface of the mine as he signaled SOS.

After a moment, the cage returned, and Patrick and Mac loaded the injured men inside. Mac pulled Patrick off the cage, secured the door and signaled again. The cage zoomed upward as Patrick said a silent prayer for the men they had found.

They turned to the right and walked down a drift until they reached a ladder. Mac pointed up or down, and Patrick shook his head. They decided to head up and climbed the ladder. Once on the new level, darkness with an eerie tinge of green enveloped them, and they stumbled as their lights failed to guide them. They turned right as the drift should have had an opening to the Speculator Mine and the cage there. Patrick tripped and nearly fell into a wall. He glanced down, breathing heavily as he fought panic at harming his apparatus.

He slapped Mac on the back, and they paused. They combined their two lights, finding the previous opening leading to the Speculator Mine had been closed off by a wall of concrete, and the bodies of four men lay in front of it, dying while clawing at it, their eyes gaped open in a death stare. "Dammit," Patrick muttered as he bent down to pat the shoulders of a few of the men. He rose, intent on finding survivors.

Mac and Patrick turned the other way, continuing down the drift when the air changed. It was a lighter gray, as though in a misty fog. Patrick saw Mac step to the side, failing to move as quickly as his partner and fell forward over the carcass of a dead mule. He grunted, grabbing at his chest to ensure his front pouch was in place and undamaged. He pulled himself forward, crawling over the mule and accepting Mac's hand as he rose. They continued down the drift until Patrick walked into Mac, who had paused. After a moment, he turned right into a small alcove and bent forward. Patrick followed, and they discovered a man clinging to life.

They hauled the miner between them, dragging him down the drift, retracing their steps to the ladder. Once there, Patrick slung him onto his back and carried him down the steps. After they reached the 2200 level again, they half-carried, half-dragged the man to the cage.

"I have to go up," Patrick yelled at Mac, motioning up with his hand. "I think I damaged my apparatus on the ladder."

Mac nodded, rushing to signal for the cage. When it arrived, they joined the man aboard the cage and sped toward the top.

At their arrival aboveground, they pushed the miner out for immediate care. Hands grabbed them and pulled them free, allowing the cage to whir into motion again. Patrick collapsed on the ground, gasping for air as he ripped off his helmet. Mac shook his head, sending droplets of sweat in every direction, and Patrick did the same.

"Godawful job," Mac muttered.

"Don't know why I signed up for it," Patrick agreed around a cough. "I think my helmet leaked there at the end. It's like I could taste the gas." He spat on the ground before his cough deepened.

"Let us know when you boys are ready to go down again," the man from Anaconda called out. "We'll get you new equipment first."

Patrick glanced at Mac and nodded. "Soon. We need to find the men soon."

They rose to speak with the foreman and the man ensuring the equipment was in working order. Time was running out for the men trapped below.

~

The following day, Patrick leaned against a wall near the mouth of the Speculator, his gaze distant as he shivered in a gentle breeze. The mine's large metal headframe heaved and groaned as the cage whirred up and down, although no new survivors had been recovered in the past few hours. Patrick ran a hand over his blackened day-old clothes before pushing back strands of sweat-soaked hair slowly drying after his most recent trip underground. Squinting at the midday sun, he raised a hand to block out the bright light.

"No use hiding from what we're doing," Mac said as he plopped down next to Patrick with a sandwich and a bottle of pop. He took a long sip of the drink before gobbling down half the sandwich. "We need strength to help any survivors. A pile of food is over there. I'd get some before we go down again."

Patrick rubbed at his reddened eyes and sighed. "I can't imagine we'll find any more survivors. We haven't found anyone since yesterday."

Mac shrugged. "You never know. They might be hiding down there, hoping we find 'em. Either way, our job's far from over. Soon we'll switch from survivor recovery to ..." He sighed and shrugged again. "The families will want to bury their dead."

Patrick squinted at him. "How many do they think are still down there?"

"Over one hundred. And I doubt many are alive." Mac followed Patrick's gaze to the steam belching from the Granite Mountain Mine shaft as thousands of gallons of water were poured down it. "Seems they decided to put out that fire."

Patrick tilted his head. "When I spoke with the foreman, they didn't think they'd get much more smoke out with the fans. I wonder how long this one will take to extinguish."

Mac shrugged. "Don't see that that matters. The damage is done. The men are dead." He flicked a glance at his partner. "You're lookin' no better than the men we've found."

"I didn't make it home last night. I had to go to the office, meet

47

with state inspectors and discuss financial concerns." His yawn cracked his jaw. "I slept at my desk."

"Well, I hope you'll make it home tonight. We need rest if we're to keep doin' this job." He rose. "We're to go back down in twenty minutes."

Patrick nodded and stood, heading to the food table. He ignored the nearby storage room—called the dry but which had been set up as an impromptu morgue—and the horde of family members who sought information as they looked there for their loved ones. They could access the storage area through a special entrance guarded by the Montana National Guard but had no means of entrance to the mine shaft or the recovery effort area.

He quickly ate two sandwiches, drank a glass of water and then penned a short note to Fiona before rejoining Mac as they prepared to venture underground again.

~

The next day Fiona Sullivan rapped on Lucas and Genevieve Russell's door, Rose wriggling in her arms. The Russells were Patrick's cousins and her only family in town. She kissed her daughter's forehead to soothe her. When the door opened, Fiona bit back tears as she forced a smile at Genevieve. "We thought to see how our cousins are."

Genevieve smiled and motioned for them to enter before calling for her husband, causing the distant piano music to cease. Lucas Russell strode into his front living room in finely tailored clothes with a distracted air as though thinking through a puzzle. His distant gaze cleared as he focused on Fiona and Rose.

"How are you, Fiona? And how is my cousin?" Lucas asked as he tickled Rose and took her from Fiona, setting down the child to roam about the living space. Genevieve pulled out a box of toys, and Lucas smiled as he praised her cleverness. He sat on the floor with Rose, playing with the dolls kept in the small box for her visits.

"Patrick left two nights ago. To help with the Granite Mountain Mine disaster." Her voice broke on the word *disaster*.

Lucas watched her a moment. "I see." He glanced to Genevieve, who nodded before joining him on the floor with Rose, who they considered their niece. "Vivie and Rose will stay here while we journey to determine if we can discover any news." He kissed Genevieve on the head before rising. He pulled Fiona into a quick hug, ignoring her stiffening. "He'll be all right. You'll see."

He shrugged into a jacket and pulled on a hat. "Vivie, we'll be home as soon as possible." When she smiled at him, he winked at her before ushering Fiona outside. They managed to leave before Rose noticed her mother's absence.

"How did you know I needed to go to the mine?" Fiona asked as she matched his quick strides.

He chuckled, slowing down as he noticed her effort to keep apace. "If I hadn't seen my Vivie in over two days, I'd be frantic. You're too controlled, Fee. At some point you'll have to let out a bit of that emotion."

She sniffed and blinked away a tear. "I hardly believe a bout of histrionics would benefit anyone at this point."

Lucas laughed. "You might feel better. And Patrick would know you care more about him than the measly paycheck he brings home each week." He pinned her with a severe look. "And he would know better than to volunteer for such dangerous work simply for money."

Fiona clamped her jaw shut, her grip on his arm tightening as she stared straight ahead.

"You can continue to freeze *me* out when you hear advice you don't like. But you should consider what you're doing to your husband. Are you more concerned you'd be left with a child and no support or are you worried about Patrick?" Lucas yowled as her handbag smacked him on his head.

"How dare you imply I only care about Patrick for money." She vibrated with fury as she now walked beside him but refrained from taking his arm.

"How would any of us in the family think any differently after two years of marriage where you treat him with such careful indifference?" Lucas handed her into a streetcar and kept silent as she found a seat while he stood. Crowds gathered around a newspaper office to read the latest headlines, while the post office flag flew at half-mast. He shook his head in dismay as he realized many walking on the street seemed to be tiptoeing, as though they feared trodding too heavily could lead to a cave-in on their missing loved ones trapped in the mines below them.

When they disembarked near the mine, they melted into a crowd of people searching for relatives. Lucas grabbed Fiona's arm and propelled her toward the gate. "This is Fiona Sullivan, and her husband, Patrick Sullivan, works for the North Butte Mining Company. He's also searching for men. We've had no word for days."

The National Guard's man pointed to a building in the distance. "Check the dry. He might be there. If not, check the list of men at hospital on the wall posted outside. If not there, I'd check the hospitals and then the funeral homes."

Lucas nodded, tugging a recalcitrant Fiona beside him. "What's the matter?"

Her cognac-colored eyes were wide, and her lips trembled. "I ... I can't go to the dry. Not there," she breathed.

He paused, buffering them from those walking past as he leaned over her, his large hands on her quaking shoulders. "You want news of Patrick. We must seek out what we can."

"The dry is where they bring the dead." Her eyes filled with tears. "I ... He can't be dead."

"Oh, God," Lucas whispered, tugging her close for a moment as she fought a sob. "I'll go through the dry while you review the list outside. I refuse to believe my cousin is dead."

She stuttered out her agreement, her control shattered. "Thank you, Lucas."

He left her reviewing the list and made his way inside the shedlike room. The building was called "the dry" because the miners kept their day clothes—or dry clothes—here for when they returned after their work in the mines, rather than having to venture forth into inclement weather in clothes soaked from twelve hours of exertion working to extract copper.

Rather than using the benches for men to sit on and change, rows of deceased miners were laid out here, awaiting identification from family members before transporting to various funeral parlors. Lucas pulled out a handkerchief to cover his nose as the smell of burnt and rotting flesh permeated the air. Many of the corpses were disfigured beyond recognition, whereas others had men and women sobbing over them.

When Lucas reached the opposite side of the long room, he heaved a sigh of relief at not recognizing Patrick among the dead.

Gulping in fresh air as he emerged from the dry, he glanced around for Fiona. She was not at the fluttering sheets attached to a bulletin board outside the shed nor was she among the small groups commiserating and praying. He frowned as he wandered the cramped area open to the public, unable to locate his cousin-in-law.

He heard a bell ring and saw cables moving, realizing men were being brought up belowground in an area cordoned off from the general public. Near the cage entrance, Fiona stood with her hands at her chest as her lips moved in silent prayer. "Fee," he gasped as he rushed to her side after slipping past the guard. "What are you doing here? You shouldn't see the men who are brought up."

"They said Patrick's down below. That he's nearly an hour overdue coming up. The foreman recognized me and allowed me in." Her terrified gaze met his. "He might be with this group."

Lucas slung an arm over her shoulders and eased her backward to allow doctors and emergency personnel to have better access. When he realized she would not leave the area, he sighed and hummed a soft song for her.

"Music won't make this better."

"I know, but it soothes me and hopefully helps you a little," he whispered. Unable to prevent Fiona from stiffening in instinctive fear at seeing more dead miners with his cousin among them, he stood on his tiptoes as the cage rattled up. He shook his head in confusion. "I don't know what I'm seeing. These men are in some kind of breathing contraption while others are foisted to the ground."

"This man needs the pulmotor!" the doctor yelled as he ripped a helmet off someone. A ventilatorlike machine was attached to him, providing oxygen as he lay prostrate on the ground.

"Mac!"

Fiona stiffened at Patrick's anguished yell. She squirmed against Lucas's firm hold on her until she could peer around those in front of her. "Oh, no," she whispered as her husband knelt next to an immobile man, tears and sweat pouring down his grime-covered face. He allowed himself to be dragged away as another doctor approached and quickly examined the prostrate man, before Patrick rose to follow the gurney as they rushed the man called Mac to a waiting ambulance.

"Patrick!" Fiona called, her voice cracking and barely audible.

He froze and turned at her faint yell. "Fee?" He grunted as she threw herself in his arms, holding him tight for a minute before she backed away. "What are you doing here? This is a restricted area."

"I've had no word. No news of you for days. What was I to think?" She swiped at her cheek and stepped back as he raised a grubby hand to her face. He dropped it at her instinctive motion away from him and wiped his forehead instead.

"That I've been busy trying to save those I could." His raspy voice faded away as he coughed. He bent at his waist, coughing deeply and spitting a few times on the ground. When he rose, he brushed away a tear from his coughing jag. "I must go to the hospital and see how my partner is. Mac."

"What happened?" she whispered.

"He tried to carry a man out. Like we've done before. But the man hit Mac's air tube and ..." Patrick's eyes became bleak. "We were a long way from the cage."

"Don't go back down, Patrick." Her voice wavered as she fought tears. "Please. Don't make me or Lucas go through the dry. Not again."

His already somber eyes sobered further. "I promise to do all in my power to return to you and Rose. But don't ask me not to aid those who could be saved, Fee. There might still be men alive down there.

We found a group just now hidden behind a makeshift barricade. There might be more in the same situation."

"But *you* don't have to find them," she whispered, grabbing his forearm.

He gripped her hand a moment before freeing himself from her clasp. "Think of their families, Fee. Their wives. Their children. Their mothers." He met her anguished gaze. "I will do what I must." He kissed her on the forehead. "Take care of Rose for me." He glanced back at Lucas. "Thank you."

Lucas nodded. "We don't need a martyred hero in the family, Pat. Remember that." He moved forward to stand by Fiona as Patrick rushed away to follow his partner to the hospital.

"He'll go back down again," she whispered. "Even though I asked him not to."

"He will. Not because he wants to go against your wishes. But because he must live with himself too. If he stopped now, he'd have a hard time holding up his head. You must know a man needs his pride."

Fiona clamped her jaw. "Pride be damned if it takes him from me."

After another moment of watching the chaos around them, Lucas tugged on her arm and turned her away from the mine. "Come. Let's return to my house. I imagine Rose is looking forward to telling you about her adventures with Aunt Vivie today." He coaxed and teased Fee as they made their slow way from the mine yard, Fiona casting glances over her shoulder for another glimpse of Patrick.

Two days later, Patrick pushed open the door to his house. He glanced around, frowning at the silence that welcomed him. He wandered through the rooms to find them all empty. "They must be at Lucas's," he muttered to himself. He entered his bedroom and pulled out a set of fresh clothes before heading to the bathroom. After he had showered and washed away five days' worth of grime, he emerged, intent on seeing his wife and daughter.

He paused a moment on his front porch, a soft smile spreading as

Fiona and Rose walked toward him. Rose took four steps to every one of Fiona's but seemed inordinately delighted at her ability to walk beside her mother. She giggled at something Fiona said and clapped her hands together. He sighed with contentment.

Fiona stiffened at the darkened shadow on her porch. "Patrick!" she gasped upon recognizing him, at first moving toward him before freezing. "You're home. Is the work done then?"

His delighted smile dimmed at her recalcitrance before he picked up Rose and spun her around. He settled her on his hip and breathed in her smell. "Hello, my little angel."

"Papa. I *miss* you!" She hugged him and kissed his cheek before squirming to be let down. He kissed her head and let her go, following Fiona and Rose into the house.

"I just got back. I showered and was going to look for you at Lucas's but then saw you walking home." He paused in the doorway of the living room as he watched Fiona set up Rose to play alone. "I helped with the recovery of those who died for as long as possible. I received word today that I'm needed at work tomorrow full time, so I had to leave the rest of the recovery efforts with my colleagues."

Fiona nodded, looking away from him as she fiddled with one of Rose's toys. "How many more days? Until they … find all the men?"

"They hope only one or two," Patrick murmured. He frowned as Fiona nodded but said nothing. "It's good to be home."

Rose settled into the living room to play with her dolls and a set of wooden trains her uncles in Missoula had built for her. Patrick ensured she was fine before following Fiona into the kitchen. "Fee? What's the matter? I came home." He grunted as she spun around and swatted him on his chest.

"You came home? That's your response?" She glared at him through tear-soaked eyes. "I asked you not to go down again. I asked you." She bit back her words and swallowed her anger.

He grabbed her shoulders, ignoring her stiffening. "I know you did. And it was one of the hardest things I've ever done, denying you that request. Can you understand why I had to continue?"

"You could have died!" she snapped. "And then where would Rose and I have been?"

"My family would always take care of you." His mournful gaze roved over her.

"What good would their money do if you were gone? You, Patrick?" She gasped as she lost her battle with her tears and sobbed. He tugged her close and held her against his chest as she cried.

"Oh, Fee. I never meant to cause you this anguish. I never thought …" He sighed, kissing her head and relishing the feel of her in his arms.

After many minutes, she whispered, "And that's my fault too. For too long, you've thought I only cared because you were a good provider."

"What are you saying, Fee?" He swiped hands over her face, frowning in frustration as she flinched at his touch. He dropped his hands and stepped away from her.

She looked away from him a moment before raising her eyes to meet his. "That I value you as more than a provider."

He watched her intently a moment and then nodded. "I'll take that for now." He smiled. "After all the time at the mine, I'm looking forward to a few days of quiet at work and at home. Do you think we could have that?"

She smiled. "I know Rose has missed you as much as I have."

"Thank you, Fee. For caring enough to come to the mine. For taking care of Rose when I was away. For being here." He traced a pattern on his thigh rather than on her arm and then eased from the kitchen to join his daughter in the living room. He sighed with contentment and battled guilt that he was home with his family when so many had been denied such a gift.

CHAPTER 5

Missoula, Montana, June 1917

*S*ummerlike weather had finally arrived in Missoula with longer, sunnier days. Although it fluctuated from comfortably warm in the day to near freezing at night, the flowers and trees were in bloom, and the birds had returned, trilling their joy. Snow remained on the distant mountain peaks, but the lower hills were changing from a lush green provided by the spring rains to their customary golden hue.

Araminta, a woman who had moved west with Savannah McLeod in 1903 after having lived in Delia McLeod's orphanage for most of her life, relished the sun on her cheeks. She paused in her round of cleaning and chores in Savannah's house to stand in the living room awash in sunlight and to bask in the warmth finally returning to Montana after a harsh winter. She sighed when a knock at the front door interrupted her quiet interlude. Her gently loping gait was a testament to a poorly healed leg injury from her childhood, although it rarely impeded her work or slowed her down.

As she opened the door a fraction, she smiled with impersonal politeness at the woman standing with a bag at her feet. "May I help you?"

"Does Savannah McLeod live here?"

"May I ask who is calling?" Araminta inquired as she faltered back a step when the woman pushed her way inside. Araminta caught her balance, flushing in agitation at the woman's rudeness.

"Oh, I'm an old friend from Boston. I know she will be delighted to see me," the woman said as she peered around doorways leading off the front hall.

"Even so, we all have names," Araminta snapped. She rubbed her hands on her starched white apron and brushed back a strand of sable hair that had come free from her bun.

The woman raised an eyebrow and looked Araminta over with an assessing glance from head to toe. "If you were my maid, such impertinence would have you cast out without a reference."

"I am not a maid, and you continue to refuse to give your name. I find that reason enough to ask you to leave," Araminta said, pushing the woman toward the door.

At that moment, Savannah McLeod walked down the hallway from the kitchen area, her brow creased with a frown. "Araminta, is there a problem?" She smoothed a hand over her sky-blue day dress with her strawberry-blond hair pulled back in a loose knot at the nape of her neck.

"Yes, this woman is insistent upon speaking with you but refuses to give me her name." Araminta pointed at the woman who stood as tall as her five-foot-four frame allowed. The light entering the front door's glass panel highlighted the gray mixed into her blond hair.

"She declined to share that information because she knew she would never be welcomed in my house," Savannah murmured, an icy undertone to her voice. "I'm surprised you'd have the nerve to come here."

"Why shouldn't I visit my only daughter?" The woman raised her chin with bravado.

"She hasn't been your daughter for years, Mrs. Smythe," Savannah said, using her guest's first married name, rather than the name granted to her when she'd married Savannah's uncle, Sean Sullivan.

Araminta gasped as she gaped at the older woman she had heard about but had never met. Mrs. Smythe stood with a regal posture, as though her presence in the room was a benediction to the household. Her gray-blond hair was held back in a chignon with a pearl clip although her clothes were years out-of-date and faded. Alert brown eyes challenged Savannah as they continued their silent stalemate.

"Mama, can you help me in the kitchen?" Melinda called out as she walked down the hallway, holding a cookbook.

Savannah's panicked gaze darted to her daughter. Although sixteen, Melinda would be unprepared for the sudden arrival of her birth mother. Frozen in place, Savannah failed to impede her daughter's entrance into the hallway and prevent Mrs. Smythe from seeing her.

Melinda looked up with a curious frown and smiled impersonally at the stranger in front of her. She shrieked as the stranger touched her, causing the cookbook to clatter to the floor. Wriggling in the woman's arms to free herself, she pushed away until she stood behind Savannah, the woman she considered her mother.

"Oh, my precious girl! You'll never know how I've longed for this moment!" Mrs. Smythe exclaimed, swiping at the tears forced from her eyes. She reached again for Melinda, but Savannah intervened, blocking her grasp while keeping Melinda behind her.

"You have no right to be here. You forfeited any parental concern when you …" Savannah snapped her jaw shut.

"I did what I had to do. As any mother would," Mrs. Smythe said in her candy-cane voice.

"You're the vile woman who sent me to the orphanage," Melly breathed with fascination. She peered around Savannah, noting the similar coloring and height she shared with the stranger.

"How can you say such a thing? I'm your mother," Mrs. Smythe sputtered. She patted at her hair, now more gray than blonde. "I remember those beautiful blond ringlets. So like my own when I was a child."

"You were awful to my siblings," Melly said. "Why should I like you?"

"Melly, go fetch your father," Savannah ordered before Mrs. Smythe could wander any further down memory lane. "You." Savannah's voice broke with fury as she faced Mrs. Smythe. "You will sit in the parlor with me as we await my husband." She followed Mrs. Smythe into the living room to the side of the front door. As she was about to sit, Savannah looked to Araminta and motioned for her to leave.

Araminta walked down the hallway, through the kitchen and out the back door. She shut the door soundlessly and paused. After a moment, she departed, walking at a near trot toward Clarissa McLeod's house to inform her of her stepmother's untimely return.

"Father!" Melly gasped as she barreled into the workshop. She slammed into a customer, bouncing off him and landing on the floor with a grunt of discomfort. She glanced around, noting that the usual noises of sanding, sawing and hammering had silenced at her precipitous arrival. A squeaking wheel approached Melinda as did boot heels on the wood floor. The customer departed, and the door creaked shut, giving them privacy.

Ronan O'Bara offered her a hand, and she smiled as he helped her to her feet. She brushed at her backside, wood dust fluttering in the air. She yowled as a splinter worked its way into her palm, and she sucked at it a second before focusing on her father. He sat on a bench in front of her, next to his brother Gabriel, with Ronan on his other side.

"Tell us what has caused you to run in here like the little hellion we know you are but hope to hide from the town," Jeremy said as he fought a smile. His tender gaze roved lovingly over his daughter.

"She's back. That woman is back," Melinda gasped. At her father's and uncle's confused frowns, she took a deep breath. "My ..." She paused and bit her lip. "My real mother."

Jeremy stiffened, and Gabriel's concerned frown turned into a glower. "She can't be. She has no reason to be," Jeremy said.

"Sophie did write last year that she suspected Mrs. Smythe would arrive, bringing mischief with her," Gabriel said to his brother. "The delay in her arrival has only led us to become complacent in our belief that Sophie was wrong."

"That woman is never wrong." Jeremy rose and kicked a stool, missing Melinda's flinch at his actions. Ronan held her hand, offering her comfort.

"Jer," Ronan said, his quiet voice commanding notice as Jeremy appeared on the verge of loosening his rage.

Jeremy spun and focused on Melinda. He marched to her and clasped her face in his hands, frowning as she battled tears. "I didn't mean to frighten you. I'd never hurt you." He pulled her to his chest, holding her close.

"I know." She wrapped her arms around him as she rested her cheek against his chest. "Does this mean I have to go with her?" Melinda's voice broke on the word "go," and Jeremy felt her shudder as she fought tears.

"Hell no," Gabriel growled. He patted Melinda on the back as he watched his brother hold the daughter of his heart. "There's no way we will allow that woman to separate you from those who love you as their daughter. As you deserve to be loved."

Melinda pushed away from her father, brushing at her cheeks. "Mother needs you at home. She's stuck with her and wants you there."

Jeremy's jaw firmed at the thought of Savannah home alone with Mrs. Smythe. "I have no doubt Savannah will hold her own until I arrive." He turned to his brother. "Gabe, will you take Melly to your house? Keep her there until we know what is occurring?"

Gabriel nodded and placed an arm over his niece's shoulder. "Come. I'm sure by now Minta has snuck out to inform Rissa, and she'll be fit to be tied at being home with the children." He nodded to Ronan. "I'll be by later with the news. Thanks for watching the shop."

Melinda walked beside Gabriel and smiled to those who called out to them. They walked quickly in an effort to discourage conversation with their friends and neighbors and soon crossed the bridge and turned toward Gabriel's house. He ushered her into his comfortable Craftsman-style house, his expression grim when he saw Clarissa pacing in the living room.

"Where are the children?" Gabriel asked as he placed his hat on the hallstand. He grunted as Clarissa threw herself into his arms and rocked her to and fro while she calmed.

"Except for the baby, they're all at the park. With Minta." She sniffled and backed away. "Come, Melly. There's nothing to be worried about."

Melinda frowned and then laughed at her sister with little mirth. "She's back, Rissa. What does she want?"

Clarissa pulled her sister into a fierce embrace. "Whatever it is, she won't get it," she vowed. "We have a long history with her and know how to outmaneuver her."

Melinda rested her head on Clarissa's shoulder but shared a worried glance with Gabriel. "I thought your outmaneuvering her was fleeing to Montana. It seems she's followed you."

Clarissa squeezed her sister's shoulder and led her to a settee, pushing her to sit down. She sat next to her while Gabriel paced to the fireplace. "Gabriel?" she asked in a soft voice.

He faced them with a reassuring smile. "All will be well." He ran a hand through his recently cut hair, standing strands of ebony mixed with gray on end. "I was standing here, trying to imagine what Mr. Pickens would say. What he'd do." His smile finally reached his eyes. "Other than slam his cane down in consternation."

He moved to the chair facing them. "Any ideas, Melly?"

Her impish smile seemed to relax Clarissa. "Oh, he'd talk about the *preposternoose* of her being here and the need for *vigilanteance*."

Clarissa and Gabriel laughed, and Gabriel relaxed against the settee. "That's exactly right. It is preposterous she's here, and we must be vigilant," Gabriel said with another chuckle. "He'd say that and then give us a toothless grin as though we were brainless to be dillydallying." He sighed. "I miss the old man."

Clarissa nodded and rubbed Melinda's back. "I would love to have seen him take on Mrs. Smythe."

Gabriel chuckled. "It would almost have been as good as watching Sophie take her on."

Clarissa sobered. "As it is, we must fight whatever malice she intends to sow." She tugged Melinda by the shoulders so she could look in her eyes. "Promise me that, no matter what she says or does, you don't doubt us or your parents' love for you." When Melinda watched her in confusion, Clarissa gripped her more tightly. "She is intent on causing mischief, and I worry that her goal is harming you. Promise me that you understand our goal is to care for you and to love you."

Melinda nodded, her brow crinkling. "Of course. I've always known that. Nothing she could say or do would cause me to doubt that."

~

Jeremy entered his house through the back kitchen door and walked through the dining room. He paused at the entrance to the living room. Instead of the heated discussion he expected to find, the two women stared each other down with a determined silence.

"If I had my way, you would not be allowed to enter my house," Jeremy said, stepping into the room and causing Mrs. Smythe to jump in her seat. He smiled with satisfaction for a moment as she had expected him to enter through the hallway door. Then he frowned as he realized how much Melinda looked like her.

"There could never be any doubt you are a McLeod," Mrs. Smythe said, looking at Jeremy. "Although what influence you McLeod men have over the women of my family, I will never understand."

"Of course you can't," Savannah snapped, "for that would mean you understood what kindness, decency and honor meant. And we aren't your family."

Mrs. Smythe settled into her chair. "It's a shame to see how you've squandered Mr. Montgomery's money. I'm certain his family would be most distressed to learn how flamboyant you have been in the displays of your unearned wealth."

Jeremy strode behind the settee Savannah sat on, her back to him, and placed his palms on her shoulders in a soothing touch. She raised a hand to lace her fingers with his, calming his anger. "He is not spoken of in our house," Jeremy said.

"Of course not. I'm certain you are afraid you will meet a similar death, living with a murderess," Mrs. Smythe said in her singsongy voice.

Savannah tightened her hold on Jeremy's fingers, preventing him from moving away from her.

"I do wonder what he'd say if he knew you were raising my bastard child."

Savannah laughed incredulously, releasing Jeremy's hands as she swiped at hair along her brow. "I can't believe you'd speak in such a way about my uncle."

Jeremy stood very still behind Savannah, watching Mrs. Smythe intently. "You're not, are you? That's your entire reason for coming here. You believe you can cause destruction and mayhem and relish in your ability to do so."

Mrs. Smythe laughed. "Oh, to see the looks on your faces. Confused, scared and incredulous."

Jeremy moved around the side of the settee and sat next to Savannah, facing Mrs. Smythe. "Tell us what you have come to say and then leave. You can say nothing that will cause us to allow you further contact with our daughter. Yes, *our* daughter," he emphasized when Mrs. Smythe protested. "You gave up all rights to her when you brought her to the orphanage when she was a child. She is ours."

"I was out of my mind with grief when I brought her there," Mrs. Smythe moaned as she swiped at a tear on her cheek.

"You can't even act as though you know what grief is," Savannah said in a scathing voice. "Any mother who had lost her child, who actually had maternal instincts, would have traveled here long before now. You are here for an entirely different reason."

Mrs. Smythe sniffled and thrust her shoulders back in a display of bravado. "I want her father to have the opportunity to know her as he should."

"He's dead, you daft woman," Savannah snapped. "He died in 1902."

Jeremy stiffened next to Savannah. "Oh. I see. You're claiming that Sean wasn't the father? That someone else was?" He shook his head. "It wouldn't matter what you claim. Her birth certificate lists Sean Sullivan as her father, and he's deceased."

Mrs. Smythe waved her hand as though the facts were immaterial and a nuisance at best. "I want there to be justice. For too long, a good man has been separated from his child."

"As though my uncle would allow you to … to … to be intimate with another man," Savannah scoffed. "He was proud and strong and would never have countenanced you carrying on an affair."

Mrs. Smythe sighed, collapsing into her seat. She remained silent a few moments. "How are my dear stepchildren? There are many days I miss their company."

Jeremy laughed. "You mean, you miss your ability to meddle in their lives?"

"I always thought it so tragic when Patrick had to leave," Mrs. Smythe said as though Jeremy had not spoken. "I wish Sean had been more understanding."

Savannah shook her head in confusion, before freezing.

Jeremy squinted as he considered the riddle of her words. "Are you insinuating … ?" he asked.

"It's no insinuation but a proclamation of the truth. The poor man, he lost everything over his infatuation with me. Including his child." She shrugged her shoulders, giving a mournful smile that was more gleeful than sad.

Savannah rose. "You vile woman, spouting your lies to provoke disharmony. Get out of my house and never return!" When Mrs. Smythe remained seated in calm contentment, Savannah nearly leaped over the tea table. She wrenched Mrs. Smythe up by the arm and dragged her to the front door. "Get out!" She gave her a push, slamming the door behind her and locking it.

She leaned against it, panting after her exertions. Jeremy remained on the settee, his mind replaying the scene. He looked up to share a confused glance with Savannah.

"What does this mean? Will we lose Melly?" Savannah crumpled to the floor, unable to fight her despair.

Jeremy rose, rushing to kneel in front of her. "My darling, no matter what, Melly is our daughter. We adopted her, although at the time we didn't believe we needed to legally. We have the paperwork from the lawyer and the judge. We did it because we loved her so much we couldn't bear being parted from her in case something like this occurred. She is our daughter. We must wait to hear from Patrick his version of this story. Don't panic, my darling."

"Yes, but …" Savannah grabbed her husband's lapel and buried her face in it. "But now Melly might choose another. And that is out of our control."

CHAPTER 6

Clarissa slammed a pile of books on a tabletop in the back sorting area of the library, ignoring Hester's hiss of displeasure. She quickly placed them in order on a small cart before moving to refile them on the shelves. She walked down one shelf, looking for the section on Jefferson, when she bumped into a woman turned the other way. "I beg your pardon," Clarissa murmured. She grunted as she moved the cart around the woman but stilled her actions when the woman turned to face her.

"Mrs. Smythe," Clarissa breathed. "At last you visit me." Her gaze roamed over her stepmother, noting the wrinkles at her eyes and around her mouth, the baggy skin at her neck she concealed somewhat with a high-collared shirt and then her graying hair. "I see that time has been unkind to you."

"No need to sound gleeful," Mrs. Smythe snapped, no hint of her singsongy voice present. "I had hoped to visit you at home, but someone is always present with you."

Clarissa's gaze turned calculating. "You mean, you had hoped to catch me off guard and alone." Her hands on the cart handle tightened, and she fought a frown. "I hope by now you've come to understand that Savannah and I are well supported here."

"That's immaterial, dear. What's important is that you realize that you have been denied the truth for too many years. I yearn for you to acknowledge why you were cruelly separated from your brother." Her eyes watered as though she battled tears. "I fought such guilt at his leaving home."

Clarissa scoffed and moved the cart, banging Mrs. Smythe in the shins when she moved to block Clarissa's path. "No, you didn't," Clarissa growled over Mrs. Smythe's grunt of pain. "You relished every second of my distress, just as you did after you left me alone with Cameron. Your desire was always to have Da and his money all for your personal use. Your bad luck was that he died too young." Clarissa maneuvered the cart again and pushed past Mrs. Smythe.

"How dare you speak to me in such a manner after how I suffered with your father? He was such a cruel man!"

Clarissa spun, her eyes blazing and hands clenched. "Don't you dare speak to me about my father like that. I know what kind of man he was, and nothing you say will ever change my opinion of him. You will never tarnish my memory of him." She stiffened when she sensed they were no longer alone in the aisle and looked over her shoulder. She closed her eyes for a moment in defeat and resignation.

"I can't believe what I am witnessing, Sister. The abuse of one of our patrons, in our library," Mrs. Vaughan exclaimed in her carrying voice. Her turquoise dress clashed with her pumpkin-colored shawl. "When I think that we asked you to return to aid us in the running of our fine establishment ..." She fanned herself as though speaking was more than she could bear after the shock of what she had just seen.

Mrs. Bouchard squared her shoulders and glared at Clarissa. "You are a wicked woman, treating your elders in such an abusive manner. I fear I'll need speak with our board about such behavior."

Clarissa watched the sisters dispassionately. "Do what you feel you must. I have no regrets about my interaction with this woman. If you will excuse me?" She pushed the cart forward, causing the sisters to leap to the side so as not to be run over. Mrs. Bouchard squelched at a ripping sound in her chartreuse-colored skirt and called to Clarissa that she'd send her the seamstress's bill.

"What has gotten into you?" Hester whispered when Clarissa closed the door in the office. Hester Loken was the main librarian, and she enjoyed the days Clarissa worked as it allowed Hester to catch up on paperwork rather than work out front. She and Clarissa were now good friends after a short period of animosity when Hester had first arrived in Missoula.

"My ex-stepmother is out there, inciting unrest. As she always does," Clarissa said as she collapsed on a stool. "She's becoming bosom buddies with the sisters."

Hester grimaced. "That's unfortunate. They don't need to add anyone else to their network of nitpicking ninnies."

Clarissa giggled. "Mr. Pickens would have liked that name for them."

Hester shrugged and shared an irreverent grin with Clarissa. "Whenever I know they plan a gathering here, I put three Ns in my datebook so I can mentally prepare. Besides, I've seen them go through my calendar a few times, and I find that having a code helps."

Clarissa laughed again. "I fear the sisters will find a way to dismiss me after they saw my rude interaction with her."

Hester shrugged. "They like to believe they have more power than they do. They are honorary members, at best. The board will listen to reason and understand you were provoked. I wouldn't worry about it." She frowned as she studied her friend. "Are you all right?"

Clarissa shook her head. "No. As long as *she* is in town, I will be uneasy. I know she's planning something. I just don't know what it is." She cringed as she heard the bellowing shrill voices of the sisters, each trying to talk over the other. "I'll sneak out the back. I must speak with Savannah."

Hester nodded. "You were almost done anyway. I'll see you Sunday."

Clarissa smiled and nodded. Hester had been adopted into their group as part of their extended family and always joined them for Sunday dinner. "It's at my house this week," Clarissa murmured as she slipped out the back door.

When she arrived at Savannah's home, Clarissa entered the

kitchen through the back door, which was always unlocked. She passed through the empty room and poked her head into the side sunroom that acted as Savannah's informal parlor, where Savannah sat on a wicker settee, her gaze distant. "Hi, Sav," Clarissa murmured.

"Rissa," she said with a warm smile. Her strawberry-blond hair was in a long braid down her back, and she wore a casual day dress in sky blue that matched her eyes. "Shouldn't you be at the library?"

"I left a little early. I had a run-in with Mrs. Smythe and needed to escape after I saw her conspiring with the sisters." She rolled her eyes as Savannah grimaced. "Hester didn't mind."

Savannah played with her wedding ring, rolling it around and around on her finger. "I still can't believe she's here."

Clarissa waited, but Savannah remained silent. "And I can't accept her story. It's almost too fantastic to believe."

"I've found that, too often, the fantastic is true, if only in part," Savannah murmured. "What if Patrick really is Melly's father? What if he wants her back?" She blinked away tears. "Do we have the right to keep him separated from her?"

Clarissa shook her head. "I don't have answers to these questions, Sav. I love my brother, but I'm so angry with him right now."

"A part of me wishes he'd never come back."

"No, Sav! I could never wish that." Clarissa took a deep breath and let it out. "I fear he's as much a victim in this whole debacle as the rest of us. Knowing Mrs. Smythe, there is much more to this story than she's told us."

Savannah shook her head, her eyes filled with disappointment. "Then why didn't he tell us first? Why would he ever leave us vulnerable to such a woman?" She watched her cousin unsuccessfully formulate a response. "There's no excuse for what he failed to do, Rissa."

She nodded. "I understand you're angry with him. But don't wish him gone. Don't wish him to not be a part of our lives. I will always be thankful he returned to us." After a few moments, she whispered, "I'll ask Colin to travel to Butte. I doubt Patrick would tell me the truth, but I think Colin will have a better chance of learning what truly happened."

Savannah watched her cousin. "I hate to be at odds with you, Rissa. You're like a sister to me. But I can't give up Melly. She's my daughter. I love her."

Clarissa gripped Savannah's hand. "I know. I'd never want you to." She took another deep breath. "Let's wait to hear what Colin discovers." She pasted on a smile as Melinda burst into the room, and the conversation changed to Melinda's plans for her summer vacation.

～

Araminta's heels clicked an uneven tattoo on the boardwalk on Higgins Avenue as she walked quickly. She held a list in her hand, with a wicker basket handle looped through one of her arms. She skirted a swinging door in front of a saloon, but her uneven step prevented her from completely evading the door. She stumbled and dropped her list.

Even as she bent to retrieve it, a hand snatched it from her grasp. She rose and held out her hand, a polite smile on her face. "May I please have my list?" she asked the stranger.

"Who are you?" asked the man, who appeared to be in his early thirties. "I've met with everyone of consequence since I arrived, and yet I don't recall you."

His friend, who Araminta hadn't noticed standing behind him, snorted. "That's because she isn't of consequence, Bart. She's the McLeod maid."

"And a cripple," another muttered as he noted his friend's interest.

Araminta stood as tall as possible on her good leg and raised her head while thrusting her shoulders back—an imitation of what Clarissa did numerous times when scrutinized. "If you'd please give me my list and let me pass?" She waved her hand up and down once in front of her.

"Aren't you curious who we are?" the man called Bart asked. He wore a navy pinstriped suit with its matching waistcoat and a cream-colored tie. "We are much more genteel than those McLeods." He snorted a laugh as he glanced toward his friends.

Araminta remained silent with no trace of amusement reaching her eyes as she studied him and his friends. She moved forward to push past them but was forced to halt when they blocked her path, stumbling as she stopped on her bad leg.

"You really are ... damaged," Bart murmured with a frown. At her mutinous gaze, he held up his hands. "I'd never call you *crippled* as you seem to move around fine." He puffed out his chest as though that consideration merited him her regard. "I'm Bartholomew Bouchard, of the San Francisco Bouchards. This is my cousin, Vernon Vaughan, and our friend, Lionel Toomey."

"I'm sure your family is delighted to have you visit," Araminta said as she leaned forward to nudge him out of her way.

"Oh, I'm not visiting. I've come here to help run the bank Uncle obtained a few years ago. I've had substantial training in San Francis-co." He hooked his thumbs into his waistcoat as he arched his back. When this failed to impress her, he frowned as though flummoxed.

During his confusion, Araminta dropped one shoulder and pushed her way past him. "Nice to meet you. Welcome to Missoula." She raised an arm in farewell as she moved down the boardwalk, entering the first store she could find. "Blast," she whispered when she remem-bered she didn't have her list, although she was thankful to have entered the grocers.

"Miss Araminta, are you unwell?" the shopgirl asked as Araminta leaned against one of the displays.

Araminta stood tall and smiled. "Of course not. Merely a bit winded. Many are about today, and the boardwalk is crowded." She moved toward the girl, her fingers tapping the top of the glass counter. "Would you mind writing down my order? I seem to have misplaced my list."

Afterward Araminta moved to a small stool in the corner and sat while she waited for her order to be filled. She looked out the store window and saw the woman causing such discord sashaying down the boardwalk. Instinctively she glared at the woman, resenting her ability to cause turmoil in Clarissa's and Savannah's lives.

Araminta looked to her hands, clasped on her lap, when the woman turned into the grocers. Araminta attempted to blend into the corner, becoming part of the shelves, but Mrs. Smythe's keen gaze landed on her. After a perfunctory greeting to the woman filling Araminta's order, Mrs. Smythe moved around the small store until she'd sidled up to the case near Araminta's corner.

"It's lovely to see you again, dear, and away from such horrid relations," Mrs. Smythe said in her sugary voice, supposedly a whisper, but her voice became louder and caused the workers in the room to lean in their direction to better overhear. When Mrs. Smythe noted their actions, she smiled in triumph. "I must say, I was dumbfounded to realize my stepdaughter and niece could act in such a shameful way to you."

"They have only ever treated me with kindness and caring." Araminta cleared her throat and glared at the shopgirl who watched their interaction with drop-jawed interest.

"Oh, but to use one such as you as they do." Mrs. Smythe sighed as she looked at Araminta with blatant pity and tsked. "I'd think they could find someone else for the hard labor."

"I am able to do the work that is required of me."

Mrs. Smythe's smile appeared benevolent, although malicious joy lit her gaze. She tapped at one of the frilly pieces of lace kept under lock and key in a case under her fingers. "Isn't this a lovely piece?" she asked no one in particular. "It must have taken so long to tat. Although I always find hand-sewn lace to have at least one deformity. Machine-sewn lace is almost always perfect. Isn't it a joy that machines can now create most of what we need and do it so much better, with little risk of such imperfections?"

She shot a look at Araminta. "I'm afraid it's the same for people. A man would never want a crippled wife, not when he knows there are healthy options. Those who are, well, less, due to deformities, will no longer be needed." She sighed as though she were mournful for her believed fact.

Araminta stiffened and rose. "The differences, the deformities as you call them, are what make us unique and interesting. Nothing in this life is perfect, and your obsession with obtaining a perfect life, a perfect family and a perfect home will only lead you to loneliness and ruin." She glanced at the shopgirl, whose previous amused interest was now one of disdain and distrust as she beheld Mrs. Smythe. The shopgirl nodded to Araminta that her order was ready. "If you will excuse me?"

Mrs. Smythe's mocking smile at Araminta's loping walk provoked a glower from Araminta, but she pushed past the woman to collect her basketful of goods. "I wish you a good day," Araminta whispered to the shopgirl. She turned, glared at Mrs. Smythe and walked out of the grocers with her head held high.

When she had walked a short distance down the boardwalk, she paused and set her basket down. A tremor went through her, and she took a deep breath before she firmed her jaw and resumed her journey to Clarissa's house.

~

Araminta slammed a pot onto the stove, causing the other cast iron pots on top to rattle. "What's got you so riled?" Colin asked as he entered Clarissa's kitchen. He approached the icebox and pulled out a pitcher of cold water. When Araminta refused to answer his question, he sat at the small table in the center of the room.

"Well, rather than me leaving after obtaining my glass of water, I'll sit here now and bother you." His smile faltered as she spun and glared at him. He choked down a sip of water and rapped his fingers on the tabletop.

"Heard about your interesting run-in today with that Bouchard buzzard," he said with a chuckle. When that earned a kick to the stove and a thwack to a kettle with a metal spoon that would have broken a wooden one, Colin raised an eyebrow. "I see you're intrigued by the man."

Araminta spun with her hands on her hip as she glowered at Colin.

Her hair was knotted loosely at the back of her head, and, although no strands were coming free, the loose hairstyle softened her features. Colin's breath hitched a moment as he looked at her before she spoke.

"Intrigued? I wouldn't be intrigued by that man if ..." She moved to the counter and lifted a knife.

Colin rose with alacrity and placed a hand over hers, preventing her from cutting anything and potentially harming herself while so angry. "What did he and his friends say, Ari?" At her stare, he lowered his hand, leaving the knife in hers and gripped the side of his pants to stop himself from caressing her face. He backed away a step so as not to lean forward and kiss her forehead.

"They called me *the McLeod cripple*." She hacked a carrot in half, then set down the knife and took a deep breath.

Any thoughts of romance fled as Colin gripped her shoulders. "Did they hurt you?" His angry gaze bored into her momentarily shocked one. He gentled his grip on her shoulders, but the anger rippled through him.

"No, it was just words. And they kept my list." She bit her lip. "I think he, that Mr. Bouchard from San Francisco, thought he was quite important and seemed surprised when I didn't show him the reaction he expected."

"Bloody buffoon," Colin muttered. "You are well?" He forced himself to drop his hands away as she backed off under the pretense of stirring the pot on the stove.

"I'm fine. Angry at what they called me. Angrier at the fact their name-calling could rouse such a response in me." She closed her eyes. "I should be used to it by now." She looked toward Colin as a growl emerged from him.

"You aren't crippled, Ari. You have a bad leg and walk with a limp. That doesn't make you crippled. You do more in a day than most women in a week." He clamped his mouth shut as though he wanted to say more but forced himself to stop. "I'm thankful you are not unduly affected after your meeting with them."

"I also saw your stepmother again. She spouted a variation of the same theme during her visit to the grocers." Araminta cut the carrot into small pieces, dropping them all into the pot.

"Miserable woman. Her greatest delight is to discover your sensitive spot and then poke a knife into it. She's always disappointed she doesn't watch you bleed to death from one of her jabs." He raised his hand and made the motion as though he were stroking her back but kept his fingers raised a few inches, never touching her. "I'm sorry you had to suffer any further interaction with her."

Araminta sighed. "So am I. I loathe that woman."

"I can guarantee, Ari, that whatever she said was a lie. I'd never trust anything from her lips."

She turned to watch him a moment, a deep hurt visible in her gaze that she generally kept hidden from him. "There's always truth amid the madness, Colin." She broke away from his searching gaze and moved toward the cutting board.

He watched her move with her own gracefulness, her gait uneven but fluid as she flitted from the stove to the cutting board and back. "Forgive me for intruding on you. I know my company is never desired." He waited a moment for her to contradict him and then nodded to himself at her silent agreement. He grabbed his glass of water and pushed through the swinging door to the rest of the house, leaving Araminta behind in the kitchen.

The screened door on the front porch slammed shut after him, and he winced at the loud noise.

"Are you all right?" Clarissa asked as he joined her on the wide front porch. The children were playing in the small front yard rather than the spacious backyard, and she was keeping an eye on them. She rocked little Colin, now sixteen months old, in his rocker next to her as he slept.

Colin traced a very gentle touch down little Colin's back and sat next to his sister. "I'm fine." When he met her doubting gaze, he rolled his eyes. "Some men downtown today made Ari feel bad. Called her a cripple."

Clarissa frowned and then sighed. "I'm afraid that's not the first, nor the last, time anyone will call her that."

"I know." Colin smiled as he watched his nieces and nephew play. "She also had a run-in with Mrs. Smythe. I don't know the details, but I also don't need them to know it must have been a singularly unpleasant interaction." He took a long sip of water.

"There's nothing we can do to make Mrs. Smythe leave," Clarissa snapped. She huffed out a breath when Colin placed a hand on her arm. "I hate that she's here. That she's invaded this place that was a haven from her and her vileness. I fear she'll stir up gossip that's better off dead."

"She'll try, and she'll succeed with some. But you and Gabe are well-liked. Those who are your true friends will listen, because people are curious, and we need to hear about something other than the war and goings on in Butte. But they also won't give her much credence." Colin shrugged. "It's the nature of things, Rissa."

"I hate when you're rational. I want you to rail against things like I do." She relaxed at his amused laugh.

They sat for long minutes, watching the children play. Neighbors passed in front of the house, short greetings exchanged or a wave as they passed by. A warm breeze blew the blooming trees. Colin sat with his legs stretched in front of him with his feet crossed at the ankles. "I hate that she won't talk with me," Colin whispered.

Clarissa paused, studying Colin a moment and the abrupt change in topic before nodding her understanding. "We've discussed this, Col. You expect everything to go back to how it was before you almost kissed Araminta. Some things can't be undone. Not for most women." She watched him with fondness and worry mixed in her gaze. "Have you ever talked to her about that night?"

Colin squirmed in his chair. "I try, and the wrong thing always comes out. I thought I'd attempt again today, and instead we talked about what happened to her when she went shopping." His characteristic upbeat nature seemed deflated. "It's as though I don't want to talk with her about what really concerns me."

"That's not like you, Col." Clarissa stroked a hand over her son's head. "I'd expect my son's namesake to be a better role model," she teased.

"I still can't believe you named him after me," he whispered, his voice thickened with wonder as he ran a finger over the whispery down on his nephew's head. "I bet he'll be a hellion, like me."

"I knew I should have named him Lucas," Clarissa said. She laughed softly as Colin acted affronted.

"How are you really, Rissa? I know you've spoken with Sav." Colin smiled as he watched his niece Geraldine command her siblings as though she were a little general.

He turned to see Clarissa swiping at her cheek. "Heartbroken." She took a deep, shuddering breath. "When I think we had welcomed Patrick back here, with open arms, and he hid this? He had to have known that *she* would come here. That *she* would cause havoc. He left us unprepared for her attack."

"I think it's why he was shocked we'd welcomed him." Colin sighed as he stretched his legs a little farther to rest on the banister in front of him. "Do you remember when you were afraid to tell Gabe about Cameron?" He watched as she froze a moment before she continued her rocking. "Why were you reticent?"

She raised angry eyes to him. "You know darned well it was because I was terrified he'd no longer want me."

Colin nodded his head. "Yeah. I think the same could be said of Patrick. After discovering his family didn't hate him, even though we didn't know the whole truth, I imagine he was as terrified as you'd been that we'd reject him once the full story was out. And he'd spent over a decade alone, Rissa."

She closed her eyes, and a few more tears trickled out. "I hate that any further injustice could be done to our family due to that woman."

Colin rocked in companionable silence a few minutes. "I agree. I have to remain hopeful that the worst damage has already been wrought, and now we have to minimize the aftereffects." He dropped his feet with a soft thud and leaned forward with his elbows on his knees as he looked at her. "I've thought a lot about it, Rissa, and I agree with you. I'll travel to Butte tomorrow. I need to hear from Patrick what happened. We've only heard her side of the story, and you know she's as reliable as a sack of cow manure."

Clarissa clasped his hand. "Tell him … Tell him, no matter what, I still love him."

Colin gave her hand a squeeze before rising and joining his nieces and nephew on the lawn.

CHAPTER 7

Colin sat in the waiting room of the North Butte Mining Company, half watching as men scurried in and out of offices. A group of men sat at desks in a far corner, although a few of the desks were empty. Colin absently read a newspaper, and, after catching up on the recent developments on the Granite Mountain Mine disaster, he focused on a story chronicling the recent uptick in antidraft activity in Butte in recent weeks.

He frowned as he read about two recent Irish immigrants who had been arrested for distributing antidraft material. A few days after their arrest, the Pearse-Connelly group had provoked a small riot in the streets of Butte as they led an antidraft protest. The condemnation of all such activities had been swift and harsh. Colin set aside the paper as a conference room door opened, and a large number of men exited, including Patrick. Colin watched as a secretary pointed in his direction.

Patrick spun to see his brother, delight then concern flashing across his face. "Col!" he called out as he approached, holding out his hand.

Colin rose, shook his hand and gave him a quick slap on his back.

"What brings you to Butte?"

"How long until you're done with your day's work, Pat?" Colin asked, adroitly dodging his question. "I must speak with you but privately before you head home."

Patrick nodded. "Give me a couple minutes to wrap up a few things." He walked toward his desk, and Colin watched as his older brother shuffled papers and spoke with a few of the men nearest him. Soon Patrick headed toward Colin again.

When they exited onto the street, Colin glanced around before steering them toward a pub for a drink. "How are things since the fire?"

Patrick shook his head. "That's a mild way to describe what happened. It's a disaster through and through. Over 160 men are dead from that fire at the Granite last weekend. And now the men are on strike."

They entered a saloon, crowded with patrons as electricians had walked out in solidarity with the miners and were also on strike. Colin and Patrick purchased glasses of beer and moved to a corner, where they could speak privately. "How many miners aren't working?" Colin asked around a sip of beer. "The papers claim that the men aren't in the mine to attend funerals."

"Well, that's partly true. It's also true that, even without funerals, they aren't returning to the mine. They want the rustling card system gone, an increase in wages and an eight-hour day." He nodded when Colin whistled at the demands. "They also want the right to a union. Many fear another tragedy could strike at any moment."

"So how many aren't working?"

"Fifteen thousand miners out of sixteen thousand have walked out, last I heard," Patrick murmured.

"That's a lot of men not working," Colin murmured as he glanced around the crowded pub. "And we need copper for the war effort."

Patrick nodded. "I know. If they are united, the miners might obtain most of what they desire. But I worry too many are influenced by the likes of the IWW. The Anaconda Company will never bargain with such radicals."

Colin nodded. "And the federal government could impose martial law again like it did in '14." He watched Patrick a moment. "You seem distracted."

"The fire was awful. I can understand not ever wanting to go underground again." At his brother's confused stare, he murmured, "I was a helmet man. Searched for survivors and then retrieved bodies."

Colin blanched. "Why? You have a good job aboveground."

Patrick shrugged. "I wanted to set money aside for Rose and Fee, and the North Butte encouraged those of us who were able and willing to learn how to do the job. They thought it would improve morale with the miners to see deskmen willing to go underground. I was the only one willing to take the training course last year." He shook his head. "It paid well. Now I understand why."

He sighed and took another long swig of his beer before focusing on his brother. "Col, it's always wonderful to see you, but you have to tell me why you're here. Is it Rissa? Sav? You and Araminta?"

"No. Yes. It has to do with Sav and Jeremy." He paused as Patrick frowned. "And Melly."

"Melly?" Patrick whispered. "What's wrong with Melly?"

"Why didn't you ever tell me, Pat?" Colin asked, unable to hide the hurt in his voice. "You've been back for years now."

"I don't understand what you mean." He watched Colin with a cautious intensity.

Colin belted him in the shoulder before leaning closer and rasping, "That she's your daughter. That you had a torrid love affair with Mrs. Smythe. That that's the reason you had to leave Boston."

Patrick choked on his drink, coughing and lowering his head toward the wall as he spit out some of his beer. He coughed a few minutes more as he shook his head in denial. "That's not how it was, Col. You have to believe me."

"Make me believe," Colin demanded. He watched as Patrick paled, still struggling for breath. "Mrs. Smythe paid a call to Sav and Jeremy a few days ago. She tried to rip apart their world. How could you leave them open to such an attack from a woman like her?"

Jeremy closed his eyes. "I never thought she'd come to Montana."

He swiped a hand over his forehead and turned, resting his forehead against the wall. "I swear to you, I never meant to cause any pain."

Colin grabbed his shoulder and spun him to face him. "Dammit, tell me the truth. Tell me what happened. Tell me why you abandoned us all those years ago."

"I didn't abandon you, dammit!" Patrick roared, his eyes flashing with pain and desolation. He lowered his voice so that they would not garner any further interest. "I was thrown out. By Da."

Colin paled as he watched the torment on his brother's face. "Da would never have done that to you, Pat."

Patrick shook his head and laughed humorlessly. "Of course he would, and he did. He wanted no one to question his abilities as a man. As a husband." Patrick swiped at his nose before slamming his hand against the wall.

Colin stood as though in a daze. "Are you saying you were with Mrs. Smythe? That you wanted to be with her?" His voice dropped. "That you are Melly's father?"

"I don't know if I am Melinda's father. I hope I'm not as I haven't amounted to much until recently." He flushed as he looked at his brother. "You remember how soundly I sleep. Like I'm dead to the world and how it takes an army to awaken me?"

Colin nodded.

"Mrs. Smythe discovered that too." Patrick cleared his throat, his flush more pronounced. "She had to awaken me a few mornings to ensure I made it to work on time. Mornings after I worked late, I had trouble waking on time." He shared a chagrined look with his brother. "You remember what it's like when you're young. Your body sometimes acts in ways you wish it wouldn't."

Now Colin flushed. "Yeah, or you'd have dreams and ..." They shared embarrassed smiles.

"Well, she took notice. And one morning I woke up to find her crawling out of my bed." His jaw tightened. "I swear to you. I never sought her out. I never liked her. I hated how she treated Rissa, how she manipulated Da."

"Jesus," Colin whispered. "She ... she ..." He cleared his throat. "She had relations with you, and you didn't even know?"

"I thought it was a dream," Patrick whispered. "And, in that dream, she wasn't the woman involved."

Colin leaned against the wall, flummoxed. "How did Da find out?" He met Patrick's resigned gaze. "She told him, didn't she?" His jaw firmed. "She got what she wanted—a baby and you out of the way."

"She wanted all of us gone," Patrick whispered. "That was her goal."

Colin hit him on his shoulder. "Why didn't you write us? Why didn't you tell us what happened?"

Patrick glared at him. "I did. I wrote you, over and over, and never got a response. I now presume she intercepted the letters." Patrick closed his eyes in defeat. "When I never heard back from you and Rissa, I considered my family, all of my family, dead to me. I thought none of you wanted to hear from me again. I thought you already knew of my shame."

Colin frowned. "We had no idea." He gripped Patrick around the nape of his neck. "Clarissa is very confused. She doesn't know what to believe." Colin shook his head in disgust. "She doesn't want to believe anything Mrs. Smythe says, but she's very worried about Savannah."

"You know I'd never do anything to hurt Sav. Besides, there is no way of knowing who Melly's father is." Patrick took a long swig of his nearly forgotten drink. "I think my role of doting uncle is the only one I should play in Melly's life. Melly can remain secure in her knowledge that Jeremy and Sav love her."

Colin's gaze was troubled. "Is that fair to you?" He cocked his head to the side, deep in thought. "I've always envisioned you involved as a father, like you are with Rose."

Patrick shook his head. "It's how it must be. It's what's best for everyone. I showed up too late, Col." He shook his head with regret before heaving out a breath. "Now I have to tell Fee."

Colin's eyes bulged. "You haven't told your wife?" He shook his head. "You don't make life easy for yourself, brother." He slung his arm around his shoulder and pointed him toward the bar's exit. "Let's head to your house. I'll entertain Rose while you talk with Fiona."

After a short walk through Uptown Butte, Patrick and Colin entered the comfortable home Savannah had purchased for Patrick as a wedding present. He shared it with Fiona and their daughter, Rose. The living room with fireplace was to the left of the entranceway with the kitchen nearly in front of the entrance. Inside the kitchen was a table where they ate their meals. Down the hallway were three bedrooms and a small bathroom. One of Patrick's favorite parts of the house was the large front porch.

As they entered, they hung their coats on pegs by the door and called out a greeting as Rose tottered toward them. Patrick picked her up, kissing her on her cheek, and then passed her to Colin as she squealed and held out her arms to him.

"*Cowin!*" she said in a happy little girl's singsongy voice, patting his whiskered face with her palms. She giggled as she traced his cheeks with her fingers and then played with his hair. Colin bent and nibbled her neck, earning a shrieking giggle. He lowered to the floor with her, helping her as her precarious balance nearly sent her tumbling. She ran toward a pile of wooden toys in the front room, looking over her shoulder for Colin to follow.

"Seems I'll be occupied for some time," Colin said with a laugh as he followed his niece. Patrick slapped him on his shoulder, walking to the kitchen.

He ran into a harried Fiona, wiping her hands on a cloth, as she was about to exit the kitchen. "*Oomph*," he said, holding her a moment as she acted like their daughter, about to teeter over. She quickly regained her balance and backed away from him and his touch. "I didn't see you." He stroked a hand over her arm, sighing as she flinched at the movement.

"'Tis Colin's voice I hear," Fiona said with a questioning lilt. "When did he arrive?"

"Just as work ended. He needed to discuss with me a concern in Missoula." He watched Fiona closely. "He'll spend the night."

Her hands firmed on the towel. "Of course. I should prepare his room." He stilled her erratic movement past him, urging her to sit on one of the low stools by the small table in the middle of the kitchen.

"That can keep. There's something we must discuss, and I want to use the time he's entertaining Rose to talk with you." He watched her tense and fought the urge to soothe her with an unwelcome caress. "It has nothing to do with Rose or you."

Her cognac-colored eyes lit with concern as she watched her husband fidget on his stool. "I've never seen you so nervous. Or indecisive. Tell me what concerns you for it can't be that bad."

Patrick took a deep breath and held very still as he spoke. "I told you about our stepmother, Mrs. Smythe." At her nod, he continued in a flat voice. "She loved to provoke discord. She wanted to separate my father from his children as she wanted Da's money for herself."

"You've told me all this Patrick," Fiona murmured, her brow furrowed in confusion.

"She's in Missoula now, and she's told my cousins, Jeremy and Savannah, that their daughter is really my daughter. With her." He met Fiona's shocked gaze. He barreled on when she remained silent. "It could be true. It probably isn't."

"How could it be true?" Fiona asked. "How could you not have told me this before?"

Patrick ran a hand over his face, now flaming red. "Do you have any idea how embarrassing it is?"

"To have a daughter?" Fiona asked, her expression one of disappointment.

"No, dammit." He grabbed her hand, while his gaze held an entreaty for her to remain seated and hear him out. "Never that. I'd be overjoyed if Melly were mine, but I'd never want to hurt Sav and Jer who love her like their own."

He exhaled. "I'm embarrassed because Mrs. Smythe crept into my bedroom one morning, and I wasn't aware of what was occurring until too late." His words came out in a rush, and she sat there a moment, blank-faced, contemplating what he said.

"She seduced you without you knowing about it?"

He flinched at the doubt in her voice. "There wasn't much seduction involved. Surely you know from your first husband, sleeping men aren't always fully sensate when their bodies are ready for ... relations."

Fiona watched him with dawning horror before clapping a hand over her mouth. He frowned as he expected her to rise, yell at him and run from the room. Instead she bent over, and a laugh burst out. "Oh, forgive me," she whispered. "'Tis inappropriate." She sat up as she wiped at her face, rubbing away a tear. He realized she was fighting a mixture of tears and laughter.

"I don't understand," he whispered.

She shook her head as her shoulders heaved until she reined in the strong emotions. She hiccupped and stuttered out a few breaths as she watched him with a yearning tenderness. He clasped his hands together to keep from reaching for her and having his actions rebuffed again. "I should have known, when you were so understanding with me," she gasped out. "I should have realized you understood what it was to be used."

Patrick frowned, his hands forming fists on the table. "How I was treated is in no way comparable to what you've suffered."

She watched him mournfully. "Are you certain? You were separated from your family for over a decade, and even now you hold yourself aloof. You won't allow yourself to live near them, desperate to maintain a distance I'll never understand. And now to learn you've been denied the opportunity to know your daughter ..." Her eyes filled with sympathetic tears now. "How do you bear it?"

Patrick sat stooped on the stool a moment, his gaze taking her in. "I don't understand you."

Fiona smiled sadly and rose. "And that's a tragedy too," she whispered as she moved from the kitchen to ready the spare bedroom for Colin.

Patrick sat alone in his kitchen while a pot of stew bubbled on the stovetop. Dishes had been set out for dinner; a loaf of bread sat on the counter, waiting to be sliced. He listened to his daughter's infectious giggle and placed a hand on his chest, rubbing at an ache.

~

F iona rose in the morning, moving barefoot and soundlessly to the kitchen. She frowned to discover Patrick at the kitchen table, drinking a cup of coffee. She forced a placid expression on her face. "I'm sorry you were forced to make coffee," she whispered, pulling out an apron. She moved to the icebox and pulled out eggs and bacon to prepare breakfast. "I didn't hear you leave the room."

"I don't know why you would have as I slept on the couch last night." He watched her with a fierce intensity, hiding a frown behind his cup when she stiffened. "Colin and I talked late into the night, and I didn't want to disturb you."

"Is he still asleep?" Fiona cracked an egg with such force that part of the egg white splattered on the countertop.

"I assume he'll sleep until Rose wakes." Patrick stood to refill his coffee cup. "No one can sleep through the racket she makes." Rather than eliciting a smile, Fiona abused the eggs. She whisked them in such an agitated manner that he settled a hand on her arm to calm her frantic movements.

"Does Colin know you didn't sleep with me?" Fiona asked, her breath emerging in an agitated pant.

"I presume he does. Although I don't know why that should bother you. He already knows he's sleeping in my usual room."

Fiona slammed down the bowl with such force he paused to ensure Rose hadn't awoken.

"Fee, calm yourself."

"You're telling me that, all this time, your brother has known that we sleep apart?" Fiona looked everywhere but at her husband.

He sighed and ran a hand through his graying brown hair. "Yes."

Fiona slapped her hands to her hips as she leaned toward her husband, glowering. "That's all you have to say?"

Patrick moved to the kitchen door, kicking aside a small stool that held the door open and swung it shut. He watched her with confused earnestness and approached her to grip her shoulders, maintaining his hold even though she flinched at his touch. "Fee, I don't understand why this upsets you. You haven't wanted me to touch you. Not since before …" He raised an eyebrow. "Why does it bother you that my brother knows?"

She bit back tears. "Your family will believe we don't have a real marriage. That I am an unsuitable wife for you," she whispered. "I hate that they have intimate details about our marriage, are discussing how we live, judging me."

He ran a finger down her cheek but dropped his hands when she jerked away from him. "No, they don't, and they never have. They believe I'm fortunate to have found such a sensible woman who is a wonderful mother." He watched her a moment, waiting for her response. When none came, he picked up his cup of coffee and left the kitchen.

Fiona watched his retreat and closed her eyes. She jerked when Colin cleared his throat. "Forgive me," Fee said. "I wasn't …"

"All will be forgiven if I can have a cup of coffee."

Fiona laughed, reaching for a cup on the shelf over the sink. She handed it to him, and he poured himself some coffee. With his contented sigh at his first sip, she relaxed and approached the eggs she meant to scramble. Colin settled onto the stool used to prop open the door, appearing more asleep than awake.

"I have a question for you, Fee," he asked as he took another sip of coffee, pausing to inhale the rich aromatic flavor. "If you want my brother, why don't you do something about it? You're already married to him. You've already lived through the dread of losing him."

She shook her head, pulling out a fry pan to start the bacon. "You wouldn't understand."

"I never said I would. Nor should I. I'm not your husband." His gaze became more alert with each sip of coffee. "I do know you're not nearly as happy as you could be."

"And you think allowing my husband into my bed will ease all my concerns?" Fiona snapped, hissing as bacon fat sizzled and popped out of the pan, landing on her arm and singeing her skin.

Colin laughed. "I wish life were that simple. Then I think we'd all be a lot more content." He watched her with exasperated fondness. "If you trusted him, shared what you truly felt with him and, yes, shared your bed with him, I think you would be much happier than you are now." He rose and refilled his coffee cup. "I like you, Fee. And I love Patrick. It saddens me to see the same distance between you now as when you married."

He gave her arm a gentle squeeze before departing. The front door closed, and it sounded as though he'd joined Patrick on the front porch. Fiona stood staring at the stove with unseeing eyes, fighting panic as she contemplated Colin's suggestions.

~

Patrick sat on the front porch, sipping his cooling cup of coffee and watching his neighbors. Children played on the sidewalk, the boys tossing balls back and forth while the girls jumped rope. He smiled at Colin as he joined him on the porch. "Sleep well?"

Colin nodded, blowing on his steaming cup of coffee. "Better than you, I imagine. Why didn't you have me sleep on the couch?"

Patrick shrugged his shoulders. "I was fine. I don't need much sleep."

Colin rolled his eyes as he propped his legs on the porch's banister. "That's a load of horse dung, and you know it." He slurped a sip of the hot coffee, wincing as his tongue burned. "What I don't understand is why you're sleeping in the guest bedroom all these years later."

"Let it be, Col." Patrick swore when Colin hit him in the arm, upending half his coffee mug on his leg. He swiped at his pants, but it did little to remove the wet stain.

"You're married to a woman you love and who cares for you. I think she might love you, but she's hard to read. I don't understand why you don't push her a little. See if you can change how things are between you."

Patrick glared at his brother. "Oh, so now you're a fount of relationship advice? How are things between you and Araminta? Have you pressured her lately? How did that go?"

Colin flushed and ducked his head. "Things are the same with Ari.

91

And you're right. I shouldn't be lecturing you when I'm as horrible at relationships as you are. However, I'm also not married."

"Numerous couples sleep in separate bedrooms."

"Generally because they can't stand each other," Colin murmured. "Why won't you try, Pat?"

Patrick set his nearly empty coffee cup on the porch floor and sighed. "For various reasons," Patrick murmured. "I remember what she was like, what our relationship was like before *he* intervened. It was sweet and almost innocent." His hopeful, yearning gaze darkened after a few moments. "And then, to have everything change, because of him. Because he saw her as a pawn."

"Are you still angry with her?" Colin whispered.

"No," Patrick said. "I understand why she did what she did. In many ways it was to protect me and our family." He rubbed at his wet pant leg. "Do you know what it's been like, ever since I married her?" His distant gaze was unfocused as though seeing scenes only visible to him. "I tried to soothe her, to show her how she could trust me. Trust that I wouldn't hurt her. To show her that my touch wouldn't be debasing like his." He clamped his jaw tight at the thought of Samuel Sanders, his former boss, abusing Fiona. The same Samuel Sanders who was also known as Henry Masterson, Gabriel's and Jeremy's cousin from Boston.

Patrick sighed once, then again, his hands unclenching on his thighs. "Even now, every time I touch her, she flinches. Every time I approach her to speak with her, she tenses. As though she's waiting for some form of abuse." He closed his eyes. "I find I have no desire to spark such fear in her."

Colin grunted and crossed one leg on top of the other. "I think you're allowing your fear to guide you as much as hers. She might reject you"—he shrugged as he met his brother's guarded gaze—"but then she might not. Have you ever considered that she's waiting for you to show your interest?"

Patrick snorted. "What else must I do?"

Colin smiled. "Not sleep in another bedroom for starters. Let her accustom herself to you next to her at night. With no expectation other than holding her in your arms. I'd think that would go a long way to soothing her nerves and to proving you're a different man than Sanders."

"I shouldn't have to prove I'm a better man than that bastard," Patrick growled.

Colin nodded. "I know. And rationally she knows that too. But fear isn't rational, Pat. Look at how you refused to discuss the truth of what occurred between you and Mrs. Smythe. You were terrified of losing us all again, even though you had to have known we would support you."

Patrick watched his brother intently for a moment before nodding reluctantly. "I'll think about what you say."

Colin stretched. "Excellent." He extracted a newspaper from next to Patrick's chair. He took a sip of coffee and then choked as he read. "Did you see what the miners wrote in their first strike bulletin?" He gasped, cleared his throat and read, "'We have nothing to lose but our chains.'"

"What?" Patrick grabbed the paper to read it himself. "Of course the Company will make much of such a comment in their papers. What could the miners have been thinking?"

"It's too much like Marx and his Manifesto. Don't they know they have to toe the line to earn public support? They can't go around spouting such drivel if they want to garner the goodwill of those who aren't in mining." Colin shook his head in disbelief.

"When did you read Marx?" Patrick asked with a quirk of an eyebrow.

"Clarissa isn't the only one in the family who had radical tendencies. Hers have persisted while mine died an early death." He winked at Patrick. "I found it to be an interesting, although impractical, read. I was also disappointed in myself to realize I'm too much of a capitalist to ever fully support such radical ways of thinking."

Patrick sighed as he heard a small cry from indoors. "Peace is over. I must go help Fee." He slapped Colin on his shoulder. "I'm sure Fee will have breakfast ready in a few minutes." Patrick entered the house, holding out his arms for a fussy Rose. "There's my beautiful girl," he crooned. He settled her on his shoulder and walked with her around the living room as she sniffled and fought fully waking. He told her stories and rubbed her back as she calmed.

Fiona entered the living room and met her husband's gaze. He nodded at her unspoken question. "She's ready for her breakfast. If she doesn't eat now, she'll be too busy playing with ..." He broke off and nodded toward the porch. He knew if he mentioned Colin's name, Rose would forgo eating to spend time with one of her favorite people.

Patrick followed Fiona into the kitchen and held Rose on his lap, feeding her bites of egg, toast and bacon. When she'd had her fill, she squirmed on his lap to get down. He stood, following Rose with her unsteady gait to the front door, smiling as she patted Patrick's leg and called Colin's name. Although Patrick busied himself with the care of his daughter, thoughts of his wife and his conversation with Colin were ever-present.

~

Lucas Russell answered the door, pulling his cousin Colin Sullivan into a hug and slapped him on the back a few times. Lucas nodded at Patrick and Fee, holding a sleeping Rose and standing behind Colin. "It's wonderful to see you, Col. Glad to have you to our home for supper. I know it's only been a few months since we traveled to Missoula for little Colin's birthday party, but it's still been too long."

Genevieve smiled as she watched her husband's joy at seeing a close family member. "Lucas is delighted when family from Missoula visits."

Colin laughed, bending to kiss Genevieve on her cheek. "Then he should move to Missoula. Sav would love to have her brother nearby."

"Preferably next door," Lucas said with a chuckle as he thought about his sister.

Patrick raised an eyebrow as he watched his brother. "I would have to disagree, Colin. We enjoy having them with us here in Butte." They finished their round of greetings with little Rose receiving the most kisses, but never work up, before they all ventured into the dining room.

"I love this room," Fiona breathed, as she placed the still-sleeping Rose into an improvised crib Lucas has positioned near the dining table. Situated toward the back of the house, the dining room had a bowed window with stained glass in the top panes. Built-in shelves and cabinets in the walls allowed for the easy storage of linens and silverware, and a large maple table filled the center of the room.

After they had passed the food around, their discussions continued. "How are things at work, Pat?" Lucas asked.

"Tense," Patrick murmured.

"I would think it would be, after the tragedy," Genevieve said. "It seems unimaginable that so many lives were lost."

"My company is concerned it won't withstand the strike and will finally be sold to Anaconda." Patrick's expression turned grim as he discussed the potential dissolution of his employer.

"I had no idea," Fiona whispered.

"I didn't want to worry you." Patrick reached out a hand to grip hers but then halted the movement halfway, and opened and closed his hand a few times. "I hope it won't come to that."

Colin tapped his fork on his dinner plate as he contemplated his brother. "Why should your company be in such financial difficulty?"

"For many reasons. The first is that the main mine is out of commission for the foreseeable future. Then there is the matter of the strike."

"You can't blame the men for wanting better working conditions," Genevieve murmured.

"I can't, especially after spending so many hours underground in the drifts." He shuddered and focused on her. "But I also think the miners don't understand that they will have no option but to work for the Company if we do go under." Patrick sighed. "Although, when I consider it, I can't see that it makes much difference. Everyone caters to the desires of the Company, including the North Butte Mining Company."

Lucas shook his head in disgust. "The days of any true competition ended years ago when Heinze left in 1906. He was the only one left to stand up to Anaconda."

Patrick shrugged. "Daly was dead, and Clark had moved on. Now no one is strong enough to take on the Company."

Colin vaguely acknowledged Lucas's comment before focusing on his brother, Patrick, again. "Is there another reason for financial difficulties?"

Patrick rubbed at his temple. "Yes. We have to pay a certain amount to the widows and for funeral benefits. With the number of men who died, it could be nearly half a million dollars."

Colin whistled. "Wow. Won't insurance cover it?"

Patrick shrugged. "Insurance companies have a way of finagling out of paying for what was supposedly covered. They have clauses that cover clauses. We've spent days going over policies until my head spins."

Lucas watched his oldest cousin a moment. "Why don't you obtain work as an architect again? I know that's what you truly love. And you'd never have to consider working as a helmet man again."

Patrick shrugged. "I have a family now, and we need a steady income."

Lucas frowned and was about to say more but saw a warning, protective glint in Colin's eyes and nodded. "So what brought you to town, Col?"

"Oh, I wanted to see my big brother. And I needed to warn him that Mrs. Smythe had reappeared in Missoula."

"That harpy?" Lucas growled. "Has she bothered Rissa?"

Colin smiled. "Oh, Rissa is able to fight back now. It was fun to watch her go toe-to-toe with her when she dared stop by Rissa's house. I'm more worried about Savannah. Mrs. Smythe's stirring up trouble with Melinda."

Lucas paled. "Oh, no. She *is* Melly's mother."

Patrick snorted. "Not in any way that matters. I've never met a woman so lacking in all maternal instincts."

Lucas watched Patrick curiously. "But you never saw her around Melly."

"No, but she treated us abysmally and took great pleasure in mistreating Clarissa. I can see no reason why she'd suddenly have turned into a maternal figure simply because she'd given birth."

"It does happen," Genevieve said with a wry tone. "I've known women who weren't the least bit maternal who then turn into the best mothers once they held their babies in their arms."

"Well, it didn't happen with her," Colin said. "She sent her own daughter to an orphanage rather than economize further to keep Melinda with her after Da died. She's a vile woman." He watched Patrick closely for a moment as though waiting to see if he would elaborate further. However, Patrick remained quiet. "She's hell-bent on causing problems again."

Lucas stroked a hand down Genevieve's back. "Let us know if you need us to do anything."

Colin nodded. "For now, it's enough that you realize she's back and stirring up trouble again. I wish you were in Missoula, but at least you aren't that far away."

~

After seeing Fiona and Rose home after supper with the Russells, Patrick and Colin entered a bar near the house. It was like entering a cave after the bright early evening light. The scarred walnut bar was long with three men manning it. Casks of whiskey and beer stood stacked behind the men, while a mirror gleamed at the center of the space behind the bar. So as to maximize drinking space, no tables or chairs littered the bar, except for a corner for musicians, where a man sat, teasing a tune from a decrepit-looking concertina.

Patrick approached the bar and ordered a drink, startled when a heavy hand landed on his shoulder. He felt Colin tense next to him as though prepared for a fight, but Patrick shook his head as he met the man's gaze.

"You saved men, risking your own life," the man said. "Lost three

97

cousins in that fire but would have lost more friends and family had it not been for the likes of you." He slapped Patrick on the back and motioned for the bartender to pour him a drink. "His drinks are on me."

When Patrick protested, the man waved away his concern. "No, you didn't have to put yourself in harm's way to help the miners, but you did. You could have remained in that office, concerned about profits. Instead you worried about the men who fought for their lives." Men who stood nearby grunted their approval or raised their drinks and said, "Hear, hear."

Patrick flushed and accepted his drink. "Thank you." He raised his drink to the men all dressed in black as they had just come from another funeral. "Here's to those unable to raise a glass with us today."

The men gave a solemn salute and lowered their heads as they considered the loss of their friends and comrades. Patrick slapped the man on the back and moved toward a rear wall, away from the mourning miners huddled near the bar.

"Is it like that everywhere you go?" Colin asked, then frowned. "That didn't happen last night after you got off work."

Patrick took a long sip of his beer and shook his head. "Some recognize me, but, for the most part, few know who I am."

Colin leaned against the wall, crossing his legs at the ankle as he watched the miners talk somberly among themselves. "I'm glad they have the sense not to be angry with you."

Patrick shrugged. "When you think about it, I'm a cog in the wheel, like they are. And, because I risked my life for them, I'm no longer seen as a stuffed shirt doing company business."

"I hope for everyone's sake you're giving up the foolish notion of working as a helmet man again in the future." He froze as his brother glared at him. "We want you safe, Patrick."

He sighed and shook his head. "I know. But you don't understand what it was like to save a man. To know that at least one woman wouldn't be a widow. Or one mother wouldn't lose her son." He shook his head as his gaze became distant.

"What was it truly like? I know you've never told Fiona the whole truth." Colin took a sip of his beer, watching his brother closely.

"And I can never tell her how horrible it was. Blinded by smoke and noxious fumes, worried I'd run out of oxygen in my tank and end up like the men on the mine floor, whose eyes were wide and mouths gaping open, like fish as they gasped for oxygen and choked to death." He closed his eyes a moment. "At first I thought I was tripping over lumber brought down to shore up the drifts. It was only later I realized I'd trampled over limbs and bodies, men who had been dead long enough to become stiff."

He took a deep breath once, then twice before he met Colin's worried gaze. "You're concerned because you believe I'll want to play hero and go back down again. Little could induce me to enter a cage and go back into a mineshaft. On a good day, it's hell on earth. Some levels are cool. Mac and I were sent to Purgatory. Hot as Hades on that level, made worse with the equipment we had to carry. Must have been 120 degrees." He shuddered, his gaze distant and voice flat. "I came across a wall, I thought it was a wall that had been constructed to close off the drift from other mines. My company has an overwhelming fear of being robbed by Anaconda."

He sighed and pinched the bridge of his nose. "I didn't know. I ... I realize now I should never have worked such a job. I was trained yet so inexperienced, not a miner. What did I know?" His brown eyes shone with agony as he relived a scene only he could see.

"I know you did your best and better than most could have done. Hell, you went down again and again, even after Fiona begged you not to." Colin's brows furrowed as his words did little to ease his brother's torment. "What happened, Pat?"

"It wasn't a wall. It was a prayer." He sighed. "It was a patchwork of timber and stones to keep some of the poison gas out so the men behind it had a chance for survival. And I ignored it. I didn't know better! And some of those men died because of my stupidity."

Colin took another sip of his beer before gripping Patrick on the shoulder with one of his strong hands. "By your own admission you were nearly blinded the moment you went down into the mine. Did the man with you think it was anything more than a concrete wall?" At Patrick's small shake of his head, Colin shook his shoulders once. "Your partner *was* an experienced miner. He knew what to look for, and he thought it was nothing. You did your best, Pat. There's nothing more anyone else could have done."

Patrick let out a stuttering sigh. "I tell myself that, but it's damn hard to be content with such an explanation as I sit at their funerals and watch their families mourn. As I look at their children and realize they won't have a father."

"You didn't cause the fire. You didn't order the drifts connecting the mines to be sealed with concrete so there was no escape." Colin clamped his jaw as he fought his growing anger at what had been done that had unintentionally made the loss of life greater. "You did everything you could to help men out of that horrible miasma."

"Did you know that the initial cause for the disaster was when a cable caught fire? It was being lowered into the Granite Mountain Mine to help create a fire sprinkler system. How ironic. How deadly ironic." He met Colin's gaze as Colin snorted in disbelief. Patrick sighed and nodded, unable to hide the guilt in his gaze. "I know I did what I could, but I wonder why I'm lucky enough to hold Rose every day and put her to bed when others have been denied that."

"There is much we'll never understand. I'd give thanks you have that chance." Colin half smiled as he watched his brother. "And I'd hope that nearly losing you would bring you and Fee closer together."

CHAPTER 8

*W*hen Fiona and Patrick tucked Rose in for the evening, Fiona whispered to Patrick that she expected him in their bed while Colin visited and that she would come find Patrick if he spent another night on the couch. So when he entered the room he would share with Fiona for the next few nights, he sighed at her, curled on her side with the blankets wrapped snugly around her.

"You'll melt," he said as he sat down and unbuttoned his shirt. When she refused to answer him, he touched his hand to her hip. She flinched but did not roll away so his hand did not break contact with her.

"You know I'll keep to my agreement," he whispered. "I had hoped by now you'd trust me." He frowned as he heard what sounded like a sniffle. He turned around to study her, but he only saw her back rise and fall with her breaths. However, his curiosity was piqued, and he rose. He kicked off his shoes, shucked his pants, and moved to her side of the bed with his underclothes on.

He paused when he leaned over her. She'd covered her face with a hand, smothering the virtually inaudible sounds of her crying. He knelt before her on the floor and ran a hand from her hairline, down her neck, shoulder, arm, and hip and back up again. "Why are you crying, my dearest Fiona?" When he noticed her slight trembling with his touch, he retracted his hand. "I never realized. I'll—"

"No!" Fiona rasped. "No, please. I'm so tired."

He pulled away her hand, allowing him to see her face. "What are you tired of? Of me?"

"No." She raised their joined hands so she could trace his jawline with one of her fingers. "I'm so tired of acting like I want our lives to continue as they began."

He settled more comfortably beside her, eye to eye. "Why have you never said anything?"

She turned her face, swiping her cheeks dry on the sheet, before facing him again. "In the beginning, every time you touched me, all I could think of was how I'd betrayed us by what I'd done. Then I became huge with the baby." She sniffled and appeared unable to prevent her tears from falling. "I never meant to put on that much weight."

"What are you talking about?" Patrick asked, his brows furrowed as he watched her.

"The bigger I got, the less you touched me, reached for me, and then, after I had Rose, ... and you thought it would help if you were in another room while I nursed her ..." She broke off as she heaved out a sigh.

"You think I no longer desired you because you gained weight to bring our beautiful daughter into this world?" He failed to hide the incredulity from his voice. He gripped her hand tightly as he stared into her eyes. "Every time I went to touch you, you'd shy away from me. A man can only suffer that sort of a reaction so many times before he changes how he acts."

Fiona closed her eyes. "I've never lost all the weight. I'm never going to."

"Is that really all you're afraid of? That I'm worried you've gained weight?" He frowned as a shadow passed through her gaze that she attempted to squelch. "Are you sure there isn't more?"

She swallowed and opened and closed her mouth a few times as though trying to speak but unable to form words. "I ... I can still feel his touch," she admitted with closed eyes.

Patrick traced her cheek, causing her eyes to open and focus on him. "I'd never hurt you, Fee. Please tell me that you know that."

She turned her cheek into his palm, rather than jerking away from him. "I do. I've known since before we married."

"What do you want, Fee? I thought you were happy with our arrangement."

"Are you?"

He gave an incredulous laugh. "Hell no. I want to bed my wife. I want to have a full relationship with you, something we've never had." He smiled at her, an aching fondness in his eyes. "For too long, we've allowed the actions of others and our fears to keep us separated. Let me love you."

"I'm so afraid," she admitted. "When I thought I'd lost you ..." She met his eyes with ones filled with a mixture of torment and relief. "It made me regret all the time I had acted out of fear."

"I love you, Fee. I love you for myriad reasons, but mainly simply because you are you. When I see you, my spirit lightens, and I know I can face anything. If you never wanted things to change between us, I would accept that, because being near you is, ... well, almost enough." He smiled as he cupped her cheek. "I promise to be honest."

"I'm afraid you'll be disappointed in me. I don't really know ... I don't really know what I'm doing. What I'm supposed to do."

He held a finger to her lips. "Your first marriage could have brought you little pleasure as your husband was only interested in having someone to cook and clean for him before using you to fulfill a life insurance policy. Your other experience could most accurately be described as, ... well, it wasn't pleasurable. And it wasn't by your choice." His gaze was filled with concerned tenderness. "I need you to tell me what you want. Show me what you want."

"Kiss me," she implored, grabbing him behind the nape and tugging him forward. He slowed the awkward tumble her hasty actions caused, balancing with one hand on either side of her upper body.

"Easy, my darling," he whispered. He clambered to the other side of her, lying on his side as he traced her head and cheek with soothing caresses. She calmed, tilting into his touch as she closed her eyes with a sigh of contentment. He traced her lips twice, then three times, before he leaned forward to give her a feather-soft kiss.

"Yes," she breathed, freeing an arm from underneath the blankets to snake around his neck and hold him to her. "More."

Patrick groaned as he deepened the kiss, his hands roaming over her body covered in the blankets and nightgown. He smiled as she pushed him to his back and leaned over him, taking control of the kiss. "Show me what you want," he murmured, tangling his hands in her red-gold hair.

She continued to kiss him, running her hands through his hair and then down his chest. Her touch was fleeting, and he arched up for more of it. When she leaned away, he growled with frustration, rolling her beneath him. He grabbed one of her hands, lacing it with his as some of the weight from his lower body rested on her.

He nuzzled her neck, stilling when he sensed her shudder was not borne of pleasure. "Fee?" he panted, pushing himself away and freeing her hand. "What did I do?" He cupped his hands around her face, running thumbs over her cheeks. The passionate flush had faded from her cheeks.

He kissed her brow, murmuring how beautiful she was to him. His thumbs traced loving patterns over her cheek and jawline. He kissed her softly as her tension slowly eased. Her eyes eased open, and the panic within cleared as she focused on him.

"Patrick," she whispered, a hint of wonder in her voice.

"Yes, my love." He kissed her nose and waited for her to explain what had happened.

Shame filled her gaze as she battled tears. "Forgive me."

He shook his head at her words and nodded his encouragement for her to continue speaking.

"When you rolled me over, grasped my arms, I felt powerless. It made me think of ... of ..."

Patrick lowered his head to the pillow beside hers and groaned.

"Forgive *me*." He pushed himself up on his forearms, balancing his weight on his arms and knees, his weight now fully off her. "I wasn't thinking. I ..."

Her tremulous smile held joy and wonder. "I know. Which is miraculous to me. You weren't touching me as though I were damaged. Or used. Or wicked."

His eyes flashed with anger. "You aren't, Fee. You are fine and good and lovely."

She stroked a shaking hand over his clenched jaw. "I try to keep him locked away," she whispered, her voice breaking as she spoke. Patrick groaned and flopped to his back beside her. She folded her hands over her lower belly, turning her head to look at him a moment. She scooted under the blankets until she was next to him and lay as close to his side as possible.

At her growl of frustration, he looked down to find her wriggling closer to him, yet her actions were hindered by the heavy layer of blankets. He sighed with disappointment as she shimmied away from him and closed his eyes. As a corner of one of the blankets thwacked him in the face, he jerked, and he fought a smile to see her fighting to free herself of the cocoon she herself had fashioned.

After nearly falling out of the bed, she turned to him with an embarrassed yet triumphant smile, pushing down the blankets on her side of the bed—as far as they'd go with him lying on the other half.

He smiled with fondness at her long white linen nightgown and thick stockings. "Did you really think you'd sleep well so covered up in June?" he teased.

She shrugged as she blushed, her hair shimmering like fire in the low lamplight as it fell over one shoulder. "Will you hold me?" she whispered.

"Of course." He outstretched his arm so she could use his shoulder as a pillow. She rested on him, her erratic breathing and pulse slowly calming.

"I've never known this," she whispered.

He traced a palm over her head to her shoulder, his focus on her.

"This quiet contentment where a man finds enjoyment merely from my company."

"I plan on giving you many firsts, my Fee," he whispered. He stilled his hand as he felt her shivering again. "Let me get the blanket. You're cold."

"No, not cold." She leaned over him with her palms on his chest, her hair tickling his face as she studied him. "I've only felt pleasure with you, Patrick." She flushed at how her words pleased him. "I ... Show me."

"I refuse to frighten you," he whispered. "I can't bear it."

"Help take away my fear. Please." A tear escaped, tracking down her cheek, and Patrick arched up to kiss it away. She relaxed into his touch as though relishing in it.

"If I do anything that scares you, that makes you uncomfortable, that makes you want to stop, tell me." He searched her eyes as though ensuring himself of her sincerity and her desire for him.

She nodded, kissing him on the lips and resting more of her weight on his chest.

He gasped to feel her breasts pressed to his chest, only her thin nightgown and his undershirt separating them. As though of their own volition, his hands rose and ran from her shoulders to her hips, pulling her more tightly to him.

"I want you, Fee," he whispered as he broke the kiss. "I can't lie to you and say I don't."

She laughed, sounding like a young woman. "Do you know what it means to me to hear you say that?" She bit her lip as she sat up to slide her nightgown over her head in a seductive manner. Instead, it got stuck, and she toppled to the side.

Patrick laughed and loomed over her, gripping her gown by the hem, where it was stuck at her hips. "Here, let me help." He waited for her to nod her consent before he eased it up her body and over her head. After he tossed it to the floor, he stilled, taking in the sight of her, naked to him, for the first time.

"Oh, my darling Fee," he murmured, his gaze caressing her. "You are beautiful beyond words." His hands traced over her in a light touch, following the path of his gaze and provoking a soft all-over body blush from her. "You were always lovely, Fee, but now you are stunning."

He leaned forward and kissed her before lifting off his shirt and stripping from the rest of his underclothes. He scooted onto his side next to her, leaning on one elbow as he used his free hand to draw patterns over her skin. "Your skin is like the softest silk I've ever had the good fortune to touch." He kissed her collarbone and her neck, tracing his hand down her belly.

"No," she whispered, squirming away from him.

"What is it?" He stilled his movements and looked where his hand was. On her belly, over silvery skin, stretched from her pregnancy. "You think I won't find you attractive because you've had a child?" He grinned at her but sobered when she battled tears.

"I hate what happened to my body," she whispered.

He kissed her hands covering her belly and the marks she detested on her skin. "Do you regret Rose?" At her instinctive gasp of denial, he smiled. "Then rejoice in your body's ability to give us a child. With good fortune, we'll have many more."

His head turned into her hands, kissing her palms as they lifted away from her belly to trace his face. After a few kisses to each palm, he turned his head to meet her watery gaze, his filled with desire. "I love you, Fee. This isn't some boyhood fantasy that will be destroyed because I realize you are human. This is a man's love. A man's passion for his wife."

She stuttered out a breath, her arms reaching for him, and he rose, pulling her into his embrace as she cried. He held her close as she sobbed. "Let me hold you," he whispered. "Tonight let me hold you."

"I know that's not enough," she whispered as she shuddered.

He forced her to meet his gaze, his palms wet from her tears. "You're always so brave. This isn't about what I want or need. Ensuring you are happy makes me happy. Seeing you smile at me makes me content beyond my dreams. I don't want you to do something merely because you believe you must." He kissed her reverently. "We have plenty of time for lovemaking, my darling Fee." He pulled her close, holding her as she relaxed in his arms. "Do you know how long I've dreamed of holding you in my arms?"

"Since the day we met," she whispered. "That's when my dreams began." Her voice trailed away as though she battled sleep.

He sighed, tugging her closer as her breaths slowly deepened. "Rest in my arms, my darling." He kissed her on her head and followed her into sleep.

$\sim$

Colin watched his brother the next morning as Fiona bustled around, preparing for church. He nodded to the front porch, and Patrick joined him outside. Patrick grunted as Colin gave a small yelp and hit him on his shoulder. "Seems you took my advice."

Patrick flushed at Colin's comment before sharing a smile with his brother. "All I will say is that things are improving between us."

Colin laughed. "Good. You and Fee deserve to be happy." He perched on the deck's brick banister. "I hate that I have to leave today."

"You've already taken too much time away from your business." Patrick watched his brother. "How is it going?"

"Oh, it's fine. I have good men working for me, although a man in town is intent on driving me insane." At Patrick's inquisitive stare, Colin crossed his legs at the ankles and raised his eyebrows as he met Patrick's concerned look. "A Mr. Caine is intent on purchasing my business, even though I have no inclination to sell."

"Why would he want your business? I'd think there'd be plenty of work in town for more than one blacksmith shop."

"Oh, there is. And there are numerous shops. For some reason he has it in his head that he must purchase mine." Colin shrugged. "I run the most successful shop in town, but I don't see why he won't start his own."

"There must be more to it than you're telling me," Patrick said.

Colin leaned against one of the pillars holding up the porch roof. "When I decided I wanted to live in Missoula permanently, I worked hard to save money and to buy my own smithy. Clarissa and I received no money as an inheritance when Da died, and his smithy was sold in Boston by Mrs. Smythe in her attempt to remain solvent." Colin rubbed at his temple. "I used to think I'd be happy working for another man, but I realized after a few years in Missoula that I wanted my own place. I'd basically run Da's smithy for a long time."

Patrick shook his head in confusion. "None of this is new to me."

"Well, when I bought my smithy, the other man interested in it was Mr. Caine. He believed he had a right to it and was irate that Mr. Jacobson sold it to me." Colin bit his lip and furrowed his brow. "I've never understood his animosity toward me nor his desire to reclaim *that* shop."

"You paid a fair price, and it was that man's to sell," Patrick said.

Colin nodded his head in agreement.

"Well, what I would say, after seeing how the Company functions here, is that you must ensure that the men working for you are truly loyal to you. Not to that Mr. Caine."

Colin frowned as he mulled over Patrick's words. "My men are loyal."

Patrick huffed out a breath. "That's what we all like to believe. However, it's not always true." He slapped Colin on his shoulder and led him inside for breakfast. When Patrick saw Fiona, he leaned over and kissed her on her cheek, smiling broadly when she moved into his touch rather than away. He ran a hand over her shoulder before lifting Rose for a kiss.

After finishing breakfast, Fiona held Rose and looked at Colin. "'Twill be sad to see you go today. We always enjoy your visits."

"I wish you could travel to Missoula more frequently," Colin said. "I know the rest of the family would love to see Rose grow." He kissed the top of her head as she played with a button on his shirt. His intent gaze homed in on his brother. "You'll travel to Missoula soon."

Patrick shared a look with Fiona and nodded. "I know. May we stay with you?"

Colin beamed. "You'll all come?" He tickled little Rose and laughed as she giggled.

"If Patrick would like us to be there as he confronts his stepmother, I'd rather be nowhere else," Fiona said. She flushed as Patrick watched her appreciatively. "Come. We must be away to church, or we'll be late." She bustled everyone out the door and slipped her arm through her husband's as Colin carried Rose.

After the service, she stood outside the church, holding Rose while Patrick and Colin spoke with a few men from the congregation as they waited for Lucas and Genevieve. She held her face to the sun a moment, enjoying the momentary fresh air as a brisk wind blew out the day's smog.

"I'd worry about forming more freckles if I were you, Mrs. Sullivan," a taunting voice said near her ear.

She stilled, lowering her face to meet the jeering gaze of her tormentor. She held Rose closer, but Rose was alert and held out her hands to pat the man. "No, love," Fiona whispered. Rose squirmed in her mother's arms as she was denied.

"Seems she knows her father already," Samuel Sanders murmured, his eyes lit with curiosity as he watched a vivacious Rose.

Fiona jutted out her chin in a challenge. "She's never known a day's sadness. I'll not allow you to sully her life with your presence." She jerked back a step when Samuel raised a hand to clasp Rose's outstretched one.

"Why deny your daughter when it seems she wants to know me?" He raised an eyebrow, his smile deepening at Fiona's growing distress.

"She's never known a harsh word or touch. She believes everyone will be kind to her. I'll not have her learn the cruelties of this world from you." She jumped when a soft hand landed on her shoulder before leaning back when she recognized Patrick's soothing voice in her ear. She spun and thrust Rose into his arms.

Rose gave a crow of delight to be in her father's arms, the new man forgotten. Patrick watched Samuel with a warning glint in his eyes. "I'd be very careful if I were you," Patrick murmured. "Please leave."

Colin stood next to Patrick with Lucas and Genevieve on the other side. The three men glowered at Samuel and formed an impenetrable wall of strength as they faced down Fiona's nemesis.

Samuel smiled before chuckling. "I wasn't doing anything. I was merely commenting on the fine day."

"Of course you weren't," Colin murmured. "You prefer to act with stealth and deceit. You'd never be open about the devastation you are about to inflict."

Samuel smiled his agreement before tipping his hat at Fiona and Genevieve and sauntering away. They watched until he had disappeared from sight. Patrick ran a hand down Fiona's arm, stuttering out a sigh of relief when she leaned into his side for support. "He's gone, love. He won't hurt us."

"He's fixated on Rose," she whispered. "The older she gets, the more interested he becomes."

"Then we'll simply be more vigilant," Patrick said as he nodded to his brother and cousin and walked to his house for Sunday dinner before Colin had to leave.

～

Fiona moved around her small bedroom and sniffed the offending odor. She paused and closed her eyes, discerning where it came from. When she opened her eyes, she moved to a corner of the room where Patrick had left a small pile of dirty clothes. She lifted his work shirts and pants and then blanched as the stench intensified. The clothes he'd worn for days while working at the mine were at the bottom of the pile.

She lifted the pants between her thumb and forefinger, held them away from her. "Burning's too good for you," she muttered at the pants as she glared at the equally offensive shirt on the floor. After taking a deep breath, she slipped her hand into one pocket and then the other. She extracted a slip of paper smudged with dirt and dropped the pants to the floor again as she unfolded the paper to find Patrick's handwriting.

My Darling Fiona,

I don't have much time to write, and I'm a horrible correspondent, so I fear you must make do with this letter. Up to now, I've had minor mishaps with my helmet and breathing apparatus. Nothing that would lead to any permanent damage.

However, should something happen to me, I want you to know that marrying you was the best thing I ever did. Rose is my greatest joy. I will always be thankful I helped you at the Gardens and that you saw me as more than Sanders's underling.

If the worst happens, know that I have loved you from the beginning. My love for you has only grown with each day.

Patrick

"Oh my," she breathed, reaching behind her for the edge of the bed. She perched on it, tracing the words on the scrap of paper. A tear trickled down her cheek, and she wrapped her arms around her middle. After a moment she rose, setting the paper by her bed stand and picked up the offending garments to dispose of. Patrick would be home soon from the pub, after seeing his brother off. Her husband, who had dared death and survived to return to her and Rose. She swiped at her cheeks as she tossed his clothes in the garbage bin and returned to the bathroom to wash and prepare for bed.

That evening after Colin left, Patrick sat on the settee in the living room, staring into space. Rose had been in bed a few hours, and Fiona had retired not long after that. He sighed and rubbed his face before rising and wandering into the bedroom he used to sleep in before Colin's arrival. He shucked his clothes before tumbling into the small bed.

After tossing and turning for many minutes, he flopped to his back to stare at the ceiling.

"Patrick?" Fiona's soft voice called out.

He pushed up onto one elbow on his bed. "Fee, what are you doing up? You should be asleep," he whispered.

"I was waiting for my husband," she said, glaring at him. "Why are you in here again? I thought we were past that."

He shook his head, sitting up with the blankets pooled around his waist. "I was sitting on the sofa, and I realized I hadn't asked you if I should join you tonight or not. I didn't want to presume ..."

She reached out a hand. "I want you next to me every night, Patrick. You don't have to ask or seek my permission." She gave him a chagrined smile. "Although I suppose you have it now." She watched as he remained seated on the bed. "Please."

"I'm not wearing any clothes, Fee," he said. "I'll be in our room in a minute."

She flushed but met his gaze. "Come. You're my husband, and our child is fast asleep. You can race across the hall with me without worrying about your dignity." She extended her hand again and beamed at him as he took it.

He rose, tugging her to him until she was flush against him. He lowered his head and kissed her until they were both breathless. "I want you, darling Fee."

"Good, because I want you too," she whispered, backing up a step. Her smile broadened as he followed her.

When they entered their bedroom, he teased the hem of her night-gown up her body and over her head. "Let me love you tonight, Fee." He kissed her shoulder, the skin above and below her breast and smiled at her groan of frustration.

"Yes, my love, yes," she whispered.

He met her passion-filled gaze, a slow smile spreading when he saw trust and desire but no fear. "I've dreamed of this since I met you." He smiled fully as she blushed at his words.

She peppered his cheeks and chin with kisses before whispering, "I told myself you were lonely and only wanted a friend."

He paused and met her gaze as he settled her on the bed and lay beside her. "I did want a friend, but I wanted more too." At her chuckle he kissed her deeply while his hands roamed over her, calming any of her nerves and provoking her passion.

"Make love with me, husband," she said as she nipped at his ear.

Soon they were lost to words.

∾

Patrick held a quiet Fiona in his arms and stroked a hand over her hip, to soothe himself as much to soothe her. He took a deep breath and then another as he fought his instinct to speak. When she nuzzled his neck, he kissed the top of her head.

After many minutes, she whispered, "Why won't you say anything? I'm sorry if I was a disappointment to you."

He snorted a startled sound, turning to his side so he could face her, to read her guarded expression. "How could you think I'm disappointed?"

Her hands played over his chest and arms, yet her gaze was downcast. "You haven't said anything."

At her whispered words, he groaned. "I thought you were upset. I … I wanted you too much, Fee. I'm sorry if you didn't find the pleasure you could have."

She frowned as she watched him. "I've never felt as cherished and desired as I did when we made love." She flushed as his eyes darkened at her words. "You'll never know what it means to me to know you still want me after everything."

He smiled and kissed her, rolling her on her back. "I'll want you until they put me in my grave." He sighed and kissed her gently before leaning away. He frowned as his thumbs traced away tears. "What is it, my love?"

"I found your letter."

He shook his head in confusion at her words.

"The letter you wrote in case you died in the mine." She pushed her head against his shoulder, wrapping her arms and legs around him as her tears fell.

"I never meant for you to see that," he whispered into her ear as she shuddered against him.

She pushed back to trail her fingertips over his face, her eyes wide with wonder as his cheek moved into her touch. "Do you know what it meant to find that letter? To know your last words to me would have been of love?" She leaned forward and kissed him. She sniffled.

"To know I didn't have to find your letter at the undertakers like so many others?"

"Oh, love," he murmured into her hair.

"I knew, deep inside, I knew you loved me. You told me how you did last night, but now, for some reason, I believe you." She met his gaze. "Thank you for never giving up on me."

His smile bloomed as his palms cupped her cheeks. "I never could. You mean everything to me, Fiona. You and Rose are my world. I will do all I can to protect you and provide for you."

"Promise me that you won't work as a helmet man again. I couldn't bear it."

He studied her a moment before nodding. "I don't think I could bear it either." He tugged her close and stroked his hand over her arm. "You must rest if you're to keep up with our daughter tomorrow. Let me hold you while we sleep." His contented sigh filled the room as she fitted her body against his side, and they slipped into a peaceful sleep together.

CHAPTER 9

Missoula, Montana, June 1917

*A*raminta walked in the shadows alongside the street in an attempt to remain cool in the long summer evening as she headed away from downtown. Maple trees planted twenty years ago had grown enough to provide some shade, and small flower gardens dozed after the heat of the day as they awaited their daily watering. She waved to a neighbor and continued her loping walk.

She ignored the calls of "Miss!" as she made her way to her new home. She had saved enough money over the years that she was confident in her ability to rent a small set of rooms near downtown Missoula. Although it had dampened her independent spirit, she had needed Gabriel to cosign both her bank account and her lease. Banks and landlords remained reluctant for single women to sign their own contracts, and she was thankful Gabriel had been willing to vouch for her.

However, she finally had a home of her own for the first time in her life. She smiled when she turned the corner for home on Pine Street, anxious to decorate and move furniture around. She gasped when someone grabbed her arm.

Bartholomew Bouchard was out of breath and sweating in the warm evening weather when he said, "Miss!" one last time. When Araminta looked him up and down in confusion, he smiled a toothy grin as though he thought that were charming. "I've been calling out to you."

She stiffened her shoulder and wrenched her arm free. "Do you have a habit of accosting women and then leering at them as though a deranged lunatic?" She huffed out a breath and turned on her heel.

"No, wait!" He reached for her again, only to have his hand slapped away.

"I don't care to be pawed by you, Mr. Bouchard." She faced him, her breath coming quickly as though she had been the one racing down the sidewalk. "I bid you a good evening."

"I had hoped you would be inclined to have supper with me." He took off his hat and pushed back a piece of hair not shellacked in place by the heavy application of pomade. His eerily light-blue eyes held a beseeching note. "I hate to eat alone."

"Then I'm afraid you are destined for discomfort," she snapped. "I'm surprised you can't find one of your friends or cousins to enter-tain you." Her gaze sharpened. "Or is it that you wanted to better acquaint yourself with *the cripple?*"

"Don't call yourself that," he barked. He blushed when he saw the confirmation in her gaze that his acquaintances referred to her as such. "I do not see you in such a way."

"How refreshing," she murmured, her sarcasm enhancing his blush. "If you will excuse me, I've had a long day."

He bolted forward as she turned to walk away from him. "Here, let me escort you." He matched his gait to her uneven lope and peppered her with questions about life in Missoula.

"I'm surprised you'd ask me such questions. Why don't you ask your family here?" She slowed her frenetic pace upon realizing she would not shake him.

"They are nice enough women but quite opinionated. I've decided I'd like to form my own opinions about the residents here, without their decades' worth of biases clouding my perceptions."

Araminta slowed further. "How interesting," she murmured. "Most are quite content to think as their families believe."

He laughed, causing her to frown as it sounded more cynical than joyful. "I find that I am more apt to survive if I trust my own instincts."

She paused at the walkway to her building. "Well, thank you for your kind escort." She smiled shyly at him before walking alone toward the front door of the building.

"Have dinner with me tomorrow," he said. "Form your own opinion of me, rather than allowing how we met or your views of my family to cloud how you perceive me."

She turned to study him, his stocky build encased in a fancy maroon suit with matching hat at a jaunty angle. "You look like a peacock," she murmured, unable to hide a smile.

"Is that a yes?" he asked with a broadening smile.

"I can't have dinner with you, Mr. Bouchard. I have my reputation in this town to consider."

He watched her, considering her words a moment. "I should have been more thoughtful. Will you join me on a walk tomorrow evening?"

"Yes, a short one." She met his triumphant gaze for a moment more and then dashed inside her building. When she closed the door behind her in her small apartment, she shook her head at her racing heart, silently chiding herself for her foolishness.

∽

The following evening, Araminta sat on her front stoop and bit back a smile as Bartholomew walked toward her building. Today he wore a navy blue suit that shimmered in the evening light. She rose from the front porch's chair and walked to meet him. She stroked the fabric of his suit, blushing at her brazen action. "Forgive me," she whispered.

He laughed. "You're the first brave enough to act on your curiosity. It's some sort of newfangled material my aunt Vaughan saw and thought would be perfect for me. I didn't have the heart to tell her that I'd look a fool."

Araminta bit the inside of her cheek. "I'm uncertain if you'd rather have me agree or disagree," she murmured.

He watched her and smiled. "I'd rather your real opinion. I have plenty around me who will tell me what I want to hear." He hooked out his elbow, waiting for her to slide her hand through his arm before turning them toward a residential side street for a stroll.

"I think you should dress how you desire, not as you believe others want you to. You should please yourself." She ducked her head after she spoke.

"Is that how you live your life? Living life to please yourself?" He nodded to a couple walking with a baby carriage.

"No, of course not. But I don't allow others to dress me up and make me look like a baboon."

He laughed. "You must work with children." At her confused stare, he said, "Your constant references to animals. Last night I was a peacock. Today I'm a baboon. I'm tempted to wear something outrageous tomorrow to see what you'd call me."

"Now you're speaking nonsense," she murmured with a shake of her head. After a few moments of silence, Araminta relaxed in his company. "What do your friends and family think of you walking with me tonight?"

He laughed. "As I don't inform them of all my activities, I don't know. Nor do I care. Last I checked, I was out of training trousers." He saw her pursed lips and frowned. "I am my own man, Miss Araminta."

They paused at a vacant lot that an industrious resident had turned into a vegetable garden. "What do you think of Montana?" Araminta studied him as his gaze roved over the mountains in the distance, now a rich lavender in the evening light.

"It's small and boring and lacking in almost all modern conveniences." He laughed as she bristled at his blunt assessment of her home. "However, the people are friendly."

"If you desire adventure, you should move to Butte." She sniffed in disdain and studied the garden.

"Come, Miss Araminta. We should all have the right to our own opinions and the freedom to express them." He sighed as she remained tightly wound next to him. "I miss the bustle and energy of a big city."

"I don't. I hated the noise and pollution and never-ending commotion as people got from one place to another." She sighed as she closed her eyes, birdsong battling for supremacy with the sounds of distant traffic. "Montana is paradise to me."

He chuckled. "You are a romantic if you believe that."

She turned to face him, her disgruntled glare earning a smile. "Why don't you return to whatever city you traveled from? We wouldn't miss you."

His chuckle transformed into a laugh. "Oh, how you wound my fragile pride."

A wisp of hair trailed over her blush-reddened cheek, but she met his gaze without a flinch.

"I have no reason to return to San Francisco and every reason to remain here. I have a job and family." He challenged her with a tilt of his head. "And friends."

She rolled her eyes and walked on again. "I would think your friends would warn you to stay far away from the Missoula cripple." She gasped when he grabbed her shoulder, spinning her to face him. Her blush intensified as she saw the anger in his gaze.

"Never refer to yourself in such a way." His intense gaze speared into hers. "We can't control how others speak or what they think. But we know the truth. About ourselves and the choices we've had to make in our lives. Don't allow another to write your story."

"You perplex me, Mr. Bouchard. When I saw you with your friends, I thought you were little more than a man intent on striding around town, puffing out his chest at his own importance. You seemed to enjoy showing off to your friends." Her brow furrowed as she studied him. "Now, how you speak, you're a different person. Who are you really?"

Her frown intensified at his triumphant smile. "You'll have to spend more time with me to discover that." He winged out his arm for her, walking slowly beside her as he escorted her back to her home.

~

Two weeks after the mine fire in Butte, Patrick Sullivan poked his head into the workshop in Missoula run by Gabriel and Jeremy McLeod. Patrick squinted at the darkened interior after walking outside in the bright midafternoon light from a late June day. The brothers joked in the corner as they sanded a piece of wood together, and he paused to watch their easy camaraderie.

"Can I help you?" a voice to the right of the door asked, jerking Patrick's gaze away from his cousins.

"Yes, I'm here to see my brother-in-law and cousin." He nodded toward Jeremy and Gabriel who had looked in his direction at Ronan's question.

They stilled their movements and watched him warily.

Gabriel threw down his sandpaper and swiped his hands on his pants. "Pat, good to see you," he said as he held out a hand.

Patrick shook it, squinting his eyes as he read a warning in Gabriel's gaze.

"I was hoping to speak with you before talking with Savannah," Patrick said to Jeremy, who maintained his distance on the opposite side of the room.

Jeremy watched and scowled as a patron for Ronan entered. Gabriel motioned with his head, and Jeremy raised his eyebrows in agreement. "Let's go upstairs," Jeremy said. Gabriel led the way up a staircase mostly hidden by finished pieces of furniture to a storage area over the workshop.

"If you can believe it, this is where Clarissa and I lived the first few years of our marriage. Until we had a child," Gabriel said as he looked around, his gaze distant as though envisioning a room filled with furniture rather than boxes and lumber. He pulled out three empty crates, turning them on their sides and forming seats for them. He motioned for Patrick to sit and then glared at his brother to do the same. After they were all seated, Gabriel studied Patrick. "Why are you here, Pat?"

"Why has it taken you so damn long to finally visit?" Jeremy snarled, cutting off Patrick's reply.

"I'm sure you've heard of the mine fire in Butte. That was my mining company's mine. Our men who were lost." He raised dazed eyes to them. "It's been a horrible few weeks, and I was needed at work. However, now that the crisis has been contained for the moment, I took a few days to come here to see all of you."

"Where are Fee and Rose?" Gabriel asked. "You can't have left them alone in Butte."

"No, they're at Colin's. She wanted to accompany me, and I'm thankful for her support."

Jeremy leaned forward, his face reddened and hands clasped together as though preventing himself from grabbing Patrick. "Why are you here? Are you here for Melly?"

Patrick paled. "I'm here because of Melly, yes. I ... Has Colin told you about our discussion?"

Jeremy ran a shaking hand through his ebony hair. "Only that it was a story you had to tell and that it showed the extent of his step-mother's cruelty." He pinned Patrick under a severe glare. "Before you see Sav, I must know. Do you plan to take Melly away from us?"

"Of course not. She's your daughter, Jeremy. You've raised her for years. You've adopted her. I'm her uncle and wish to have a part in her life." He sighed. "I'd like no secrets between us so Mrs. Smythe may no longer stir up doubts and trouble between us."

"She's been doing a darned good job of it lately, as she's had us jumping to her tune for years," Gabriel grumbled.

"Will you tell us how you're Melly's father?" Jeremy asked.

Patrick nodded. "If it's all right with you, I'd prefer to tell you, and then you can tell your wives in whatever fashion you deem ... accept-able. It's not something I'd care to discuss with my sister or cousin," he said, flushing.

Gabriel lost his battle to fight a grin. "No offense, Patrick, but the way you and Colin are building this up, it has the makings for the story of the century."

Patrick glared at him. "Just remember that I'm the one who suffered through it."

Gabriel sobered at his words and nodded for him to continue.

Patrick spoke, his words hesitant and voice low as he related the same events he had told Colin earlier in the month. He fought an all-over body blush at Gabriel's incredulous chuckle at the part where he related waking and finding Mrs. Smythe crawling out of his bed.

"Nasty surprise," Gabriel muttered.

"There's no way to know for certain that Melly is my daughter. My father is dead. We will never know if he was … unable to perform his duties." Patrick held his head in his hands as though ashamed to even discuss such a thing.

"Besides, anything that raving lunatic tells us is bound to be at best only a half-truth," Jeremy said. He cleared his throat. "I can under-stand why you'd not want to relate such a … a"—he waved his hand around—"to Sav and Rissa."

"Now do you understand why I would never alter how things are for you?" Patrick asked Jeremy beseechingly. "Melly's happy. She's well-loved, and she knows who she is. Why would I ever want to jeop-ardize that? If she is my daughter, I could ask for no more."

Jeremy heaved out a huge sigh. "You have no idea what a relief this will be for Savannah. For me," he whispered. "Melly has been ours since the moment we held her on the train ride west fourteen years ago."

~

Patrick wandered Colin's small back yard, ignoring the slamming of the back door. "I'm fine, Col," he called out as he studied the bushes and stared into space. He jolted at the soft hands touching his arm.

"Patrick." Clarissa tugged on his arm, pulling him to face her.

When he still refused to meet her gaze, she pushed herself into his arms. "Oh, Patrick."

"I'm fine. I'm glad there are no more misunderstandings or secrets between us." He ran a hand over her hair and pulled her tight. He shuddered as she gripped him to her with as much might as he held her.

After a few moments, he pushed himself away from her. "I don't understand why you'd believe me. Why you'd immediately accept what I said."

"You don't lie, Patrick. When we were children, you were annoyingly truthful. Don't you remember all the times we could have gotten out of scrapes, but you told the truth?"

"It wasn't fair for the servants to take the blame," he said, standing taller and more stiffly.

"Exactly." A soft smile spread as she watched her eldest brother. "Since I was a girl, you've acted with decorum and honor. I know you wouldn't lie to me, to your brother, to your cousins. Not about something this important." She gripped his hand. "Not when it caused you to be cast from our family for so many years."

She pulled him as she moved toward the back door. "Come. Everyone's waiting for you inside. We want to celebrate."

He planted his feet, as though having grown tree roots. "Why? I've been back for a few years."

"Yes, but now we know the truth. We know that Melly will always be with Sav and Jeremy and also the reason for your odd, searching looks at her." Clarissa tugged him, propelling him into motion. "Besides, you survived that horrible work as a helmet man. And your relationship with Fiona must have improved as she's traveled with you. We have many reasons for a celebration."

Patrick was unable to hide his contented smile.

Clarissa's grip on his hand tightened.

"Yes, those are all wonderful reasons."

After sharing a grin, Clarissa sobered. "We also know Mrs. Smythe will return to speak with us. We must prepare for the upcoming confrontation. This is a small town, and she will hear of your arrival."

"We can discuss what we hope to say," Patrick murmured, "but we all know nothing ever goes as planned with that woman."

～

"**W**hy are you in such a foul mood?" Patrick asked, his feet propped on the banister on Colin's front porch. He sat outside with Colin, enjoying the long warm evening as it slowly cooled off. Fiona was inside with Savannah and Melinda, helping to put Rose to bed. When Patrick had offered to help with the evening ritual, he'd been shooed away, the women wanting to share time together. Colin remained silent, chewing on the end of a toothpick.

Patrick stretched as his brother gave no indication of answering his question. "I'm not looking forward to another train ride, although I'm glad it's only for a few hours."

Colin grunted. "Was it worth it to you?" He turned to meet his brother's inquisitive stare. "Marrying a woman who didn't love you?"

Patrick stiffened before forcing himself to relax. "I believe Fee does care for me. She's simply having difficulty expressing that emotion."

Colin made a deep noise and stared out at the street again. "I wonder, if you take too much time declaring how you feel, if her feelings for you will have eroded due to your silence."

Patrick dropped his feet to the ground and leaned toward his brother. "I don't think we're talking about me. We're talking about you and Araminta." At Colin's tortured glare, Patrick gave a small *humph*. "I've never understood why you haven't told her that you love her." When Colin remained silent, Patrick sighed, settling into his chair again. "Araminta looks different."

"She's being courted," Colin whispered. "By bloody Bartholomew Bouchard, that bastard from the Bay."

Patrick laughed. "How long did it take you to come up with that phrase?" He grunted when Colin hit him on his shoulder. "I don't know why you're torturing yourself. Tell her how you feel. Once she knows the depth of your feelings, she'll drop the bloody bay man."

"I wouldn't be so sure. I've never seen her so content." Colin ran a hand through his hair, leaving strands standing on end. "I've been a fool, waiting too long. Worrying that I would ruin the relationship we do have."

Patrick huffed out a sardonic laugh. "I don't know why you've worried about ruining something that's been horrible since Lucas visited in '14. Ever since you almost kissed her." He raised an eyebrow at Colin's shocked stare. "Do you think siblings don't talk? Rissa told me all about it."

Colin covered his face with his hands and groaned. "This is why I dream of living far from meddling family!"

Patrick instantly sobered. "No, Col. You never want to live far from family. It's horrible and lonely. The worst experience you could imagine."

Colin dropped his hands and rolled his eyes. "You know I'm not serious." He sighed. "I suspect you're the only one who knows what it's like to be frozen out by the woman you care about."

"Have you ever considered that the reason Araminta acts as she does is because she cares too much about you and doesn't want to be hurt by a rejection from you? You've had years to declare yourself, and you never have." Patrick shook his head in bewilderment. "It makes no sense to me."

Colin sighed as he scrunched down into his chair. "Nor to me either."

"Something will happen to force you to act, Col," Patrick said, his warning tone causing Colin to shiver.

Colin gave his brother a warning glance, signaling he wanted no further discussion of his relationship with Araminta. "What are we to do about Mrs. Smythe?" Colin asked.

Patrick's expression became even more serious as he clamped his jaw at her name. "I have no desire to speak with her, but I fear I must. Let's arrange a meeting either here or at Rissa's. Savannah and Jeremy have been through enough."

Colin closed his eyes as though in deep thought. "Even if the meeting isn't at their house, I think they'll want to be present. If for nothing else to support you." Colin opened his eyes to look at his brother. "An injustice was done to you by that woman. She needs to understand the family is united in its support of you."

~

The family had crowded into Clarissa's living room, while the children, including Melinda, were at the park with Araminta. Patrick stood by the fireplace with Colin at his side, while Jeremy sat next to Savannah. Clarissa sat on a chair next to Fiona with Gabriel behind her, his hand on Clarissa's shoulder. Ronan had joined them in solidarity, sitting in his wheelchair by the settee. They shared long glances at the loud knock on the front door.

Colin strode to the door, flinging it open with a glare as he beheld his stepmother. He stepped back to allow her to enter but refrained from offering to take her coat or hat. She sauntered into the room, looking around at the united front awaiting her. After tense moments of silence, she huffed out an agitated breath.

"So this is how I'm to be treated?" Mrs. Smythe said in her sugary, high-pitched voice. "As though a criminal on trial in front of her family?" She glanced around and huffed out an exasperated breath.

Clarissa looked at everyone in the room. "I see no family of yours present."

"How dare you, you little hussy!" Mrs. Smythe screeched. "You tricked me into agreeing to visit your home by telling me my daughter would be here. That she was eager to make my acquaintance." She swiped at an eye as though scrubbing away a tear and frowned when she saw Colin roll his eyes. She focused again on Clarissa. "After all I did for you, ensuring that a respectable gentleman would want you. Would offer for you and provide you a place in Boston society, this is how you speak to me? This is how you treat me?"

Gabriel placed a hand on his wife's trembling arm. "You know exactly the reasons each one of us in this room despises you. None more than I do." He glared at the woman who promoted Clarissa's abuse at Cameron's hands. "Never believe, for one moment, that you have been absolved of your sins for your mistreatment of Clarissa. There is no absolution for what you did."

Mrs. Smythe watched Gabriel with patent loathing and superiority. "You have always been a worthless upstart, and I will never understand my stepdaughter's unfortunate fascination and alliance with you." She sniffed as she looked at Clarissa and then at the simple, comfortable home she had made with Gabriel. "It seems life in this pathetic backwater has brought you little joy. When I think of how you could have lived ..." Her voice faded away at the tragedy of the thought.

"You never had any consideration for my being or my care. It was all about you. How much you could garner from any alliance I made with a man deemed acceptable to the grandparents," Clarissa hissed. "I am only thankful I was able to evade your trap."

"Your grandparents have missed you terribly," Mrs. Smythe said, frowning when her remarks earned scoffs and amused smirks from Colin, Savannah and Clarissa.

"They've only ever cared for themselves," Clarissa said. "I shouldn't worry about them."

"You unfeeling monster," Mrs. Smythe declared. "Do you have any idea what it did to them to know they would have no family, no one present when they died? That none of their offspring would honor them with their presence?"

"Why should we mourn what we never had? There was no affection, love or consideration of our desires," Clarissa said with a taunting smile. "They would gladly have seen Savannah beaten to death by her first husband, if only for the upkeep of the family name and the enrichment of the family coffers. They—and you—would have wished no better for me with their encouragement for me to marry Cameron."

Colin watched his sister with a mixture of concern and admiration, knowing that discussing her forced separation from Gabriel and any allusion to Cameron's rape was difficult for her. However, understanding lit the gazes of those present as Clarissa garnered Mrs.

Smythe's attention and ire as she strove to distract her from Patrick's presence.

"You've always believed yourself to be cunning," Mrs. Smythe said, her sugary sweet voice gone. "And you." Mrs. Smythe focused on Savannah. "Pathetic, docile Savannah, doing her family's bidding. Losing her first daughter and then claiming she was abused so she could murder her husband. I'm surprised you could convince the gullible police you were acting in self-defense." Mrs. Smythe sniffed again as though in disgust. "It's horribly unfair you were allowed to inherit his millions when you killed him."

Savannah raised her chin. "I'd give thanks daily, Mrs. Smythe, that you never had to suffer as I did."

"Suffer? Suffer?" she shrieked. She glared at Colin as he touched one of his ears as though having experienced hearing damage. "You'll never know how I suffered. Not in my first marriage nor in my second. Married to that oafish Irish immigrant who could barely string two words together and had the manners of an ape."

"How dare you speak of our father in such a way," Patrick said.

Ronan shook his head at Patrick's words as he walked into her well-laid trap.

Mrs. Smythe smiled, as though she had successfully baited a response from her intended target. "Oh, my dear Patrick. You'll never know how I mourned when your father sent you away. Such nights of passion we had together."

"You're delusional, and you know it," Patrick growled. "There were no nights and certainly no passion on my part. Just shock and mortification one morning when I saw you crawling out of my bed." He flushed at the last sentence.

She smiled indulgently as she watched him blush in mortification. "Oh, how it pains me to hear you deny what we had." She preened in front of his family members, delighting as their postures became more guarded. "I doubt any of you here know the pleasure that was …"

"Enough!" Patrick roared. "You are a lying filthy horrid woman, and everything you say is a blatant falsehood. I never wanted anything to do with you. Not then and not now. You took advantage of me. To my everlasting shame."

"So you admit you and I share a child?" Mrs. Smythe said, her gaze calculating.

"No, I don't. I have a beautiful niece, daughter to my father, Sean Sullivan." He clasped Fiona's hand as he stood behind her in solidarity. "I have a daughter with my wife."

Mrs. Smythe scoffed. "A daughter. You claim to have a daughter with that harlot? We all know it wasn't you who planted a baby in her belly." She smiled with joy as Fiona flinched. "I've heard that her real father is intent on regaining what he lost. I'm certain he would do a better job in the raising of such a beautiful little girl." She sighed with feigned sadness. "I know her grandmother is eager to meet her. She dreams of showing her the wonders of life in Boston."

"Stay away from Rose!" Fiona yelled, quivering with fear and indignation as Patrick rested a hand on her shoulder to keep her seated in front of him.

Mrs. Smythe's focus moved from Fiona to Patrick for a moment. "You accepted damaged goods, as is to be expected of the men in your extended family." She watched with delight as Fiona paled further under her intense scrutiny. "I must admit that I'm disappointed to learn you appear to have reconciled with your husband. I delighted in knowing of the discord between you."

Fiona raised indignant eyes, lit to the color of warmed cognac. "Why? Because you believed you'd induce my husband into some sort of a liaison with you?" Fiona laughed. "You are delusional. He only desires me."

Mrs. Smythe leaned forward. "I'd remind you that I had his baby, something you've failed to do."

Fiona glared at Mrs. Smythe, leaning into Patrick's touch.

"Have you spoken to my cousin Henry?" Gabriel asked, his voice lethally quiet.

"Oh, Henry is such a lovely young man. When Mrs. Masterson learned I was to travel here to reunite with you, she insisted I correspond with Henry." She leaned forward as though imparting an important secret. "He's an essential member of the Anaconda Company. And a wonderful ally to have."

"What are you plotting?" Jeremy asked. He relaxed slightly when Savannah stroked a hand down his arm.

She looked around at the occupants in the room with feigned innocence. "Why should I be plotting anything? I merely wanted to right a wrong that was committed years ago. I've had trouble living with myself, knowing that a good man had been denied his child." She smiled with triumph at all of them present. "I am eager to speak with my daughter." She glared at Savannah and Jeremy as they contradicted her. "She is my daughter as I carried her for all of those horrid months and then went through the pain of birthing her. I can't wait to impart the truth to her about her father."

She glared at Jeremy who remained seated. "I bid you a good day. However, this is far from good-bye." She sailed from the room, slamming the front door behind her.

∽

After Mrs. Smythe left, Patrick sat in a daze. He noted Fiona rising as though through a fog but failed to follow her. He focused on Savannah and Clarissa who tapped him on his arm a few times.

"Patrick?" Savannah whispered. "Patrick, we must talk," she whispered.

Patrick met Savannah's gaze and saw Jeremy sitting nearby. Gabriel had joined Colin in the kitchen, and Patrick heard the back door slam as they went to the backyard. "Where is Fee?" he whispered.

"She went upstairs to take a nap. I think she needs a break from all of us," Clarissa said. "We need to talk, and we must talk quickly before the children return with Minta."

"What more is there to say?" Patrick asked. "I will never challenge you, Savannah, or Jeremy for Melly. She is your child. I've accepted that."

Savannah gripped his hand and smiled through teary eyes at him.

"Thank you," she whispered. "But we need you to speak with Melly when she arrives. She's very confused and worried, and I don't want her to doubt her place in our family. If Mrs. Smythe talks to her before we do, I worry what damage that could do."

Patrick nodded. "I can't lie to her," he whispered. He looked over Savannah's shoulder and met Jeremy's gaze. "I ... I think I should tell her a portion of the truth."

Jeremy nodded, his gaze grave. "Savannah and I agree with you. We'd like to be present, in the background as you speak with her, in case she has questions we could answer but that you can't."

As the door burst open with the children pouring in, Patrick took a deep breath. He watched as Melinda entered, carrying Rose and laughing at something Billy said. "I don't believe you, Billy-boy."

"I tell you, it's true! Mama uses a *slaughtered* spoon in the vegetables. Just ask her." He beamed at his mother as she turned a beet red.

"It's *slotted*, Billy-boy," Jeremy murmured as he stifled a chuckle.

Melly laughed again as she set Rose down and took off her hat. She smiled at her parents, stilling when she saw their serious gazes. "Is something the matter?" she whispered.

"No, my dearest girl, nothing's the matter," Jeremy said, rising to give her a quick hug. "Your uncle Patrick, your mother and I need to speak with you a moment." Jeremy motioned for them to follow him onto the front porch. As he held open the front door, Clarissa herded her children into the kitchen, granting the rest of them more privacy.

Melinda wrung her hands as she looked from one adult to the next. "What is it?"

"We had another visit today from Mrs. Smythe. Mrs. Sullivan," Patrick said, stumbling over her married name. "I don't know how many memories you have of her."

Melinda frowned. "Why has she come back? Why is she interested in us again?" Her worried gaze roved from her uncle to her parents and back.

"She is an unhappy woman who strives to cause discord." Patrick paused and closed his eyes. "She hoped to cause a rift in the family."

Melinda's brows furrowed. "I don't understand."

"She wants us to doubt that my father was your father," Patrick whispered. "She wants us to believe that I'm your father."

Melinda stiffened and shook her head. "How could you be?"

Patrick stared at her a moment, his mouth opening and closing a few times before he puffed out his cheeks and exhaled a deep breath. "In a complicated manner, there is a remote chance I am your father, but we have no way to know for sure."

At his whispered words, she backed up a step. "You didn't want me either?"

"No!" he yelled, grabbing her hand. "Of course I would have if I'd thought for an instant you were mine. But I wasn't in Boston. I was … I don't even know where I was when you were sent to an orphanage. Kansas City? Cleveland?" He shook his head. "I was in no fit state to care for you." He looked at her beseechingly as he met her confused gaze. "I was thrown out of my father's house months before you were born."

"Why?" she whispered.

"Because my stepmother lied to my father. She claimed we had a love affair. Which we never did." He gripped Melinda's hand. "I know this makes no sense to you as there is a slight possibility I am your father. But I never wanted to be with Mrs. Smythe." He motioned for Melly to wait a moment to let him finish speaking. "Although that does not mean I would not have wanted you had I known you were my daughter."

"What does all this mean?" She looked from her uncle to her parents, then back again. "Do I move to Butte with you?"

Patrick shook his head. "I consider you my beloved niece. You've had the greatest of good fortunes to be raised by two such loving parents. My hope is that you continue to live with them, never doubting for a moment who you are and what you mean to us."

"You don't want to be my father," she whispered, ducking her head.

Patrick cupped her cheek, using his thumb to trace away tears that silently coursed down her cheeks. "It would be one of my life's greatest honors to be your father, Melly. But you already have a wonderful father. I could never take his place." He waited a few moments in silence until she raised confused, wounded eyes to meet his. "I care deeply for you as your uncle, as one of many members of this family who love you. I could never love you more than I already do."

Melinda looked from Patrick to her parents and then back again. "You still don't want me," she whispered, rising and rushing down the porch steps as she raced away.

"Melly!" Savannah screamed after her.

Jeremy rose, running a hand down his wife's arm. "It's all right. I'll follow her home and ensure she's safe. Stay here with our family, love. You must be with them right now." He kissed her on the forehead and took off at a run after his daughter.

"I'm sorry, Sav," Patrick whispered as he watched her gaze down the street. "I would never have told her if not for the threat from Mrs. Smythe."

Savannah nodded. "I know. I just wish you'd told us sooner what had really happened. About who you really were to her." She raised her gaze to meet his. "I understand fear, Patrick." She grasped his hand. "I don't blame you."

"Thank you," he breathed. He released her hand and reentered the house, in search of his wife.

～

Fiona lay on Clarissa and Gabriel's bed, her fingers tracing the needlepoint patterns on the quilt, staring out the window. She watched big white puffy clouds move across the sky and tried to occupy her mind by picking out shapes. However, nothing worked to calm her racing thoughts, and she curled into herself on the mattress.

"Are you all right, my love?" Patrick's fingers traced down her back, and she shivered at the light touch. "I'm sorry about Mrs. Smythe."

"What now, Patrick?" Fiona remained on her side, turned away from him. She allowed herself to be tugged against him as he spooned against her back.

"I spoke with Melly," he whispered in her ear. "I wish you'd been there with me, but I understand why you didn't want to be. I told her an edited version of the truth."

Fiona took a deep stuttering breath. "Is she coming to Butte with us?" She instinctively arched into his touch as he kissed her neck.

"No. She's remaining here with her parents. As she should."

Fiona pressed against him until she'd turned to face him with her skirts tangled about her waist. "But you're her father."

He traced long fingers over her cheeks, his intense gaze meeting hers. "I know I am. Deep inside, I know it." He pressed his forehead against hers. "But I have no right to rip her away from everything and everyone she knows. She's confused enough as it is."

"But what about you?" Her whispered question emerged plaintive.

"I have you and Rose." He kissed her nose.

"A daughter who isn't yours," she said as she fought tears.

Patrick growled. "She's mine in every way that matters." He met her gaze. "Don't allow a vile woman to fill you with doubts. Not about us. Or about my family." He ran his hand over her head, tangling his fingers in her hair. "We won't disappoint you like your family did."

Fiona wrapped her arms around him, tugging him close. "Oh, my love, hold me and make me believe," she whispered.

Patrick laughed. "I'd like nothing better than to hold you forever right now. But we must go downstairs and have dinner with the family."

Fiona flushed. "Of course." She kissed his neck. "I worried you'd be more interested in Melinda than Rose," she admitted.

He cupped her face with his large hands, canting her face up to him. "Rose is my daughter. I could never love her any more or any less than I love Melinda." He kissed Fiona's nose and then her forehead, before sighing and tugging her against his chest. "I wish I could lay with you here and forget dinner."

"We'd scandalize your sister," Fiona whispered.

He chuckled and pushed himself up. "We would," he said with a soft smile, reaching a hand down to help heft her up. "Tonight, though, is ours."

CHAPTER 10

*P*atrick wandered into Clarissa's living room and glanced out the front window. Ronan sat in his wheelchair as he watched the children run and play in the front yard. Patrick joined Ronan on the porch, sitting next to him in a rocking chair as his nieces and nephew ran around the side of the house to the back. They sat in companionable silence for a while before Ronan shifted in his seat.

"Seems like you've had a rough month." He shot a curious glance at Patrick before maneuvering his wheelchair to better see him. His strong arms and shoulders were a striking contrast to his emaciated, withered legs.

Patrick huffed out a laugh. "I was thinking about returning home after I was relieved from helmet duty." His low voice was a quiet counterpoint to his gentle rocking, the sounds of birds chirping and the distant children's calls. "I barely had a few days peace before Colin showed up with news about Mrs. Smythe."

Ronan snorted. "That woman. No matter how much you plan, she still has you jumping to her tune." His sherry-colored gaze met Patrick's.

Patrick sighed and rubbed a hand through his graying hair. "I can't think of what else we could have done." He looked down the street toward Savannah's home to where Melly had retreated. "I hate that I might have hurt Melly."

"She's young. She's resilient." He waited until Patrick focused on him again rather than the yard and street. "You are resilient, and I imagine she'll be quite a bit like you."

Patrick stiffened, his cheeks flushing at Ronan's words. "I won't do anything to harm her relationship with Sav and Jeremy."

"Keep saying that, and you might believe you have some control in this messed-up situation." Ronan lifted himself to shift in his chair. "Have you ever thought that by doing nothing, as it appears is your plan, you'll hurt Melly more? She needs some sign from you that she was more than a mistake and now an embarrassment." He frowned as Patrick's flush deepened. "She's young. She reads those romance novels and makes up even more wild stories in her head. I hear all about them when she visits me at the shop. She needs to be grounded, and you can help her."

Patrick gave a stiff nod, his jaw clenched.

Ronan heaved out a sigh and traced a hand over one of his weakened thighs. He watched Patrick a moment and slapped at his leg. "Thank you for what you did for those miners."

Patrick's gaze shot up to meet Ronan's sincere look. "You're welcome," he muttered, his voice confused.

"I didn't rely on helmet men, but I like knowing men like you are willing to help those working in such perilous conditions." Ronan tapped at his thigh again. "We had more risk of cave-ins and poorly timed explosions than fire in my day."

Patrick canted forward at Ronan's soft words and distant expression. "They still have plenty of those."

"What's it like, wearing one of those breathing apparatuses?"

Patrick sobered as he thought about the helmet he had worn for days. "Heavy. You feel like you're entombed in this enormous contraption that is so delicate you worry about rubbing against anything." He shrugged. "Which you know is inevitable in a drift. I fell over more horses and mules than I could count. And I dislodged my tubes a few times."

"But you were still able to work," Ronan said with open curiosity.

"When I felt light-headed or if I could taste gas, I knew my mask was leaking. I'd head to the cage and go up to have it fixed." He paused, his gaze distant. "Only once did I pass out. My partner had to drag me out."

"Does Fee know?" Ronan asked.

Patrick shook his head. "She knows I had minor mishaps. But not that I would have died if I hadn't been close to the cage. I'm a big man to drag." He sighed. "That was the last time I went down. I spent a few hours under a doctor's supervision with a pulmotor pumping oxygen into me, and I made the decision to return to my regular job full-time. They didn't argue with me because I'm a low-level executive with my mining company." He shared an embarrassed smile with Ronan. "Fee thinks I was ordered back, but I chose to return to my desk job."

"There's no shame in not wanting to go down the cage again, not after nearly dying." Ronan smiled. "I still remember going down the first time with Matthew, Liam's partner. Tickled him with a feather the whole way down."

Patrick laughed. "Oh, that's cruel!"

Ronan nodded. "Don't worry. He found ways to get even." His smile faded as his gaze became introspective. "I never really knew what happened to me. One minute I was working, the next I was flying through the air, and then I woke up at the hospital." He patted his wheelchair. "Gabe would argue I was the lucky one as I came out alive."

Patrick watched him solemnly, with somber eyes.

"Living a half-life, stuck in a chair, as I wait for my kidneys to fail, isn't what I imagined when I arrived in Butte all those years ago. But it is better than no life. For I would have missed the joy of Gabriel's family." His eyes clouded. "I'll never understand why I lived and Liam and Matthew died."

"If I learned one thing, crawling around the bowels of a poisonous mine, it's that there's no use looking for a reason. Nothing makes sense. Why does the man who's two feet from the cage die and the one a half mile away still cling to life and survive?" Patrick shook his head.

"And you feel the same guilt for returning home to your family as the rest do." He shared a long look of understanding and comradeship with Patrick. "In the beginning, after the accident, I willed myself to die. Why should I live when Amelia lost her husband? Gabriel, his best friend?"

"What happened?" Patrick whispered.

"Your sister badgered me with baskets and kindness, and Gabriel bullied me with his love." He shook his head. "Between the two of them, I never stood a chance." Ronan sighed as he released his memory's hold on him. "I hope you realize how fortunate you are in your family."

Patrick nodded.

Ronan stretched as best he could, changing the topic with a chuckle. "Now Butte is embroiled in a citywide strike. I have to admit, that's something I'd like to see, although it can't be much fun working for a mining company throughout it."

Patrick half smiled. "They don't hate me much as some recognize I was a helmet man. Besides, their true hatred is pointed at the Anaconda Company, not my little mining company. Although, if they had any sense, they'd realize we follow the Company's lead."

They looked toward the front door as it opened. Fiona poked her head out. "Patrick, you were to spend time with your sister before dinner." She flushed when she saw Ronan. "I beg your pardon. I thought he was out here alone."

Patrick rose and held the door wide so Ronan could wheel himself inside more easily. "No, you're right, Fee. It's time for us to join the family." He kissed her on her forehead and smiled.

∼

After a long meal with his family, marred only by the absence of Melinda and Jeremy, Patrick squeezed Fiona's shoulder as a silent good-bye before escorting Savannah home.

"There's no need for you to walk me home," Savannah protested.

"Fee and Rose will settle in for the night after returning home with Colin. I'll meet them there soon." He glanced at Savannah before clearing his throat. "I'd like to speak with Melly if I could."

Savannah stiffened before she could control her reaction. "Of course. You have every right to speak with her."

Patrick gripped Savannah's arm, stilling her increasingly frenetic pace. "Sav, stop. I'm not trying to change your relationship with Melinda." He studied her panicked expression in the fading evening light. "However, Ronan helped me to see that Melinda might feel I'm embarrassed or ashamed of her, and I don't want her to believe that. I couldn't be more proud of her and the young woman she's become." He let go of Savannah's arm. "Thanks to you and Jeremy."

Savannah sniffled as she fought tears. "It seems, no matter how many times you reassure me, I can't fully believe that my relationship with her won't be altered." She squeezed his hand. "Come. Jeremy will be worried."

They returned to her large home on an oversize corner lot. The light in the turret room, Melinda's room, was on, and Savannah led Patrick inside. He waited in Jeremy's den, pacing in front of the window as he glanced at the door every other minute. He exhaled a deep breath when he heard rapid footfalls on the stairs.

Melly slunk into the den and flopped onto one of the leather chairs. Her hair was tied back in a loose braid, and she wore the same dress from the park. "Why are you here?"

He leaned against the front of Jeremy's desk a moment before realizing he towered over her in that position. He grabbed the other leather chair and tugged it where he sat facing her.

She glared at him as he figured out what to say. Her arms were crossed over her chest, and she curled into herself. "It's not as though you wanted me. You managed to get rid of me. I'd think you'd be upset your escapade was discovered."

Patrick huffed out a laugh, his hand shooting out to hold her in place. "Melly, stop." He raised an eyebrow as she glared at him mutinously. "Please stay here so we can talk and please cease speaking such nonsense." He watched her with warm fondness. "Ronan said you had a vivid imagination."

"You're here because of Ronan?" Her eyes filled before she blinked away the tears.

"I'm botching this." He rubbed at his head. "I'm here because Ronan, a good friend of the family, helped me to see that I was hurting you by not speaking with you." He canted forward, his long fingers almost touching her arms wrapped around her middle. "You must know I could only ever be proud of you."

"Why?" Her raspy voice elicited a wince in him.

"Because you're bright, curious, kind." His gaze roved over her. "You're beautiful, but you don't look to your beauty as the means to accomplish your goals." He smiled. "How could I not be proud of you?"

"You didn't want me!"

He took a deep breath. "I didn't know you existed. Not until I arrived here four years ago. And I'm still not certain you are mine." He flushed. "I'm delighted you have such wonderful parents who love you as you should be loved."

Melinda shook her head as a few tears leaked down her cheek. She jerked away when he reached forward to swipe at them. "You had years to tell me the truth, and you did nothing. Do you think because I'm young, I'm gullible?"

Patrick stared at her with a deep intensity, his brown eyes boring into her. "There is no certainty that you are mine. That I am your father. Yet I remain your uncle. Of that I am sure. I could never love you more than I already do, Melly."

She rose, her gaze defiant as she panted with her agitation. "You have a weird way of showing it! You marry another and have a baby with her, forgetting about me! I don't need you! I'll never need you!" She pushed past him and spun, storming from the library.

Patrick sat in stunned silence and ran a quaking hand over his face.

$\sim$

olin's legs stretched out in front of him in his cozy living room. He twirled a piece of string he'd torn off the cuff of his shirt and listened as Fiona coaxed little Rose to sleep. He raised an eyebrow as Fiona emerged from the bedroom and collapsed on the settee across from him. "All settled?" he whispered.

Fiona hugged a pillow to her middle and smiled. "She hates going to sleep. Thinks she'll miss out on an adventure. Then, when she falls asleep, it's as though she never fought sleep."

Colin smiled. "Pat still sleeps like that."

Fiona chuckled, her gaze softening at his mention of her husband.

"I'm happy to see things have improved with my brother, Fee. You make him happy." He cleared his throat. "I hope you can understand today's events were out of his control."

Fiona frowned. "She's a vile woman who knows exactly what to say to provoke harm. I wonder why your father married her."

Colin chuckled. "We men aren't always rational. And she didn't show her true nature until after the ceremony." Colin sobered. "I'm the only one who didn't suffer from her actions."

Fiona watched him a moment. "You suffered. You helped your sister heal, and you were separated from your brother for over a decade. And I can't imagine she'll let you go without trying to harm you in some way."

Colin shivered at the thought, causing Fiona to focus intently on him.

"You don't worry about yourself, do you? You worry about someone else." Her gaze flitted away a moment as she thought before meeting his again and smiling. "The woman who's always watching the children. Her." At Colin's nod, she smiled. "Well, I'd keep your interest hidden as long as that woman's in town."

She broke off from saying anything further when Colin's door creaked open. "Patrick," she murmured. She scooted to the side on the settee so he could sit down and she could snuggle in his arms.

"How did it go?" Colin asked.

Patrick slung an arm around his wife's shoulder and sighed. "Terrible. Melly hates me."

Colin chuffed out a laugh. "Of course she does. You've been back for years and ignored her the whole time. You couldn't stand living near her, so you lived in another town, the ugliest she's ever seen. Then you married another and replaced her with another child, so you have no need of her." He raised an eyebrow. "How am I doing so far with her delusional thoughts?"

Patrick groaned. "Not all are delusional, but that's the basis for what she yelled at me."

Fiona snuggled into his chest. "You can't expect to show up, tell her you might be her father and have her accept it without some questions. Not after you've been back for four years."

"She's smart. She's resourceful, and she's fanciful." Colin shrugged his shoulder. "One of her favorite people was Mr. Pickens and even he couldn't keep her completely grounded."

"I'm glad she has an imagination, but I hate that it's conjuring all sorts of falsehoods and making her doubt who she is and how much she is loved by her parents and all of us." Patrick ran a hand down Fiona's arm.

Colin sat up and stretched. "Well, that mess will still be there tomorrow. I'm to bed. See you in the morning." He brightened a moment. "Ari might come by and help with breakfast since you are here." He went to bed with a spring in his step.

Fiona giggled. "He's enamored of that Araminta."

"Not nearly as much as I am of you," he whispered. "Come to bed with me, Fee. These worries will keep for tomorrow."

She ran her palms over his chest before leaning up to kiss him. "Yes, love. You did promise me that tonight was ours." She rose, reaching for him, and they walked to their room hand-in-hand.

∿

M onday morning Ronan sat tapping away at a pair of shoes. The shop was quiet as Gabriel and Jeremy had gone to the train station to see off Patrick, Fiona and Rose as they headed back to Butte. Ronan paused, stretching his back as he had leaned over his workbench for too long without pause. When he glanced at the door, he frowned to see Melinda hovering outside.

"Melly, what are you doing out there?" He motioned for her to come inside and wheeled around his workbench to be near her. She wandered the room, her fingertips tracing pieces of furniture her father and uncle were in the process of building. Ronan rubbed his hands on a towel and waited for her to settle. Finally she moved toward him and plopped down on a bench next to him. They sat in companionable silence as they watched passersby on the boardwalk and street outside.

"Minta has a suitor, Uncle Ronan," she blurted out. She'd called him uncle since she could remember, and he'd always loved the honorary title.

Ronan chuckled. "I'd heard that. One of my customers mentioned he'd seen her walking with a gentleman last week. Wonder how your brother'll take it."

Melinda shrugged. "It won't bother him. He knows Minta would never want anyone but him."

Ronan nodded and tapped his fingers on the armrest of his wheelchair. "Must be nice, having such confidence in another person."

Melinda ducked her head, her shoulders stooped. "I wouldn't know."

"Wouldn't you?" He tilted his head to one side and then waved at a customer as he walked past. "I'd think you'd have more confidence than your brother or sister. With your family and all."

She snorted, before swiping at her nose and cheeks. "What family?"

He spun his wheelchair so he faced her and not the street. "The family who's loved and cared for you since the moment you were born. The brother and sister who rescued you from the orphanage and the parents who loved you so much they begged to have the chance to raise you." He met her defiant, turbulent eyes. "The uncle who wanted to see you settled so he set aside his needs and desires to ensure you were happy."

She choked back a sob. "You were supposed to be my friend!"

He grabbed her arm, causing her to spin toward him. He held her tighter than he would have liked but had no other recourse to prevent her from running away from him. "I am. Just as I am your father's and uncle's friend." He smiled as she glared at him. "Being friends doesn't mean I always agree with you, Melly. It gives me the right to tell you when you're being a fool."

She failed to bite back a laugh. "That sounds like something Mr. Pickens would have said."

He smiled and let out a deep breath when she sat down across from him again. "Now you're turning into a flatterer." He gripped her hand. "I can imagine why you are upset with Patrick, your parents, your siblings." He waited until she gave a small nod. "It all reminds you of how your birth mother gave you to an orphanage. And now your birth mother has brought up questions as to who your father is. No one can take away your anger or confusion, and you must work through that on your own time."

"I don't know if I will ever forgive him for ignoring me since he returned four years ago."

Ronan sighed. "From what I heard, his da sent him away. Even Rissa and Colin didn't see him for over ten years." He met her hurt, confused gaze. "Do you understand how fortunate you were to have Colin save you from that orphanage? And then to have Savannah and Jeremy desperate to raise you as their daughter?" He watched as she blinked away tears. "Even your novels can't compete with your own life, Melly."

She shook her head in mutinous denial. "He didn't want me."

Ronan held her hand. "You have parents and family who love you. For the past four years, you've had another uncle who adores you. A man who loves you enough, who worries about you enough, to want you to be happy more than he wants to cause you doubt and confusion. I would consider that a tremendous gift." He watched as she flushed. "All I'd ask, Melly, is that you not be rash."

She rose, hugging him before turning toward the door. "I'm expected at home. Thank you, Uncle Ronan." She disappeared as quickly as she arrived. Ronan sighed and rubbed his head before returning to his work.

CHAPTER 11

Butte, Montana, July 1917

*L*ucas sat at the piano, tinkering to find the correct chord and rhythm for his composition. He hummed to himself as his fingers moved from key to key and shook his head in defeat. He sighed, and his fingers effortlessly moved over the keys, playing the first part of the piece again as he coaxed the missing notes from his brain to his fingers. He closed his eyes at the sweet, tender music and played for a few minutes. He played the final section, hoping it would inspire the next part of his composition, but it remained elusive.

He glanced to the doorway and smiled at Genevieve. "Vivie," he called out. "Come join me." He stopped playing and held out a hand for her. "Do you like my new composition? I'm trying to envision it with a violin as accompaniment, but I'm not good at writing violin music."

She sat on a nearby ottoman and smiled. "It's as beautiful as all the others you've written. And don't worry about writing a part for the violin."

He frowned at her platitudes. "That's not helpful. Criticize it. Tell me what's repetitive or weak. I can take it." He leaned toward her as though eager to hear her critique.

She shook her head, spreading her hands over her forest green skirt. "I'm sorry, Lucas. I wasn't really paying attention to your music tonight. Will you play it again for me sometime?"

He frowned at her distant expression. "I wrote it for you, Vivie." He met her startled gaze with a tender smile. "Of course I'll play it again. I doubt I'll ever publish it as I'll want to tinker with it my whole life to ensure I have it just right." His frown transformed into a glower when he saw her near tears. "Vivie?"

"Oh, Lucas, I have to tell you something." At her whispered words, she scrubbed at her cheeks. "I don't know if you'll be happy or not."

"Tell me either way," he pleaded. "I can't bear your sadness." He raised her hands, kissing each one.

"I'm having a baby." She met his surprised smile. "We're having a baby."

He clasped her head between his palms, his expression transforming from exultation to concern. "Why were you afraid to tell me? Why would you think I wouldn't be excited?"

She sniffled. "It's a change. We have a wonderful life. I worried ... I worried you'd resent a child taking away from your piano time. Or my time with you."

"Vivie." He sighed, resting his forehead against hers before he pushed away from her and kissed her lower belly. "Our child will only know love. And acceptance."

He rose up, kissing the tears off her cheeks. "She'll never wonder if I will use her as a pawn to gain family respectability. He'll never worry that his career choice will bring shame to the family. Our child will only know how proud we are of him or her."

"Oh, Lucas," she whispered, crying into his neck. "Thank you."

"As for me worrying that a baby will take away piano or composing time, our baby should. I want to be present in our child's life." He met her surprised expression with an impish grin. "You'll be sick of me, my love, and will send me off to the pubs for musical inspiration."

"Never," she vowed, clinging tightly to him. "Never."

~

A strong breeze blew, nearly ripping off Genevieve's hat pinned to her hair. She rushed home, a hand to her head to keep her hat in place. The points of the recent speech she had witnessed echoed in her mind as she sought to find anything of merit in the IWW speaker's arguments. She slipped into her house, grimacing when she heard Lucas playing the piano in the front parlor. She eased out of her jacket, unpinned her hat and shut the door with a soft *click*. She stood in the front hall a moment, uncertain if she should tiptoe upstairs or enter the living room.

"I know you're there, Vivie," Lucas called out. "Come join me."

She sighed with defeat and walked into the living room brightly lit by the rays from the late evening sun. "What are you working on?"

He smiled. "A new piece for you and our babe. I'm hopeful it will be appropriate for a lullaby." He tugged her close, settling her next to him on the piano bench. "Where were you, Vivie?"

"I went to hear a speaker," she whispered, her hands playing a few chords.

Lucas stilled next to her, his hand on the piano keys motionless. "Not Frank Little."

She rose and moved to the settee. "Yes, Frank Little. I was curious to hear what he had to say. The papers were incendiary in their dislike of him, and I wanted to form my own opinions of the man who is here at the behest of the IWW."

"You're not a Wobbly, Vivie."

She flushed. "You know I'm not. However, I am interested in the rights of all people, something the Company is eager to squash. Without a press free to print what it desires, rather than what the Company tells it to print, I needed to attend to hear what he truly said."

Lucas frowned. "I hate to think of you amid a crowd that could have turned into a dangerous, violent mob. You know the rumors that the Company infiltrates such gatherings with paid thugs and gunmen. You must take care of yourself. For yourself and for our baby."

She flushed. "I know it was foolish of me. The moment I arrived I wished you were there with me."

He smiled at her. "How do you know I wasn't there?"

Her eyes rounded in surprise as she gaped at her husband. "You were there?"

He nodded and then laughed at her amazement. "Yes. I heard he was to speak again, even though his first speech a week ago was a debacle. I wanted to hear him speak too. Besides, I worried you'd attend, and I had the naive belief I'd find you in the crowd. I never imagined thousands would attend one of his speeches." He rose to sit next to her on the settee. He stretched an arm over her shoulder, sighing with relief and pleasure when she leaned into him. "What did you think?"

Genevieve *tsk*ed. "I think he was a grave disappointment. Raving on about President Wilson betraying his pacifist promise. Then I almost fell over when he said the Constitution was simply a piece of paper and could be torn up like any other scrap of paper. How can he have such little respect for the laws that govern this land and that guarantee he can speak as he does with impunity?"

Lucas chuckled. "He seemed more interested in inciting the crowd and furthering his own rhetorical firebrand message than actually having any purposeful agenda for the miners. They'll rue the day they ever invited him to speak to the miners. This is the sort of thing the Company and its papers will love."

"I agree. He couldn't have alienated more people unless he set fire to half the town." She let out a huff of air. "What could the miners be thinking, welcoming him here when they have such little bargaining power with the Company?"

"Many of the miners are sympathetic to the IWW," Lucas murmured. "Now that the electricians have settled with the Company, the miners are truly on their own."

"Which prevents them from gaining the support of the rest of the community. They must know that the radical ramblings of a man like Little does nothing to further their cause."

Lucas kissed her head. "I'm relieved you were offended by him. I feared you'd think him a kindred spirit. Or his cause anyway."

Genevieve clasped her husband's hand. "I might believe in progressive causes, Lucas, but that doesn't mean I desire to overturn everything I know or to radically change the world I live in. I simply want the world I know to be more just."

Lucas squeezed her hand in return. "Unfortunately even that sentiment is extreme to many. Besides, take heart that the Keating-Owen Act passed last year."

She was silent a moment as though considering the bill passed by Congress in 1916. "It's a good bill," she murmured.

"Yes, it is. Prohibiting the purchase of any interstate product produced by a child under the age of fourteen and limiting working hours to eight a day for those sixteen and under is a great improvement."

She nestled into his embrace. "Thank you for supporting me last year when I was lost in letter-writing to various members of congress." She kissed his neck when he chuckled. "I worry about those who will circumvent it."

"There are always those who will do what they can for a profit," Lucas said. "Too often it's at the expense of the weakest or poorest among us."

~

Genevieve rushed home a few evenings later after spending the afternoon with Fiona and Rose. She burst into the house, pausing at the smell of roasted chicken and potatoes. "Lucas?" she called as she unpinned her hat and took off her gloves. "Who made dinner?"

Lucas played in the music room on one of his pianos, and she frowned as the music was more melancholic than usual. Since she'd informed him of her pregnancy, his music had been lighthearted and whimsical. She jolted when his fingers slammed onto the piano keys in a fit of pique.

"Lucas?" she whispered, approaching him on silent feet and stroking a hand down his back. "Are you all right?"

He relaxed at her touch. "Vivie." He spun, tossing his legs over the piano bench and pulling her between them. "I've missed you." He gave her a quick kiss. "You look lovelier every day, Vivie. As for dinner, I hired a cook yesterday, and I wanted to surprise you today with a cooked meal."

She stared at him, momentarily dumbstruck. "You hired a cook? Why? Don't you like my cooking?"

His eyes widened in panic as he watched her. "Oh, no, I mean, I love your cooking." He stammered, gripping her hand. "I merely wanted to give you the freedom to pursue what you want without feeling as though you had to race home every day to prepare a meal or to go to the grocers."

She squinted at him and was silent a moment. "There's more you aren't telling me."

He flushed and gave her a chagrined smile. "Her mother is a widow from the Spec. She hasn't received any sort of compensation from the North Butte Mining Company yet and has seven children to feed." He held up his hand. "And before you start your interrogation, she's the oldest at seventeen."

Genevieve smiled before she kissed him on his cheek. "You should have seen your panic when you thought I was mad at you for not liking my cooking."

He laughed. "A husband never wants to be in the bad graces of his wife." He raised her hand and kissed it. "You really don't mind?"

"I wish I'd had a chance to meet her before you hired her, but I don't mind having a cook. I enjoy being in the kitchen but not every day." She looked around their comfortable home. "Besides, I'd like to support the miners in a small way."

Lucas nodded and tugged her to the settee. "There's something else, Vivie."

She froze as he became even more serious. "You're leaving to tour."

He shook his head in confusion. "No, of course not. I wouldn't leave you now, when you're with child. In fact, I don't know when I'll tour again."

Although she caressed his head and shoulders, she tensed. "Are you having second thoughts?"

He furrowed his brows as he tilted his head to meet her worried gaze. "Second thoughts?" he frowned.

"The sad music," she whispered. At his nod and shrug, she murmured, "Are you upset about the baby?"

"Oh, Vivie, you must learn not to read too much into my moods." He pulled her close to him. "I'm ecstatic we are to be parents." He met her shadowed gaze. "Petrified too, if I'm honest." He leaned forward and kissed her still-flat belly. "No, that's not what's put me in a mood to play such music."

He retrieved the evening newspaper from a small table next to the settee. "I need you to promise me that you won't go to any more labor meetings." When she glared at him mutinously, he held up a palm. "At least not without me. I couldn't bear it if something happened to you or the baby."

"Lucas, what happened?" she whispered.

"Frank Little was murdered last night." He raised her hand and kissed it as she paled. "He was pulled from his boarding house at 3:00 a.m. and forced into a car. They … did horrible things to him. They found him, strung up, with a warning pinned to his clothes."

She breathed heavily as she massaged at her temple with her free hand. "But I—we—just saw him speak a few days ago. He was fine." She raised horrified eyes to her husband. "Who would do such a thing?"

"It's unknown who killed him, although it's being reported that patriots are responsible for ridding the town and country of a traitor."

"What did the note say?"

"It's somewhat cryptic. On top of the note, it says 'Others Take Notice! First and Last Warning!'" He looked at the front page of the paper. "Then some gibberish appears. The numbers 3-7-77 and then the letters L-D-C-S-S-W-T, with the L circled."

Genevieve looked at her husband and shook her head. "Haven't you studied any Montana history since you arrived? Those numbers were the hallmark of the Vigilantes."

"What do the letters mean?" Lucas asked with a challenging lift of one eyebrow. At her shake of her head, he kissed her cheek. "The newspapermen speculate that it's a warning to others who these Vigilantes are targeting. Especially labor organizers. And the circled *L* means that the job was accomplished with regard to Little."

She plucked the paper from his hands and quickly thrust it on the side table. "I don't care to read how they tormented him before he died. What have we come to that this is how we treat those who dissent with our way of thinking?"

Lucas sighed. "He did more than dissent, Vivie. He promoted the overthrow of capitalism and railed against everyone in power, including President Wilson. The sad fact is that we are at war, and we need copper for our munitions and communications. One way or another, the mines will be functional again."

She leaned into his shoulder. "I understand what you say, Lucas, but I fear the Company will never listen to the miners or consider their concerns as valid. Leaders like that horrid Samuel Sanders don't have to worry about their safety every day when they go to work, neither is their pay cut at the whim of the Company."

He shook his head. "It isn't fair, Vivie. It isn't right. But things are bound to get worse in Butte before they improve. I don't want you caught up in the struggle." He kissed her palm. "We'll do what we can to support those around us, but we can't openly defy the Company. Not now when we have so much to lose."

She sat in quiet contemplation for a few moments. "I agree with your concern about my safety and remaining healthy for the baby. However, I want to attend Frank Little's funeral. I want to be a witness to the horrible tragedy that occurred and in some way show that these sorts of actions are never condoned."

Lucas nodded. "As long as I may attend next to you."

CHAPTER 12

Missoula, Montana, August 1917

*A*raminta entered Savannah's kitchen, piles of dishes and pots strewn on the countertops. She picked up a dishcloth and slapped it on a chair a few times before she stormed from the room and up the stairs. She knocked on Melinda's door and glared at it when no response came. She pushed it open, frowning at the tornado that appeared to have hit Melinda's previously pristine room.

After writing a short note for Savannah, Araminta headed downtown. When she arrived at Gabriel and Jeremy's workshop, she took a deep breath before entering. Ronan's space was unoccupied, and Jeremy worked in the back by himself. "Hello, Jeremy. Where is Gabriel?"

Jeremy turned to face her, frowning with confusion when he saw her. "Minta, …. wonderful to see you." He waved at Gabriel's empty space. "Gabe went with Ronan to see the doctor."

She shifted from foot to foot, catching herself a moment before she tumbled to the ground as she leaned too heavily on her weak leg. "I need to speak with you." At Jeremy's nod, she moved to an unvarnished bench and sat down. He leaned against his workbench and crossed his arms as he waited for her to begin.

"I'm worried about Melly." She saw pain and regret flash in his eyes. "She isn't doing any of her chores, and her room is a mess. She speaks with insolence to me when I ask her to help me." She took a deep breath. "I know I am little better than a maid, but she was raised to treat those around her with respect."

"How long has this been going on?" Jeremy asked.

"Her room has been a mess for a little over a month. She stopped her chores around then too."

"And her insolence?" Jeremy raised an eyebrow, his arms tense across his chest.

"The same amount of time, I guess." Araminta watched Jeremy and shook her head. "I know I have no right to criticize your daughter. I … I …" She broke off as she lowered her gaze. She jumped when he slammed his hand on his workbench.

"I'm very displeased, Minta," Jeremy growled.

"I'm sorry, sir. I never meant …" She broke off her words when he glared at her to be silent.

"Why did you wait, Minta? Why wait a month?" He looked at her as she watched him with dazed confusion. "Why not tell me the instant she treated you without respect?"

"I thought it was a passing phase," she whispered.

"Did you believe I'd countenance my daughter treating you without courtesy?" He shook his head, his gaze filled with disbelief and displeasure. "I'm disappointed, Minta. How can you believe, after all this time, that you are little better than a maid? You are a member of our family. How can you not know that?"

He approached her and sat across from her on a newly finished chair. "You are as a cousin to us. And we cherish you." His jaw tightened when tears fill her eyes. "I wish you'd told me the moment you took over her chores. Why cover for her?"

Araminta closed her eyes for a moment as a tear trickled out. "She told me that I had no right to complain because my parents wanted me less than hers wanted her." At Jeremy's incredulous stare, she whispered, "She said we were both orphanage brats, but at least she hadn't spent her entire childhood there, unloved and unwanted."

The tic in Jeremy's jaw was visible as he reached forward and gripped her hand. "I can only imagine the pain her words caused you. I hope you know they aren't true."

Araminta sniffled. "But they are. My parents didn't want me."

Jeremy smiled at her with tenderness and compassion. "You don't know that. You'll never know what causes a person, a mother or a father, to give up a beloved child. Very few are as heartless and cruel as Mrs. Smythe. Most would do anything for their child." He watched Araminta closely. "Including giving them to the care of an orphanage so that they are clothed, educated and fed." He frowned. "I'm sorry for Melinda's cruel words."

Araminta nodded, unable to speak.

"From now on you are not to do any of her chores. I want to know exactly the cruel things she says the moment she says them. And I will speak with Savannah so she understands what has been going on. This is unacceptable, and we will right this wrong."

Araminta swallowed. "Melly is unsure of her place in the world."

Jeremy nodded. "I know. I wanted to provide a place for her to feel safe and cherished, and instead she doubts who she is and those who love her."

Araminta watched him with envy. "She's fortunate to have a man like you care for her as a father."

He half chuckled. "I'll remind her of that."

∽

Savannah sat in Jeremy's study in stunned silence after what he'd told her. She grimaced and shook her head. "And to think I was upset with Araminta. I thought she'd created the mess in the kitchen."

The front door opened, and Jeremy leaped from his seat behind his desk. "Melinda." His voice boomed through the room and into the front hall. He looked up the front hall steps and called to her again. "Come here. Now." He waited as she sighed and rolled her eyes. After she clomped down the stairs, he closed the door behind them.

"I don't see why you closed the door. We're the only ones here." She plopped into the other seat beside Savannah and tapped her fingers on the armrest.

"Why have you been cruel to Araminta?" Jeremy asked without preamble.

She raised startled eyes to her father. "I don't know what you are talking about."

"Taunting her with her time in the orphanage. Gloating about the fact that you were wanted more than she was." His jaw tightened as he beheld her. "How could you be so cruel?"

"It's not as though anything I said was a lie," she muttered. At her mother's horrified gasp, she spun to glare at her. "We all think it."

"What is the matter with you?" Savannah whispered. "You've always treated Araminta with respect, as though she were a member of our family."

"But that's just the point. She isn't a member of our family. And she never will be." Melinda rose. "If that's all?" she asked with another roll of her eyes. She jumped when her father slammed his fist to his desk.

"No, that isn't all. You've been lax in your chores, and you've been wandering around Missoula unchaperoned after school. What have you been doing?"

"Why should you care? It's not as though you're my father!" Her eyes went huge the minute she said the words. She projected a false bravado, but she could not hide her body's slight trembling nor a faint flush on her cheeks.

"I'm not your father? I'm not your father?" Jeremy asked in a low, anguish-tinged voice. "Who held you when you had croup and had trouble breathing? Who cleaned your skinned knee when you fell, trying to keep up with your uncle Colin's antics? Who read you bedtime stories every night for a year to keep away your fear of monsters under your bed?"

Melinda ducked her head and shook it, refusing to answer.

"And Savannah. Are you saying she isn't your mother? The woman who taught you to cook, taught you about love and loyalty and compassion. Encouraged you to laugh and embrace life's joys." He shook his head. "You are our daughter, Melinda. You've been ours from the very beginning, and we love you."

She raised mutinous eyes to meet his irate gaze.

"And I couldn't be more disappointed in you. Go to your room and clean it. I expect it to be tidy before supper, or you will have nothing to eat." He nodded to the door. He heard her quiet sob as she left the room. He collapsed into the chair behind his desk.

He scrubbed at his face and heaved out a sigh. "Forgive me for being so harsh." When Savannah didn't respond, he looked at her, frowning at the tears coursing down her cheeks. "My love," he murmured.

"My aunt Betsy said that sometimes tough love is needed. What you served Melly was just that. And she needed it. Desperately." She scrubbed at her face with her handkerchief. "That doesn't make it any easier to watch."

"It hurts that she doesn't understand how much we love her," Jeremy whispered. "I'd do anything for her."

Savannah nodded. "I know. She's confused and lost. Just as Mrs. Smythe wanted."

Jeremy growled. "I hate that woman. I know I shouldn't allow myself to feel any emotion toward her, but I do. I hate what she's accomplished."

Savannah's smile was tremulous but hopeful. "I hate what that woman is attempting. I'm uncertain she's accomplished her goal—or ever will—because Melly is strong and smart ... maybe even stronger and smarter than we give her credit for."

Clarissa sat with Savannah in her kitchen, sharing a cup of iced tea. "What's bothering you, Sav?" Clarissa took a sip of her cool drink, her assessing gaze on her cousin. "You've been out of sorts for days."

Savannah gave a false smile that faded under Clarissa's unimpressed stare. "Lucas and Genevieve are expecting their first child." She took a deep breath. When Clarissa remained quiet, Savannah frowned. "I hate being jealous of my own brother."

"I'm sorry it brings up old hurts, Sav." Rissa patted Savannah's hand. "But I'm delighted for Lucas and Genevieve. To finally have a baby on the way. I know she's longed for a child."

Savannah's gaze sharpened. "Do you? How?"

"We've discussed it a few times when they've visited. I doubt it's something she would have brought up with you." Clarissa rolled her eyes as Savannah bristled. "If this is how you truly feel, she had every right to be wary about discussing it with you."

"Do you believe I was upset when you had your children?"

"No, I never once suspected you were envious. And you never stayed away. If I could have made you godmother to them all, I would have." Clarissa stilled as she studied Savannah in her misery. "There's more to this. What is it, Sav?"

Savannah buried her face in her hands. "I'm losing Melly."

Clarissa gasped and moved to sit next to her cousin, pulling her into her arms. Savannah cried on her shoulder. "You can't be. You're her mother."

"She hates Jeremy and me. She thinks we took her out of pity and that we are pathetic because we can't have our own child." She stuttered out a sob. "Says she's counting the days until she can leave us."

"No!" Clarissa breathed. "That doesn't sound like Melly. That sounds like ..." Her eyes rounded. "Has she been spending time with Mrs. Smythe?"

Savannah rubbed a hand over her face. "I fear she has. She doesn't come home directly after school, and, when she does, she's filled with this defiant anger and half-baked truths." She swallowed a sob, but a low keening sound still emerged. "I love her so much, and I don't know how to reach her."

Clarissa held Savannah as she cried, rubbing her back. "Perhaps you should grant her what she wants. She says she wants to leave you. Let her go."

"I can't!" Savannah wailed. "She's not even seventeen yet."

Clarissa gripped Savannah's shoulder. "She won't appreciate or understand what she has with you and Jeremy until she is away from it. Her mind's been filled by that horrible woman, and somehow that spell must be broken."

Savannah's crying slowly abated as she thought through Clarissa's plan. "It's a terrible risk. She might decide never to return to us." Another tear fell.

"I understand, but you're all miserable now. You can't continue like this, forcing her to remain here when she believes she'd rather be somewhere else."

Savannah rose and wet a cloth, swiping at her face before pressing it to her eyes. She sighed with relief as it soothed her reddened, sore eyes. The front door slammed shut, and Melinda's footsteps sounded as she walked toward the kitchen.

"Hello, Clarissa," Melinda said, a challenging glint in her eyes.

"How is Mrs. Smythe, Melly?" Clarissa asked.

Melinda glared at her and then shrugged. "My mother is fine although always devastated when I must depart to return to this house. She eagerly awaits my arrival every day."

"*Hmm*, I'm sure she's most anxious to see you," Clarissa murmured, her gaze sharpening as she noted the subtle changes in Melinda's appearance, from the eye makeup to her new hairstyle, all fashioned after Mrs. Smythe. "She always did enjoy playing dress up."

"I will not allow you to speak badly of my mother!" Melinda shrieked.

Savannah turned and faced her daughter. "And I won't allow you to speak to your sister that way. I've always considered you my daughter, Melly. And I *never* would have consigned you to an orphanage." Her severe look silenced any of Melinda's protests. "Your father and I would *never* have left you there. Your brother and sister would *never* have abandoned you in such a place."

"She had no other option." Melinda tilted her chin in defiance.

Savannah snorted in disbelief, her gaze filled with disappointment. "You obviously don't remember your early years with Mrs. Smythe.

And, for that, I am grateful. However, I have no desire to cause you pain. Or to separate you from a woman you wish to know better." She took a deep breath and swallowed. "If you would like to pack a bag and leave, I will not fight your decision."

Melinda's mouth dropped open, and she paled for a moment. She shot a look at Clarissa, and then met Savannah's gaze again. "I'd like that, Mo … Savannah. I'd like to leave."

Savannah nodded, her shoulders tense and hands gripping the washcloth to the point of rending it in two. "I understand. I trust you will discover the truth. But remember, this is your home, and I will always welcome you." She took another deep breath. "It will be your decision if you want to return. I wish you well, my beloved daughter."

Melinda stood there dumbfounded for a moment before she spun on her heel and raced up the stairs.

Clarissa leaped from her seat and enfolded Savannah in her arms. "That was very brave, Sav."

"And very stupid. Jeremy will be irate with me."

"Once he calms down, he'll admire how brave you were," Clarissa soothed. She helped Savannah to a chair and watched as she stared into space.

"She wouldn't call me mother," she whispered. "That's the first time since we arrived in Montana fourteen years ago that she hasn't called me *mother*." She dropped her head in her arms and sobbed.

~

Jeremy paced their bedroom as Savannah lay on her side, watching him. Every few moments he mumbled something, ran his hands through his hair, kicked the wardrobe and then continued his frenetic movements. They had dressed for bed long ago, yet sleep would not come.

"How did this come about?"

She sighed. "I've explained this already." Yet Jeremy's earnest gaze in her direction had her repeating it all again. "Clarissa and I were talking in the kitchen. I told her of my suspicions about Melly and Mrs. Smythe, and she suggested that I—we—had to let her go."

"Why wouldn't you discuss such an action with me first?" He flopped to the foot of the bed, facing her direction but not touching her.

She curled around so that she could face him. "I'm sorry, Jeremy," Savannah whispered. "It was impulsive, and I know I should have waited for you. But, when Melly entered the kitchen, all dolled up like a mini–Mrs. Smythe, I was past reason."

Jeremy closed his eyes at the vision. "Oh, Sav," he murmured, scooting up the bed to pull her in his arms. They lay crosswise on the bed, entangled in each other's arms. "I don't know what we could have done differently."

"We gave her all our love. If she doesn't want that, there's nothing more we can do," she stuttered out, burying her face in Jeremy's shoulder. "I hate every bit of that despicable woman I see in her."

"Melly is sensible. She'll soon see there's nothing but a thin varnish of charm over an ugly soul. She'll come back to us." Jeremy crooned to Savannah as she cried. When she calmed, he turned them so they stretched out properly in bed. "Come. Let's try to sleep." He coaxed her into his arms again and sang to her until she drifted to sleep.

The following morning he woke, stiff and heartsore. Easing from bed and leaving Savannah sleeping, he stretched and yawned. He donned an old pair of pants and a well-worn shirt before heading downstairs to read last evening's paper and brew coffee. He moved around the kitchen, whistling softly until he heard a soft thud near the back door.

He wrenched open the back door and stared outside. He shook his head, moving to reenter the kitchen and to enjoy his coffee when his gaze focused on a heap by the stable wall, nearly hidden by a bush. He approached it, his pace quickening to a run.

"Melly," he breathed, running his hands over her until he had her turned faceup. "Melly!" he shouted, shaking her.

"Father," she whispered.

"Tell me where you are injured." He pulled her into his arms, groaning as she was no longer a little girl and rose, carrying her in his arms into the house. "You'll be all right. I promise. We'll take care of you."

"Oh, Father," she whispered, shaking before she started to sob.

"Shh, my darling girl. It will be all right. You're home. You're safe," he soothed. He carried her through the kitchen and upstairs to her room. After kicking open her door, he settled her gently onto her bed, running a hand through her unkempt hair and then down her arms. He frowned at the sooty eye makeup that made her look like a raccoon, his gaze searching for any wounds.

Savannah appeared at the door. "Jeremy, what is going on?" She looked around his shoulder to a rumpled, disheveled Melinda and flew into the room. "Melinda!"

"Mother," Melinda said as her tears poured out. "I ... I ..." She turned to her side, crying as she curled into herself as if to disappear.

Jeremy sat in front of her, holding her hand and rubbing her arm and shoulder. Savannah climbed onto the bed behind her, wrapping her arms around her.

"How can you welcome me home? After how horrible I was?" she stuttered out.

"We love you," Jeremy whispered. "You are our daughter, and we love you." Her incredulous gaze met his. "We always will."

"But I've been so mean," she wailed. "And I hurt you."

"We sometimes hurt those we love." Jeremy ran a hand over her soaked cheek. "It doesn't mean it hasn't been tremendously painful for your mother and me, but it hasn't stopped us from loving you."

"I couldn't understand why you'd love me and the woman who had me didn't." Melly closed her eyes. "Doesn't."

"Oh, Melly," Savannah murmured. "I'm so sorry."

"Why?" she asked. "I thought you hated her."

Jeremy and Savannah exchanged a look before Savannah spoke. "Melly, although it is true we will never like Mrs. Smythe and will feel negatively toward her, you must know that, if we thought you'd be happiest with her, we would never stop you from being with her."

Melinda pushed away from her parents and sat up, her eyes blazing. "You knew how horrible she is! How could you have sent me to her?"

Savannah sighed. "I didn't send you to her. And you wouldn't have made a fully informed decision for yourself where you wanted to be unless you spent more time with her. Time that she hadn't carefully coordinated to highlight herself at her best."

Jeremy watched as Melinda quivered on her bed. "What happened, Melly?"

She shook her head as though refusing to talk of the past afternoon and evening. After a few moments of silence, however, she spoke in a low voice. "I packed my bag and thought of myself as wonderfully grown-up as I came downstairs. I heard you sobbing in the kitchen, Mother, and snuck out the front door."

She plucked at a loose thread on her dirty skirt. "When I arrived at Mrs. Smythe's, she was irate I'd returned. Said I was interfering with her plans. When I informed her that I'd decided to live with her, she screeched that I was nothing but an imposition and a leech. How was she to make her way in the world with an adult daughter?" Melinda mimicked Mrs. Smythe's mannerisms and diction. "How was she to get a man when he'd want her daughter instead?"

"Oh, Melly," Savannah whispered.

Melinda continued as though in a trance, not registering her mother's words. "She finally said I could spend the night but that I had to return home tomorrow—today—as she had no desire to care for me." Melly bit her trembling lip. "She prepared for an evening out and then left without acknowledging me. There was no food, and I finally fell asleep on the settee."

Jeremy watched Melinda as her story petered out. "What caused you to flee and sleep in the stables last night?"

Melinda covered her face and shook her head.

Savannah gripped her daughter's hand and lowered it. "There is no reason to be ashamed or embarrassed with us. We will always love you and do everything we can to protect you."

"You sent me to that woman!" Melinda screamed.

Savannah clenched her jaw shut, refusing to be goaded into an angry response. "I didn't send you anywhere. You chose to go to that woman, Melly. Now tell us what happened."

"She came home. But she wasn't alone." Melly trembled. "I woke to their laughter. She was with two men." She shook her head with confusion. "Why were there two men?"

Jeremy growled out, "What happened next? What did they do to you?"

She shook her head as a few tears leaked out. "She knew I was awake. She saw them glance at me and must have seen they were interested in me." Her jaw trembled as she fought tears. "She offered me to them for money."

"What did the men do, Melly?" Savannah whispered, one of her hands gripping Jeremy.

"I … I think they were half drunk or more. One seemed keen on the idea. The other worried, and I bolted at their moment of indecision. Ran out the door with her screeching behind me that I'd cost her good money." Tears coursed down her cheeks. "I ran and ran through the streets. I never realized how scary it could be in the middle of the night, alone." She swallowed back another sob. "I didn't know where else to go."

"Why didn't you knock on the door when you arrived home?" Savannah whispered, running a hand over her daughter's head and cheek.

Melinda looked down at her clenched hands. "I didn't know if I'd be welcomed."

In an instant, she was sandwiched in a hug from her parents. "When I think of what could have happened …" Jeremy shook as he held her tight.

When they had calmed from their fright, Jeremy eased away from Melinda while Savannah held her daughter in her arms.

"Melinda," Jeremy began, "we need to know what you want. Do you wish to remain here, as our daughter, a cherished member of our family? Or do you prefer to leave us?" He watched as Melinda battled deep emotions. "We can't continue on as we have these past weeks, going on months. We love you and want you. But your mother was correct yesterday in giving you a choice. You must decide what it is you want."

Melinda looked with wonder from Savannah to Jeremy. "You'd still want me, after everything I've done? All the horrible things I've said to you and to those you care about?"

Savannah kissed her daughter on her temple. "We understand you've been confused since Mrs. Smythe arrived, and it only worsened after your discussion with Patrick. It never changed our love for you."

A sob burst forth, and Melinda turned to burrow into her mother's shoulder. "I want to be here with you and Father. You want me. You chose me. You love me. This is where I want to be. This is who I am."

~

Jeremy marched into the workshop he shared with Gabriel and slammed shut the heavy wooden door. Gabriel looked up from his work and frowned.

"Generally we encourage business, Jer," Gabriel teased. He sobered when he saw Jeremy was ready for battle. He shared a look with Ronan, and they moved to the area near Ronan's workbench. "What happened?"

"Melinda is home," Jeremy said, his tone still tortured.

Gabriel nodded. "Good." When Jeremy remained quiet, Gabe asked, "Is she accepting of you and Sav as her parents?"

Jeremy gave a curt nod and yet paced like a caged tiger.

"Who do I have to prevent from getting killed?" Gabriel asked with an intentional inflection of humor.

"This isn't humorous, Gabe." Jeremy spun and took a deep breath to prevent himself from launching at his brother, prepared for a fight.

"I know it isn't, Jer, but I won't sit by and allow you to end up in jail." He met his brother's stormy gaze. "Not now. Not ever."

Jeremy growled. "*She* deserves to suffer. After all she's done to the members of our family."

Gabriel nodded and sat with quiet patience as his brother worked through his rage.

"Melly ran to her yesterday. Had some nonsensical romantic belief that she'd be welcomed with opened arms by that harpy of a woman who gave birth to her and promptly gave her away. Instead, Melly was advised that she was an unwanted burden." Jeremy spun and kicked a small table Gabriel had just finished constructing, shattering one of its legs. Gabriel sighed at the destruction but didn't protest his brother's actions.

"Do you know what that woman did then?" Jeremy demanded after a few moments. When Gabriel and Ronan remained quiet, Jeremy stopped, and his breaths came out in stuttering gasps. "She came home with two men and offered to sell Melly, *my daughter*, to them."

Gabriel swore, and Ronan hit his table with a hammer. "That bitch," Gabriel snapped. "What happened to Melly?"

"She was smart enough to use the men's momentary surprise to race out of there, her so-called mother screaming at her that she'd cost her money." Jeremy rubbed at his face in weary anguish. He finally collapsed onto a bench near Gabe. "When I think about what could have ..." He shook his head and lowered it into his hands.

"But nothing happened?" Gabriel whispered.

Jeremy shook his head. "No. Melly got away." He shared a wry smile with Gabriel. "She was confused why Mrs. Smythe would come home with two men."

Ronan chuckled. "She won't always be your innocent little girl, but I'm glad no harm came to her." He tapped his tabletop with his small hammer. "However, something must be done to that horrible woman. She can't frighten Melly as she did and suffer no consequences."

Melinda entered the front sitting room and came to an abrupt halt. "What are you doing here?" She glared as Mrs. Smythe settled onto the comfortable settee. "I never heard the knock, and I know no one would have allowed you entrance into this house."

Mrs. Smythe smiled at Melinda and patted the seat next to her. She stiffened when Melinda remained standing away from her. "I did knock, but there was no answer. I let myself in to wait."

"You have no right to be in our home." She stiffened her shoulders as she'd seen her sister, Clarissa, do on many occasions, and her expression sobered further. "Please leave."

"You don't really want to throw out your own mother, Melinda. After a small misunderstanding, I can't believe you'd be so harsh."

"You horrid woman," Melinda rasped.

Mrs. Smythe glowered at her. "I hate how they've turned you against me. That they've destroy the relationship we could have."

Melinda shook her head and scoffed with incredulity. "Do you truly believe me so foolish as to ever believe anything you say again? After last night?"

Mrs. Smythe waved her hand as though Melinda's concern were of no more importance than an irritating gnat flying near her. "You know what a little drink does to a person. Makes them act in a way they wouldn't normally."

"You claimed you were part of the temperance movement. Thought Carrie Nation was a role model for all women." Melinda waved her arm before realizing she mimicked Mrs. Smythe and dropped it to her side. "Just like everything else about you, it was all bluster and nothing of substance."

"Now listen here, darling daughter, you are allowing your anger to rule you. Something you inherited from your father's side of the family." She ran a hand over her lap and smiled sweetly at Melinda. "I was caught off guard yesterday when you arrived unexpectedly."

Melinda shook her head. "Were you equally surprised to find me asleep on your settee when you brought two men home? And then offered me to them for a price? Like I was nothing better than the women on Front Street?"

Mrs. Smythe watched her with a calculating smile. "You must

know that's all we are, Melinda dear. The women on Front Street just aren't caught up in the societal niceties we bind ourselves with."

Melinda gaped at her and shook her head. "I will never forgive you for your disregard of me. For seeing me as something to profit from, never as a person. Never as a daughter."

Mrs. Smythe slapped her hand onto her lap. "If you'd been a son, you'd have been valuable!" She smiled at Melinda's gasp of pain. "Yes, I would have taken joy in you if you were a boy, rather than a weak, useless daughter."

Melinda swiped at her cheek and met her triumphantly cruel smile. "I will forever give thanks you sent me to the orphanage. You allowed me to be cared for by those who love me, by responsible and strong men and women." Mrs. Smythe sputtered, and Melinda smiled. "Your act of selfishness was the greatest act of caring you could have done for me, and, had you known it, I'm sure you would never have done it. I'm only thankful that you were too self-absorbed to realize that my family has more honor and more integrity than you will never fathom."

She strode to the door and flung it open. "I want you to leave and never return. You are not my mother, and you never were. Giving birth to me doesn't give you the right to call yourself my mother. You're a cruel, vindictive, heartless woman, and I want nothing to do with you ever again."

Mrs. Smythe rose with as much grace as she could muster as she vibrated with anger. "If you think you can throw me out of your house and issue ultimatums ..." She laughed at Melinda as she approached the open door.

"I can. My parents will stand behind me and support me." Melinda jolted when she heard Savannah's voice.

"She has my full support and that of every member of our family here and in Boston. You are outmaneuvered, Mrs. Smythe. I suggest you leave and never return." Savannah leaned against the wall in the hallway, hidden from view in the sitting room. She shared an intense stare with Mrs. Smythe.

"This isn't over. I will find a way ..." Mrs. Smythe blustered but didn't finish her sentence as Melinda pushed her out the door and slammed it behind her.

Melinda leaned against the closed door and looked at Savannah, the woman she'd always known as her mother. "How much did you hear?"

Savannah smiled and walked toward her daughter, pulling her into a comforting embrace. "Enough. I wanted to intervene but realized you needed this opportunity to tell her off." She pushed Melinda back and cupped her cheeks. "You were brilliant, darling. I just wish your father could have heard you."

Melinda smiled before her lips trembled. "I hate how I hurt you both." She fell forward again into her mother's embrace, crying.

"It will take time for your wounds to heal, darling. But we all have growing pains from our youth. I know I wish I'd acted differently." Savannah stroked a hand down Melinda's back. "The one person you must speak with is Araminta."

Melinda nodded, accepting the comfort that was offered.

The following afternoon, Melinda walked over to Araminta's rented rooms. She knocked on her door, frowning when there was no answer. She decided to wait on the porch, hiding in the shade on the hot afternoon rather than heading home only to return later. After watching random townsfolk pass by, she stilled when Araminta approached, walking alongside a man. Frowning at them as he evoked a laugh from Araminta, Melinda canted forward to watch as, at the foot of the walkway, he kissed Araminta's hand. Araminta stood there, watching him depart for a few moments before she turned to enter her rooms.

"Minta!" Melinda whispered from her hiding place on the porch.

Araminta jumped, tumbling to the ground as her weak leg gave out. She grumbled as she pushed herself up and then glared at Melinda. "What are you doing here? Spying on me?"

"I wasn't spying. I was waiting for you and getting out of the heat. Who is that man?"

Araminta blushed. "He's a friend."

Melinda looked in the direction he'd gone and shook her head. "No, I think he wishes he were more. He dresses funny."

At that, Araminta laughed. "That's because he's Mr. Bouchard. He works at one of the banks here with his uncle."

Melinda nodded as though waiting for more details. When none were forthcoming, she frowned. "I don't understand why you'd take walks with him when you're meant to be with Colin."

Araminta made a low growling noise and shook her head. "I'm not meant for any such thing. It's abundantly clear Colin and I will never be more than mere friends." She wrenched open her front door and motioned for Melinda to follow her. After she unlocked the door to her rooms, she hung up her hat and light coat. "Why are you here, Melly?"

Melinda shook her head. "I think you're wrong about Colin, but that's for you to figure out. As Mr. Pickens would say, I think you're being *pomptuse*." She looked around Araminta's sparsely decorated space with a crate for a table, two wooden chairs and a lumpy settee. "Why haven't you asked us for furniture? You know we have extra in the attic."

Araminta sighed. "I've already received too much from your family. I can't ask for or expect anything more."

Melinda gripped Araminta's hand as she moved away from her. "No, Minta. You're a member of our family. You should never feel embarrassed to seek our help or to ask for something." Her eyes filled with tears as Araminta kept her head bowed and refused to meet her gaze. "I'm so sorry for the horrible things I said to you."

Araminta sniffled and then raised her angry eyes to meet hers. "Then why'd you say such awful, mean things to me? You knew exactly what to say to hurt me the most."

Melinda paled at the anguish in Araminta's expression. After a moment of opening and closing her mouth to find words to explain herself, she shook her head. "I know you'll hate me forever. I'm so sorry, Minta."

Araminta half laughed. "Oh, Melinda, stop being so theatrical." She shook her head and rolled her eyes. "I won't hate you forever, but I want you to tell me why you acted like you did."

Melinda released Araminta's hand and collapsed onto the lumpy settee. "I've always been secure in who I was. Melinda McLeod with two parents and a wonderful family who all love me. That *woman* made me doubt everything." Melinda wrung her hands together on her lap. "And I hated that you, who really was an orphan, seemed more secure in your place in the world than me. I wanted you to feel as out of sorts as I did."

Araminta let out a gasp of air before sinking onto one of the hard wooden chairs. "You knew how much you'd hurt me, and yet you did it anyway?"

Melinda nodded. "I wanted someone else to hurt worse than I did." She swiped at one of her cheeks. "I'm sorry, Minta. You've always been like a sister to me, and I treated you worse than I would treat a sworn enemy."

Araminta rolled her eyes again. "Melly, you don't have a sworn enemy."

"No, but Father does," she argued.

Araminta shook her head. "You read too many of those romantic novels. Life isn't like it is in books. It's painful and boring most of the time. You have to accept life as it is and find the joy where you can."

Melinda shook her head. "That's not true. You can make your own joy, Minta. And you should fight for the joy you want." She studied Araminta and frowned. "Is that why you aren't willing to show Colin you want a future with him? Because you accept life as it is, not as you want it to be?"

Araminta glared at her. "You're talking nonsense. Once you've lived a little, you'll know what I'm saying is true. Grab the joy you can, but accept life as it comes."

Melinda sighed and shook her head. "I'm bound to be a disappointment then. I refuse to accept life as it is. I'll always want more, for me and those I care about." She pinned her close friend with an intense stare. "Which includes you, Minta. I'll always want more for you. Which means I want more than a puffed-up buffoon who'll never make your eyes light with joy the way Colin does."

Araminta closed her eyes in defeat. "We'll not agree on this, Melly. What I will say is that, although you hurt me, I will be able to forgive you. It may take me a little while, but this won't do any lasting damage to our relationship."

Melinda beamed at her and threw herself into Araminta's arms. The wobbly chair collapsed with their combined weight, and they toppled to the floor. Araminta grunted with discomfort while Melinda burst out laughing. "This is why you need better furniture." She rose, holding out a hand to help Araminta from the floor. "I'll speak with Father. We'll have furniture delivered within a few days."

She whooped when Araminta gave a reluctant smile of acquiescence. "Someday Colin will visit you here, and we want it looking nice."

Araminta sputtered and glared at Melinda. "He'll never visit me here. It isn't proper for a single man to visit a single woman in her rooms." She glared at Melinda. "Don't give him ideas."

Melinda shrugged her shoulders. "I won't have to. He's my brother and more sensible than you give him credit for." She hugged Araminta again and then headed for the door, her expression once again serious. "Thank you, Minta, for forgiving me."

CHAPTER 13

Washington, DC, August 1917

*T*eddy sat on the doorstep of an apartment building in Washington, DC. From the receipts of expenses incurred, he believed this to be where Zylphia and Rowena had a small apartment. Any correspondence he sent her went to the suffragist headquarters at Cameron House. He shifted as the concrete step made an uncomfortable seat and glared down the shrub-lined walkway as if to make Zylphia appear. After thirty minutes, he rose and massaged his backside, walking the few steps to and fro in front of the building. He stilled when he heard laughter.

"Teddy!" Zylphia proclaimed as she turned down the walkway. "Whatever are you doing here?" She leaned forward and kissed him on his cheek.

"Hello, Zee. Rowena." He smiled at her friend. "I've heard alarming tales in Boston, and I wanted to ensure you were well."

Zylphia held out her arms to her side. "As you can see, I'm quite well." She linked her arm through his and walked toward the front door. "Come. I'll show you our small apartment."

Upon entering the tiny living space, Teddy roamed around. It had

177

a miniscule entranceway big enough for two coat pegs and a small table. The living room had a settee, two chairs and windows on two walls, as it was a corner unit. One door led to a bedroom, the other to a bathroom. Along the wall that had the small entrance table was a curtain concealing a sink and a hotplate.

"Isn't it grand?" Zylphia asked.

"I'd hoped, for what we were spending, you'd get more than this," Teddy said, shucking his jacket and throwing it over the back of the settee. "At least you have decent light." He looked out the front window to a small garden area below. He absently noted Rowena leaving with a small bag.

"Well, I think it's grand, and I'm not here that often as it is." She hung her coat and hat on a peg by the door. "I spend most of my time at Cameron House." She watched him curiously. "Why didn't you come there to see me?"

"I did, but you weren't there. I waited for a while and then decided to come here." He sat on the settee and watched his wife closely.

"I hope you were well received at the House." Zylphia played with a loose button on the front of her dress.

"I was. I met a friend of yours. Mr. Hooper. He seemed most interested in making my acquaintance." He leaned forward, his elbows on his knees. "Why would that be, Zee?" At her persistent silence, he tilted his head to one side. "Why would he look at me as though I were the scum of the earth and accuse me of being a wife-beater?"

Zylphia paled. "He's overreacting. He saw me when I returned from Boston a few months ago, when my wrist was bruised." Teddy flinched as he recalled gripping her forearm. "I assured him it was my fault—"

"No, it was solely mine as I was the one who bruised you. I promise it won't happen again."

"I almost wish it would."

He stilled at her whispered words.

"It means you care enough to become upset with me."

He watched her with a fierce passion lighting his eyes. "Why would such a man take an interest, Zee?"

ment, arching up to him. She cried out in pleasure as he joined with her, leaning up to kiss him again. "I love you, Zee," he said before he was lost to their passion.

~

"Where did Rowena go?" Teddy asked. His hands roved over Zee's soft skin, eliciting shivers.

"She whispered she'd spend the night in a hotel."

Teddy flushed. "That was thoughtful of her. We should have gone to the hotel, rather than consigning ourselves to this tiny bed." He shifted as Zylphia giggled, curling into his embrace as he struggled to not fall off the single bed.

"How long can you stay?" She traced her hand over his chest.

"I must return tomorrow." He kissed her frown away. "But I had to see you, ensure you were well." After a few moments of silence he let out a big sigh. "What is it like, on the picket line?"

She lay with her head cushioned on his shoulder. "Exhilarating at first. To know that we are expressing our beliefs and demanding to be heard. ... Oh, Teddy, it's almost intoxicating. But then it became a test of endurance. The cold and wet and constant abuse." Zylphia shuddered. "I had hoped to be done with picketing by now, but it's important for those who arrive here to see that we remain enthusiastic about it. They must see some of what they call the 'old guard' continuing with it."

"What happens when you are on the picket?" Teddy asked, arching down to kiss her.

"Sometimes we are attacked as we march there from the house. Other times, they wait to see what we'll proclaim in our banners." She sighed as she snuggled against him. "I love our banners. They're beautiful, with gold silk fabric and purple lettering."

"I've read about how you are treated," Teddy whispered, unable to hide the concern from his voice.

"We're yelled at, spit on, and we have things thrown at us, yes. The worst is when they grab the banners and tear them up. Sometimes they believe they can do the same to us and our clothes." She sighed. "We never fight back. Miss Paul has instructed us that no matter what is said or done to our person, we must never fight back. We are to remain peaceful."

"How can you when others are abusing you so terribly?" He stroked a hand down her arm as though to ensure she was well next to him.

"It goes against my nature." Zylphia giggled. "A few times I wanted to punch and give as much as I received. However, I realize Miss Paul is correct. If we fought back, they'd have valid charges against us. As it is, they have to use weak charges that no one believes, such as obstructing others' access to the sidewalk. Although none who attack us are ever charged with anything."

He ran a soothing hand over her arm and shoulder. "What can Miss Paul hope to achieve with the picketing? All it seems to do is turn more against you and the cause."

"At the moment, I fear you are correct. However, I know at some point, something will happen that will shift the tide of public sentiment, and it will be due to the picketing. For some reason, the pickets are central to Miss Paul's plans."

"Promise me that you'll keep yourself safe," Teddy whispered. He rolled Zylphia so he could meet her eyes. "Promise me, if you ever find yourself with child, you'll protect yourself and our child."

Zylphia smiled. "Of course I will." She kissed him again, her easy affection assuaging any of his concerns.

~

The following morning, after Teddy had left to catch an early train back to Boston, Zylphia waited for Rowena. At the soft knock on the door, she opened it, smiling at her friend. "Why such a timid knock?" Zylphia asked as she pulled her hat off the peg.

"I didn't want to disturb you and Teddy," Rowena said with a teasing smile, dropping her overnight bag by the front door.

"He's already left. Some business emergency in Boston called him away," Zylphia said as she pinned on her hat.

"You seem happier since his visit." They emerged onto the sidewalk to travel the short distance to Cameron House.

"Nothing is settled between us, but it helped to have him show his concern for my welfare. He refuses to change his stance on beginning a citizenship application." Zylphia tilted her head to enjoy a few moments of sunshine before the oppressive heat returned as was forecast for the next few days.

"Did you argue with him before he left?" Rowena asked, earning a scowl from her friend.

"Yes. He asked me about the pickets last night. I thought he understood how important it is. I thought he was proud of my courage and determination."

Rowena slowed as they walked through the small square. "What did he say?"

"This morning he said he'd only support me here if I promised to never picket again. That he couldn't live with himself if something happened to me and he'd financed my ruin."

"Oh, Zee," Rowena breathed, gripping her friend's arm.

"It's not the money, Ro. I have plenty of money, and I know my father would support me." She swiped at her cheek. "I feel betrayed by the man who I thought would always support me." She took a deep breath. "He intended to visit Cameron House with me before he left, but I encouraged him to take an early train."

"You didn't want him to meet Mr. Hooper."

Zylphia grimaced. "He already met him. Yesterday."

Rowena arched an eyebrow at her. "Seeing as there isn't anything between you and Mr. Hooper, and never has been, I don't see why that is a concern."

"Too many believe I've been indiscreet. Teddy met Octavius yesterday, and I had to swear I had been true to Teddy." She shared a worried glance with her friend. "I think he believed me, but I didn't want him to spend more time at the Cameron House and hear any more whispering."

Rowena nodded.

Zylphia bit her lip and flushed. "Besides, I never told Teddy that I'd been arrested in July."

Rowena gaped at her. "What?" At Zylphia's shrug, she choked out an incredulous laugh. "You're joking. You never told your husband that you'd been one of those women imprisoned after Bastille Day?"

"I feared it would make him more insistent about his demand I cease picketing. That I'd be consigned to return to Boston for insipid painting and balls." She kicked at a small rock on the pavement before her. "I couldn't go back, not now. Not when the movement needs us."

"You lied to your husband, Zee." When Zylphia protested, Rowena shook her head. "A lie of omission is still a lie. Besides, don't you think he knows? The papers in Boston would have printed the names of those imprisoned."

Zylphia shook her head, deflated that Teddy had not been following the cause more closely. "He would have said something if he'd known. His largest concern was that our banners would cause us to appear treasonous. He's overly worried about the Espionage Act and that we are in blatant defiance of it."

Rowena nodded. "Which they very well might be treasonous, and we most certainly are blatantly defiant."

"The banners are not illegal, and we are speaking the truth."

"It's our version of the truth, and you know the president isn't very keen on dissenters." Rowena shook her head in wonder at her friend.

Zylphia waved her hand to change the subject and focused on her friend with a false cheer. "How are you, Ro? I realize how selfish I am, always focusing on myself and never thinking to ask about you."

Rowena shrugged. "I'm fine. I no longer have any communication with many members of my family." She looked around at those passing by and then gave Zylphia a pointed stare. "I understand that is how it must be now." They turned up the walk to Cameron House. "Have you heard from Parthena lately?" Rowena asked.

"I receive sporadic letters from her. Seems she's still molding herself into the wife Morgan envisions rather than being who she is and allowing him to adapt to her quirks."

Rowena chuckled. "So they're both still miserable?" At Zylphia's nod, Rowena sighed. "Well, I hope something changes for them soon. They've been married two years. It's long enough for them to determine what they want from their marriage." She opened the door to Cameron House, and their personal concerns faded away as they focused on the needs of the cause.

CHAPTER 14

*P*arthena stood in her parlor, staring at her piano. Her straw-blond hair was tied back in a loose knot and she wore a casual pink day dress. She leaned toward the piano, encouraging an inclination to play. Fingertips tracked down her back, and she shivered at the unexpected caress. "Why are you here, Morgan?"

He chuckled, his brown eyes shining with amusement. "Isn't it acceptable for a husband to visit his wife in her parlor?" He stood to her side so he could study her face, nearly half a foot taller than she. "Why aren't you serenading me with some brilliant composition you've just created?"

She huffed out an exasperated breath and pushed past him. Rather than sitting on the piano stool, she plopped onto a settee. He joined her, grasping her hand and stilling any further restless movements.

"What is bothering you, Hennie?" He frowned when she refused to meet his gaze. "I would hope by now you are used to my presence here."

She fought against a smile but failed. "You know I am."

He traced the hint of a smile on her cheek and the small indentation it formed on her chin. "I am quite used to our ritual of relaxing before dinner with a drink while I listen to you perform." He frowned.

"However, I only want you to play if you want to. Not because I enjoy it."

She flushed. "I never dreamed you would admit to enjoying hearing me play the piano."

He chucked her under the chin, the gentle pressure encouraging her to meet his gaze. "You know by now, two years after our marriage, that I do." His gaze warmed as he saw his words pleased her. "Hennie, tell me what bothers you."

She closed her eyes and shook her head.

He dropped his hand from her chin and clasped her elbow. "Are you ill?"

At the panic in his voice, her eyes sprang open. "No! Of course not."

"There is no 'of course not' about it." He sighed as he studied her mounting tension. "Whatever is bothering you, please don't be afraid to tell me. I won't be angry."

Parthena shook her head. "You say that now, but I know you'll misinterpret what I say." She cut him off with a hand over his mouth. "I received a letter from Viv today. She's still adapting to life in Montana. I fear she never will."

Morgan sighed. "I'm sorry if my actions forced your sister to live away from you. I had hoped they'd feel comfortable returning here by now. No one concerns themselves with women who elope during a time of war. They're too concerned with hating their neighbor."

Parthena frowned at his cynicism. "I hope that's not true."

He laughed and rolled his eyes. "You read the papers like I do. Every day there's something in them about Germans in America, and what could they be plotting? What more should we take away from them so they won't harm us?" He shook his head in disgust. "I fear we'll never learn as a people and will always search out strife."

Parthena watched him with wide eyes at his prescient statement. She took a deep breath. "Yes, well, as we were talking about Viv and my letter from her." At his subtle nod for her to continue talking, she said, "I think she hoped to return to Boston before now. But Lucas enjoys Montana. Relishes living near his sister and his extended family. And he seems to thrive playing low-class music in those bars. What a waste." She leaned against Morgan and eased into his embrace when he slung an arm over her shoulder. "She's pregnant," she blurted out in a voice barely stronger than a whisper. "She'll have a baby the end of January or beginning of February."

Morgan froze, the tender caress on her upper arm transforming into a tight clasp. "What?"

"Genevieve is pregnant. With Lucas's child." She shuddered out a breath as though forestalling tears. She swiped at her cheeks as Morgan's arm fell away, and he stood.

"I can see why you feared discussing this with me." His voice had the warmth of a glacier.

She grabbed his hand, preventing him from storming out of the room. "Don't do this. Don't you dare turn into that icicle again." She rose and grabbed his other hand to pull him toward her. However, his greater strength kept him at arm's length.

"I thought you enjoyed the icicle," he snapped. "Then you weren't forced to feel. Or to choose."

"Damn you," she choked out. "You know I chose you. I chose you when I married you." Tears streamed from her eyes. "I've never been unfaithful to you."

"No, never—except in your thoughts, dreams and hopes for your future," he snapped. He clamped his jaw shut when Parthena flinched. "I beg your pardon. That was uncalled for."

"But that's how you see me. How you believe I see our marriage." Her voice cracked on the word *marriage*.

"How would I see it any differently? At best you tolerate my presence. You laugh at my jokes because you think that makes you a dutiful wife." He cut off any protests with a sharp look. "You accompany me to business functions because you desire to appear faithful and you disdain gossip. You host events to further the fallacy we are a contented couple. And yet you refuse me into your bed. I never thought to have separate sleeping quarters from my wife, but now I do."

"Morgan, I'm sorry," she whispered.

"I can only imagine what that apology covers." Morgan closed his eyes a moment and then took a deep breath. "Why are you so upset? I'd think you'd rejoice that your sister is to have a child. That at last you'll be an aunt."

She forced a smile. "Of course. How could I possibly be upset? I've always wanted a niece to dote on. To teach her all the lessons I failed to learn." She released him and moved to the piano, finally sitting on the piano bench. She played a sweet, yearning composition and lost herself in her solitary performance. She looked up to share a smile with Morgan and to bask in his appreciation of her talent, her smile expressing her desired hope for conciliation and her yearning to heal whatever damage had been wrought that evening, only to find the room empty.

~

M organ stood outside Parthena's room the next morning. He rapped on her door and forced himself not to pound on it with his clenched fist as his anger mounted. "Parthena," he whispered. When no response still came, he opened the door and peered inside. The curtains had been flung open, and he frowned as the bed was freshly made and unoccupied. After entering and softly closing the door behind him, his quick perusal of the room gave him no insight into his wife's whereabouts.

On the verge of storming from the room and interrogating the staff, he noticed a letter on her bedside table. He picked it up and growled as he opened it.

Morgan,

It seems we are destined to be discontented with each other. I'm sorry to continually cause you pain. I need time to consider what I want. Don't worry about me. I'll be fine. I'll spend time with Zylphia Goff.

Parthena

Morgan bunched up her note in his fist and barreled down the hallway and stairs, bellowing for his butler. "Strand!" He held out the crumpled note but not so his butler could read it. "Do you know where Mrs. Wheeler has gone?"

"She left early this morning, sir. Said she had important business to attend to."

"Business, my foot," Morgan snarled as he spun, grabbing his coat and hat before racing down the steps of his home onto Commonwealth Avenue. He pushed past those taking a leisurely morning stroll, striding toward the Charles River and Beacon Street. He failed to notice the cloudless day lacking in humidity or the neatly trimmed gardens in front of the brick homes and glared at those who dared call out to him.

He burst into the tidy brownstone on Beacon Street, refusing to await the butler's appearance. He shrugged from his coat as the butler grabbed at him, eluding his grasp, and pushed into the office off the main hall.

Teddy looked up from the papers he examined on his desk. "Wheeler," he said, waving off the butler and servant who had rushed in to drag Morgan away. Teddy bit back a grin to see Morgan accept his hastily discarded coat from the butler and don it once more. "What brings you by?"

"Did you know about this?" Morgan asked, slamming the crumpled note onto Teddy's desk.

Teddy raised an eyebrow and glanced at the other man sitting to the right of his desk before reading the note.

Morgan scowled. "Of course, you'd be here." He glowered at Aidan McLeod.

"Of course I'm here. He's my son-in-law, and we are working on business matters. What's got you so riled, Morgan?" Aidan asked. He remained seated, with an air of relaxed ennui about him.

"Parthena's left him to join Zee," Teddy murmured as he set the note down on his desk.

"Ah," Aidan said. "That would rile any husband. Especially if such departure was precipitous." Aidan waved at Morgan to sit, and Morgan collapsed into a chair next to him. "I presume she had a reason to leave." At Morgan's silence, he said, "Or she believes she does."

Morgan raised a hand to his head, swiping away sweat after his race across the Back Bay. He extracted a handkerchief from his lapel pocket and rubbed his hand and then his face clean. "We argued again last night. I didn't think it was any different from our previous arguments," he admitted. "Although I say things when I'm angry ..."

Aidan sighed, and Teddy settled back into his leather chair, causing it to squeak. "We all do," Teddy said. "Although I think you have a tendency to say more than you'd ever mean to." He watched Morgan with blatant curiosity. "Why are you here and not in DC?"

Morgan stared from one to the other and then laughed mirthlessly. "She's in DC?" At Teddy's nod, Morgan groaned and held his head in his hands. "I thought she wanted a few days respite from me. To run to your wife as a protest."

Aidan chuckled. "Well, I'd say she's done that. It's simply that her protest has brought her to Washington. And, I fear, notoriety. For, if she's visiting Zee, she will end up on the picket line."

Morgan glared at first Aidan and then Teddy. "Do you expect me to believe you countenance your wife's actions? And her ability to drag my wife into her dangerous plans?"

Teddy smiled with a nod in Aidan's direction. "I've been convinced that there is little danger in standing in front of the White House, holding signs in protest. They aren't breaking the law, and they are peaceful. If men are afraid of women speaking their mind, then that's their concern." He took a deep breath. "I can't say I'm delighted to know Zee carries out such activities, but my protestations were ignored. Thus, it's what she wants to do, and I must support her."

"Why?" Morgan asked. "Why, when it will only bring her pain and suffering and will do little to further the cause she espouses?"

Aidan chuckled. "You still have a lot to learn about your wife and marriage, Wheeler. You must grant them the freedom to do what they believe."

Morgan watched Teddy with frank confusion. "But your wife isn't even considered a citizen of the United States. Why would she continue to struggle for women here when her country has disavowed her?"

Teddy stiffened. "Zee refuses to accept the limitations on her citizenship imposed by her government. Although they don't consider her an American, she does." He shook his head. "She's never been to England. Why would she consider herself English?"

Morgan watched Teddy closely, but he said nothing further. Aidan's countenance, while friendly, failed to encourage further personal conversation.

"Doesn't it bother you that your wife has already been arrested three times?" Morgan asked Teddy.

Teddy glared at him. "Of course it does, but those arrests didn't lead to much. She was released almost immediately. They were perfunctory, and I'm certain the judge is well aware of the dangers of incarcerating women who haven't broken any laws."

Morgan scoffed. "You know how the courts work. They'll find some meaningless charge as a way to lock them up." He sighed. "I can't imagine Parthena in jail."

Teddy sighed. "Zylphia would not be swayed, and she is under the belief I am unaware of her imprisonments." He ran a finger over his eyebrow. "I saw no reason to mention it to her as I knew it would not aid my argument. She was healthy and well, and I should not concern myself about a few days spent in prison."

Morgan watched him with dawning horror. "It's as though she sees it all as a lark. And now Parthena has been drawn into her web."

Teddy's jaw tightened a few times before he nodded. "I fear Zee has yet to recognize the gravity of their situation should public sentiment, or the judge's, turn further against them."

After a drawn-out silence, Aidan cleared his throat. "I would recommend you give Mrs. Wheeler and yourself time to calm after this latest argument. When you feel enough time has passed, and, if she has not returned from DC, I'd consider visiting her there."

"I want her home by the holidays," Morgan murmured.

Aidan nodded as though his demand were reasonable.

"It's only September, Morgan. Give her time to cool down and to miss you," Teddy said with a wry smile. "I visited Zee last month and learned I hadn't given her enough time to miss me yet."

Morgan shook his head, perplexed as he watched Teddy. "But your wife has been away for the better part of eight months. Since that drastic picketing started in January."

Teddy's eyes flashed but otherwise remained composed. "I know how long my wife has been away." The soft pitch of his voice silenced any protest from Aidan or Morgan. After a tense moment, the conversation turned to business, and the tension thrumming through Teddy and Morgan eased at the impersonal topic.

∼

Parthena waved away the cab one block from her desired destination. She carried her small suitcase with her and found the address to the National Women's Party headquarters at Cameron House. She peered at the three-story brick building and paused on the walkway. As she stood there, dithering about what to do, the door burst open, and a line of women poured out. Parthena jumped to the side of the walkway to watch the stream of women pass her.

∼

Seeing Parthena on the walkway, Zylphia halted as she walked from the building, a bundle under her arm. Zylphia spoke to a woman in her group and handed her the bundle, motioning them to go without her. "Parthena?" Her incredulous voice jolted Parthena out of her perusal of the goings-on of the street. "What are you doing here?" She pulled her friend into a hug.

When Parthena pulled away, Zylphia frowned at the tears in her friend's eyes. "What's he done?"

"Oh, Zee," Parthena whispered. She waved at the backsides of retreating women fading in the distance as they marched down the sidewalk. "I see I've interrupted something important. I'm sorry."

"It's all right. Bev took my place. I'll have to switch with her another day." At Parthena's confused stare, Zylphia laughed. "We're picketing. We picket every day." Zylphia glanced up and down the street in front of Cameron House. "I'm actually surprised people aren't here protesting our departure. That's become an almost daily occurrence."

She looped her arm through Parthena's and led her in the opposite direction of the picketers. "Come. Let's go to a tea shop, and you can tell me what's happened." She stopped and held up a finger. "Wait a second. I'll see if Ro is free."

Parthena watched as Zylphia raced inside. Within a few minutes, she returned with Rowena in tow. After giving Parthena a hug, Rowena said, "Rather than a café, let's go to our apartment, Zee."

When they arrived, Zylphia held the door for Parthena, welcoming her into their small rented rooms. "These aren't much, but everything is quite expensive in Washington. Besides, we spend most of our time at Cameron House. We're thankful we don't have to go down the hallway for the bathroom."

Parthena shook her head. "I hate to admit I hadn't even considered that possibility. How do you stand this?"

"It's like being in the nursery again," Rowena said with a wink. "Zee and I share a bedroom."

"I want to be in Washington, and this is what I can afford," Zylphia said as she took off her hat and hung it on the peg by the door. "That's not true. I could pay for something much grander, but I don't know how long I'll be here, and I want to economize as I'm not sure how long Teddy will help me."

"I can only imagine that Teddy would give you adequate money so you could live a bit more grandly." Parthena watched her friend with a worried furrow in her brow. "And that your father surely would not make you live like this either." She nodded to Rowena, who shrugged.

"Teddy and I fail to agree on much these days." Zylphia waved her hand as though such a comment were of little concern. "Please, sit and tell us what has brought you here. What did Morgan do?"

Parthena roamed the room, picking up framed pictures of Zylphia and her parents, Zylphia with her cousins in Montana. Parthena paused as she studied a photo from the previous holiday of Teddy, Zylphia, Morgan, Rowena and herself. "It's more what I did."

Zylphia collapsed onto the settee, kicked off her shoes and curled up in comfort. "I'm sure he provoked you into acting like a madwoman."

"And you couldn't help but respond and say awful things," Rowena said as she sat on a chair near Zylphia.

Parthena turned to study her friends, both of them sitting with an air of calm composure even though they'd spent the day writing articles against the government for denying women the right to vote and had supported women who had defied the law and picketed that day. "Why do you always take my side? Why do you never believe I could be at fault?"

Zylphia laughed. "I know you could be at fault. You're human. But you're *my* friend, and I will always think well of you."

Rowena smiled. "We know you, Parthena, and we accept you as you are. We also know your husband, and he could provoke a saint to violence."

Parthena sank onto the chair next to the settee and shook her head. "I don't know what to do anymore. One moment I think we'll have a normal marriage. A fulfilling marriage. And then he turns all cold again. And he loves to taunt me with Lucas."

Rowena frowned. "You must have said something to make him feel insecure if he brought up Lucas again."

"Genevieve and Lucas are to have a baby." She watched as Zylphia smiled with joy at the news. "I told Morgan that, and he immediately jumped to the conclusion that it meant I wished I were the one pregnant by Lucas. Not Viv."

"Oh my." Zylphia sighed. "Did you disabuse him of that foolish notion?" When Parthena sat dejectedly on her chair, Zylphia shook her head "Of course you didn't. The two of you would rather choke on your own pride than actually speak to each other and explain what you are feeling."

"That's not fair, Zee."

"Of course it is. Why can't you simply tell Morgan you want a baby? That you're envious of your sister and wish to not only be an aunt but a mother too?" She frowned with frustration as she watched her friend. "Or is it that you still bar him from your bedroom?"

"I don't bar him," Parthena snapped. "He's chosen to distance himself from me in that manner."

"Because you froze him out and didn't want him touching you!" Zylphia tossed her hands in the air in exasperation. "You talk about Morgan acting as an icicle, but I think you learned that lesson well too, P.T. You must decide what you want. Lucas is lost to you. He's never returned to Boston in all this time, and I wonder if he ever will. He's happy with your sister. From what he writes, he's been in love with her since almost the moment they married. You must find your own happiness."

Rowena canted forward as her two friends talked avidly about their marriages, her eyes lit with curiosity. "Zee's right, P.T. You have to stop clinging to the hurts from your past and find the happiness of your present." Her gaze was filled with compassion as she watched Parthena battle tears. "I'd hate to have the same conversation with you five or ten years from now."

Parthena scrubbed at the few tears that escaped. "You don't know what I fear." She gripped Zylphia's hand when she felt it on her knee. "I know he'll see any overture I make to him as a sign of weakness, and I couldn't stand to have him believe he has such power over me."

Zylphia sighed. "Loving someone gives them power over us. The power to hurt us. The power to bring tremendous joy. If he loves you, he won't see your love as a weakness, but as a strength. And a precious gift."

After a few moments where Parthena sniffled, Rowena said, "In the beginning, I can see why you were worried he would react in such a way. But not now, P.T. He's overall a good man, and he's been very patient. If you truly want nothing to do with him, tell him. Free yourself, and him, so that you can find joy."

"I ran away," Parthena whispered. At her friends' confused stares, Parthena closed her eyes in regret. "I ran away when I promised I never would."

Zylphia's confused expression didn't clear up with Parthena's statement. "We all run when we're afraid. I think it takes tremendous courage to acknowledge that we were wrong, that we should have acted differently. And then to change how we act."

Rowena raised an eyebrow at her friend's words, her gaze filled with ironic humor. However, Zylphia remained focused on Parthena and refused to meet Rowena's gaze or practice any introspection.

Parthena swiped at her cheeks. "I know I must face him at some point, but I'm not ready. I need time," she whispered.

Zylphia shared a smile with her friend. "Don't worry. We'll keep you plenty busy with the cause. You'll have time to consider what you want to do, but you'll also have your opportunity to become more involved." Her smile held a touch of deviltry. "What are your thoughts on picketing?" She shared a laugh with her friends.

~

Parthena returned from the picket line with a hem torn loose and her hair down. Her banner had been ripped from her hands, and she sported a bruise on one of her shins. She attempted to walk without a limp but feared she failed. When she reentered Cameron House, Zylphia saw her and smiled.

"I can see it went well," her friend said.

Parthena glared at her friend's sarcasm.

"No, I'm serious. You're still clothed." The outrageous comment shocked a laugh from Parthena who rolled her eyes.

"Come," Zee said, gripping Parthena's arm and tugging her to a back room where tea and cakes awaited the picketers. "Help yourself and then tell me all about it."

Parthena placed a few treats on her plate, filled a cup with tea and then followed Zylphia to her desk. Parthena pushed aside papers to make room for her plate and cup and settled into her chair with a sigh. "It feels good to sit."

Zylphia laughed. "I know. Even though we're only out there for hours, it can feel like days sometimes."

"I don't know how you can continuously return to the picket. It's boring, and, then in an instant, it can turn terrible." Parthena took a sip of tea, blushing as she accidentally made a slurping noise.

"I tried to give you the least inflammatory banner for your first day," Zylphia said. "I think it might have helped."

Parthena shook her head in disbelief. "Some men spit on women. Can you imagine?"

Zylphia nodded. "Yes, I can. It's disgusting." She shuddered as though recalling it. She stiffened, her demeanor cooled and sent a warning glance to Parthena. "Hello, Mr. Hooper."

"Mrs. Goff, always a pleasure to see you." He turned his bright smile to Parthena. "I believe I've yet to have the pleasure of making your acquaintance."

"I'm Mrs. Wheeler," she said in a flat, crisp tone. "From Boston." She jerked her hand away from his as he lifted it for a kiss.

"I'm Mr. Hooper, a special friend of Mrs. Goff." His smile widened as Zylphia watched him with a feral glint in her eyes. "She's always reluctant to speak of us in public," he whispered.

"Mr. Hooper, if you would please leave, preferably forever, I would be most thankful." Zylphia fisted her hands at her waist and blushed as she beheld her unshakable suitor.

"Oh, I know women don't always mean what they say," Mr. Hooper commented as he perched on the edge of Zylphia's desk.

"I find that statement offensive," Parthena snapped. "You are here, in Cameron House, and theoretically in support of universal enfranchisement. However, if you truly believe that women don't always say what they mean, then how can you believe we are in earnest when we proclaim our truths? When we go to the picket line each day and unfurl our banners?" She set down her teacup with such force that the saucer cracked. "You are offensive, and I'd think those in charge of this movement would prefer you not enter here."

"But I'm in support of your movement," he sputtered.

"In words only. You aren't truly in support of women and what we hope to achieve once we are enfranchised. Men like you hope we'll remain in a convenient little box, easily labeled and controlled. You'd do well to learn that this is just the beginning of true equality for women." She glared at him. "If you will excuse us, we have important matters to discuss that don't include you."

Mr. Hooper stood, stupefied for a moment before he tugged on his waistcoat and stormed off. Zylphia giggled as he nearly ran over Rowena in his haste to exit Cameron House. Rowena joined them, pouring a cup of tea.

"What riled Mr. Hooper?" she whispered.

Zylphia smiled. "Parthena told him off. I'm hopeful he'll cease in his pursuit of me now." She grinned wickedly at her friend. "Or he'll find Parthena more to his liking."

Parthena shuddered. "I hope he'll take the hint and leave us all alone."

Rowena shrugged. "Whether we like it or not, we'll need his help at some point. He is a brilliant lawyer, and we're bound to need legal counsel."

Zylphia rose and arched her back. "Come. It's time to finish the day. Let's go for a short walk to show Parthena some of the local sights before heading home."

"Plus I should find a hotel room as your apartment is cramped already with the two of you."

"Or," Zylphia said, "you could rent rooms in our building."

Parthena laughed. "I am spoiled enough to want more during my stay here."

They gathered their hats, light jackets and purses and departed Cameron House. They walked at a leisurely pace toward the Tidal Basin where many locals enjoyed the comfortable fall evening as they passed the Washington Monument. They glanced in the distance where a memorial to President Lincoln was being constructed. As they walk on, they had entered a verdant park, with no buildings and few cars on the roads that intersected the area.

"When I arrived, I explained what had happened between Morgan and me." Parthena shot a quick look at Zylphia. "Yet you've been absent from Boston for over eight months, and, when you're home, you never visit. Why is there such a distance between you and Teddy?" Parthena asked.

Zylphia's step faltered a moment before she righted herself as though she'd never hesitated in her step. "He needs to work on his business dealings with my father in Boston, and I desire to be here during this important time in the movement," Zylphia said.

"There's more, Zee. Tell me," Parthena coaxed. Rowena nodded her agreement to Parthena's prodding.

Zylphia motioned them to join her on a bench on the warm late September afternoon. They sat in the sunlight, soaking in the warmth. "I want to be an American citizen. Teddy doesn't want to be an American." She shrugged her shoulders as though that described her situation.

"I don't understand," Parthena said.

"When I married Teddy, I unwittingly lost my citizenship. Due to the Expatriation Act of 1907, my citizenship is tied to that of my husband's. It doesn't matter where I was born. Thus, since Teddy is a British citizen, now I am seen as British. I have no legal protections here."

"I thought a case a few years ago settled all this," Parthena argued, her brow furrowed.

"No, the Supreme Court found in favor of the government, and that merely reinforced the law from 1907." Zylphia balled up her hand and bounced it off her thigh repeatedly in agitation. "Men never fear losing their citizenship! They can marry whomever they please, a citizen or not. But I marry for love, and now I am seen as an alien to my own country." She swiped at a tear.

"And Teddy?" Parthena asked hesitantly.

"And Teddy has the power to help me regain my citizenship but will do nothing!" She took a deep breath. "He's lived here for years. I fail to understand why he clings to being British when he's more American than many I meet."

"Except for his adorable accent," Parthena said. She flushed when Zylphia glared at her.

"I can apply for naturalization, as though I had never lived here and want to become a citizen. However, because Teddy doesn't desire to be a naturalized citizen, it doesn't matter what I do. As long as he remains a British citizen, I will never be an American citizen."

"Is that why such a distance is between you? Because you punish him for not seeing your side?" Parthena asked. "Sophie mentioned it to me when I visited a few weeks ago."

Zylphia slouched against the back of the bench. "Yes. I'm so angry at his implacability. Why won't he do this for me?"

Rowena shook her head. "I think you should understand that being British is as important to him as being an American is for you. Neither of you will have what you want. One of you must accept this, Zee."

Zylphia sniffled and rubbed at her nose. "I hate that I had no choice."

Parthena sighed in understanding. "That's it, isn't it? You want to have had a choice, and you resent that he does." Parthena scooted forward and moved so that she could face Zylphia better. "Zee, you have to realize that life is unfair the majority of the time. It's how we respond to all of these situations we wished were different that will determine whether or not we will be happy."

"I can't believe you'd lecture me with that drivel when you're in a worse situation with Morgan," Zylphia snapped. She immediately blanched and grabbed at Parthena's arm as P.T. moved to rise. "Forgive me. That was uncalled for."

"You're right, Zee. I'm having a difficult time determining what I want to do about the mess I've made. Perhaps because of that, I see you doing something similar, and I want to prevent you from making the same mistakes."

"You and Teddy love each other, Zee," Rowena argued. "It doesn't matter what country you call home."

"I know what you say is true. But can you understand what it's like to all of a sudden be considered a foreigner in your own land? Simply because I married a man from England? And how I had no desire to lose my citizenship. I want to be an American. I want to vote here when we win equal rights for women."

"I am not going through what you are right now," Rowena said as she stroked a hand down Zylphia's back. "But being angry with Teddy isn't making either of you happy. It's no more his fault than it is yours."

They sat in contemplative silence as they stared at the Tidal Basin. Vendors peddled ices, peanuts and newspapers. Nearby a father played with a son, attempting and failing to fly a kite in the sparse breeze. The child seemed undeterred, screeching with joy as he chased the kite around.

"Do you regret marrying him?" Parthena asked after a long pause in their conversation.

Zylphia closed her eyes, as though in defeat. "No. I could never regret marrying Teddy."

"The way you're acting would give him that idea," Rowena said. She gave Parthena a pointed glance, and Parthena blushed in agreement. "I'd think you were both fortunate in the men you married. You knew you were immediately upon your marriage, Zee, as you chose him. You've had to discern your luck, P.T., but I think you have by now."

Rowena watched as both her friends mulled over her words. "Now I'm wondering when I'll be abandoned here in Washington when you both rush back to Boston to your husbands."

"I won't leave until I'm certain that we've fulfilled Miss Paul's goals with the picketing. I have a sense that things will soon come to a head." Zylphia watched her friends. "After that, I can make no promises."

"I'd like to help, Zee," Parthena said. "I want to remain a while longer. However, I will return to Boston by December. I have no desire to be away for many months on end like you. And I fear a long separation will give Morgan the wrong idea."

Rowena smiled. "Well, I have you both here for a while at least."

They settled onto the bench to watch the passersby and to enjoy the evening for a little while longer before venturing to find dinner and then returning to their apartment and finding a place for Parthena to stay while in DC.

CHAPTER 15

Butte, Montana, October 1917

Genevieve walked into her living room and paused. She took a
deep breath to calm her racing heart as a strange man paced
inside near her front door. His suit was tattered at the seams,
while the previously white shirt appeared ivory colored at best. "May
I inquire as to why you are in my front hall?" She stood tall as the man
spun to face her.

He stood taller than Lucas, nearly as tall as the McLeod cousins,
although he had a lanky frame. His brown hair, longer than fashionable, hung over one blue eye, and his full beard needed a trim. "I'm
your butler." He bowed, scraping the floor with his fingers.

Genevieve bit back a smile. "My butler?" Her gaze raked over him
again and shook her head. "Do you know my husband?"

"Of course. Luc is a wonderful friend to those in need," he said.

She was unable to bite back a laugh at this man's nickname for her
husband. "You're the first person who's ever called him by anything
other than Lucas or Mr. Russell." She speared the stranger with a
fierce glower. "I believe it proper for a butler to address his employer,

for lack of a better word, as Mr. Russell." She placed quivering hands over the subtle bulge of her belly.

"Mr. Lucas it shall be," he said with a bow of his head.

Genevieve sputtered out an incredulous laugh. "Who are you? What are you doing here?"

He pulled at the lapel of his jacket and stood as tall as his lean frame allowed. "I'm Marc Legionnaire."

"And you're French." At his slight hesitancy, Genevieve's smile widened. "Or you wish to appear French and thus more sophisticated." At his sniff of disapproval, Genevieve laughed. "Oh, come. I wouldn't think such airs and graces should be necessary in Butte. And certainly not in my home."

"For a musician, one's persona is nearly as important as one's talent."

"Hogwash," Genevieve snapped. "Lucas could be a mealy-mouthed ingrate, and he'd still be sought after due to his extraordinary talent. The fact he's charming is merely a bonus." She glared at the stranger in a severe a manner, like a disapproving schoolmarm. "Now what is your name?"

"I'm Joseph Rigionneri." His shoulders stooped in defeat. "But I don't want you usin' that name outside this 'ouse!" He flushed as his rough accent emerged as he became flustered.

Genevieve nodded her approval. "Good. You're Italian?" At his nod, she continued. "I assume you're used to hard work?" As the question was rhetorical, she barreled on. "If you are to act as our butler, you will have to earn your wage. You will not merely pace in front of the door in hopes of answering it. First of all, that isn't what a butler does. Second, I hope you didn't think you'd merely act busy in the belief you'd have the rest of the time to use my husband's fine pianos to practice on?" When he flushed and then shook his head, Genevieve smiled. "Good. I'm glad we understand each other. Please go to the kitchens, and I will meet with you there in a few moments."

"But the door—"

"Lucas has already been so kind as to hire a hall boy." Genevieve looked around and sighed. "Although I imagine he's either flirting with one of the new maids or eating his second breakfast." She tilted her head in the direction of the back staircase and watched Joseph make a hasty retreat. She sighed as she sat on a settee.

After a few moments, when she heard Lucas's heavy steps descending the stairs, she inhaled deeply again. "How much of that did you hear?" she asked.

"How did you know I was there?" Lucas asked, chuckling. He approached her, leaning in to first kiss her on the side of her neck and then to massage her shoulders.

"Smells are accentuated for me right now. Including your after-shave." She sighed as she bent her head forward to give him better access to her shoulders. "How much did you hear?"

"Almost all of it. I should have known you'd see right through him from the start." He gave her a last gentle squeeze and then sat across from her on a piano stool. "You don't mind, do you?"

She frowned. "Do we truly have enough money to keep such a large staff?"

Lucas nodded. "I couldn't bear to watch him starve, Vivie. He's talented but hasn't anyone to mentor him. And he has a mother and sisters to support."

"Why wasn't he in the mine?" she asked.

"His father and brother were, but they died in the disaster four months ago." Lucas scrubbed at his forehead. "When they were going underground, they could eke out a survival. Now that no money is coming in …" Lucas shrugged. "And, with the strike, no one's inter-ested in using money they don't have to pay for a musician to play a tune in a pub." His shoulders stooped.

"You can't support the whole city, Lucas." She watched him with fond exasperation. "We have two maids, a cook, a hall boy, a butler and a gardener." She waved her arm around. "We don't even have a garden! We could manage on our own if we had to."

"That's just the point. We don't have to." He flushed and tapped his fingers on his leg as he met her amused gaze. "I know, just as it would be best if I became an unfeeling bastard who didn't see the suffering all around me. But I can't be that man, Vivie."

Her eyes filled with tears. "I wouldn't want you to be."

"Good," he whispered, leaning closer to grab her hands so as to play with her long fingers. "How do you feel about having a personal maid?" He laughed as she hit him on the shoulder. "I'll take that to mean you're not convinced you need one yet."

She giggled and tugged at him until he sat next to her on the settee. "I'd be very careful before you hire another servant, Lucas." She ran a hand down his arm. "I know you want to aid those in need and that hiring all these people helps prevent abject poverty on their part. But, for me, it takes away the joy of my home. I feel as though a visitor now."

"I'm sorry, Vivie," he whispered. "I never thought what it would mean to you. I thought all women liked help around the house and to be waited on."

She clasped his face between her palms to ensure he focused on her. "I am not your mother, Lucas." When he nodded, she relaxed. "Would Sav enjoy living like this? Rissa?"

He shuddered. "No, they'd chafe at it." He gave her a pleading glance. "I can't ask them to leave, not when they finally have hope of a job and a meal or two a day."

Genevieve turned to lean against him and snuggle into his arms. "I'd never demand you ask someone to leave your employ. Just don't hire anyone else. Please?"

He squeezed her lightly around the middle and kissed her on her head. "Of course. Although you might be happy for their help once the baby arrives."

She sighed in defeat at her husband's stubbornness. "Perhaps I will."

~

Fiona sat at the table in the kitchen and glared at the empty seat across from her. She ate her meal of potatoes, carrots and boiled chicken as methodically as she always did. When she finished, she rose, covering Patrick's plate with a cloth and placing it in the icebox.

She hummed to distract herself as she washed the dishes, the open window allowing the late evening breeze into the small room.

She dried her hands, checked on Rose sleeping soundly in her room and moved to the front porch, leaving the door ajar to hear Rose if she cried out. Fiona eased into the rocking chair and watched as neighbors acted as though it were normal to have their husbands, fathers and sons home when they should have been busy working in the mines. The constant background noise from the mines was mostly absent with the air clearer as the smelters no longer spewed an incessant stream of smoke into the air. As a herald of the fresher air, a patch of green grass had taken root next to the walkway leading to the house, along with a few dandelions.

She closed her eyes and rested her head against the rocking chair, ignoring the letters she needed to write, her knitting to finish and a book she had just begun. She relaxed as the warm breeze cooled the evening after an unseasonably warm day and listened to the sounds of children playing. Someone nearby sang part of the song "Over There," and she hummed along. She stilled when she heard footsteps on the walk.

"Hello, Fee," Patrick said as he dragged himself up each step. "How was dinner?"

"Fine." She clamped her jaw together and resumed rocking. "Your plate is in the icebox."

He nodded, resting a hand for a moment on her shoulder before moving into the house. He emerged a few minutes later with his dinner and a glass of water. He perched on the brick banister on the side of the porch and wolfed down his dinner. "This is delicious. Thank you, Fee." When she only nodded, he frowned. "I'm sorry I missed dinner again."

"I fail to see how you are needed extra hours at that company you work for. No one is working," Fiona whispered. "I'd think you'd want to see your daughter more than once a week on Sundays."

Patrick rose and motioned for her to join him inside. "We can't have this discussion outside. Too many are interested in any scraps of gossip." He held the door wide for her and followed her in. After setting his plate and glass in the kitchen sink, he joined her in the living room.

He pulled up a chair and sat across from her as she held a rigid posture on the settee. He grasped her hands, his fingers playing with hers and intermittently tracing her wedding band.

She frowned at the fatigue and guilt in his expression. "What is it, Patrick?"

"They've found a loophole in the miners' compensation law passed in 1915." He rubbed at his forehead. "The North Butte has to provide $75 for funeral costs for all men who died, although most funerals run between $150 to $200. Instead of paying either the lump sum death benefit of $3,380 or the $10 weekly death benefit totaling $4,000, my company has spent months finagling its way out of paying what is owed to the survivors of those men." His bleak gaze met his wife's horrified stare. "If the miner wasn't a citizen of the United States—or, even if he was a citizen, but his dependents live outside the United States or if his dependents were anyone other than wife and children—then he is being denied the death benefit."

Fiona gasped in horror. "That's outrageous."

Patrick nodded. "It is. Instead of paying out more than half a million dollars to the miners' families, the North Butte will only pay about $150,000." He dropped his head into his hands. "Only 39 of the 163 miner families will receive death benefit compensation."

"Why the long hours at work?" She traced her finger over his hand.

"They know I'm displeased, and I have to prove my worth to them. They're looking for any reason to reduce staff and overhead costs. I don't want them to look to me as expendable." He raised worried eyes to meet hers. "I want to continue to provide for us."

She freed a hand and traced it over his cheek. "I thank you for that." A tender smile escaped, and her features softened. "I miss you when you work long hours. I miss hearing you play with Rose as I work in the kitchen. I yearn to hear you read the paper aloud to me or tease me about my embroidery."

He froze, perplexed by her words. "I never realized you cared if I was here."

"And that's my fault. I've always wanted you here but had a hard time showing it." She leaned forward and kissed him softly on the lips. "I understand your need to work, but know that, when you are free, Rose and I are waiting for you."

His eyes lit with radiant joy as he beheld her. "I never dared hope you'd feel this way."

She tugged on him so that he sat beside her on the settee. After he'd settled, she nestled into his embrace, tucking herself into his side. "I'm slow to find my courage again, Patrick. Please be patient with me."

"Always, my love," he murmured, kissing her head.

She drifted in his arms a few moments before speaking again. "We had a letter from Clarissa today." She paused.

"Was there any news about Melinda?"

She stroked a hand down her husband's arm clasped around her waist. "She receives your letters, but no one knows if she reads them. I'm sorry, darling."

He stuttered out a breath and tightened his hold. "I'll continue to hope she writes me someday."

Fiona sighed. "The main news is that your stepmother has departed Missoula for friendlier environments." She stroked a hand down his arm again as he tensed and kissed his shoulder.

"I wonder what that means. The woman always was cryptic." Patrick ran his hand over Fiona's head as though to soothe himself as well as her.

"Do you think she'd come to Butte?"

He cooed to her as she was unable to hide the fear in her voice. "There's no reason for her to travel here. She has nothing to gain by seeing me again."

"I'm sure she'll concoct one."

$\backsim$

Genevieve slipped from her house, escaping the butler, Joseph, as he peppered her with questions about his role. She sighed, thankful to be outside even though the air was thick with smelter smoke as more and more miners trickled back to work with copper extraction creeping up to near normal levels. She turned toward Fiona and Patrick's house, smiling to those she passed.

As she neared Fiona's house, a woman approached her, carrying a crying child. She smiled at the woman, surprised to see she did little to soothe the crotchety child. "She's not having a good day," Genevieve soothed, running a hand down the back of the little girl.

"She'd be fine if she stopped her whining," the woman snapped, inching the girl away from Genevieve. "If you'll excuse us, we must be on our way." As she stepped past Genevieve, the little girl lifted her head, and Genevieve gasped.

"Rose!" Genevieve grabbed the woman's shoulder, wrenching her around and tugging Rose into her arms as she caught the woman off balance. When the woman reached to take Rose back, Genevieve gave her a swift kick in her shin. "I don't know who you think you are, but you have no right to this child."

Genevieve saw a young boy run away from their fracas before she focused again on the woman, who on closer inspection was older than she had first appeared. "Who are you, and why are you stealing Rose?"

"I'm not stealing the child," she snapped, her blue eyes flashing with anger. "I was returning her to her father."

Genevieve stared at her a long moment. "You're that horrid woman from Boston. That Mrs. Smythe."

Rose had settled into Genevieve's arms and rested her head on her shoulder. She arched away from Mrs. Smythe, only calming when Genevieve spoke soothing words in her ear.

Genevieve jumped when a man spoke. "What is the matter here?" a policeman asked.

"This woman snatched my niece from her home. I happened to pass her on the street and saw her with my niece as I was to visit her house." Genevieve stroked a hand down Rose's back.

"What a preposterous accusation. Her mother asked me to care for her this afternoon. We are quite close." Mrs. Smythe flung back her head in indignant righteousness.

"Bad woman," Rose mumbled, pointing to Mrs. Smythe. "Bad woman!"

Genevieve laughed and kissed Rose's head. "I think we should trust my niece's assessment. She is a bad woman. I must travel to their home with Rose as I'm certain her mother is distraught."

Another policeman arrived, and, after he conferred quietly with his colleague, they escorted both women and Rose to Fiona's house. When they arrived, one policeman and Mrs. Smythe waited on the porch while Genevieve and Rose entered with the first policeman.

"Fee?" Genevieve called out when she entered. She frowned at the silence that met her. "Fee?"

She heard a banging noise and moved toward the hallway near the bedrooms. When she arrived, she noted a closet barred by a chair under the handle. The policeman removed it and a weeping Fiona tumbled out. Her mouth was stuffed with a rag, which was quickly removed. "Viv, I've lost her," she sobbed.

"No, you haven't," Genevieve soothed, dropping to her knees and freeing Rose from her embrace.

Rose toddled to her mother, patting her mother's wet cheeks with her palms and giggling at the wetness. "Mama! Mama! You're wet!" She giggled as her mother pulled her into a tight embrace.

Fiona sobbed, holding her tight and rocking to and fro as she remained in the hallway.

Genevieve stood, paused a moment before asking the policeman, "If you would be so good as to send a man to the North Butte Mining Company to ask Patrick Sullivan to return home? His wife and daughter need him."

The policeman nodded. "That woman on the stoop will have quite a few questions to answer," he muttered before storming out.

Genevieve watched Fiona a moment before she moved to the kitchen to brew a pot of tea.

~

Patrick glanced up at the commotion in the hallway at work, frowning when he saw a policeman. He stiffened when a colleague pointed in his direction before forcing a welcoming smile as the policeman approached.

"Excuse me, are you Patrick Sullivan?" At his nod, the policeman lowered his voice. "You're needed at home, sir."

Patrick rose, grabbing the jacket off the back of his chair. He waved to his boss while pointing at the policeman and followed on his heels. When they emerged on the street, they set a fast pace. "What has happened?"

"An attempted abduction of your daughter. She is fine, as is your wife by all appearances."

Patrick swore and then burst into a sprint as he raced toward home. He dodged through those meandering down the sidewalk and evaded cars as he jaywalked. His lungs and muscles burned as he ran even faster to return home as quickly as possible.

"Fee!" Patrick bellowed as he thrust open the front door. "Fee!" He ran into the living room to find it empty. He saw Genevieve in the kitchen before seeing his wife and child in the hallway, collapsing before them to his knees, panting and panicked. "Oh, my loves." He pulled Fiona and Rose into his arms, shuddering and shaking. After his mad dash across town, he slowly regained his breath.

After a few moments, Rose squirmed from being squished between her parents and pushed to escape. He eased back, holding her on his lap as he ran a hand over her as though inspecting her. "Are you all right, my little angel?" When she giggled, he let out a stuttering sigh and shared a grateful look with Fiona.

Genevieve emerged from the kitchen and picked up Rose. "You need a few moments alone," she murmured as she tickled and played with her niece and moved to the living room.

"If Genevieve hadn't been walking by ..." Fiona shook her head as she lost her battle with tears. "We could have lost her."

Patrick tugged Fiona into his arms again, shuddering as he felt her shiver in his arms. "What happened?" He stroked long fingers over her shoulders and back to soothe her.

"That woman barged in here when I was in the kitchen while Rose napped. Insisted she was here to make peace. I tried to push her from the house, but, the next thing I knew, I was locked in a closet."

He rubbed a hand over her head, stilling the motion when she grimaced. His hand felt sticky, and he frowned to find his fingers covered in blood. "You were knocked out, my love. I imagine you have a terrible headache."

She rested her head against his chest. "Now that I'm not worried about Rose, I feel awful. And so tired."

He gathered her close, glaring at the policeman who appeared with a chagrined look on his face. "You may not question my wife at this time. She needs a doctor and rest after what she's suffered."

"I understand, sir. I ... I wanted to apologize that the woman in question seems to have disappeared."

Patrick flushed with anger, his brown eyes a molten chocolate as he glared at the policeman. "If I were you, I'd obtain a warrant and search the home of Samuel Sanders. I doubt he'd allow you entrance without one."

The policeman's eyes flashed with curiosity. "Why should he be involved in this scheme? He's an important man in this town."

Patrick murmured soothing words to his wife before focusing on the young policeman again. "He has taken an unhealthy interest in my wife and daughter. I believe he is the one you should focus on, even though he will bluster and claim I'm delusional."

"Is there anything else I should know?"

Patrick paused as he considered his answer. "He is also known as Henry Masterson. That's his real name, and that's what he was known by in Boston before he moved to Butte and reinvented himself."

The policeman nodded, his small pencil tapping his pad of paper. "Reinvention is common in a town like Butte. There is no crime in that." He tapped one last time at his pad. "But I'll keep in mind what you've said. I, or one of my colleagues, will return tomorrow to speak with you, ma'am." He nodded deferentially in Fiona's direction and then departed.

A few hours later Rose had eaten dinner and was in bed, while Fiona had seen the doctor and was also resting. Patrick sat in the living room with Lucas and Genevieve, although he rose every few minutes to pace before sitting again. "I can't thank you enough, Genevieve." Patrick ran a shaking hand over his face.

"There's nothing to thank me for. I wished to visit, and Fee was expecting me. I simply wish I'd arrived when I was expected. I was detained at home." She frowned and gripped her hands together on her lap.

Lucas massaged her tensed hands. "What is it, Vivie?"

She shook her head. "I shouldn't even think it. But today has not been an ordinary day. I hate to accuse someone of mischief when it's unwarranted."

"Now you must tell us what concerns you or we'll die of curiosity," Lucas half teased to coax her to continue speaking.

"Joseph was acting odd today, peppering me with questions about his role, although he had learned his role already." She paused as she shook her head with a distant gaze. "He seemed frantic when I finally pushed past him and departed the house this afternoon. As though he'd failed at something."

Patrick paled before rising to pace once more.

Lucas gripped her hand tightly. "I fear I may have been a gullible fool and hired a spy." He met Patrick's worried gaze. "I wonder if he works for Sanders?"

"Would make sense. I'd think more than Mrs. Smythe would be involved. Although I wouldn't put it past her to knock Fee senseless, I'm not sure she has the strength any more to drag her down the hall and stuff her in a closet."

Lucas swore before slinging an arm over Genevieve's shoulders. "Forgive me for making us vulnerable to him. I merely wanted to help a poor musician and his family."

"You did nothing wrong, Lucas," Genevieve soothed. "If he had an ounce of loyalty, he never would have betrayed your trust."

Lucas took a deep, calming breath. "First, we must speak with him and determine if he truly did betray us before we condemn him. If he did, he is out on his ear. Agreed?" He nodded as Genevieve blinked her agreement.

"I've never understood why you have so many employees," Patrick muttered. He waved his arm around. "How do I keep Fee and Rose safe from Sanders?"

"I know it's not a solution you will like, but you can always move in with us. We have plenty of room." Lucas studied his cousin's frenetic movement around the room. "That way, you'll know that someone from the family is within shouting distance at all times."

Patrick shook his head. "Fee would hate it. So would I." He flushed. "Not that I mean any disrespect. It would feel like a cage, when we're used to our own home and privacy and freedom." He ran a hand through his hair. "But I will discuss it with her and will let you know what we decide."

Lucas nodded and rose, giving Genevieve a hand to stand up. "We'll be in touch tomorrow."

$\sim$

Patrick opened his daughter's door, tiptoeing inside to ensure she was well. She slept on her back with her arms flung out and her head to one side. He rubbed a gentle hand over her hair before leaning down to softly kiss her. "Sleep well, my darling girl."

He eased into his room down the hall, toeing off his shoes as he slipped out of his shirt and pants. Fiona stirred on the bed, and he made soothing noises to coax her back to sleep. However, she rolled to her side, her eyes tracking his movements as he finished undressing and then slid under the covers. "Come here, love," he whispered, pulling her toward him. He sighed when she rested her head on his shoulder.

She sat upright, as though remembering what had happened, and his grip on her waist tightened. "I just looked in on Rose. She's fine. Sleeping with abandon as only the young can."

"Oh, Patrick, forgive me," she whispered against his shoulder.

His featherlight kiss to her hair gave comfort but no pain as he remained mindful of her wound. "There's nothing to forgive. You fought valiantly to protect our Rose but were overpowered." His hold on her tightened before he forced himself to ease his grasp of her. "I give thanks you weren't more severely injured."

She shuddered in his arms.

He murmured to her softly but could tell from the tension in her body that sleep eluded her. "Lucas and Genevieve have invited us to live with them. For as long as we would like." He waited many moments as she remained tense and silent in his arms.

"I hate that my first instinct is to accept their invitation."

He frowned at her whispered admission. "There's no shame in wishing to feel safe after suffering what you did today, love."

She pushed against him and sat up, clinging to his arm and shoulder as she closed her eyes. "Dizzy," she muttered. After a minute she opened her eyes and met his gaze. "I'd feel a coward were I to accept. We should be strong and remain in our own home."

He watched her with worried eyes. "I can't always be with you, Fee. I wish I could, but I must go to work."

Once more she settled against his shoulder with a sigh, her fingers playing in his chest hair. "I know. And I shouldn't want you home. You need to be off, feeling pride as you provide for us."

He choked on a laugh. "Somehow that didn't come out as a compliment."

She giggled. "I never meant it as a criticism. I merely want you to know I find true peace when you are home." After a pause, she added, "Now more so than ever."

She sighed and linked her hand with his large one. "I appreciate their offer, Patrick, but I want to remain here. In our home. I will have a few rough days, but I will overcome them."

He kissed her temple. "I agree. However, I believe we should accept for a few days as you recover from your head injury. Then we will remain here, strong and independent."

She snuggled into him and kissed his neck. "I fear independence is an illusion, my darling."

He chuckled as he held her close while she slipped into sleep again.

~

Lucas played the piano in the main living area, the piece more somber than usual. Genevieve acted as though she read the newspaper, although her gaze darted to the side at any noise. Joseph appeared, looking well-fed and content as he strolled into the living area. He paused near the piano.

"Joseph," Lucas said with a friendly smile as Genevieve watched the scene unfold from around the newspaper. "Have you had a chance to write any new songs?" He scooted over on the piano bench as though in a friendly manner to allow Joseph to sit next to him.

"No, I'm workin' too hard 'ere an' at ..." His voice trailed away.

"I'm glad you've found plenty of work to help your family," Lucas said. "I'm surprised you'd need two jobs." He played a soothing sequence of notes.

Joseph cleared his throat, also ridding himself of the rough street cant as he mimicked Lucas's refined accent. "My mother's ailing. She a—isn't able to take in the washing like she used to, so I'm trying to help with more work."

"I'm sure your other employer is understanding of your situation."

"Sanders is a right mean bastard, but 'e pays well." Joseph froze and shot a concerned look at Lucas. When Lucas continued to play with no evidence of concern, Joseph relaxed and watched Lucas's fingers as they nimbly moved over the keys.

"Would that be Mr. Samuel Sanders? The successful manager from the Company?" At Joseph's nod, Lucas changed the tenor of the piece. Rather than a soothing lullaby, it was harsher and more strident. "I'd think a man as successful as he is would pay quite well, and you wouldn't need two jobs."

"Oh, it were a short-term deal."

Lucas slammed his hands down on the piano keys and spun on the piano bench to face Joseph. "The kind of deal that means you spy on us? The kind that means you delay my wife's departure to my cousin's house so his daughter can be kidnapped?" He clamped a viselike hand over Joseph's wiry arm. "Is that the short-term deal you mean?"

Joseph stared at Lucas with dawning horror. "I never meant—"

"Was that your goal, Joseph?" Genevieve asked, coming to stand near him.

"No! I needed money. For bills an' food." He squirmed and kicked, growling in frustration to realize he wouldn't break free from Lucas's hold. "I never meant no 'arm to no one!"

"Why wouldn't you ask us? You know we would have helped you," Genevieve whispered.

Lucas watched Joseph with pity and sadness. "We would have helped you in any way we could have. Instead, I must ask you to leave this house and never return. You betrayed our trust, and you are never welcome here again."

"No," Joseph called out. "It ain't like he got what he wanted. The little girl's still at home."

Lucas clamped his jaw tight as he fought his anger. "Only because Mrs. Russell escaped your incessant questions and distractions yesterday to foil the kidnapping." Lucas rose, dragging Joseph with him. "Come. Let's get your things as you are banned from this house." He tugged a complaining, explaining Joseph behind him as they walked toward the back stairs.

Lucas returned, disheveled and out of breath. Genevieve moved over on the settee and he plopped down next to her. "That was singularly unpleasant."

She shuddered. "What he was complicit in was even more so." She snuggled into his shoulder a moment. "I still can't believe he acted in such a way."

Lucas ran a hand down her arm, the motion calming him as much as it did her. "I fear he'll have no job by the end of the day. With yesterday's debacle, it can only end poorly for him."

She sighed and laced her hand with his. "I wish I could feel sympathy for him. But I can't. When I think of what could have happened ..." She scrubbed her face against Lucas's shirtfront. "It's inconceivable."

"I fear this won't be the last dealings we have with Sanders. I think he has tentacles everywhere." Lucas kissed the top of her head and finally relaxed with her on the settee.

"Just like the Company." Genevieve shuddered and then froze at the knock on the front door.

Lucas sighed and heaved himself up. He wrenched open the door with a glower that transformed into a grin when he saw his cousin and his family on his doorstep. "Come in!" He stepped aside so they could enter. He tickled little Rose on her belly, earning a giggle that eased his tension.

Genevieve rushed to Fiona, embracing her. "Oh, Fee, you look well. I've been so worried."

"I've a bit of a headache, but otherwise I'm well." Fiona blushed under the close scrutiny.

Patrick cleared his throat. "If you wouldn't mind, we'd like to stay here for a day or two as Fee recovers. Then we'll move home again."

Genevieve clapped her hands together with excitement. "Oh, how wonderful. We rarely have guests in this large rambling house. And I have just the room for you, Rose." She led Fiona and Rose upstairs to choose rooms, her chattering easing Fiona's tension.

Lucas and Patrick remained in the living room, a tense silence between them. "I've fired Joseph," Lucas offered.

Patrick's rigid shoulders relaxed, and he sighed. "Thank you. I worried on the walk over if I was placing Fee and Rose in further danger. Fee didn't know about him."

Lucas nodded and slapped his cousin on the back. "I'd offer you a drink, but it's barely midmorning, and I imagine you must go to work." He smiled as Patrick agreed. "Don't worry. We'll relish spoiling little Rose and will ensure Fee rests."

"I might be back late tonight as I had to leave work early yesterday, and I'm arriving late today."

Lucas waved away his concern. "No matter. We'll have a plate of dinner waiting for you, no matter what hour you return."

"I'll make sure Fee has Rose settled, and then I must be off. Thanks again, Lucas. I promise it will only be a few days." He strode from the room and up the stairs, the sound of Rose's delighted laughter echoing down the stairs at his arrival.

~

S amuel Sanders paced his library, a darkly paneled room with mahogany wood. A small bar stood at the far end of the room, near a desk. Heavy burgundy curtains half covered the windows, allowing in only a fraction of the day's bright daylight. A plush oriental carpet covered the floor, silencing the sound of Samuel's pacing. "How could you have failed?" His low snarl elicited a sniff of disdain from the other occupant in the room. "I had this planned perfectly."

"Not well enough clearly," Mrs. Smythe snapped, her scornful glare watching his figure-eight movement around his desk. "If I'd had two more minutes, no one would have been the wiser."

"Now I have police demanding entrance to my home. Threatening me with a search warrant!" He glowered at the middle-aged woman long past her prime, lounging in a chair pushed away from his desk which allowed him to pace around it.

"I imagine they are looking for me."

"No need to sound pleased, Mrs. Smythe. For, if they find you, then we are in deep trouble. I have little faith you'll withstand their rounds of questioning."

"How dare you imply I am not up to the task." Her cheeks flushed with indignation.

"Oh, spare me your displays of so-called womanly strength. Your supposed cunning and deviousness did little except allow you to escape that impressionable policeman." He prowled around the room, only stopping his movement to glower at the door as it flung open. His scowl darkened as he beheld a breathless Joseph standing there.

Joseph shut the door behind him and shook at Samuel's glower as he sat in a chair next to Mrs. Smythe. "I—I had nowhere to go, sir."

"So you decided to run here? You failed in your duties, Joseph. You had one thing to do. One!" He slammed his hand on the top of his desk, causing Joseph and Mrs. Smythe to jump in their chairs. "You were to ensure that Mrs. Russell remained home yesterday afternoon. I don't believe that was too much to ask."

"You never said nothin' 'bout stealin' no baby," Joseph said.

"It isn't stealing when the child is mine." The low, lethal tone provoked a shiver in Joseph. "Now you can redeem yourself by ingratiating yourself further with the Russells. I want to know anything of interest with their family in Missoula." Samuel paced again with a distant expression as though plotting out a new scheme.

Joseph's shivering intensified. "That ain't possible, sir. I's not workin' there no more."

Samuel halted, a rare look of surprise on his face. "You no longer work for Lucas Russell?" At Joseph's shake of his head, Samuel gave a bark of mirthless laughter. "And to think I thought you were a perfect candidate." He sighed and waved for him to leave. "There is no further reason for an association between us."

"But, sir ..."

"Leave, Joseph, before I find other ways to hurt your family." Samuel's deadly cold eyes overruled any of Joseph's complaints, and he scampered out the door.

Mrs. Smythe shook her head. "That's what you get for relying on incompetent schoolboys who are desperate."

"The desperate ones are usually the most resourceful. They have too much to lose if they fail." Samuel sighed and ran a hand through his hair. "Now I merely must concern myself with you."

Mrs. Smythe stiffened and raised her chin in a haughty manner. "You must know I am not a thing like that young man. If you abandon me to the police, I'm taking you with me." She sniffed and gave one definitive nod.

Her tension eased when he gave a stiff nod of agreement. "I'm still perplexed as to why you'd desire your daughter's presence in your home. They are such feeble, useless beings at this age. I'd think you'd wait until she's older and able to earn you some sort of profit, prefer-ably from an advantageous marriage."

Samuel snickered. "I can see why my mother enjoyed your friendship."

Mrs. Smythe raised an eyebrow. "Of course she did." She paused as though considering her own advice. "Once you've wooed her with your charm and money, then you can influence who she desires to marry." She flicked her wrist as though it were an easy matter. "Sell her off to whoever will give you the greatest benefit, and there's no more concern about upkeep, and you can forget about her as she'll be her husband's concern."

"Seems you failed in that regard with your own daughter." He watched her with gloating satisfaction at her miscalculation.

"I admit I didn't factor in the potential reward for keeping the mewling, bothersome creature all these years. Instead I made the gravest error and allowed her to be raised by a McLeod." She raised an eyebrow as she met Samuel's thunderous expression. "I'm sure you can understand my disappointment."

Samuel snorted his agreement. "I can think of no worse a punish-ment, although they are delusional in believing they are fortunate to be a part of that familial group." He glowered. "I'll find a way to shield you from the police this time." As she preened with satisfaction, he leaned against the edge of his desk with his arms crossed over his chest. "In exchange for my aid, I want your promise to help me in my future endeavors to wreak havoc on all who associate with my cousins in Missoula."

Mrs. Smythe smiled with pleasure. "That is no favor at all, dear boy."

CHAPTER 16

Washington, DC, November 1917

$\mathcal{Z}$ ylphia prepared a banner in the main conference room of Cameron House, rolling it up tightly. She smiled at another woman who had joined her in jail for a few days that fall. "Don't worry. If all else fails, we'll meet Miss Paul in prison." She winked in encouragement to the woman before she ate a small teacake and took a sip of tea.

Parthena sidled up to Zylphia and spoke in a whisper. "How can you be so nonchalant? You know the judge gave Miss Paul six months in jail. I don't think I could last six days."

"P.T., if this is too much for you, don't picket." Zylphia smiled in encouragement at another woman across the room. "For I'm certain we'll be arrested. However, I doubt we'll earn anything like Miss Paul. At most we'll be in jail a couple days."

"You make it sound as though it is a grand adventure." Parthena glared at her friend.

Zylphia gripped her friend's elbow and tugged Parthena to a corner of the room. "Listen. This isn't an adventure. For, in adventures, there's generally a happy ending. Being spat at, yelled at and having refuse thrown at you isn't fun. It isn't my idea of a good time. However, I believe these tactics are important and will aid us in earning the right to vote." She watched Parthena with an impassioned intensity. "I smile to bolster spirits because we all have doubts and fears. But we can't be ruled by them." She took a deep breath as though convincing herself of the validity of her next statement. "I can't sit by and let others do the work I know I can do."

Parthena nodded. "I know. I'm just afraid. Miss Paul's already in jail."

Zylphia squeezed Parthena's hand. "It's only because, this time, you know we'll most likely be sent to jail too. The other times were more of a lark in comparison."

"Calling the President 'Kaiser Wilson' will never be considered a lark!" Parthena whispered, earning a giggle from Zylphia.

Zylphia stood tall as Lucy Burns called out that it was time. Each woman grabbed her banner and formed two single-file rows. As they marched from Cameron House, they passed by an honor guard of women encouraging them. When the door closed behind them on the cold mid-November afternoon, Zylphia shivered under her long wool coat before resolutely marching among her thirty-one friends and comrades.

When they arrived at the White House and Lafayette Square, they spread out to occupy the space between the front gates at the White House. Soon an angry mob surrounded them. Zylphia remained stoic as passersby screamed at her, and she barely flinched as another kicked her shins. She gripped the banner proclaiming, *Mr. President, It Is Unjust to Deny Women a Voice in Their Government When the Government Is Conscripting Their Sons*. Almost instantly a man in uniform grabbed it. She grunted as she fiercely pulled it to her chest, but she failed to fight him off. He yanked it from her, smiling with evil delight as he tore at it, eventually rending it in two.

She watched him toss the pieces to the ravening crowd before she tugged another banner from the lining of her boots. She attached it to the pole she had reclaimed and stood tall again. A police officer saw her actions, a glimmer of respect in his eyes for a moment before he called forth his reinforcements to arrest Zylphia and the other women. Zylphia was exhilarated as they were led to the courthouse.

~

"Six weeks in jail," the judge ordered, his gavel slamming down and echoing around the courtroom.

The protesters chattered about the excessive amount of time and were quickly herded together to be brought to jail.

Zylphia looked up to the gallery and nodded at Rowena, who sat taking notes. Rowena nodded back to her and Parthena, her face solemn and resolute.

"Rowena will inform our husbands," Zylphia whispered. "I asked her to this time. I fear we may need their help as I had a feeling the sentences would be harsher, and I doubt the president will aid us this time." She clasped Parthena's hand. "We'll be all right, P.T. I promise."

"I doubt they'll do much." Parthena gripped Zylphia's elbow and followed the herd of women. "What did Teddy do the last times you were imprisoned?"

"As far as I know, he isn't aware I've ever been in jail. He needed no further reason to encourage me to cease my activities here."

"You're a fool if you believe Teddy isn't following your antics even though he's in Boston. I'm sure he knows each and every time you were arrested and exactly when you were released. He must have his reasons for not speaking with you about it."

Zylphia shrugged as the group of women were herded into the large waiting area of Union Station. She gripped Parthena's hand so as not to be separated from her and moved with her fellow suffragists as they were forced into a packed railcar.

They stood in the aisles as no seats were available. "Why are we heading south?"

At Parthena's whispered question, Zylphia looked around at the dawning understanding on the other protesters' faces. "We're not going to jail. We're being sent to Occoquan. The wretched workhouse run by Mr. Whittaker." As the whispers spread of where they were going, they crafted their plan that Dora Lewis would be their spokesperson and that they would demand to be treated as political prisoners.

As dusk fell, they were led into the workhouse. Zylphia sat next to Parthena in the matron's office, Zee's head held high but her gaze lowered as she and all her fellow protestors refused to answer the roll call. Their chosen speaker had informed the matron that they would not respond to any inquiries until the warden arrived, even if that meant sitting here for days. A soft snore rent the tense silence in the room as the hours ticked by, and Zylphia stifled an inappropriate giggle.

When pounding footsteps approached, she stood up straight and thrust her shoulders back. A man with stiff white hair and penetrating eyes burst into the room with a bevy of orderlies behind him. As Dora Lewis rose and proclaimed that she and the other women were to be considered political prisoners, he ordered his men, "Take her!" She was grabbed and yanked from the room.

"Now I will have order and obedience," he barked as he walked with menacing steps in front of the women. "When your name is called, you will respond." Zylphia exchanged a glance with Parthena and subtly shook her head. As the names were again called out, a resounding silence echoed through the room.

"Take that woman and that woman," Whittaker snapped, pushing his orderlies into action. They held clubs and dragged the women from the room, wrenching shoulders and lifting them off their feet to propel them away as though they were nothing more than rag dolls.

Zylphia fought initially but then gave up as she was overpowered by two large men. She shied away when one raised his large club with a threatening, eager look. As she was hauled after Parthena, she focused on her friend who seemed to be flying through the air. Rather than dragging them into the workhouse, they were hauled outside to the men's jail and then downstairs. Zylphia saw Parthena tossed into a far cell, and Zylphia was unceremoniously dumped into one closer to the stairs, the guard giving her a slap on one cheek for good measure.

She knelt as she watched woman after woman thrown into cells—

some alone, others sharing a cell. Zylphia was kept alone and stood to peer out her cell. Lucy Burns was a few cells down from her and began a roll call. As each woman answered, Mr. Whittaker stormed in. "Quiet!" he screamed. When Lucy continued to speak, a guard grabbed her arms and handcuffed her to the cell door with her arms over her head.

Zylphia whispered to Lucy but jumped away from the bars of her cell when a guard yelled at her for quiet or she'd suffer the same fate. Zylphia stifled a sob and curled into herself as the adrenaline faded. She leaned against the wall of her cell, the concrete soothing her cheek. With no blanket to cover herself and a window allowing the cool November air to seep into her cell, Zylphia trembled. Soon she was shivering, and nothing she did warmed her.

The following morning a matron unlocked her cell. She dropped a plate of food on the floor and then scowled as she looked at Zylphia on the floor. "Doesn't even have sense to get on the cot," she grumbled. When she backed from the cell, her sharp gaze focused on Zylphia, and she called out to a female orderly, "Let's begin with this one!"

Zylphia was pulled up and dragged to the bathroom and forcibly stripped of her clothes. They were tossed in a bin, and she was pushed into a public shower. She attempted to cover herself, earning snickers from those watching her discomfort. She shivered at the cold water and grimaced at the communal piece of soap she was given. However, after a poke to her back, she washed before standing, dripping for a few minutes, as she waited on a towel or cloth to dry herself. Finally a threadbare rag was thrown at her, and she sopped up the water as best she could. She caught a worn blue dress and donned it, chafing at the rough fabric. After dressing, two orderlies gripped her by her elbows and dragged her from the room. Her feet scraped along the floor, unable to keep pace with the stronger orderlies.

She heard the whispered words, "Hunger strike," as she was pulled back to her cell from the restroom. She met Parthena's worried gaze, in a cell at the opposite end along the same side where she was held. She nodded her understanding and collapsed to the floor after she was flung back inside. She curled into herself again as she fought tears and prayed for strength.

~

R owena answered the door on the first knock. She stepped aside as Teddy and Morgan stormed into her small apartment.

"We left as soon as we could after the telegram arrived," Teddy said. He shucked his coat and slung it over the back of the chair. "Can you tell us anything?"

Rowena shook her head as she fought tears. "Very little. They were supposed to be at the district jail. Instead they were sent to the Occoquan workhouse."

"I'd think a workhouse would be much better than a jail," Morgan said as he paced behind the settee. He stopped and gripped the back of it with such strength it appeared he was on the verge of tearing the stuffing from it.

"The women who have been in both the jail and the workhouse say that the workhouse is the worse of the two." Rowena flushed as she suddenly had the attention of both men. "The food, the conditions and the treatment by those in charge are much worse at the workhouse."

"Bloody hell," Teddy said. "Of course Zee and Parthena would get caught up in such a scheme." He massaged his injured hand and spun to face a window, although he saw little as he stared into the darkened night.

"They had—have—every right to protest and to demand their rights," Rowena said as she stood tall. At their persistent silence, she sank into a chair. She frowned as Teddy clenched and unclenched his hands, with no relief in the tension in his shoulders. "What worries you, Teddy?"

"I know how little esteem most of these women have in the eyes of the public. Any mistreatment will be seen as their due," he whispered. "The papers already snicker about the rich society matrons deprived of their maids and unadorned by jewels as they spend time in jail. I wonder if Zee thought through her actions or only reveled in the thought of becoming a martyr to her cause."

"She won't die, Teddy," Rowena said. She jumped as Morgan collapsed on the settee he had been mangling with his hands.

"She won't come back unchanged." Teddy shuddered. "I saw what prison did to my cousin Eugenie in England." He let out a deep breath and leaned his forehead against the cool windowpane. "I hate to imagine how this will affect Zee."

"Or Parthena," Morgan said. Guilt seemed to emanate from his pores as he sank farther into the settee, his head resting against the back of it. "I should have come here sooner."

"None of us knew this was coming," Rowena argued.

Teddy scoffed and turned to face them. He rubbed at his forehead, massaging a scar on his hairline. "I doubt that. I'm sure that woman in charge of this debacle of a movement knew exactly what would happen to the women who dared to picket." He cut off Rowena's protest. "And I'm certain she's delighted her protesters are in custody."

"As she's already in jail, I think that's unfair," Rowena said. "We all knew the risks."

Morgan sat as though in a daze. "I'll never understand why going to jail would be seen as successful."

Rowena shook her head in disappointment. "Of course you wouldn't. It's a sign of our determination to this cause. Of our dedication. It's essential we change public perception of us."

Teddy laughed without a trace of humor. "You think that going to jail will erase the public's memory of you standing outside the White House in a time of war calling our president the Kaiser?" He shook his head. "Our country is at war with Germany. You should never have made such banners." At Rowena's disappointed stare, he muttered, "I understand your determination, but your methods are mad."

"We've never provoked violence. We've never lied," Rowena snapped.

"You twist the truth to your way of thinking, just as any politician does," Morgan said. "I read your newspaper every week. I find your articles to be the most illuminating."

Rowena flushed at his praise before focusing again on Teddy. "What do you plan to do for Zee?" Her gaze moved to Morgan. "For Parthena?"

The two men exchanged a long glance and shook their heads. "I'm not sure," Teddy said. "I'm not sure what can be done when they've refused to pay a fine and have chosen to go to the workhouse."

Rowena leaned forward. "That's just it. They didn't choose the workhouse. They chose jail."

Teddy's silver eyes shone. "Aah, … then I think we have the beginnings of a case."

~

Four days later, Zylphia lay on the cot, her mind wandering aimlessly as she fought hunger. The overwhelming scent of bacon wafted through the air, and she pinched her nose so as not to smell it. Tears leaked out as she imagined eating again.

A lassitude pervaded her, and she barely had the strength to braid her hair. She glanced at the door as a tray with buttered toast and milk was dropped on the floor. She ignored the offering, her inherent indignation waning with each passing day that they believed her resolve so weak they could corrupt it with a piece of buttered toast. She awaited the creeping sound of rats approaching her untouched food.

Her mind wandered as she had increasing difficulty focusing on the reality of her situation. Visions of her time at the orphanage, of playing with children her age, of drawing and realizing she had talent. Her mind flitted around from memory to memory as though watching a motion picture in slow motion, images fading in and out of focus. Sitting in a steaming coffee shop as she spoke with her father. Moving into his home after he wed her mother. The first time she told him that she loved him. Her joy at seeing a room set up as her painting studio, arranged by her father. Meeting Teddy. Watching him watch her as she twirled around a ballroom in Newport with Owen Hubbard. She shifted uncomfortably after thinking about Teddy, preferring to doze and not remember, rather than focus on him and their relationship.

Two days later, she was nearly insensate. She had had little contact with any of the other prisoners, and the few times she had crawled over to peer out her cell, she had been unable to see Parthena. She heard rumors that she and a few others were to be transferred to the jail due to their weakened states. When the workhouse cell door scraped open, she watched with a bleary-eyed indifference as they approached her. "This one'll die if we do nothing," the guard said with a shake of his head. "Stupid woman. Hasn't learned to accept her place."

"Then she must be forced to accept the consequences of her actions," another said with gleeful malevolence.

Zylphia squinted as the sound of a chair scraping against the concrete floor echoed through the cell. She blinked a few times to bring the goings-on into focus. When her arms were grasped, she kicked and bucked. Two more men came from outside, forcing her into movement as they hauled her into the chair. She kicked out, landing a strike on one man's shoulder. Strong arms gripped her legs, and she lacked the strength to fight them off. After her legs were strapped to the chair and her arms tied behind her back, she continued to buck and fight.

"Don't be wasting the little energy you have left," one of the guards scolded. "The doctor will be right here."

"No!" Zylphia screamed, moving with such force she toppled the chair backward. Another guard jumped and pushed her upright before she collapsed and smashed her skull on the concrete floor. With a few hand motions, he instructed the other guards to hold her in place.

The doctor arrived with a nurse beside him. She carried a long tube, and he held a small black bag. He approached Zylphia with tired eyes and frowned as she struggled against the guards. "If you would accept your fate, this will be much more pleasant for you."

"Thrusting a tube down my throat will never be pleasant, no matter how docile I am," she hissed. She gasped as one of the guards gripped her hair and yanked her head back. That small gasp allowed the doctor to pry apart her jaw with a metal instrument. He tightened the screws, holding her jaw open against her attempts to close her jaw, the metal digging into her lips and gums.

One guard sat on her legs to prevent any movement of her lower body while two others held her shoulders back so she would remain as still as possible. Tears poured down her cheeks, and she gagged as the cold rubber tube was thrust down her throat. Her imploring gaze turned to one of hatred as the doctor forced a thick liquid gruel down the tube into her stomach. After a few minutes, he nodded with satisfaction and eased the tube from her throat. Afterward he removed the tube and he patted her on her shoulder. "There, that should keep you going so you reach the jail."

He removed the metal instrument from her mouth, and she turned her head, vomiting all over the doctor's feet. She clutched her stomach, ignoring the commotion as the mess was cleaned up. Rather than crawl into bed, she was tugged into the hallway where another orderly awaited her. She swiped at her bleeding lips with the rough cotton of her workhouse gown and leaned against the wall, her legs shaking and barely holding her weight.

"I'm not carrying you, so don't expect special treatment 'cause you refused to eat," the orderly snapped. "Follow me." He motioned to Zylphia, and, when she was slow to move, he grabbed her arm and dragged her down the hall to a set of stairs and to the awaiting vehicle.

She fell on the seat in the back of the trucklike transport with two other women already present. She had a bench to herself and curled onto it, shaking, willing herself not to cry.

"It's all right, Zylphia," Lucy Burns said, her voice roughened and raw. "Things will be better at the jail. Alice is there. You'll see."

"I never imagined ..." Zylphia whispered. "With everything I've read, I never ..." She shuddered and pulled her knees to her chest.

"The important thing is to keep resisting. To keep fighting. They think we don't know our place. The problem is that they don't understand that their vision of the world must change." Lucy stroked a hand over Zylphia's head. "And we'll help them acknowledge that."

"I don't want to die," Zylphia murmured.

Lucy laughed. "You won't. They'll keep you alive. Through forced feedings. Through any means possible. The death of a previously healthy young woman in jail is not the notoriety the government needs. You're doing well, Zee. Keep up the struggle."

"I can't imagine that happening again." She scrubbed at her tear-soaked cheeks.

Lucy sighed. "The truth is, it *will* continue. It will occur up to three times a day. You must find the strength to fight but know that whatever happens is worth it because it furthers the struggle."

"I'll try," Zylphia whispered before she grabbed Lucy's hand. "Do you know how Parthena is?"

Lucy gripped her hand to calm her. "She's brave. Like you, Zee. She'll most likely follow us to jail in a few days. She'll need feedings soon."

Zylphia sensed Lucy move away from her to settle on the other bench. She dozed during the trip to the jail on the outskirts of Washington, DC. The transfer from the back of the police wagon to her new jail cell was a blur. Dimly lit hallways, stale air and curious eyes peering from inside cells were fleeting impressions before she tripped and fell to the floor in her new cell. She crawled to the bed in the corner, hugging her knees to her chest as exhaustion overwhelmed her.

CHAPTER 17

*T*eddy sat beside Morgan in the courtroom's spectator balcony. Jam-packed with reporters, suffragists and curious citizens, they had opted to sit in the balcony rather than down below so as not to draw attention to themselves. Teddy sighed when a reporter watched them with keen interest, jotting down notes as the case progressed as though analyzing their responses to share with his avid readership.

Teddy shifted in his seat again as the proceedings dragged on. The judge showed little inclination to reduce the prisoners' sentences and release them early. Teddy glared at the lawyer he and Morgan had contributed a large sum of money to as the attorney remained ineffectual in his arguments.

Finally he called forth women to describe their treatment in the workhouse. They detailed the filthy conditions, the taunting by the guards, the screams they heard from the women who were force-fed. As they spoke in blunt words, an uneasy murmur rose among the spectators watching the hearing.

When the jail warden gave testimony, the suffragist lawyer said, "I would like to hear from one of the ringleaders. That Lucy Burns or Zylphia Goff. They've been arrested enough times."

"I'm afraid they were deemed too weak to be present today," the warden said.

"Too weak?" The lawyer raised an eyebrow as he peered over his spectacles at the man. "Have you not just informed me that they are on a hunger strike?"

"Yes, sir."

"And did you not just say that they are force-fed?" At the warden's nod, the lawyer squinted as he tapped the papers in front of him. "How many orderlies hold them down to feed them every day?"

The crowd gasped and instinctively leaned forward to hear the warden's words. Teddy stiffened next to Morgan, and his hands clenched at any description of Zylphia's mistreatment.

"I've been told it takes four to hold down Miss Burns, while only three are necessary for Mrs. Goff." The warden's face reddened as he glared at the triumphant lawyer.

Morgan nudged Teddy in the side when he subtly shook after hearing three men held down his wife to force-feed her. "She's strong, Teddy. She'll be all right."

"How would you feel if they were describing Parthena?" Teddy asked, their wild, worried gazes meeting.

Morgan blinked his understanding before returning his attention to the proceedings.

The lawyer whipped off his glasses and pointed them at the warden as though in confusion. "You're telling me that they weren't allowed to testify because they were deemed too weak, but it takes three or four grown men to hold them down to feed them?" He shook his head in feigned befuddlement. "I seem to have a different definition of *weakness*."

The judge glowered at the warden and intoned, "I am deeply displeased at this show of malfeasance at this hearing."

When the hearing was over, no resolution had been agreed upon, and the women were to remain in jail or the workhouse for the foreseeable future. Teddy strode from the courthouse, pushing past nosy reporters and refusing to comment. He hailed a cab, escaping the curious onlookers.

Later Teddy sat in Rowena's sitting room, staring into space as he relived the hearing. Lamps were lit as darkness descended earlier on these the late-November evenings. He sighed his thanks as Rowena handed him a cup of tea. Morgan had followed the lawyer to his office in hopes of ascertaining any further information and pressuring for an immediate release. He planned to meet them at Rowena's after his meeting.

"She'll be all right, Teddy," Rowena whispered.

Teddy shook his head. "That's what Morgan said. But I don't believe she'll ever be the same Zylphia as when she went in." He ran a hand over his face. "Do you know I haven't seen her since August?" He set aside his tea and rose, moving to stare out the window. "I thought it kinder to the both of us if I stayed away. All we seemed to do was bring each other pain."

"She enjoyed your visit here, Teddy," Rowena murmured.

Teddy laughed mirthlessly. "She did for a few hours. Then the bickering started again. If we could gag each other and not talk, we might get along." He sat down on a wingback chair and rested his head against its high back. "I wonder now if that wasn't her goal. To induce an argument with me so that I'd leave her to do what she pleased."

"Why is it so important that you retain your British citizenship?" Rowena asked. "You've lived here for years."

Teddy shrugged his shoulders and flushed. "It's one of those things that's a part of who I am. I've lost so much in my life. I didn't want to lose that too."

"Is it worth keeping if you lose Zee?" Rowena asked.

Teddy bolted upright to face Rowena, who'd become a close friend during Zylphia's incarceration. "I can see why Zee enjoys your counsel," he said. "All I've focused on is what I'd initially lose. Not what I'll gain if I change my mind."

Rowena smiled. "If you mean what you said, Zee will be delighted, not because you've changed your mind, but because you'll have harmony again. She's missed you dreadfully."

"I thank you for saying that, but I fear you're being overly optimistic." Teddy's eyes clouded as he watched Rowena.

She frowned. "What is it?"

He ran a hand through his sable hair. "I shouldn't even contemplate what worries me." He rose again as a restless energy filled him, his hands grasping the back of a tall chair. "I've heard ... rumors ... that Zylphia has become close to a man who frequents Cameron House. An Octavius Hooper." He paused. "I met him in August. He seemed overly concerned about Zee's welfare."

Rowena paled. "Teddy, you have to understand ..." She paused as she bit her lip. "You have to understand that many men find your wife attractive. And because she's been here for so long without your presence, there are those who believe that she is open to dalliance."

Teddy's jaw twitched. "And was she?" He met Rowena's troubled gaze. "Open to dalliance?"

"No. She flirted, but she never wanted anything to do with any of them, Teddy. You must believe me." Rowena frowned as he broke his gaze from hers and moved to lean against the windowsill.

He sat in silence a few minutes, the only sound in the room the clock ticking on the side table. "I'm afraid I don't know what to believe anymore. I know what I hope to be true. But no longer what I believe."

Morgan burst into the room, his eyes lit with hope. "I believe there is a possibility for them! One of the judges, the one who sent them in and who's had the most interaction with them, is pressuring for the women to be released. He believes the death of any of them would be more than the government and city officials could overcome."

"When would this release occur?" Teddy asked, his previous melancholy banished.

"I'm not sure as today is Friday. Hopefully sometime this weekend. I'd think Monday at the latest. The women on hunger strike aren't getting any stronger." He nodded as he watched Teddy pale. "Parthena's striking too, Teddy."

Teddy gripped his shoulder and took a deep breath. "Then we'll have to add our voices to this judge's reasonable recommendation."

"I'll see what is planned when I'm at Cameron House tomorrow," Rowena said. "I'm certain the leaders who aren't incarcerated will keep us informed."

~

The following day, Morgan strode into their replacement lawyer's office with Teddy on his heels. The glass in the door rattled as it slammed shut behind them. "I've been told you're one of the best, Hooper, and that you are in favor of what the suffragists espouse. I hope both sentiments prove true."

Octavius smirked at Morgan before studying Teddy. "I'm better than they think I am." He motioned for them to sit. "I thought you had a lawyer." He raised an eyebrow in an inquisitive manner.

Morgan sighed. "We do, but I'm afraid he's not as competent as I would like. He's yet to speak with the judge, and he believes we must wait for something drastic to occur to ensure the freeing of our wives and the other women prisoners."

Octavius shook his head. "Incompetent fool. I've spoken to the judge twice today and expressed the mounting concern that numerous women could die or require daily force-feedings to remain alive. He's appalled at the potential for bad press, and I'm confident that they will be released early next week."

"Will it be too late for some of them by then?" Teddy asked, his shoulders tensed.

"They won't allow one of those women to become a martyr to the cause. That would galvanize even those who are only mildly interested in enfranchisement. That's the last thing they want—believe me." Octavius steepled his fingers as he watched Teddy with blatant curiosity.

"Public support seems to be shifting toward the jailed suffragists," Morgan murmured.

"A death would be unpardonable," Octavius said in a flat voice. "It would also highlight the incompetence of these prisons and work-houses in last year's congressional investigation."

"How is it that a successful lawyer as yourself has the time and inclination to aid the women of the movement?" Teddy asked.

"I have a personal interest in ensuring the women are released, having suffered minimally for their beliefs." He smirked as he quirked an eyebrow at Teddy. "As you know, I'm a particular friend of your wife. She's a remarkable woman."

Teddy stiffened at Hooper's words before forcing himself to relax after noting the pleasure his reaction brought Octavius. "Zylphia is a woman to be esteemed, and it's fortunate you were able to see her fine qualities."

Morgan's gaze flit between the two men engaged in a staring match and frowned. "Mr. Goff and I are thankful you are dedicated to the cause and that you are using your influence to ensure our wives and their colleagues are freed." Morgan elbowed Teddy in the side as he rose and held out his hand to Octavius. "I trust you will notify us with any news?"

Octavius nodded and shook Morgan's hand. He nodded to Teddy, who refused to offer his hand.

Teddy followed Morgan from the office and speared him with a severe look to remain silent until they were out of the building. When they'd emerged onto the street and walked toward the Willard Hotel, Teddy took a deep breath. "Now you can tell me how I was an ass."

Morgan chuckled. "I think you were remarkably controlled when he implied an impropriety between him and Zee. I would never have been that restrained."

Teddy let out another breath, and the remaining tension leaked out. They turned off F Street to Fourteenth Street and into Old Ebbitt's Saloon. "I hear this is a good place for a drink." After ordering drinks in the Old English Room, they moved to a table in the corner.

"Do you think he's as good as he believes he is?" Teddy took a swig of whiskey. "He seemed cocky."

Morgan laughed, almost spitting out his sip of beer. "That's because you'll never like him, no matter what he does. You'll always hate him for his friendship with Zee. And you must consider it a friendship until you've been told otherwise. It isn't fair to your wife."

He glanced around the room at the eclectic decor of animal heads mounted on the wall and antique beer steins lined up over the bar. "I do think he is as capable as he believes. The fact he's spoken to the judge twice today is a positive beginning."

"But is that a good sign? I'd think one conversation would be enough."

Morgan shook his head. "For a taciturn Englishman like yourself, it would be. However, it never hurts to add pressure. Besides, if the judge didn't want to take Hooper's call, he wouldn't have. I think it indicates the judge must be growing desperate to find a way to save face and the women who've been imprisoned."

Teddy sighed, shifting so he could cross his legs. "I fear both sides will declare victory in this battle of wills. All I care is that Zee and Parthena are freed." He stared at Morgan. "And I want my wife home, away from all this."

Morgan nodded. "I agree. However, I refuse to force Parthena. I know well enough she'll not bend to my will, and I want her to return of her own volition."

Teddy took a long drink of his whiskey. "I hope we are both fortunate to have our wives at home without any further trauma to them or to us."

Morgan raised his glass in a salute, and they sat in silence as they contemplated what more could be done for their wives.

∿

Zylphia lurched to her feet, falling almost instantly to her knees before crawling to the side of her cell. She curled into a ball in the corner when she heard footsteps approaching, her arms clasped around her ankles, like a turtle retracting into its shell. She shivered at the sound of the keys clanking against the orderly's belt, her stomach in knots as she knew what it meant. The scraping of metal against the floor caused her to hug herself even tighter as the shaking began.

"It's that time," a taunting voice called out as the cell door slid open. "I can see you're excited to see us." His laugh sounded throughout the cell.

Zylphia peered out of a small gap between her arm and knee and watched them set the chair in the center of the room. Unable to stop her quivering when the other male orderlies entered the room, she hugged into herself with all her might. She grunted when someone tugged on her arms and another pulled at her shoulders, dragging her toward the chair as she fought them with her meager strength.

"No!" she yelled. "Let me go!" Tears streamed down her cheeks as she kicked out, knocking the chair over.

"Cease!" a booming voice decreed. She was dropped to the ground with a thud. "She is to be released today and will undergo no further forced-feedings."

Zylphia curled into herself again and peeked to determine if this was a ruse or not. Her strength waned, and she did not have the energy to fight them for much longer. When she was commanded to stand, she let go of her legs and uncurled herself. She met the gaze of the person giving the orders and relaxed to the floor.

When he motioned for them to lift her up, she screamed. "You liar! You fiend!" Tears poured down her cheeks again as they tugged her closer to the chair. Instead of forcing her to sit, they dragged her from the cell and down the hall to a communal shower. The male orderlies left, and female orderlies approached her. They stripped her of her jail clothes as frigid water poured from the shower spigots.

"Bathe," one of the women orderlies demanded, with a finger pointing at the shower.

Zylphia shook her head and sat on a bench. She flinched as clothes were thrown at her, the clothes she'd worn when she had traveled to Occoquan nearly two weeks ago. She fingered the fine fabric before slipping the dress over her head. It hung on her, at least two sizes too big, and her hands shook as she did up the buttons on the front of her dress. She looked for her fine jacket, but it was nowhere in sight.

When another orderly motioned to her, she rose, splaying a hand on the wall to maintain her balance. She walked with ginger care down the hallway to the entrance of the jail with seven other women.

She looked for Parthena but did not see her. Once outside, the doors clanged shut behind them. No crowds awaited them. No journalists were present to note their appearance or mistreatment in the jail. A few members from the NWP were here, and they ushered the women into waiting cabs to return to Cameron House for care and evaluation by a doctor.

After climbing into one of the taxis and crawling under a blanket, Zylphia looked out the window at the gray late-November morning. She massaged her throat and held her other hand over her abdomen and marveled at all the people continuing on with life as though nothing momentous had occurred. Unsuccessful in blinking back her tears, Zylphia watched the world speed by as though through a rain-drenched window and wondered how life would ever return to normal.

CHAPTER 18

*T*eddy wandered the small sitting room that was part of the suite of hotel rooms he'd rented in Washington. Zylphia had been released from jail five days ago to be cared for initially at Cameron House. Two days ago, he had moved her to the hotel and had ensured she was comfortable. He scratched at his four-day growth of beard and tugged at his hair sticking out in odd places. He turned toward the bedroom door as it creaked open. "Good afternoon."

Zylphia's smile barely curved her lips, and she crept from the doorway to the settee, keeping her hand on assorted pieces of furniture the entire way to provide support. Her lips were chapped and scabbed in places, and her cheekbones protruded more than the last time he had seen her in August. She eased onto the settee and pulled a throw blanket over her. "What day is it?" she murmured.

"Friday." He remained standing by the window, his expression now hidden by the influx of bright light behind him.

"When was I released?" Her words were scratchy, but she smiled her thanks as Teddy handed her a glass of cold water, sighing with pleasure as it soothed her throat.

"Monday. You spent two days at Cameron House, and then I brought you here."

She shivered, and he placed another blanket over her legs. "But why did you bring me here?" she asked softly. "They would have cared for me there."

He raised an eyebrow at her whispered question. "I wanted to care for you, Zee, and there's no place for me in the apartment you share with Rowena." He crossed his arms over his chest. "I refused to be denied seeing you again, Zee. No matter how you may feel, you are my wife."

"I would never deny wanting to see you," Zylphia protested. She scooted over on the edge of the settee as though to lean against the armrest. It also gave him plenty of room to sit beside her. Instead Teddy perched against the windowsill.

"Those women you've aligned yourself with would," Teddy said in a flat voice. "They barred me from speaking with the doctor who cared for you. Could you explain why they'd do such a thing?"

"Teddy," Zylphia whispered, holding out her hand to him as she fought to hide the anxiety in her eyes.

He watched her closely and remained across the room from her, not taking her hand.

"They're overprotective is all. I was sick when I left jail." Her smile failed to soothe him. "I want you to care for me here."

Teddy sighed, his arms crossed over his middle. "I'm trying, Zee. I'm trying very hard."

"What do you mean?" She turned her head, squinting to make out his expression.

"Everything in me screams to pack up everything here and bring you back to Boston. To take you away from women who would readily plan for any harm to befall you." His arms tensed as he spoke, as though forcing himself to remain motionless.

Zylphia rolled her eyes. "I'm my own person, Teddy. I decided to join those pickets. I knew the risks. I knew, if I was arrested, that I'd be sent to jail."

"Well, it seems you succeeded, and public sentiment turned, just as your Miss Paul had hoped." He tossed the recent copy of the *Suffragist* onto the table between them, with a picture by Nina Allender of women peering out from behind jail bars on the cover. "Seems that the thought of so many women on the verge of starving themselves to death for the cause has made many rethink their position."

"I wonder if the president has," Zylphia whispered, her eyes lit with excitement. "It means it was all worth it." Her smile faded as she fought tears.

Teddy frowned as he noted her tears before nodding and moving from the window to sit on a chair facing her. "I knew you'd say that. Do you know how hard we worked to release you?" At her blank stare, he shook his head in frustration. "Every minute you were in jail, Morgan and I were searching to find a way to ensure your release."

"Morgan is here? How is Parthena?"

He frowned as he watched her. "I'd think you'd know. You were jailed with her."

She shook her head. "They separated us from the very beginning. And then, once the hunger strike started, I barely had the energy to worry about myself." She shook her head as though ashamed.

"She's with her husband in a room here. He was insistent on caring for her when she was released from the workhouse." Teddy sighed. "Morgan was a good partner to have as we worked for your release." He studied her as she nodded with little interest in the work that had entailed. "We met your Mr. Hooper."

Zylphia glared at him. "He isn't my anything."

"He seems to believe you were close friends. Much closer than when I met him in August."

She fidgeted under his severe stare. "Then he's delusional. Not all men who believe they are my friends are my friends."

Teddy watched her closely for a moment. "I have to know, Zee. Did you even once think of me? Of what you being harmed would do to me?"

Zylphia sighed. "This isn't about you. This is about me, proclaiming my rights as a woman in this country."

"In a country that no longer sees you as a citizen because you married me," Teddy snapped. He clamped his jaw shut and leaned forward, his hands held together as though he were in prayer, his face leaning against his hands. Finally he raised his head and looked at Zylphia. "Did you think of me?" He enunciated each word, as though they were torn from him.

She sank into the settee as the fight left her. "No. Not in that way."

Teddy tilted his head to the side. "Then in what way, Zee?"

Zee rubbed at her cheek and seemed surprised to find it dry of any tears. "You used to take such pride in me. In my wild antics. In the thought of me obtaining the vote." The eloquence of her flat voice spoke to her despair. "When I decided to picket that last time, I thought of how angry I've been with you. My defiance was against you too. It gave me further strength of purpose."

Teddy rocked backward in his chair. "Of course. You, in all your juvenile tendencies, had to find a way to strike back at me." He met her irate glare. "Congratulations, Zee. You succeeded."

"You have what you want. Why can't I work toward what I want?" Zylphia demanded, grimacing and holding a hand to her throat. She raised the cup of water and took a long sip. "I'm only thankful I'm recovering enough to testify next month."

Teddy rose, and he now gripped the back of the chair. He seemed to contemplate if he would lift it and fling it against the wall. After a long moment, his grip lessened. "Do you have any idea what it did to me to learn you had been jailed? That it took three men to hold you down to force-feed you? To then be denied entrance to your sickroom?"

Zylphia glared at him. "Yes, be offended because you, as a man, were denied something." She flushed as her husband flinched.

Teddy watched her with disappointment and disillusionment. "Do you truly believe that, if I gave up my citizenship as an Englishman, your life would improve? I know you wouldn't cease with these actions, putting yourself in harm's way." He shook his head. "I know you are angry with me. You're angry with the world because you believe a wrong has been done against you against your will. And it has. But that anger won't change anything, Zee. Congress won't care next week when you convince them of the fallacy of their law. The Supreme Court didn't care in 1915. It won't turn you back into an American. It won't allow you to vote when women do obtain the right to vote here. Because you will still be seen as an alien."

"Yes, because I'm a woman, and I have no voice, and I have no rights! Why can't you see that? You, a man, can do whatever you damn well please. You can attack me on the street for speaking my truth, and I'm the one who is sent to jail. You can marry whomever you want, with no threat of losing your citizenship. Why can't you see that it's unjust? That there's nothing wrong with wanting more?" Tears now streamed down her face as she watched her husband with open heartbreak.

Teddy sank on the settee next to her but did not touch her. "I am not that man you speak of. Please tell me you know that." He watched her with devastated eyes. "Zee, I love you. The one truth in my life is that I love you." He waited a moment for her to say something, watching as her tears fell.

"I'm sorry you feel such anger inside you, my darling. I know you do. I hate that I've caused you pain. That you feel as though I've ... betrayed you." He took a long breath. "I realize your work here is important to you. I ... I shouldn't have come. I see that now. You don't need me here." He watched her with fading hope for a contradictory sign, but none came.

She watched him with wide, luminous blue eyes but remained mute.

He rose and moved toward the bedroom. "I'll leave you, Zee, to recover and regroup with your colleagues. Forgive me for intruding and thinking you'd want me here."

~

Parthena woke in a warm bed, her body cushioned on a comfortable mattress with a soft pillow underneath her head. She squinted as she deciphered where she was. The walls painted a soft yellow, the white crown molding and the blue curtains were foreign to her. She closed her eyes as she heard a door close and feigned sleep.

Soft footsteps approached the bed, and she forced herself to remain relaxed as though she slumbered. A deep sigh came, and then the mattress dipped beside her on the large bed. Morgan's scent wafted over her, and she fought tears at his nearness.

"Oh, Hennie," he whispered. He kissed her softly on her forehead before settling beside her.

After a few moments, Parthena opened her eyes and turned her head toward him. He lay on his back with his hands linked over his stomach and his feet crossed at his ankles. Her eyes widened as a tear leaked out before his hand chased it away.

"Don't cry," she croaked. If she'd had the voice, she would have squealed as Morgan reared up and loomed over her.

"Hennie!" He grasped her by her shoulders for a moment before releasing her when she winced at his touch. "Forgive me. I shouldn't have touched you."

"No, it's fine. I'm just a bit bruised. And sore," she breathed. "Is there any ice?" At his confused stare, she continued to speak softly. "Anything cold to soothe my throat?"

He traced a hand over one of her eyebrows before leaping from the bed and racing to the door to bark an order outside. Soon he entered with a bucket full of ice. He set it down on the table beside the bed and then eased her to a sitting position. He slipped a piece into her mouth, and the worry lines bracketing his eyes eased when she groaned in relief.

"Thank you," she whispered. He continued to place chips in her mouth until she motioned for him to stop. He rose, and she reached out a hand for him to rejoin her on the bed. He eyed her warily but climbed atop the bedding and rested beside her. He laid on his side, his head on one of his hands.

"How are you?" he asked. He stiffened and then curled an arm around her as she snuggled into his embrace. He pulled her close, keeping his arms around her loose so as not to provoke any pain. As he held her, the tension left his body as she relaxed into him.

"Why are you here?" she asked against his chest.

"When I learned you'd been arrested and sent to jail, I immediately traveled here," he said as one of his hands rose to play with her long hair.

"Why? I ran away." She pushed her head harder against his chest. "I don't ..."

He eased her away from him, sadness in his gaze at her grimace with the movement. "You don't ..." he coaxed. He closed his eyes for a moment in frustration. "Forgive me. I shouldn't expect you to talk when your throat hurts."

She raised trembling hands to his face and eventually covered his mouth. "No. Stop talking." A tremulous smile flitted across her lips. She grunted as she pushed herself away so that she could see him better. She gripped his arm, and her legs moved to keep contact with him. "I ran away, and I promised I never would."

"No, you didn't, Parthena," he rasped.

"Maybe not out loud to you. But I made that promise to myself." She stroked a hand over his cheek before dropping her hand. "I'm sorry. I'm so tired."

"We don't need to speak now. It's enough for me that you are in my arms." He eased her forward again. "Let me hold you."

"Forgive me," she whispered in a groggy voice. "Forgive me for giving into my fears." She said no more as she fell asleep in his arms.

~

Parthena sat curled on a chaise longue in the sitting room of the suite she shared with Morgan. She thought about the previous two days and nights, where he had rarely been far from her. He'd read to her, told her stories about his youth and held her as she slept. Each morning she awoke more rested, with her head on his shoulder. She placed a hand against her stomach, fighting panic and another foreign sensation she refused to name.

"Come in," she called out at the knock on the parlor door. "Zee! Rowena!" she exclaimed. She remained seated when her friends entered and waved at her to remain on the chaise. Her astute gaze roamed over Zylphia, and she frowned. "It's been one week, yet you look terrible."

Rowena's inquisitive gaze roved between her two friends, her gaze sharpening to see the difference in recovery between Zylphia and Parthena. Whereas Parthena appeared close to prime health again, Zylphia seemed to be near collapse. "What more happened to you, Zee, to prevent you from recovering like Parthena?"

"I'm fine," Zylphia said in a low voice. She shared a look with Parthena. "I'm still not able to speak at my full volume."

"I imagine Teddy is appreciative of that," Parthena teased. Her smile froze when Zylphia stiffened.

"My husband has returned to Boston." She met her friends' shocked gazes. "He left the day before yesterday."

Rowena gasped at the news.

Parthena gripped Zylphia's hand. "Why? He had to have been as worried as Morgan. They helped fund the lawyer who freed us."

Zylphia shook her head, her gaze focused on the windows. "We fought, like we always do. I barely gave him a chance to speak before inciting his anger." She laid her head back against her chair.

Parthena watched her friend closely. "Why didn't you seek his comfort? I can't imagine not wanting my husband's comfort." She blushed at Zylphia's startled gaze and Rowena's intrigued glance.

Zylphia closed her eyes. Tears leaked out, and she swiped at her cheeks. "I don't even know what he would have done if I hadn't angered him. If I hadn't agreed with the women from Cameron House."

"Teddy was beside himself," Rowena said, "from the moment he arrived in DC. He worked tirelessly to find a way to ensure your freedom." Rowena shook her head incredulously at Zylphia. "Do you know how tormented he was upon hearing about your treatment at the workhouse? About your force-feedings? I've never seen a man so miserable. Why would you continue to argue with him? It makes no sense."

"How could you side with them when they kept you separated

from your husband?" Parthena asked, not allowing Zylphia to answer Rowena. "Morgan advised me they kept Teddy away for an entire day."

Zylphia shrugged. "I'm sure they had their reasons. They were caring for me and only wanted what was best for me."

"Zylphia, you're not speaking sense," Rowena said. "That's Teddy's role. No matter how much you've argued, he loves you. He wanted to care for you. He wanted to hold you as you recovered. You denied him that." Rowena shook her head in confusion at her friend. "I know I'm not married, but I've always envisioned that was part of the reason for marrying—to depend on the other in times of grief or trial. I thought you would have realized what was truly important during your time at O."

Rowena and Parthena watched as Zylphia seemed to shrink into herself. Rather than fight back and justify her actions, she curled into herself.

"If you'd bothered to listen to him," Rowena said, "to seek out his aid rather than to incite his anger, you would have realized he had every intention of bowing to your wishes." Rowena's cheeks reddened from her irritation.

Rowena's proclamation roused Zylphia. "That's patently false, and you know it."

Rowena met Zylphia's glare and shook her head. "No. He regretted the constant arguing, the distance between the two of you and had decided that he loved you more than his British citizenship."

Zylphia paled as she stared dumbly at Rowena. "When?" she croaked out. "When did he decide that?"

Rowena shook her head. "I can't tell you exactly when he made that decision, but he told me of it after he heard of your mistreatment in the workhouse and jail. He tormented himself with the belief that he could have prevented your abuse there had he only acted sooner."

Zylphia sighed. "He should know me better to realize nothing would have kept me away from that picket line. Being considered a citizen again would only have fueled my desire." She shared a chagrined look with her friends. "I never thought he'd change his mind."

Parthena took a sip of cold water, sighing as it soothed her throat. "You missed your anniversary with him. You picked a fight with him nearly the moment you woke up after your hunger strike. I don't understand why you act as you do, Zee." When Zylphia shrugged, Parthena sighed. "I know you plan on remaining here in Washington. On testifying next month in front of the House, and I applaud you for your commitment, Zee."

Zylphia frowned as she watched her friend. "Will you remain to support me?"

Parthena shook her head. "No. I must return home. It's been nearly three months since I left, and I want time with Morgan. I want to prepare for Christmas and to be at home." She leaned forward and gripped Zylphia's hand. "I wish you luck, Zee. But, more than that, I hope you reconcile with Teddy and that you're happy again."

Rowena nodded her agreement as Zylphia took a sip of tea, her gaze distant.

CHAPTER 19

*P*arthena entered the home she shared with Morgan on Commonwealth Avenue, her gaze wide and steps slow as she entered the opulent front hall. She glanced at the grandeur of the large staircase at the end of the hall, its black walnut wood shining under the chandelier's light. Her gaze roved over the gray marble floor covered in a plush red velvet carpet, the elaborately carved hallstand and the elegant chairs placed near the door. She paused, handing her coat to the butler.

"Are you all right?" Morgan asked when he saw her wide-eyed stare. "Nothing has changed since you departed."

She shook her head. "Everything has changed," she whispered. She followed him as he grasped her hand and walked into her front parlor. He closed the door behind them and then pulled her into his arms as she swayed on her feet.

"Are you overtired? Do you need to rest after the long train journey?" he whispered into her ear as he held her.

"I am tired. I should rest." Rather than ease away from him, she snuggled closer into his embrace.

He ran a hand up and down her back. "Why has everything changed? The house has not been altered."

"I'm different," Parthena whispered. "I see everything in a new way." She scrubbed her cheek against the fine wool of his jacket. "After prison, this is a palace."

"It's not a palace. It's our home." He kissed the side of her neck. "I hate what you suffered, Hennie. I don't want you to suffer like that again."

"I never thanked you for traveling to DC to fight for me." She kept her gaze downcast when he pushed her back and stroked a hand over her warm cheeks, surely reddened by her embarrassment.

"You're my wife, Hennie. When you are threatened, I will do anything I can to ensure you are safe." He kissed her forehead. "I can see you are exhausted. Why don't you rest? If you are awake later, I'll have them bring up a tray to you."

She kissed his cheek, murmured, "Thank you," and left.

~

Later that evening, after a nap and a small meal, Parthena stood at her bedroom window and thought about her marriage with Morgan. She remembered those first few weeks when they had shared a bed. The pleasure his touch had wrought, even if undesired because he was not Lucas. She sat on the window seat and brushed out her hair, lost in her memories.

Of him watching her with intensity in Newport after he had encouraged her to play the piano. Of his impassioned admission he had wanted her for years. Of his rescue of her sister Genevieve. Of Rowena's story of his arrival in Washington. She rested her head against the window's cool glass and fought tears. Her shoulders stooped at the realization she had hurt him, wittingly and unwittingly, throughout the two and a half years of their marriage. She shuddered as she feared it was a daily harm.

"Oh, Morgan, why do you still want me?" she whispered. She rubbed at her head. "Why have I denied the truth all this time?" She quivered at the thought of opening herself to him. She closed her eyes as she fought an intrinsic fear.

Parthena rose, tossing the silver-backed hairbrush onto the soft window seat cushion and marched into her adjoining closet. She pushed through stacks of clothes until she found what she desired. Her hands shook as she took it off the hanger and returned to her room before she lost her nerve.

～

M organ paced inside his bedroom, hoping that he'd eventually be fatigued enough to fall into a fitful slumber. He nearly snarled at the soft knock on his door. "What?" When there was no response, he marched to the door and wrenched it open. "Parthena?" he whispered, his gaze studying her from head to foot. His fingers gripping the door turned white, and he fought his instinctual inclination to slam the door shut. Or drag her inside. "What are you doing here?"

She brushed past him, her emerald silk dressing gown brushing against his arm as she moved. "I needed to speak with you. And, no, I couldn't wait until morning." She raised an eyebrow as though anticipating his next question.

"Hennie, this isn't a good idea." He shut the door behind her. His hungry gaze roved over her clingy wrap, and his hands clenched. "You need rest, and you are still not fully recovered from your time in the workhouse."

Her triumphant smile eloquently contradicted him. "I think it's a very good idea. And about time." She approached him, swaying her hips with each step. Her smile broadened as he suppressed a shudder. "And I'm fully recovered."

"I want you to leave now," he said in a deep, almost angry voice.

She froze as she studied his face to understand all he did not say. "No. I'm not leaving. I'm finally here." Her smile faded when he failed to reach for her or share in her smile.

"Fine. You won't leave." He pushed past her to move into the room. He sat on a hard chair and glowered at her. "What's come over you? Why have you decided to invade my room?"

259

She flushed and moved to the matching chair by him. After she sat, blushing as the gown slipped open and flashed a long expanse of leg, she covered herself and cleared her throat. "Morgan, I'm tired of our marriage—"

"Well, this is a damned funny way of showing it," he snapped.

"No! I'm tired of how our marriage has been," she said. "I want more from our marriage."

He froze in his movement to rise and settled into his chair again. "Why? Why now?"

She broke away from his penetrating gaze. "You won't like what I have to say. At least not all of it."

He sighed. "Of course I won't. You're Parthena. We never agree on anything."

Her shoulders arched back, and she glared at him. "That's not true! We agreed when you helped Viv." She sputtered as she sought to remember another time when they had agreed. He raised an eyebrow at her, and she glared at him.

"I know you misunderstood me when I was upset about Viv having a baby. I think you believe I wished to have Lucas's baby." She met Morgan's gaze and saw the flash of pain in his gaze that he tried, and failed, to conceal. "That's not why I was upset," she whispered. "I suddenly realized I was a coward, and I was desperately sad."

She raised a hand over his mouth and shook her head. "No, don't say anything. I'm not desperately sad because I'm with you, Morgan. I'm sad because I've done this to myself. I've done this to us. I've spurned you, your touch. Your ..." She broke off.

She jolted when Morgan traced her cheek, smudging away tears she had not realized were falling. "My love," he whispered around her fingers.

Her gaze met his, fearful yet hopeful. She leaned into his touch.

"I need you to forgive me," he whispered. "I say hurtful, hateful things when I am afraid. Like that evening before you ran away to Washington in September. I was terrified you didn't really want me but desired Lucas. I know of nothing more to do to earn your esteem, Hennie."

Tears fell unchecked down her cheeks at his broken admission. "You don't dare to dream for yourself, do you?" She stuttered out a breath. "I want to know your touch again, Morgan. To feel the pleasure you can give me. I hope to give you pleasure in return." She flushed at his appreciative stare at her robe.

"Why come dressed like this to my room?"

"Zee told me, when we first married, that I should shock you and seduce you. That maybe that would bring us marital harmony. I remembered her words tonight." She kissed his palm as he cupped her cheek.

"Do you truly want this?" He studied her with a fierce intensity, his muscles bunched tight as though barely keeping control of his movements.

"Yes. I want more than a considerate marriage with you, Morgan." At his smirk she grinned. "Or whatever you'd call it. I want to be honest with you and for you to feel you can be honest with me. I want to trust you." She smiled self-deprecatingly. "I want more than playing heartbroken piano songs that I hope induce some sort of passion in you. I want—"

She gasped as he gripped her by the nape of her neck and kissed her passionately, pulling her off her chair onto his lap. She giggled as she almost fell to the floor, but then she realized her flimsy gown made it easy for her to straddle his legs, and she moved into that position. She arched into him as he groaned.

"Tell me you want this. That you want my touch. After over two years without you, I fear I won't have any patience once I finally touch you." He paused as he held his lips over her bared collarbone.

She threaded her fingers into his hair. "For God's sake, Morgan, I want you. I want this. You're my husband. Make me feel like your wife."

"Gladly," he growled as he rose, carrying her to his bed.

～

Morgan traced a hand over Parthena's bared shoulder, sighing with relief when she moved into his touch rather than away. He slung his arm around her belly, anchoring her to him. "How do you feel?" he asked.

"Like a well-loved wife," she murmured.

He chuckled. "Well, you are that," he whispered as he kissed the back of her head. "Hennie, will you be honest with me?"

"I'll try." She arched into him and pulled his hand to her mouth for a kiss before releasing it.

"Why were you so upset that your sister was to have a child?" The instinctive tensing of his muscles relaxed when she didn't pull away from him physically or emotionally.

"I was jealous," she said in a low voice.

He leaned up on an elbow and eased her to her back so he could see her expression. "Explain that for me so that *I* don't become jealous." He attempted a teasing note in his voice, but knew he'd partly failed when she raised a hand to trace the worry lines around his eyes.

"I'd always dreamed of having children. Of being a mother. I was jealous my younger sister would be a mother before me." She stared into his eyes. "I realized tonight that no one but myself was holding me back from my dreams."

Rather than alleviating his tension, he stiffened and frowned. "Are you saying you only wanted my company tonight because you hoped to become pregnant?"

Her eyes widened with shock. "Of course not! I thought it was rather evident I wanted you for ..." Her voice cracked as she fought embarrassment. When he watched her steadily, she took a deep breath and fought her discomfort. "I wanted to feel pleasure. Pleasure from *your* touch. No one else's. If I became pregnant due to our enjoyment of each other, then I would consider us fortunate."

He watched her with a fierce intensity. "Did you really write those morose songs to induce me to comfort you?"

She flushed before giggling. "Yes. I had hoped it would provoke some sort of response in you. All you did was clap and comment that I had a rare talent for melancholy." She rolled her eyes as he laughed at her disgruntled glare.

"You know I'm not artistic," he said as he kissed her shoulder. "Why you'd believe I'd discern your true motive is beyond me."

Parthena sighed and arched into his touch. "You're more artistic than you believe." She opened her eyes when his soft caresses stopped and met his startled gaze. "You are capable of appreciating what artists create, which is a wondrous gift. You never complain when I spend hours at the piano."

An embarrassed flush lit his cheeks. "Of course not." He met her curious stare. "It makes you happy."

"What makes you happy?" Parthena asked as she leaned up and kissed him gently on the lips. "What is it that you want?"

He ran his gaze over her, laying in rumpled, sated contentment in his bed. "All this time, all I've ever wanted was you. Your touch. Your care," Morgan whispered as he kissed her on her neck, then her breastbone. "Now you're finally here."

~

The following morning Parthena reached for Morgan only to find his side of the bed empty and cold. She frowned even as she rolled to his side of the bed before sighing with pleasure. His scent was strong against the pillow, and she breathed it in appreciatively. As she remained between wakefulness and sleep, she relived the previous night. Gentle caresses. Soothing murmurs. Passionate pleasure. She smiled with contentment as she curled on her side.

"I love seeing you smile," Morgan whispered as the bed dipped with his weight. He met her sleepy gaze as she opened one eye. "Why are you on my side of the bed?" He traced a finger through her hair to her shoulder.

"I missed you," she whispered, flushing at the flash of delight in his eyes. "Your scent is strongest here." She ran a finger over his tie. "Why are you already up and dressed?"

He chuckled. "It's nearly noon. I had a meeting I couldn't cancel." He raised her hand and kissed it.

"Come back to bed, Morgan," she whispered before her cheeks turned beet red. Although he could see her embarrassment, she met his startled gaze. "This is like our honeymoon. I want time with you."

"Parthena ..." He sighed. He leaned over and buried his face in her hair. "I have work."

She turned so that she faced him, twisted at her waist. "You always have work. It will always be there. Please, Morgan." She brushed hair off his forehead. "Dare to be spontaneous." Her eyes challenged him, and he stiffened at her words. She ran a finger over his eyebrow as she gave him an encouraging nod.

He pushed himself up, and her groan of disappointment turned into an approving smile as he worked to free himself of his clothes. She pushed herself up to kneel on the bed, the sheets falling around her, uninhibited by her nakedness in front of him. She tugged at his tie and eased his shirt off. He gave her a gentle nudge back into bed as he kicked off his shoes and shucked his pants.

"Come here, Hennie," he murmured, tugging her to him. "God, you feel good." He ran a hand over her shoulders and back. "Like the finest satin and silk." He kissed her collarbone and met her smile. "I was a fool not to woo you sooner."

She cupped his cheek. "Let's not play that game of who was more foolish," she whispered as she leaned forward and kissed him. "Let's be thankful we're no longer so misguided."

He groaned his agreement as he deepened the kiss, pulling her closer. "Never leave me, Hennie. I wouldn't survive."

She gave him a nipping kiss on his chin and then ear before meeting his gaze. "I promise. This is where I want to be."

She shrieked as she toppled to her back and threw her arms around his shoulders, lost to their passion.

CHAPTER 20

Zylphia recalled the first time she had walked through the halls of congress. The excitement she felt at meeting Congresswoman Rankin. The pride filling her as she thought of her Montana family for having elected a woman to congress. Now she walked with purpose as she marched down the halls of congress, ignoring the questions from reporters who remained curious about her time spent in the Occoquan workhouse and jail. She wore a new suit in a deep violet, the cut of the dress and the fine corset underneath hiding the extent of her recent weight loss. Her hair was pulled back in a tidy chignon, with a yellow rose pin holding it in place. When she approached the hearing room for the Rankin Bill, she took a deep breath as she met another woman's gaze, Kate Devereaux Blake, and nodded as they entered the room together.

Representatives sat in comfortable green leather-backed chairs in a semicircle facing an unoccupied desk. Their aides and minions mingled behind them, while the gallery above was filled with reporters and curious onlookers. This was the second half of the day of questioning, and Zylphia hid her nerves as she fought to forget the women's tales from the morning session.

She sat, setting her short prepared speech in front of her. She smoothed a hand over her violet skirt and sat with perfect posture as she awaited recognition from the representatives. After listening to them recap the morning's session, they turned to her. She smiled at Representative Raker, known to be a friend of the suffrage cause.

"I thank you for the honor of speaking with you today. I am Zylphia McLeod Goff. I was born in Boston, educated at public schools before I attended university. I have worked to alleviate the suffering of orphan children in Boston. I am also a painter and a firm believer in the women's suffrage movement."

She paused and cleared her throat. "I married my husband in November 1915, and, in doing so, I lost my citizenship. Although I consider myself to be a United States citizen, the laws of my country no longer consider me an American citizen merely because my husband is from the United Kingdom. He is proud of his citizenship, having fought and been wounded in the war raging in Europe."

She took a deep breath and looked from representative to representative. Some listened intently; others took notes, while the rest conferred with their staffers and paid little attention to what she said. "I am a loyal member of this country and wish to call myself a citizen of my home country. The 1907 Expatriation Act has denied me a basic right, and I am asking you to consider the Rankin Bill so as to right a wrong committed against many American women." She clamped her jaw shut as one representative scoffed at her and rolled his eyes.

"I can hardly credit one with your wealth and standing as having suffered a great blow," one representative said with an arched eyebrow as he peered at her over his half glasses.

"This isn't about my wealth or standing," Zylphia said. "This is about my rights as a citizen of the United States. Rights unjustly taken away from me."

"I fail to see why we as a body should be concerned about a disloyal woman," another piped up. "If you chose to marry a man from outside this country, a man who refuses to become a United States citizen, then you should forego citizenship in this fine land."

"Then so should the men who marry alien women!" Zylphia snapped. "Why should they have citizenship conferred on them when

266

mine is stripped from me? How can you determine that she will be loyal to this country merely because she married a citizen?"

John Raker, a man Zylphia had looked to as an ally, watched her with mocking condescension. "My dear, under the tutelage of her kind American husband, she has become an American patriot at heart." He pointed at a sputtering Zylphia. "Your actions, by marrying a foreigner, were a clear, open, broad-daylight voluntary surrender of citizenship. I feel no sympathy for you."

"Hear, hear!" another member shouted. "Let this be a lesson that good American girls marry good American boys!"

Zylphia sat there in mute rage as they berated her and her fellow speakers for daring to question the legality and morality of the law. When the session paused for a break, Zylphia rose, collecting her papers in front of her. She emerged into the hallway, her confident step and posture reemerging as newspapermen swarmed. She pushed past them and walked down the long hallway. When one asked what she had hoped to accomplish as a noncitizen imprisoned in the United States, she bit back a response to remain stoically quiet.

Once outside the Capitol building, she took a deep breath. Her anger gave her strength, but she knew she had not recovered to the extent she could walk to Cameron House. She hired a cab and escaped any further questioning from persistent reporters.

Upon her return to Cameron House, she slammed her hat to her desk and kicked the chair before she sat down.

Rowena raised an eyebrow as she watched her friend. "I don't need to ask how it went."

"They were insolent and superior in their beliefs that women should be punished for daring to marry anyone other than an American citizen. As though we are recalcitrant children and they feel it their duty to teach us a lesson." She growled as she bowed her head forward and massaged her scalp with her fingers. Her neat chignon was ruined, and the yellow rose pin fell to the floor.

"You knew it unlikely they'd see how they had mistreated the women of this country," Rowena said. "The sad fact is that many women agree with them too." She watched Zylphia with concern.

"What will you do now?" Rowena asked. She bent forward and picked up the hairpin, setting it on Zylphia's desk.

"What is there for me to do?" Zylphia asked. When Rowena remained quiet, Zylphia laid her head on her arms on her desk. "I'm tired, Ro. So tired. I want to go home."

"Then go home. You haven't been yourself since you were released from jail." Her worried gaze roved over her friend who seemed nearly asleep on the desk. "You've never fully recovered from your time there, and I hope being with Teddy will help reinvigorate you."

Zylphia sighed. "If what you say is true, that Teddy is considering changing his opinion on his status …" Zylphia sighed and cleared her throat to remain awake. "Although at this point, I'm not sure I care after that House hearing. Rude buffoon men, lording over their so-called superiority."

"Go home, Zee. Make your peace with Teddy. Rest. Recover. See your parents." Rowena's voice acted as a sleeping tonic. "You've earned a break after nearly a year here."

"Tomorrow," Zylphia whispered. "Tomorrow I return home."

～

Teddy sat at his desk, papers spread out in organized piles. A small fire in the grate warmed the room, while the weak December rays did little to brighten his office. A lamp on the corner of his desk provided illumination that would allow him to work long into the night. He waved to a small side table when the door opened, indicating the maid could leave his afternoon tea there. "I'll pour it myself when I want a cup."

"I don't have tea." Zylphia wavered as though buffeted by a windstorm, moving forward and back.

Teddy threw his pencil on the stack of papers in front of him, watching his wife's unconscious movements. "Either enter or leave, Zee." She flinched at his flat words.

She shut the door behind her and leaned against it. The subtle shaking in her limbs lessened as she seemed to gather strength the longer she rested against the door. She wore a simple navy dress with a pin on her lapel.

"Sit before you fall down. You've barely had time to recover." He waved to a chair across from him, and she collapsed onto it. He refused to rise and join her on the nearby settee.

She stared over his shoulder for a moment before meeting her husband's gaze with one of confusion. "Where did my painting go?" She glanced again at the faded square on the wall behind him where the cherry blossom painting had hung, ever since moving into this house upon their return from their honeymoon two years ago. The painting had often shone as though under a spotlight as the afternoon sun entered his office.

He watched her coolly. "The frame was damaged. It's out for repair." He watched as she shivered at his words. "Why did you come here, Zee?"

Her cheeks flushed, and she glared at him. "Because this is my home. Where else was I to go?"

Teddy huffed out a laugh and shook his head. "After all these months, you'd have me believe you consider this your home? When you've preferred DC to here? To any amount of time you could have spent with me?" When she remained silent, he said, "I read about your testimony in front of the House Committee." He watched as she flushed. His angry demeanor softened for a moment. "I'm sorry they tabled the resolution."

Her blush intensified, and she leaned forward, her index finger tapping a pile of papers. "As it will not affect your life, I don't know why you're sympathetic." She glared at him as his neck mottled with anger. "You continue as you always have and hope I'll simply grow tired of struggling for what I want."

"Do you ever consider that others' considerations, dreams or desires are as valid as yours?" Teddy asked, his low voice laced with rage. "Do you ever consider anyone other than yourself when you think about how you've been wronged?"

"You knew who I was before we married. You knew how important this cause is to me. Don't act a martyr now because I've dedicated so much of my time to it."

He clamped his jaw shut to the point it twitched a few times. After glaring at each other, he said, "What does that pin mean?" He nodded to her lapel. "I've never known you to wear pins before." The pin was a silver latticelike pattern that resembled a jail door.

"Miss Paul gave them to us a few days ago. She had one made for each woman who was jailed for picketing." She stroked a finger over it as though in pride or remembrance. She raised her head and met his gaze with one of defiance.

Teddy leaned back in his chair, the creaking sound rending the air as they stared once more at each other. "I believed I loved you enough to accept being second best most of the time." His silver eyes were colder than steel on a January day in Pittsburgh. "I've since learned I was mistaken."

Her indignant blush faded at his words. "What do you mean, Teddy?"

He rose and ran a hand through his sable hair. "Do you want to know what happened to your painting?" he asked, waving in the direction of the barren wall. At her nod, he paced behind his desk. Rather than relaxing him, he became more agitated with each step. "I rushed to Washington when I learned you were in jail. In the workhouse. Whatever they wanted to call it, the end result was the same to me. You, my Zylphia, were locked up, and I couldn't reach you."

He turned to face her, his eyes filled with torment, rage and regret. "Do you know what that does to a person? To a man? To be completely impotent to aid the one person you love most in this world?" His jaw clenched as tears tracked down her cheeks.

He pushed his chair into the seating well of the desk and leaned against the back of it with his forearms atop the chair. "Do you know what it's like to be advised by various women in Cameron House that I'd have to wait to see you upon your release? That I was looked at with suspicion simply because I was a man?" He cleared his throat as his eyes shone as though bright with tears.

"They were cautious," Zylphia protested. "They always are when women return from jail or a workhouse. Too many times, reporters and the like try to finagle their way into the house." Her explanation trailed away when she realized it did little to soothe Teddy.

"Then, even when I had you safely in our hotel room in Washington, you wanted nothing to do with me. You picked fights until I finally left, tired of arguing with you." He watched her guilty blush and clenched his hands. "When all I wanted was to care for you."

"I'm sorry, Teddy," Zylphia whispered.

He waved away her apology. "After I vacated our hotel room in Washington, I went to a pub. I have no acquaintances there, so imagine my surprise when a man called out a greeting to me." He speared her with an irate look. "One of the doctors who'd cared for you. He somehow knew who I was. He was most solicitous and concerned about your health."

Zylphia stilled as she watched her prowling husband. "How kind of him."

Teddy's half-smile was one of self-mockery and regret. "Imagine my surprise to learn you'd betrayed me." His ice-cold voice sent a shiver through her.

"No!" Zylphia cried out, her voice thickened by tears.

"How could you, Zee?" His gaze raked over her with contempt. "How could you put yourself in a position where you could be sent to jail when you knew you were pregnant with our child?"

"I didn't—"

"You promised." He leaned forward. His cold gray eyes held a hot fury as he studied his wife. "You promised me, if you ever found yourself with child, you'd cease your reckless behavior. For your sake as well as our baby's." He exhaled a stuttering sigh. "Tell me you didn't know you were expecting our child when you volunteered to picket." He met her defeated gaze. "Tell me that, dammit."

She shook her head. "I can't," she whispered as her voice broke. "I suspected I was but hoped I was wrong." She swiped at the tears on her cheeks. "I had to participate. I don't expect you to understand."

"You think that's a good-enough explanation?" he roared. "That you don't expect me to understand? That that will somehow rid me of my anger and induce me to … to …" He broke off as he panted for breath.

Teddy took a step backward until he was braced against the wall behind his desk. "Do you want to know what happened to your painting? I turned it into kindling in a fit of rage when I returned from DC." He met her shocked gaze at the destruction of a cherished gift from before they were married.

"You barred me from your room at Cameron House because you were miscarrying, and you never wanted me to know you'd lost our … a child. You denied me the opportunity to comfort you."

She gave a guilty nod as she glanced away. After a minute, she raised her gaze and met his irate one. Moments of silence stretched between them.

"Leave, Zee. And don't come back. Not until I ask for you. If you stay, I will say things to you that can never be unsaid." He clamped his jaw shut as he saw her pale at the unspoken truth behind his words.

"Teddy, please," she said as she fought tears.

"Get out, Zee. I don't want to see you. I don't want to hear your voice. I don't want anything to do with you. Not until this rage has passed."

He watched as she rose and stumbled once before she regained her balance and fled the room without a backward glance. When he heard the front door slam a few minutes later, he moved to the sideboard and poured himself a tumbler of whiskey. After one sip, he spun and flung it at the fireplace. He crumpled to the floor, as shattered as the crystal, with as little hope of being rendered whole again.

CHAPTER 21

*Z*ylphia sat on the chaise longue in Sophie's guest bedroom, her gaze distant as she faced the rear garden. Her black hair was in disarray as it tumbled down her shoulders and back, and she'd failed to dress for the day. A nearby church tower tolled the hour of three o'clock in the afternoon, and she sighed as she rolled to her side and stared at the furniture in the room. A loud knock interrupted her silent musings, but she refrained from speaking. When the door burst open to an irritated Sophronia, marching forward in indignant glory, Zylphia closed her eyes and curled into herself.

"Enough!" Sophie barked as she *thunk*ed her cane onto the plush carpet. She frowned as the loud noise failed to rouse a response from Zylphia. She pointed for a maid to place a chair in front of the chaise longue and then waved her away. After waiting to hear the door close behind the maid, Sophie focused on Zylphia. "This is not who you are, my girl. What happened to your determination? Your dedication? Your fire?"

She ran a shaking hand over Zylphia's head and cheek, but Zylphia refused to speak. "If you don't speak with me and explain why you came here seeking refuge rather than with your parents, I will seek out your mother." The implied promise in her words had Zylphia's gaze focusing and meeting Sophie's.

"You wouldn't," Zylphia whispered.

"Of course I would. I've never understood why you came to me rather than returning to your parents' home. They'd love and care for you during this difficult time. I imagine it would be a strain on your father as he has become quite close to your husband since your marriage. However, you can't doubt that their first loyalty is to you." She watched Zylphia with blatant curiosity and confusion as she seemed to shrink into herself on the chaise.

"Come. Sit up. Brush your hair. I've found when we perform the daily rituals of life, they can help us continue on when we believe we are incapable." She gave Zylphia a gentle tug but was unable to budge her.

"You don't understand," Zylphia whispered. "Your husband died. You knew he loved you when he died." Sophie nodded as Zylphia met her gaze with an inquisitive one. "My husband lives, and I know he despises me."

"Theodore Goff is no simpleton. He does not despise you for your dedication to the cause," Sophie barked.

Zylphia grasped Sophie's hand, its skin thinner and bones more fragile with each passing day. "I wish I had your faith. He knows what I did." Tears leaked out, unbidden. "I've been so angry with him. I thought I hated him. Why wouldn't he do what I wanted?" She rubbed her face into the small pillow on the chaise. "I realize how childish that was now."

Sophie's aquamarine eyes were clouded with worry as she watched Zylphia. "What happened in Washington? I visited Teddy soon after his return, and he had little inclination to talk about you and how you were."

"Ever since I met my father and have come to accept that he loves me, I've lived a charmed life. I know that Teddy and I were separated during the first part of the war, but that turned out well. We married. We were happy. In many ways I remained a spoiled child, even though I believed I'd matured. When Teddy refused to bend to my wishes about his citizenship, I wanted to punish him. Show him I was my own person and wouldn't bend to his will."

Sophie paled at Zee's words. "I can understand desiring to remain your own person, even though married. I hope you didn't do anything foolhardy."

"Oh, Sophie. I was determined to protest. To show that women deserve the right to vote. At any expense." Tears coursed down her cheeks.

"Teddy knew you believed in this cause when you married. He wouldn't be this angry simply because you protested and were sent to jail," Sophie said, her scratchy voice expressing her confusion.

Zylphia pushed herself up to a sitting position. Her cheeks were splotchy and her nose red. She accepted the handkerchief Sophie handed her and rubbed at her nose. "I was pregnant, Sophie. I should never have protested that last time. I knew that we'd be arrested, but I never thought it would be as bad as it was."

"Oh, God," Sophie breathed. "And your husband knows this?" At Zylphia's guilty nod, Sophie leaned back in her chair, dropping Zylphia's hand. "How could you, Zee?"

"I ... I never thought we'd be there so long. That there'd be a hunger strike. That that would be enough to ..." she whispered.

"Surely, once you told them about your pregnancy, their treatment toward you changed."

Zylphia shook her head. "I never told a soul." She held a hand to her belly and hung her head as tears poured out.

"Why in God's name did you participate in the hunger strike if you refused to tell the truth about your condition?" Sophronia shook her head in consternation.

"I led the women who picketed. I couldn't be seen eating. To break morale."

"Your pride cost you your child," Sophronia snapped, her eyes sparkling with anger. "And perhaps your marriage."

"Until I lost the baby when I arrived at Cameron House, I hadn't realized how much I wanted it." She swallowed her sobs and sniffled, looking toward Sophie who sat as though dumbstruck. "It's why they kept Teddy away from me for a few days after I arrived there."

"I pride myself on not being easily shocked. But this is … this is …" Sophronia shook her head as she looked at Zylphia. "You've done this to yourself, Zee. I thought you more astute than that."

Zylphia flinched at the disappointment in Sophie's gaze and voice. "I'm mad at myself too." She rubbed at her face. "I know I hurt Teddy. Far worse than he ever hurt me. I don't know how to make it up to him."

Sophie shook her head, her gaze distant. "For once I have no words of wisdom, Zee. You must discover your own way back to your husband. I pray that you are able to." She turned her head to focus on Zylphia. "However, I insist that you speak with your parents. If you wish to stay here, I have no objections. The one requirement for you to remain here is that you explain to your parents all that has transpired."

$\sim$

The following afternoon Delia sat with stiff formality in Sophronia's front sitting room with her hands clenched in her lap. She wore a rich burgundy gown that enhanced her aging beauty. Aidan stood, staring out the front windows, absently watching the pedestrians as they made their way through the Boston Common. "I told you there was a rift between Teddy and Zee," Delia muttered.

"I agreed with you. However, she's married now, Delia. She must find a solution to her problems. We must allow them that freedom, without our interference. They won't thank us for butting in when they must work through their growing pains on their own." He looked over his shoulder, one eyebrow arched as he watched his wife fidget on the settee.

The pale blue-gray of the wallpaper clashed with the aquamarine satin coverings on the furniture while the paintings on the wall were bold proclamations rather than soothing components to the room's decor.

"This is a remarkably ugly room," Delia said, earning a startled chuckle from her husband. When he sat next to her, she eased into his side.

"It is," Aidan said as he took her hand and kissed it. He looked to the door as it opened, his gaze friendly and inquisitive. He kept a firm grip on Delia's hand that prevented her from rising and rushing to their daughter as she entered, Sophie on her heels. When the door shut, and they were ensured privacy, Aidan's smile of encouragement seemed to bolster Zylphia. "Hello, Zee. We've been worried about you."

Her long black hair was tamed in a heavy braid that fell more than halfway down her back. The simple navy dress she wore enhanced the deep blue of her eyes and the paleness of her skin. She nodded to her parents and sat on one of the chairs opposite them. "I'm sorry if I've worried you."

Delia frowned. "Of course we've been worried. Rumors about your fight with Teddy and your flight from your home have spread like the plague through Boston. Why didn't you come to us?" Delia bit her lip at any further recriminations as Aidan murmured, "Hush," and squeezed her hand.

"I came to Sophie's because I knew she'd take me in, and I didn't want to cause problems between you and Teddy," Zylphia said, her gaze lowered.

Aidan released his wife's hand and leaned forward with his elbows resting on his knees. "Zee, look at me." After a few moments, she finally raised her eyes and met her father's gaze. "I value Teddy's brilliance in business. I consider him a trusted friend. And, yes, I love him as a son. But you are my daughter. You are my first priority. It saddens me how you still don't accept that."

She bit her lip and gripped her hands together on her lap. "I didn't want you to feel ashamed of me and to have to hide that shame," she whispered.

Delia's concern evaporated, transforming into anger. "How dare you condemn your father and me before even speaking with us. Do you know what it's been like, knowing you've chosen sanctuary at

Sophie's house rather than turning to your own parents? Do you know what it's like to act as though your decision doesn't bother us when neighbors and acquaintances make cutting remarks?"

"Mother, I'm sorry," Zylphia whispered. She covered her face a minute, then took a long breath and looked from her father to her mother and back again. "Will you please listen without interrupting?" When they nodded, she haltingly told her story as she'd told Sophie the previous day. "I'm ashamed, angry, mournful, confused," she whispered as she finished speaking. She met her father's tormented gaze.

"Did you believe we'd condemn you for your actions?" he asked. His blue eyes shone with regret and impotent fury. At Zylphia's nod, he muttered a curse. "Dammit, Zee, we all make mistakes. Some we realize are inconsequential. Others are life-altering."

He rose and pulled an ottoman to perch on as he grasped his daughter's hands. "You are my daughter. You are impetuous, passionate and loving. You have a strong sense of righteous indignation that, at times, can get the better of you, as I fear it did this time." He raised one hand to swipe at her tears. "You've more than paid the price for your folly."

"I want … I want …" she stammered as the words clogged in her throat. She collapsed forward into her father's strong embrace. "I feared you'd tolerate me at best because I'm your daughter."

At her whispered admission, Aidan groaned and kissed her head. "Never, Zee. I love you. Your mother loves you. When you doubt our love …" He sighed into her hair. "I can't describe to you the pain."

After many moments Zylphia pushed away and met her mother's gaze. "I'm sorry, Mother," she whispered.

Delia shook her head as tears silently coursed down her cheeks. "I hate all that you suffered … without my—without our—support," she stuttered out. "You *must* know … we would have comforted you."

Sophie cleared her throat. "As we all know, fear makes us irrational. Besides, when we've lost the support of one we desperately love, it makes us doubt those we also believed loved us unconditionally."

Aidan's jaw clenched as he released Zylphia to settle into her chair as he remained on the ottoman. "I don't know what this will mean for my business venture with Teddy."

Zylphia's eyes widened with alarm. "Oh, please, Father, don't alter how you treat Teddy. This isn't his fault. It's all mine." She sniffled and fumbled in her pocket for a handkerchief.

"I would agree that a large portion of this debacle is due to your prideful nature. However, he has some responsibility in this matter," Sophie said when Delia remained silent.

Delia studied her daughter for a long moment, her hands clenching and unclenching in her lap before she rose and departed the room.

Zylphia's head turned, tracking her mother's movements.

"Give her time, Zee," Aidan murmured. "Give us all time." He kissed her on her forehead and followed his wife from the room.

~

The sound of a letter tapping on a table was the only indication the room was occupied. Aidan stilled as he glanced around the room, his gaze settling on his son-in-law sprawled in a comfortable chair in front of a roaring fire. He frowned at the letter in Teddy's hand and his contemplative expression.

"What has you so pensive?" Aidan asked, breaking the quiet spell of the late afternoon. Snow spit outside and anyone with sense was as Teddy, ensconced in front of a fire and escaping the elements.

Teddy glanced at his father-in-law a moment before waving him to a chair next to him in front of the fire. "I received a letter from an old friend today," Teddy said.

Aidan sighed as he settled into the worn leather and stretched his legs in front of him. "Dare I hope it was from an old school chum?" His gaze sharpened at Teddy's subtle shake of his head. "I hope it has little to do with that nurse."

Teddy's gaze remained unfocused as he stared into the fire. He shrugged before stilling the tapping of the letter. "I haven't had much energy to put into the Equalizer project."

Aidan sighed as he rested his head against the back of his chair. "I didn't come here to talk about some damn project, Teddy." He waited until Teddy nodded. "I saw Zee today." When Teddy froze, he continued. "She looked like hell."

A long silence stretched between them, with the fire crackling and a tree branch scratching against the office window with each gust of wind. As it became apparent that Teddy refused to speak, Aidan made an irritated noise in the back of his throat. "This is what comes of a battle of wills. No one wins, and everyone loses."

"Aidan, I respect you as my business partner. I admire you for the role you play in your family. I'm thankful for your acceptance as your son-in-law." Teddy's silver eyes shone with anguish and a pent-up rage. "But I refuse to be talked round by some nonsensical twaddle about battle of wills. You and I both know Zee was fully aware of what she was doing. Very little consideration was given to our child. Her only thought was for herself, with a sprinkling of malice at the thought of defying me."

Aidan sat upright, his upper body braced on his knees as he breathed heavily. His nostrils flared with agitation as he glared at his son-in-law. "I may concede that point. However, you must acknowledge that you pushed her to act in such a manner." His anger faded at the desolation in Teddy's gaze. "It always takes two, Teddy, in an argument."

"I thought I could never feel more agony than what I suffered in the war," he whispered. "These past days have shown me how wrong I was."

They sat in silence a few moments as they contemplated the fire. "What will you do?" Aidan asked.

Teddy sighed as he tapped the letter again. "I'm uncertain. She's been at Sophie's for a little over a week. I never thought she'd stay away so long."

Aidan stretched his long legs in front of him and crossed his hands over his belly. "She's not the same person as before she went into the workhouse, Teddy. Anyone who truly looks at her can see that." Aidan turned to look at Teddy. "Just as I can see you aren't the same."

Teddy nodded but refused to meet his father-in-law's gaze. "I appreciate your concern, but I'm fine."

"I'd hardly call you fine when you turned Zylphia's painting into kindling," Aidan murmured. "Have you told her that yet?" At Teddy's shrug, he grabbed the letter from Teddy to garner all his attention. "You're angry. Disappointed. Disillusioned."

He looked into his son-in-law's tormented eyes. "We all are. Her mother became so upset at today's visit that she stormed out of the room on her." Aidan's gaze eased when a flash of concern crossed Teddy's face before he could conceal it. "Nothing will change the past. All you must do is decide how you want the future to unfold."

∼

Parthena sat in her parlor and played a mournful piece of music. The solemn music eased her tension but failed to lighten her mood. Hearing the chuckle from the doorway, she stilled her hands and glared at the intruder.

"I had hoped we'd moved past the mournful stage," Morgan teased. When his joke failed to brighten his wife, he frowned. "Hennie, what's the matter?" He shut the door behind him and strode to her. He pulled over the ottoman and sat on it, facing her as she spun on the piano bench.

She shook her head. "I'm being ridiculous. I received a letter from Viv today. I won't see her until after she's had the baby. Maybe not for another year or two." She swiped at her cheek. "I can't imagine not seeing her for so long. That she'll become a mother without anyone in her family there to support her."

"Oh, my love," Morgan soothed as he pulled her into his arms. "When is the baby to arrive?"

"Sometime in late January or early February," Parthena whispered into his collar. "I'm sorry. I should have expected a separation like this when she left two years ago. I just never imagined … never imagined she wouldn't come back." Her voice broke on the word *back*. She relaxed as Morgan held her tighter.

"Do you want to go to her?" he asked, his voice tight.

She pushed away so as to meet his gaze. She searched his face for clues to how he felt but frowned with consternation at her inability to read him. "Please, don't freeze," she implored as she ran a hand down his cheek. When she felt him relax slightly, she nodded. "Yes, I'd like to go to her." She watched as he fought panic. She gripped his face between her hands and held on to him, refusing to allow him to rise. "I want you with me. I want my husband with me."

A startled, delighted smile lit his face. "Truly?" At her nod, he swooped down and kissed her. "I'd be thrilled to travel with my wife, my Hennie, to visit her sister." He sobered a moment. "My only request is that we stay in a hotel."

Parthena watched him and nodded. "Until we see the situation there, that is fine," she whispered. "My hope is that they will see us smitten, and I will see them devoted, and there will be harmony among us all again." She shared a deep smile with Morgan before sighing. "I fear I'm not ready for tonight's entertainments."

Morgan leaned forward and kissed her neck. "I have a different sort of entertainment in mind." He leaned away and arched an eyebrow, smiling when his wife flushed in agreement. "Come. Let's away to our bedroom before we embarrass the staff."

He rose, tugging Parthena to his side, unable to hide a contented sigh as they walked from the parlor arm in arm.

～

Aidan searched another room in the large house he owned on Marlborough Street, only to find it empty. He huffed out a frustrated breath and marched next door. When that room was also empty, he turned on his heel and returned to his library. He stopped short at the entrance to find Delia curled on the sofa. "When did you get here?"

"I've been here since I left Sophie's," she said in a deadened voice. She watched the dampened fire, her head resting on a pillow, a throw rug tucked around her.

He approached her and nudged her closer to the back of the sofa so he could sit beside her, hip to hip.

"Where have you been?" she asked.

"I went to Teddy's. And then I've searched the house for you. For some reason I never suspected you'd be here. My darling," he whispered, pausing at the desolation shown on her face. He stroked her cheek, opting for his quiet presence as solace rather than any empty platitudes.

"We could have been grandparents, Aidan," she whispered. "We could have held a baby in our arms together." She raised her anguished gaze to his. "Something I denied you all those years ago."

"Oh, my love," Aidan choked out, curling himself around her. "Do not be saddened on my behalf. Think of Zee and Teddy. They need our comfort, our care, right now."

She pushed him up and then stood, allowing him to lay on the sofa so she could rest along his front with her head on his shoulder. "Must you always think of everyone else and ignore your own sorrow?" She shuddered in his arms. "I feel terrible for Zee. And yet I'm so angry with her. I couldn't remain in that room a moment longer for fear of what I might have said to her."

Aidan held Delia's head against his heart, his hand playing in her graying hair. "I love you, Delia. I love your strength and your sense of right and wrong. I love how you've raised our daughter, always showing her love and compassion. Don't change now." He kissed her head as she soaked his shirtfront with her tears.

"She's hurting, my love. Hurting more than we ever wanted her to." He breathed deeply into Delia's hair and closed his eyes. "If we are this upset and disappointed, imagine how Teddy must feel."

Delia gripped Aidan's arm, stroking her hand down his arm until their hands were clasped. "I've been terribly disappointed in him, Aidan. And now to realize it's my own daughter who caused this rift between them."

Aidan tugged her tighter to him. "Our place is not to judge but to support and love." Delia grumbled against his chest, and he chuckled. "I admire how fiercely you love and how loyal you are." He tilted her head back so he could gaze into her hazel eyes. "Taking sides will not help either of them, love. Not at this point."

Delia flushed and nodded. "If they don't resolve their differences soon, I can offer no promises."

He kissed her head again. "I can agree with that." He held her as she relaxed into him, gaining comfort from her embrace.

CHAPTER 22

*D*elia sat in Sophie's rear parlor, an untouched cup of tea cooling on the marbletop table in front of her. She met Sophie's disgruntled stare but remained silent.

After a resounding *harrumph*, Sophie shifted in her seat. "I can see where your daughter came by her recalcitrance," Sophie snapped. "How could you act so shamefully yesterday when you left your daughter crying in her chair?"

Delia stiffened but spoke in a calm tone. "I refuse to act like a child sitting in the principal's office. You have no right to scold me."

Sophie *thunked* her cane on the floor. "Of course I do. I know you've always wondered at the close relationship I have with your daughter and with other members of your family, but you must realize that your daughter is in distress. She needs your support."

Delia huffed out an irritated breath. "Just as you must understand that I have the right to my feelings." She blinked away tears. "I'm deeply hurt that she came to you, that she hid the details of her discord with Teddy from us and that she acted in such a foolish manner."

Sophie looked at Delia with fond amusement. "Are you telling me that you've never done anything you don't wish you could have changed? That you are happy you raised Zylphia alone for fifteen years by denying Aidan the right to even know he had a daughter?"

Delia flushed.

Sophie *harrumph*ed. "You acted as you thought you must, and Zee did the same. We all wish she would have behaved differently, but the fact remains she didn't. We must now help her and Teddy as they realize what this means for them."

Delia bit her lip as the door opened. Zylphia stood at the threshold of the room, her gaze wary as her mother had tea with Sophie. Zylphia stepped back, mumbling her apology for interrupting them when Delia leaped to her feet and tugged her into her arms. "Zee," she breathed, pulling her close and holding her tightly to her. At first Zylphia remained stiff, but, after a moment, she crumpled into her mother's arms and cried. "Shh, ... my darling daughter. Forgive me," she whispered.

She sat on the settee with Zylphia burrowed into her side. She hugged an arm around Zylphia's shoulders and crooned soft words to her as though she were a child. Delia shared an alarmed look with Sophie, who nodded. "Forgive me, Zee," Delia murmured as she pulled her daughter even closer to her side. "Forgive me."

"I understand why you'd find it hard to forgive me," Zylphia stammered out.

Delia ran a hand over her daughter's shoulder and to her wrist. "Zee, you must learn to forgive yourself." She sat in silence as Zylphia's crying jag ebbed. "I won't lie to you, Zee." She eased Zylphia away so she could meet her reddened eyes, lacking in all her customary passion and inquisitiveness. "I was very hurt by your actions. By what you did in Washington and by your failure to come to us afterward here in Boston."

Zylphia ducked her head. "I'm sorry to be a disappointment, Mother."

Delia waited long minutes until Zylphia raised her eyes, the anger in Delia's gaze causing Zylphia to flush. "You are not, nor will you ever be, a disappointment to me. I want you to understand that." She waited until Zylphia gave a tiny nod. "I asked you for forgiveness, Zee, because in all you told us yesterday, I could only think about how your actions had affected me. Not about how you were suffering. Forgive me my selfishness."

Zylphia watched her mother in confusion. "You're not selfish. You never have been."

Delia smiled with unutterable tenderness at her daughter. "You needed my compassion and love yesterday, not to feel as though I disapproved of you and your actions." She swiped away her daughter's tears. "However, none of this really matters unless you begin to forgive yourself."

Zylphia sighed and curled up on the settee, her cheek resting against the arched back and turned away from Sophie.

Sophie grumbled but rose and sat in a chair nearer the window so she could see Zylphia's expressions. "What will you do?" Sophie asked Zylphia.

"I don't know. Try to get through each day. Try not to live with such overwhelming regret." She bowed her head as she scrubbed away a few tears.

Delia frowned and watched her daughter curiously. "Do you want to return to Teddy?"

Zylphia's head shot up, and her startled gaze met her mother's. "Of course. But he doesn't want me there, and I've realized I don't want to intrude where I'm not wanted."

"Rubbish," Sophie intoned. "We never get what we want if we don't intrude and inopportune those around us. What else is our movement?" She shared a long glance with Zylphia. "If you want to return home, you have every right."

"I fear I'll prove a disappointment to you, Sophie. I simply don't have the energy for a fight right now." Zylphia closed her eyes as though in defeat.

∼

F lorence entered Sophie's rear sitting room and smiled, finding Sophie bent over her desk, writing a letter. Florence paused, imagining the dictates and advice Sophie put to parchment. "I wonder who is the lucky recipient of your wisdom."

Sophronia turned to face a smiling Florence, her silver hair tied back in an artful chignon, her light-blue dress enhancing the aquamarine blue of her eyes. "I'm glad you could come today." She set down her pen and rose to step toward the sitting area in the room. A fire burned in the grate, and she rang for tea.

After Sophronia and Florence settled, and tea had been served, Florence took a deep breath. "Well, you summoned me. I only have a few hours while the boys are at school." Florence took a sip of tea and sighed as she relaxed, momentarily free of obligations.

Sophie laughed. "You know your neighbor will watch them if you are late returning home." At Florence's nod, Sophie asked, "What news on the movement here?"

"Well, as you know, New York was successful in obtaining the vote for women last month. They managed another referendum after the debacle of 1915. I worry that it will be much harder to convince the legislature to put the issue to vote again here in Massachusetts." She pursed her lips in consternation. "The antisuffrage league is very strong and has the ear of influential lawmakers."

"*Bah*," Sophie grumbled. "We must ensure Rowena writes us a few articles when she is home for the holidays. I had no idea of her talent until she joined Zee in Washington last year."

Florence smiled. "It's the highlight of the *Suffragist* for me, reading her articles and seeing Nina's drawings." Flo paused for a moment. "Do you think she would write an article for us?"

Sophie shrugged. "We may always ask, although I imagine she looks forward to a break while she's here for Christmas and New Year's." She *thunk*ed her cane on the floor. "We must find a way to alter the president's way of thinking. Then congress will vote accordingly as it is still a Democratic majority."

Florence sighed. "I fear what may happen if the elections of 1918 do not go in his favor. Many in the movement are fearful of a resurgence in the Republican party, and its ability to gain seats, due to the president's intolerance for anyone who speaks out against the war."

Sophie nodded as though lost in thought. "The Espionage Act was severe enough. I hope he is sensible and does not attempt any more stifling legislation."

Florence sighed. "From what I hear from Clarissa and Savannah, many believe the Espionage Act isn't nearly strong enough. A man was murdered in Montana this summer, and many believe he would have been saved from death if he could have been arrested for his comments against the war and the president."

Sophie *harrumph*ed her disapproval. "Utter nonsense. We must have the ability to speak out when we believe our leaders are acting against our best wishes. Conformity has only ever led to calamity."

Florence raised an eyebrow and nodded. "I agree, although many are angered at anyone who questions the war effort."

"That sentiment will only worsen as our boys return home wounded." She raised her eyebrows. "Or not at all."

Florence shivered. "I give thanks the draft doesn't call up any of the McLeod brothers, nor Colin or Patrick or Lucas. I never thought I'd be thankful my husband was in his forties!" She shared a tremulous smile with Sophie. "Who were you writing?"

"I'm ascertaining that Carrie has seen sense and that she now believes a constitutional amendment is the only way to proceed. I would prefer if the women's groups could unite during this time to ensure that we are successful."

"Carrie and Alice can't stand each other," Florence said. "I doubt they'd combine forces now, especially because Alice believes in such bold actions that infuriate Carrie." Florence yawned behind her hand. "However, I agree. I think all groups realize an amendment is the only way to ensure enfranchisement for all." Florence closed her eyes a moment. She flushed when she relaxed and saw Sophie watching her closely.

"You must take care of yourself, Florence," Sophie murmured in her gravelly voice.

"I am. I've promised Richard that, no matter what, I will not overtax myself." She shared a long look of understanding with Sophie and then smiled in triumph.

Sophie nodded in agreement. "When is the baby due?"

"May." She laid a hand over her lower belly.

"How is Richard taking the news?"

Florence grimaced before sporting a smile. "He tries to act excited, but I think he's terrified. He's been going on and on about money lately."

Sophronia laughed. "Don't worry. His uncle will set him straight. As he always does."

Florence smiled a moment before sobering. "How is Zylphia? I heard she was staying with you for a while. Has she returned home yet?"

"If you mean, has she returned to the home she shares with her husband, no. She is napping at the moment. I believe she plans to move to her parents' home soon, as she'd like to spend Christmas with them." Sophie tapped her cane a few times on the floor without making much noise. "I worry about them."

"I can't imagine living through jail and the workhouse and then not having my husband's support. I'd be very angry and disappointed in him." Florence took a sip of tea, stilling when Sophie shook her head in agitation.

"They've each hurt the other, and they must make peace with one another. I fear they're too stubborn to find common ground."

"Perhaps Zee would benefit from time spent with the boys." She frowned as Sophie paled.

"I think not, Flo." Sophie appeared uncharacteristically uncertain for a moment before she met Florence's gaze. "She lost a baby. I fear being surrounded by your rambunctious group, and learning that you are expecting a child, could prove too much for her right now."

"Oh, poor Zee. How could Teddy abandon her like this?"

"When you are aware of all the facts, then you may decide whether or not your indignation is called for."

~

D elia walked into Aidan's office but stopped short when she saw the room's occupant. "I beg your pardon," she breathed.

Teddy looked up from a document and met her startled gaze. "Mrs. McLeod. Always a pleasure to see you."

Delia glared at him for his meaningless platitudes. "When did I become Mrs. McLeod again? And I know it hasn't been a pleasure for over a year, not since you and Zee started fighting." She sat in a chair facing him. "If I recall, you've avoided working here, intent on having my husband work in your office."

Teddy set down his pen and tapped a finger on the papers in front of him. "Having meetings in my office seemed prudent." He met her disapproving stare. "Forgive me if my presence is unsettling for you. Aidan encouraged me to work here this morning on a project with him."

Delia squinted as she studied Teddy and his feigned calm. "I know you aren't this nonchalant about the fact your wife has sought refuge at Sophronia's. Although you've never cared what Boston gossip has to say about you or your life, I can only imagine the ongoing speculation bothers you."

Teddy's jaw tensed, and he sighed. "I'm surprised you think me so vain as to care what the witless masses think about me."

"No, but I know you care when they slander Zee. For, by harming her, they harm you."

Teddy eased back in his chair, the papers forgotten in front of him. "Once, you would have been correct. Now, how she is perceived is of her own making."

Delia frowned. "Are you saying you are unconcerned that they say she is unhinged and would benefit from a stay in a mental hospital?"

Teddy shrugged. "They say that about all women who challenge a man's perceived authority and dominance in society. Zylphia will reemerge, stronger than ever, to squash any rumors and prove her competence."

Delia paled at his words. "No trace of pride was in your voice when you spoke of her just now." She pulled her shawl more tightly around her as though chilled.

"Delia, I thank you for your visit. Aidan was called away on business for Mr. Wheeler. If you prefer me to leave, I will. Otherwise I'd like to return to my work." He nodded his head in dismissal as he again focused on his papers.

Delia rose and stood still in the room a moment before slamming her hands down in front of him on the desk. She smiled at his irate glare. "Do you care that Zee is suffering at Sophie's? That, with each day away from you, a little more of her spirit, her will to fight, dies?" At Teddy's blank look, she kicked the foot of the desk. "Do you care that she terribly regrets what she did?"

Teddy closed his eyes and exhaled twice before rising. He grabbed his papers, thrusting them haphazardly into his briefcase. "I'm sorry to have invaded your husband's office. I will incommode you no longer." He grabbed his jacket hanging on the back of his chair and flung it on. "And, no, I don't care what you have to tell me about Zee. Not yet." He strode from the room, slamming the door behind him.

～

A idan glanced up from his desk at the soft knock on the door. He beamed as he beheld his nephew. "Come in, Richard. It's always a joy to see you."

Richard shook his head at his uncle. "How can you always be pleased to see me?"

Aidan settled back into his comfortable, well-worn leather chair and watched his nephew. "I find your comment curious. You know I take great joy in family."

Richard flushed. "I often bring concerns and worries that I set on your desk with the hopes you'll find a solution for me."

Aidan frowned as he settled his long fingers over his stomach. He arched an eyebrow at Richard and nodded for him to speak.

"Flo is expecting again." He appeared bilious at the words and swiped at his sweaty forehead.

"That's wonderful news, Richard. A reason to rejoice." Aidan's calm, carefully modulated voice eased the silent tension thrumming through Richard, and he relaxed back into his chair.

"I need to know you'll take care of them. That you'll support them should it be necessary."

Aidan frowned and scratched at his forehead. "Are you planning to leave us?"

"Times are precarious, Uncle," he said with a frustrated glare. "I have to ensure my family, my large family, is well provided for."

"You own three successful blacksmith shops. You earn a handsome profit on their running alone each year. Florence will never want for anything." He raised an eyebrow. "Except her husband's company."

When Richard seemed to tense further, rather than relax at his uncle's soothing words, Aidan sighed. "What's brought this on?"

"My father was forty-one when he died," he whispered.

"And you turned forty-one this summer." Aidan rubbed at his eyebrow. "There is no reason to be concerned, Richard. Your father died in a tragic fire accident. I'd hardly think you'd suffer the same fate."

"That's just it. Horrible accidents happen every day. I'm lucky I wasn't maimed working in the smithy all those years."

"Stop it," Aidan barked, causing Richard to jolt in his chair. "You cannot live your life filled with fear. For, if you do, any chance for joy will leech away until the ability to appreciate happiness will disappear." He watched his nephew. "Embrace the unknown. Savor the unexpected."

Richard sighed and rubbed at his face. "What will I do if I lose Flo?"

Aidan steepled his fingers and studied his nephew. "That's your real concern, isn't it? That you'll lose Florence in childbirth."

Richard raised tortured eyes to meet his uncle's compassionate gaze.

"No one can take away that fear, Richard."

"How did you overcome the loss?"

Aidan's gaze became introspective as he remembered his first wife, who had died in childbirth—as did their child—from a hemorrhage. "I was a ghost for months. Haunting the baby's room, imagining I heard a cry. Sequestering myself in my wife's sitting room, merely to surround myself with her scent." He closed his eyes. "Finally I realized I was alone, as alone as I'd ever been, and I buried myself in work." He opened his eyes and watched his nephew. "You'll never be alone, Richard."

Richard swallowed at the soft avowal. "In all ways that matter, I would be if she died."

Aidan sighed. "I imagine Florence is afraid too. Excited, yet fearful. Support her, spend time with her, listen to her, as you've always done. Don't drown her in your fears as this should be a joyous time." He paused and took a deep breath. "Then, if we are truly blessed, we will have a new member of the family to love in May."

Richard nodded his agreement. "Thank you, Uncle. Thank you for seeing to the heart of what truly bothered me."

Aidan smiled. "When you're giving your sons and nieces and nephews similar advice in the years to come, think of me."

CHAPTER 23

*Z*ylphia lay on her side on the chaise longue, watching as the snow fell. She felt as barren and devoid of apparent life as the trees outside. At the soft knock on her bedroom door, she ignored it, knowing the maid would enter anyway with a tray of food. She curled further into herself, huddling under her blanket. When she heard the door shut, she stiffened as footsteps roamed the room. She rolled over and froze, meeting her husband's gaze.

"Teddy! What are you doing here?" she asked, aghast.

"Visiting my wife," he murmured. He pulled the vanity stool closer to the chaise longue and gingerly sat as it creaked under his weight.

Zylphia sat up so she was propped up on the chaise with blankets pulled closely around her. Her black hair hung in clumps, and she pushed it back to hide some of her dishevelment. "Why now?"

He sat with impeccable posture in a gray suit that matched his eyes. The burgundy of his tie eased the starkness of his ensemble. He clasped his long ink-stained fingers together on his lap while he clenched his jaw a few times. The silence stretched between them. When their gazes met, she flinched to see the despair in his, matching her own.

"I had a visit from your father. He was concerned I'd yet to ascertain you were comfortable in your new home." He paused. "And then your mother lashed into me."

Zylphia flinched at his words, imparted in a cold, clipped manner. She pulled the blanket more tightly around her. "Do you care at all?" Her voice broke, and she shook her head.

Teddy leaned forward, the facade of a composed, cool businessman shattered in an instant. "Do I care that you acted recklessly and cost me my child? Do I care that you would rather live here than at our house? Do I care that I'm not even certain that child was mine?" he rasped, his eyes molten in their fury.

"Teddy," she whispered. "I ... of course it was." She shook her head in disbelief as tears poured down her cheeks. "How could you think otherwise?"

He clamped his jaw shut as though angry with himself for having revealed so much. "We'd made love one time in the past six months, Zee. Why now, when every other time hasn't led to a pregnancy?"

She shrugged, ignoring the tears that fell. "I don't know. That's part of the reason I doubted ..."

"Don't lie to me!" he roared. "You promised." He took a deep breath to calm himself. "You promised that, with any suspicion, you'd cease your activities for the good of our child."

Zylphia nodded, her chin wobbling. She raised a hand to cover her face as a wail emerged. Her other hand she held at her waist as she slid down the chaise longue, curling into herself as she sobbed.

Teddy watched her a moment before rising. He bent over her shaking form, kissed her forehead and turned away.

"No, Teddy, please," Zee sobbed. She reached for him, but he stepped away from her. As she heard his footsteps retreat from the chaise longue, her sobs intensified. Suddenly his arms were about her, and he eased her upright, cradling her against his chest as he coaxed her to walk beside him.

"Come, my darling," he whispered. He led her the short distance to the bed, where he'd pulled down the covers. He laid her on the bed, tugged off his boots, shrugged out of his coat and waistcoat and climbed in after her. He pulled her against him, holding her as her sobs slowly abated. "I've got you, my love," he murmured, kissing her nape.

When she had calmed to random hiccoughs, his hold on her remained strong. She squirmed against him until he released her enough so she could face him. He traced fingers over her tear-ravaged cheeks, her eyes red-rimmed and swollen from crying.

He leaned forward and kissed her forehead, evoking another shudder. "I'm still furious with you," he said, although his voice was warmer and held no trace of the earlier rage.

"I know." She rubbed her face against his shoulder. "But there's no one who could be angrier with me than I am." She blinked, and two more tears leaked out. "Will you ever forgive me?"

He sighed. "I don't know as I'll ever be able to fully." He leaned away to meet her hurt gaze. "I won't lie to you, Zee. This has affected me profoundly. I thought I could trust you. That faith—in you, in us— has been shaken."

"Teddy," she whispered, grabbing his injured hand and pulling it to her heart. "I love you."

He closed his eyes at her quiet avowal. "And I love you." He met her terrified gaze. "But I wonder if that's enough."

"No!" she shouted as loudly as she could amid her tears. "You will not throw me over for this. We will make it through this."

He watched her with tired, sorrow-filled eyes. "Then I fear you have more faith than I do." He ran a hand over her head, frowning at the knots in the long strands. "Look at what our relationship has done to you, Zee. I hate that loving me has led you to this point."

She pushed at him until he fell to his back, and she leaned on his chest, as though she were strong enough to hold him in place. "Loving you, being loved by you, will help me out of this horrible darkness I've descended into. Losing you would consign me to it forever. Don't ..." Her voice broke. "Don't give up on us, my love."

His melancholy smile did little to reassure her. "For now, rest in my arms," he soothed. He relaxed as she scooted to pillow her head on his shoulder.

"I will find a way for you to trust me again, Teddy. I will prove myself worthy of you," Zylphia whispered, her voice thickened with sleep.

~

Teddy wandered downstairs a few hours later, leaving a sleeping Zylphia nested in her bed. He poked his head into the cold, vacant formal sitting room before wandering down the hallway to the rear parlor. A fire warmed the sitting area, with soft lamps lit throughout.

"It's about time you decided to show your face here," Sophie barked from her chair near the fire.

Teddy jolted at her voice. "I didn't see you there." He sat in a chair across from her, meeting her perceptive, piercing gaze without flinching.

Her mouth trembled as she appeared to bite back words. "I thought you cared more for your wife's well-being than letting her languish in her misery for over a week."

Teddy heaved out a sigh. "I know you relish your role as a wise advisor, but I fear those around you will always be a disappointment."

She glared at him, her aquamarine eyes gleaming with dissatisfaction. "Don't be flippant, young man. You had every opportunity to make things right. Instead you've licked your wounds. Do you have any idea what it has been like for that poor girl, worried you'd never come here?"

"And in all of this"—he waved his arm around to indicate Zylphia sleeping upstairs—"have you given any thought to me? To how I feel? To the fact I suffered too?" He met her stormy gaze with his. "Or has all your concern been for Zylphia? I should have known you'd first champion your women friends. Us men will only be second best in your world."

"Don't take that tone with me, young man."

"I'll take whatever tone I like, Mrs. Chickering. You've failed to consider what I have suffered. What I fear." He rose. "If you are so inclined, please tell my wife she knows where to find me if she would like to talk further. I bid you good night."

"Stop right there, young man," Sophie barked, her cane *thunk*ing twice on the floor with her agitation. "I thought you knew me better than to throw such accusations my way." She glared at him as he flushed beet red. She motioned him to sit down again and waited a few moments before speaking. "I have a tendency to parse out advice to my acquaintances and friends. I like to believe those close to me seek out my counsel." She raised an eyebrow at Teddy, causing him to squirm as he had been one of those she spoke of.

"However, you are delusional if you believe I place more value on any of my friendships because the friend is a woman. It is an appalling accusation." She tapped her cane on the floor again. "When have I failed you? When have I treated you unfairly?"

"You've harbored my wife!" His flush intensified at his roar.

"If you care to recall, you threw her out." She pinned him with a stare, daring him to contradict her. "When any friend comes to me needing succor, I will offer what I can. I'm fortunate enough to have a large home and sufficient income to open my home to those in need."

She sighed, her grip on her cane's handle easing as her ire lessened. "Now stop all that nonsense and tell me what is bothering you." She sat back in her chair, her gaze eagle sharp as she studied the man in front of her. His coat and waistcoat were haphazardly buttoned, and his hair was disheveled.

"I think ..." He stared into the fire a long moment. "I believe I must petition for a divorce."

Sophie gasped and dropped her cane. It *clack*ed against the small table in front of her before bouncing on the carpet. "You can't be serious."

He rose and wandered to the mantel. He played with a few of the trinkets she had there, tracing the smooth enamel before gripping the marble mantel. "I'm dreadfully serious." He spun to face Sophie. "I hope you can see how earnest I am." When she gave a reluctant nod, he continued speaking. "I love Zee. I believe I always will. However, I fear I'll never trust her again. Not with the things that truly matter."

Sophie cleared her throat. "Do you ever consider the role you had in this debacle?"

He sat again across from her. "My obstinacy cost me my child. If I'd swallowed my pride and traveled to Washington earlier, this could have been avoided." He pinched the bridge of his nose.

Sophie harrumphed. "I don't see how. Zee has been irate with you for over a year about your unwillingness to apply for citizenship here. A trip to Washington wouldn't have made it better."

He raised sorrow-filled eyes to meet Sophronia's gaze. "I'd already decided to comply with her wish. I merely wanted her to come home to tell her the news. I never thought she'd stay away so long."

Sophie frowned. "When was the last time you saw your wife?"

"The end of August," he whispered as understanding dawned in Sophie's gaze. "She swears the baby was mine, but ..." He rose again and paced to the window.

"She should have had more than doubts by mid-November," Sophie murmured.

Teddy nodded, his head lowered as his shoulders shook. "I would have cherished any child," he gasped out. He took a deep, stuttering breath. "Forgive me."

"Ah, my dear boy, I know you would have. It does my heart good to see how much you care. And, because you care as you do, I know you aren't in your right mind when you say you are contemplating divorce." She frowned as his shoulders heaved a few more times with deep breaths.

"Do you know what it is to wonder if you've been betrayed? To know that the one you love could ... could chain herself to a cause and deem it more worthwhile than the life you dream of building with her?"

Sophie nodded sadly. "I do. I'm certain my husband fell in love with a nurse when he worked as a surgeon in the Civil War. Just as it took me many years to overcome my anger that his desire to serve in that gruesome conflict overrode my desire to have him here with me." She gave a nod of understanding to Teddy. "We all must overcome fear and doubt to learn to trust again. Those we love will fail us. It is inevitable. They are human."

She paused as she took a deep breath. "But never forget, we will fail them in equal measure. We must hope, every day, that our love is stronger than our fear."

~

Parthena played her piano in her front sitting room, swaying to the gentle music she played. She smiled to herself as she realized she had been unable to play anything but sweet music since the improvement of her relationship with Morgan. She ceased playing when she sensed someone watching her. She spun on her bench and smiled. "Zee!" she called out and stood, then neared the settee. "Come in." She nodded to the maid behind Zylphia. "Tea, please." When the door closed behind the maid, Zylphia remained near the mahogany door.

"Come. Sit by me," Parthena coaxed, patting the seat next to her on the settee.

Zylphia nodded and moved listlessly, her usual grace and vivacity missing.

"What's happened, Zee? I haven't seen you or Teddy at any of our regular entertainments, and my recent cards have gone unanswered." She paused as the maid returned with the tea tray. When they were once again alone, she ignored the tea and clasped her friend's hand.

When Zylphia remained quiet, Parthena shook her head in confusion. "Well, I'll share my news." She frowned at Zylphia's panicked gaze. "Morgan and I are traveling to Montana after the New Year to see my sister and Lucas. She is to have a baby soon, and I want her to have family around her to support her."

"A baby. I'd forgotten they were to have a baby," Zylphia said with a weak smile. "How fortunate."

Parthena frowned at Zylphia. "Yes, well, as you've traveled to Montana before, I was hoping you'd guide me in what I should bring and what to expect on the journey." She waited expectantly and glared at Zylphia as she stared into space. "Zee?" she demanded.

Zylphia jolted at Parthena's harsh tone. "Teddy and I fought when I arrived home from Washington. He's very angry with me for what happened there," Zylphia said in a flat voice as though a recitation in front of a classroom.

Parthena squeezed her friend's hand and then shook it to elicit more emotion from her. "Morgan told me that Teddy was beside himself with worry for you when we were arrested. He can't be angry with you for that. I'd think he'd be rather proud for what you attempted." She smiled with a hint of pride. "As Morgan is of me."

Zylphia raised haunted eyes to Parthena. "Aren't you ever beset by nightmares? By what we lived through?" When her friend paled and nodded, Zylphia licked her lips. "I can still hear the women near me screaming. The moaning as the hunger set in. The thuds as another was kicked for insolence. The clinking of the key against a chain as they approached to force-feed me again." She closed her eyes. "Nothing takes away those memories."

"We all have them, Zee. We all lived through similar experiences." Parthena paused and closed her eyes, sniffing the air dramatically. "I can still remember the smell of bacon, as though I can always smell it, and I'm taunted by it."

Zylphia half smiled. "I feel guilty eating it now." She shared a look of understanding with her friend.

Parthena poured two cups of tea, preparing Zee's with plenty of milk and sugar. She handed Zylphia her cup and then sipped hers with a quiet sigh of contentment. "I'll never take these simple pleasures for granted again." After she set down her cup, she studied Zylphia. "We were separated almost from the very moment we entered that horrible workhouse. What did they do to you, Zee?"

Zylphia's eyes glazed over as she became lost in her memories. "Nothing worse than they did to anyone else. A few slaps here and there. The horrible cells. And the hunger." Her voice faded away at the word *hunger*.

Parthena cocked her head to one side. "I'd think Teddy would be proud of you for sticking to your convictions."

Zylphia let out a stuttering breath. "I was pregnant, P.T. And my foolishness cost us our child." She met Parthena's horrified gaze. "And, yes, the doctor told Teddy when he met him in a bar in Washington."

"Oh my," Parthena breathed. "That's why Teddy wasn't allowed to see you at Cameron House. None of that meaningless blather about concern with reporters." At Zylphia's guilty nod, Parthena paled. "He wasn't to know."

"I don't know what he's most upset about. The fact I endangered our baby and lost it. Or the fact I didn't tell him about it."

"Oh, Lord." Parthena's eyes rounded with shock as she stared at her friend. "I can't imagine any man getting past such a … a …"

"Betrayal," Zylphia breathed. "He even doubted it was his baby." She laughed before covering her face as it turned into a sob. "Can you imagine? Things have become that dreadful between us that he would consider I'd be unfaithful."

Parthena nodded and shrugged. "You've been unforgiving in your anger toward him, Zee. I can see why he'd believe you'd do something rash. And then, when you didn't tell him, I could see why he'd have his suspicions. Men's minds don't work like ours." She picked up her teacup for a sip. "Besides, there've been plenty of rumors about you and Octavius."

Zylphia rested against the back of the settee, gripping a pillow to her chest, her teacup long forgotten on the table. "It's so ironic to me that I used to believe the worst that could befall me was Teddy refusing to change his citizenship. Now I fear he dreams of a divorce."

Parthena choked on her tea and coughed for a few moments. "You can't be serious," she said between choking fits. "He loves you, Zee. Anyone can see that."

Tears tracked down her cheeks. "He doesn't trust me. He doubts he ever will again. And he says he'll never fully forgive me." She closed her eyes in defeat. "I told him that I'd find a way to earn his trust and to prove myself worthy of his trust again, but I don't know how."

Parthena stroked her friend's forehead. "It never works, you know.

Trying to change yourself to earn someone's regard. You both end up miserable." She shared a long, commiserating glance with Zylphia. "You must recognize what you did caused harm not only to yourself but to all those who love you and trust you. Especially Teddy. And then you must show him that you are sorry." Parthena shook her head in frustration. "But you can't change who you are, Zee. You can't give up your struggle for the vote or your painting or any of it. It all makes you who you are. You'd be miserable, and so would he."

Zylphia closed her eyes and shook her head. "I don't know. I've never been more miserable than I am now. I think I'd do about anything to ensure he loves me."

∾

Rowena wandered the sparsely lit living room near the front door, her head tilted to one side as she listened to the deep voice of the butler speaking with Teddy in his office. This room had a stilted, stifled sense to it, as though decorated and forgotten. No evidence of a life lived here was found, and she swiped a finger over a tabletop, sniffing with displeasure when she discovered a thin film of dust. She spun to face Teddy as his footsteps sounded in the hallway.

"Hello, Teddy." Her smile was hesitant as she catalogued his disheveled appearance and confused expression. "I never meant to disturb you."

"It's never any trouble to see you," he said with his veneer of British charm. He waited for her to sit on a chair before sitting across from her. He grimaced. "I always forget how uncomfortable this room is."

"Why don't you have it refurbished?" She ran a hand over the red silk fabric of the chair.

"Not worth the bother." He shrugged before focusing on her, his eyes a cold steel. "I imagine you're here to see Zee." At her shrug of agreement, he sighed. "You should go to Sophie's. Last I knew, that's where she was."

Rowena paled, opening and closing her mouth a few times before

304

finding her voice. "Why would she be there, rather than at home with you?"

"That's for Zee to discuss with you, if she chooses to do so." He rose, but, rather than retreating to his office, he ambled to the fireplace and warmed his hands. "Our differences have only seemed to multiply since the last time you and I spoke."

Rowena gripped his hand and tugged him to face her, blushing when he watched her curiously. "Why would you want to be separated from her now when all you wanted when we were in Washington was to free her and reunite with her?"

Teddy shook his head. "Some betrayals are impossible to overcome."

Rowena paled and then firmed her lips, her brandy-colored eyes snapping with indignation. "You are delusional if you believe Zee has played you false. I lived with her. I know she has remained true to you!"

Teddy sighed and retook his seat. "Rowena, it's the sorry fact that, unless you are part of the marriage, you will never fully know or understands what transpires."

Rowena growled with frustration. "Of course I know that. And I don't appreciate your implication that, since I'm not married, I couldn't possibly understand." She gripped her hands together on her lap. "Whatever she's done, you have to know she loves you."

Teddy watched Rowena a moment with an expression of curious stupefaction. "Why is it that everyone believes love will be enough?"

Rowena frowned. "Because it is. It must be."

"No, Rowena. Other things are as important. Trust. Loyalty. Honor." He silenced her with a severe look.

After a moment Rowena huffed out a breath and looked around her. "So Zee is like this room then?" At Teddy's confused stare, she glared at him. "Not worth the bother?"

"That's not fair."

"Why isn't it fair? You seem as equally disinclined to alter the furnishings as you are to improve the discord in your relationship with your wife. How is that assessment not fair?"

Teddy rose and slammed his hand on the mantel. "Speak with Zee. Learn what happened. What she did and what she failed to do. And then presume to accuse me of not bothering." His low voice sent a shiver down her spine. "I have no patience for lectures I am not due, Rowena." He spun and stormed from the room.

Rowena sat for a moment in stunned silence before gathering her outer garments to journey to Sophronia's house.

CHAPTER 24

*T*eddy steepled his fingers as he watched his cousin of sorts, Richard McLeod, sitting across from him. "Are you here for investment advice? I thought your uncle handled that sort of thing for you."

"He does, but he thought I could benefit from another viewpoint. He worries that he is too conservative with his advice as he ages and thought you should look through his recommendations to ensure I wasn't missing any potential profits."

Teddy laughed as he fingered through the meticulous notes his father-in-law had sent with Richard. "If there's one thing Aidan is, it's thorough. You won't miss out on a profit. But you will most likely escape a loss." He frowned as he concentrated for a few minutes. When he focused again on Richard, he shrugged. "I would consider altering very little. It's a solid investment plan, especially considering your family situation. I wouldn't want to be too aggressive and cause hardship for you, Florence or the boys."

Richard sighed and relaxed into the chair. "Thanks. I'm nervous about ensuring that they want for nothing."

Teddy titled his head as he closed the file and stared at Richard. "Is anything amiss?" At Richard's prolonged silence, he murmured, "Are you ill?"

Richard flushed. "I know you'll think me crazy. But my father died around this age. His father didn't live to be much older. I worry I'll die soon, and I want to leave them plenty."

Teddy studied him. "Aidan's much older."

"So Flo tells me often." Richard ran a hand through his hair. "I can't shake the feeling something bad is coming. That soon we'll be surrounded by loss."

Teddy sighed, settling back into his chair with a creaking sound. "We are at war. You'll know men who are going to fight. You'll lose friends." His voice was matter-of-fact, with no sorrow in it.

Richard nodded, kicking out his long legs to one side of the desk. "I tell myself that's it, but it doesn't take away the worry."

"Be thankful you're too old for the draft." At Teddy's murmured words, Richard focused on him absently rubbing the missing stubs of his fingers.

"Yet."

Teddy's gaze zeroed in on Richard's whispered word.

Richard said, "You know as well as I do that, if the war continues, they'll have to expand the draft, and they won't take younger men. They'll take older men."

Teddy blinked his agreement. "We must hope it ends soon. Although, after over three years of insanity, it's hard to imagine anyone will see sense." He cleared his throat. "How is Florence?"

Richard flushed. "We are to have another child." He frowned when Teddy froze. "I'd hoped those around us could be happy after what we suffered last time."

"No, forgive me." Teddy's voice emerged choked, and he blinked rapidly. "I ... I'm so very happy for you. Perhaps you'll have a daughter who looks just like Florence."

Richard held his hands as in prayer. "I merely want Flo and the baby to be healthy and safe. No matter what."

Teddy was silent a long moment. "How ..." He broke off and shook his head.

"How what?"

He speared Richard with a gaze tormented by grief and disillusionment. "How did you recover from the loss?"

Richard sighed, his gaze distant a moment, then sharpening on Teddy. "Oh. Is that what happened?" He ran a hand through his ebony hair, only a few strands of gray visible. "There is no blame when something like that happens, Teddy. It's misfortune or bad luck or whatever you want to call it."

"What if something she did caused it to happen?"

Richard shook his head. "No, that's not Zee. She'd never do that. You might believe that now to help you with the pain, but you have to know that's not true. Refusing to console her and being consoled by her in turn will only multiply your misery." He sighed. "When something like that happens, you must accept there is no blame."

"I'm so angry." Teddy lowered his head to his hands for a moment. "I no longer know at whom or at what."

Richard nodded. "It's easier to have a target for your anger. For your distress." He studied Teddy, his misery clearly evident now that he no longer focused on business matters. "Has your anger brought you peace? Has it brought you anything but misery?"

Teddy huffed out a laugh. "Now you sound like Aidan." He ran a hand through his hair while surreptitiously swipe at his cheeks.

"That's a fine compliment. And I've had to listen to plenty of Aidan's advice. He's the one who counseled me after the loss of my daughter." Richard leaned forward with his elbows on his knees. "What I would say, Teddy, is that first you must reconcile yourself with the fact that something terrible befell you and Zee. It was out of your control. You both seem to cling to the illusion of control, never more so than in the past year."

He met Teddy's defiant gaze. "Then you must make peace with what happened. With Zee. With yourself."

Teddy returned home from his afternoon meeting and sequestered himself in his home office. After pouring a glass of whiskey, he sat in front of his fire, his feet stretched toward it to warm them. He attempted to take a sip from his glass, but his hands shook, and he set aside the glass rather than spill the amber liquid.

A stuttering sigh escaped as he ran a hand over his face. Unable to think about anything except what had been said during his recent meeting with Richard, he brooded as he stared into the hypnotizing flames. The recent conversations with those he trusted also played through his mind.

He took deep breaths as the anger he had clung to withered into a profound sadness. Tears trickled down his cheeks as he acknowledged all he had lost and all he stood to lose. Unable to prevent it, a sob burst forth at the image of holding his child, the tears wetting his shirtfront. When he emerged from his bout of cathartic grief, he stumbled to his feet, making his way to his desk. He ripped out a piece of paper to write a letter from his heart.

∾

My Darling Zylphia,

December 26, 1917

I've spent the last hour at my desk, with pen and paper in front of me, uncertain what to write. Afraid you no longer care to receive a letter from me.

Do you remember those letters we wrote when I was in England? I've kept each one, and they are among my most treasured possessions. For, in them, you professed your love. You declared your loyalty and desire to build a future with me. For those letters alone, and the emotions expressed within, I dared brave the Atlantic, hopeful the American truce with the Germans was more than a publicity ploy. For the dream that our love was stronger than any fear.

We've been married two years, Zee. We missed our last anniversary because you were in jail. For nearly the past entire year, we've known only conflict due to our stubborn natures. I want peace, Zee.

More than anything I want you to return home. I want a home with you. I hate that you are in Boston but not here. I know I asked you to leave. Demanded, really, that you leave. I would have said vile words that I could never have recanted. Now I must repent for my anger that thrust you away from me. However, if you so desire, I want you home. With me.

I dream of holding you in my arms again. Of the times when words are insufficient to express all we mean to each other. Of hearing you laugh. Of smelling your paints and knowing you've had a good day. Of hearing you proclaim your outrage at the latest setback for your cause.

I miss you. I think I miss you more than when I was in England. For now I know what a harmonious married life with you can be. Living without that has been worse than any wound I've ever suffered.

Your

Teddy

∿

Teddy lounged on a sofa in the sitting room of his house. The Christmas tree remained in a corner with none of the candles lit. A few presents were still under the tree, haphazardly wrapped. Two stockings hung from the mantel, backlit by the fire, with wilting sprigs of holly and dusty pinecones on the mantel. He listened as the hall clock ticked, his eyes closed as he waited for midnight to sound before heading to bed. He rubbed his eyes and sighed, muttering, "What a lonely way to ring in the New Year." When the chimes tolled the hour, he raised a hand to his eyes, swiping at a tear that leaked out.

"Happy New Year, Teddy."

He jerked to a sitting position and faced the person shrouded in darkness, standing at the doorway's threshold, and he rose. "Zee? Are you really here?" He saw her nod. "When you didn't respond to my letter, ... I thought you didn't want to return home. That you no longer wanted me."

"I just received it tonight. I've been at my parents." She cleared her throat. "Sophie forwarded it to me."

He nodded a few times, his gaze raking over her as he discerned her expression, hidden in the shadows. "Come in, Zee. Please." Unable to mask his disappointment when she refused to take his proffered hand, he closed the door behind her. After draping her coat over a chair, he watched as she sat on the edge of the settee he'd vacated at her arrival.

"Zee, I know there is much we need to discuss. Much we have yet to fully reconcile." He sat next to her but refrained from touching her. He felt her tense at his nearness. "May we take tonight and tomorrow to be together again as a couple? To celebrate the New Year?"

"Waiting to discuss our problems won't make them go away." She studiously stared into the fire, her arms wrapped around her middle.

"It might help remind us why we are together," he whispered.

She looked around the small family parlor, at the unlit tree and the pile of presents she assumed were for her and shook her head. "I have no presents for you," she whispered and bowed her head. "Some Christmas you must have had."

He knelt at her feet, his quick movements startling her. He grasped her knees to still her and to soothe her at the same time. "You're here now, Zee. I couldn't ask for anything more. I don't want anything more." He watched as she battled tears and blinked rapidly. "I know I've caused you pain, and I'm asking for you to give me time to hold you in my arms as I used to. To allow me to comfort you."

"Teddy," Zylphia croaked, as she collapsed forward into his embrace. "I don't deserve—"

"Hush," he commanded, holding her tight.

∼

A few days later, he stood in the doorway to her studio. He watched as Zylphia stared at a blank canvas, paints drying on the palette with her brush raised. He frowned as she appeared rooted in place but with no drive to create art.

"Zee?"

She shrieked at his whispered word and upended the palette onto the pristine canvas. She dropped the paintbrush, and the palette slipped from her hand to land with a thud on the sheet covering the floor. She stared at the mixed-up jumble of colors on the canvas. "That's one way to get me to start painting," she whispered.

After shutting the door behind him, Teddy approached her, perching on the arm of a plush purple velvet chair. "Why can't you paint?"

"I can't see the way I used to." She waved at the canvas. "I used to stare at it, and an image would appear, and I'd be consumed with creating that image. Now there's nothing."

He reached out for her but dropped his hand as she shivered and moved a step away from him. "It will return to you, Zee."

"Of course it will," she said, although her voice lacked all conviction. "Why are you here?" She sat in a chair across from him with a table between them.

"We need to talk. You've been back a few days." His gaze roved over her. "It doesn't seem to be doing you much good."

Zylphia curled into herself at his subtle criticism. Her raven black hair was tied in a braid down her back but was not nearly as shiny as it had been before she had been sent to the workhouse. She remained much thinner than before and had little appetite. An air of desolation clung to her that Teddy feared was impenetrable.

"Why don't you tell me what you will do? I know you desired a divorce." Zylphia maintained a lowered gaze. "Sophie told me."

Teddy ran a hand through his hair and moved to sit in the chair rather than on its arm. "Did she also tell you that she argued against such a foolish idea?"

"Why would it be foolish? You've said yourself that you fear you'll never trust me again." She swiped at her eyes and then met his concerned gaze with one of anger and despair. "I've thought and thought of all the ways I could convince you to love me again. Of how I could earn your trust. And there aren't any. I betrayed you, Teddy."

He paled at her words. "What are you saying?"

She stilled at his confused question. "I have always been true to our wedding vows. I hate that my actions gave rise to such doubt. That my stupid flirting caused gossip." She clenched and unclenched her hands together on her lap. "I acted in such a way as to cause the loss of our child." She lowered her head and sobbed, wrapping her arms around herself.

"Did anyone physically harm you when you were in the workhouse?" When she remained silent, he pushed aside the table separating them and knelt at her feet. "Did a guard hit you in your stomach?"

"No. I was slapped a few times but nothing in my belly," Zylphia whispered.

He pulled at her arms until she held them in front of her, and he grasped her hands, easing them open to stroke her palms. "I had visited a doctor friend of mine earlier that day when I wrote you that letter. He used to be interested in some of my experiments, and now I help him with his investments. He works at the Free Hospital for Women and is a specialist in pregnancies." He swallowed and took a deep breath. "He says it is impossible to know what happened because each pregnancy is unique. However, the likelihood that your hunger strike led to the loss of our baby is small. You were healthy when you went in, and you were force-fed."

Zylphia shook her head in confusion. "I don't understand what you are saying, Teddy."

"It means that, even without your stay in the workhouse, we probably would have lost the baby." His voice broke on the word *lost*, and he blinked so as not to cry. He raised a hand to swipe away the tears that coursed down her cheeks.

"You can't absolve me of this. You can't," Zylphia rasped. "I acted recklessly. With only the thought of hurting you and progressing the cause as my goals." She bit back a sob. "I gave no thought to what I put in jeopardy."

Teddy took a deep breath and exhaled it. "Zee, I can't say that I'm not upset with how you acted. You made me a promise and broke it." His gaze was unreadable. "It will take me time to rebuild my trust in you." He played with her hands, as though needing that contact with her.

"However, I know it will take you time to trust me again too. I let you down, Zee." At her instinctive denial, he let go of her hands and gripped her shoulders to prevent her from moving away. He stroked her cheek and allowed her to see the guilt and despair in his gaze. "You needed comfort, love and understanding from me, and I gave you none of it."

"Oh, Teddy," she cried as she slid from her chair and into his arms. She shook, crying as his arms pulled her tightly to him. "Hold me. I've missed you."

He kissed her hair as he rocked her and whispered in her ear. "I love you, Zee. Forgive me for losing my faith in us. For not having the strength to face what happened and for throwing you from our house."

She beat at him with her fists against his back. "I needed you! I needed you, and you abandoned me."

He choked back a sob. "I know. I focused on my belief that you had failed me when I had failed you in equal measure." He tugged her even closer, to the point she gasped for breath before he eased his hold on her. "I need you to forgive me. Please, Zee."

When her sobs quieted, she leaned against his chest, quivering from her emotional outburst. "We hurt each other, Teddy," she whispered. "I forgive you, my love." She stroked her hand over his cheek, surprised as her palm met the dampness on his cheek. "Don't cry. I won't make you sad again. I promise."

He laughed and closed his eyes. "Yes, you will. Something will occur in the next fifty years, Zee, to bring strife into our lives. Most likely within the next few months." He stroked a hand over her head, dislodging pins. "I will be saddened again, and I hope you will be there to provide succor, as you are now."

His hold on her eased as she leaned against him, and he sighed with contentment. "Having you here again in my arms, Zee, is all I need," he whispered into her ear.

~

Zylphia stood in their large living room, holding Teddy's hand as their guests arrived. He raised their clasped hands and kissed hers before leaning down to whisper into her ear, "We are having friends and family visit us, Zee. There is no reason to be anxious."

"I want everything to be perfect tonight." She squeezed his hand. "I want the rumors about us put to rest."

"There will always be rumors about us," he teased as he brushed a finger over her cheek and smiled. "Nothing is ever perfect, Zee. When we find joy in the imperfections of life, we know we will be fine." He waited until she smiled in agreement before greeting Aidan and Delia.

Just six days after Zee had reunited with Teddy, having moved back into their home, the large front room had been decorated with fresh pine boughs and holly, in celebration of Little Christmas. Red candles and evergreen-colored tablecloths enhanced the holiday feel of the adjoining dining room.

Delia kissed her daughter's pale cheek, unable to hide her concern. "I worry that you are not regaining your strength as you should after your ordeal."

"Now that I am home, I know I will fully improve." Zylphia smiled, her gaze tracking her husband's movements as he greeted Rowena and the Wheelers.

"It seems you and Teddy have made your peace," Aidan murmured, kissing her forehead.

"We have, although it will take time to completely mend our wounds." She smiled as Parthena and Rowena approached, hugging them and then moving to a corner of the room to gossip and chat. Her spirit lightened as Teddy watched them with a delighted glint to his eyes as though they were young women in a ballroom again.

Sophronia entered the parlor, her sharp gaze brightening when she saw the harmony in the room. Teddy welcomed her with a kiss to her cheek and whispered into her ear. She cackled at whatever he said and then took his proffered elbow. He led her to a comfortable chair, winking before he left to speak with Morgan and Aidan.

Soon Delia, Parthena, Rowena and Zylphia sat around Sophronia. "I hear you're to leave us soon?" Sophronia asked with a raised eyebrow in Parthena's direction.

"Yes. Morgan and I are to travel to Montana to be with my sister and her husband as they await the birth of their first child." Parthena fidgeted at Sophronia's incredulous stare. "I want my sister to have family around her at such a time."

"I'm amazed your husband has the sense to know he's won the battle," Sophie murmured.

Parthena smiled and flushed. "I believe he hopes he has but doesn't want me traveling alone."

Sophie laughed and *thunk*ed her cane. "I'll be quite interested to learn what is occurring there. I want to be informed if you hear any talk about a Mrs. Smythe."

Delia stiffened and shook her head in consternation. "She wouldn't dare try anything further."

"I fear you have too much faith in the police or in her sense of decency. That woman will do whatever she can to cause havoc in her stepchildren's lives, and I fear that little girl is far from safe from her."

The younger women frowned in confusion.

"Mrs. Smythe attempted to kidnap Patrick Sullivan's daughter in October. He's Clarissa's eldest brother. I imagine you were too busy with your concerns in Washington to stay abreast of the news in Montana." She stared pointedly at Zylphia.

Zylphia flushed. "I fear I ignored letters as we planned our next moves."

"It seems I'll have more of an adventure than merely having my husband see Lucas again," Parthena murmured.

Sophronia *harrumph*ed before cackling out a laugh. "You've always been intrepid in getting out of scrapes. I have no fear you'll do quite well while you are out there." She pierced Parthena with a fierce frown. "You must promise you will return to Boston. No more of this romantic twaddle about Montana. I will not have more of you abandoning me for that horrid place."

Zylphia laughed. "It's really rather beautiful, in an unkempt, wild way." She winked at Sophie. "Besides, you could vote there."

Sophronia fought a smile and failed, yet her eyes gleamed with pleasure at Zylphia's teasing. "As for you," Sophie nodded at Rowena, "I need you to write a conclusive article about the merits of universal suffrage that shatters any arguments the antis can throw at us."

Rowena laughed as she shook her head. "Good to know your expectations are as realistic as ever." She sighed as she met Sophronia's gaze. "I'll write an article, but it's impossible to defuse all their arguments. They'll have a meeting and come up with another preposterous reason why women shouldn't vote."

As Morgan settled near Parthena, and Aidan pulled over another chair to sit near Delia, Teddy joined their conversation. "I heard the president is to address congress in a few days. Perhaps he'll surprise you and say he's in favor of suffrage."

Zylphia snorted and shook her head. "You're delusional." She relaxed as he stroked a hand over her shoulder, leaning into his touch.

Morgan sighed, his hands crossed over his lap. "Well, something needs to change as he can't risk more women going to jail and having hunger strikes. It seems the picketing has ended for now, but I wonder how long the truce will last if the president fails to act."

Sophronia smiled as she looked at her close friends she considered family. "We will succeed. Defeat is not an option when so many are dedicated to this cause." She raised her full glass of champagne in a toast. "May we always know the joys of friendship, the love of family and the thrill of a cause to champion."

After a resounding *clink* of their glasses and a call of "Amen" from all, the room quieted, each person seemingly in deep reflection.

Parthena leaned into Morgan's side and added, "To home and hearth."

Zee nodded, grabbing Teddy's hand, murmuring, "To safe harbors."

Rowena smiled as she watched her two best friends, content and at peace with their husbands at last. "And to the mighty pen. May it end wars, both big and small."

AFTERWORD

Thank you for reading *Resilient Love*! I am hard at work on Book 8 in the series, and I can't wait to share it with you.

If you would like to receive sneak peaks, early cover reveals, and bonus stories that I write only for my newsletter subscribers, please sign up for Ramona's newsletter.

If you enjoy my novels, please consider leaving a review at the retailer you purchased my book from. Reviews help authors sell books, and they help other readers discover new authors.

AUTHOR'S NOTES

As with all historical books, a multitude of research is required to insure historical accuracy and find interesting story lines.

The dilemma facing Teddy and Zylphia regarding her citizenship was faced by thousands of women in the United States from 1907 to 1923. Even when the law changed, allowing women to keep their citizenship, the women who had been affected during that 16 year period did not have their citizenship reinstated.

The hearing that Zylphia attended after her time in jail did occur. The quotes by the representatives are actual quotes that they said to women during the hearing.

The Granite Mountain/ Speculator Mine disaster occurred in Butte on June 8, 1917. It remains the deadliest, underground, hard rock mining disaster in U.S history.

ACKNOWLEDGMENTS

No novel is written in a bubble. Thank you to everyone who consistently supports me so that I can continue to write.

Thank you to my family, who is accustomed to me disappearing for hours on end as I seek to reach my word counts. Thank you for always listening as I become excited about obscure research that I have discovered that I know is probably not that interesting!

Thank you to my friends, who are wonderful cheerleaders and always boost my spirits.

Thank you, DB, for your wonderful editing and insight into the novels.

Thank you, Jenny Q for the beautiful cover.

ABOUT THE AUTHOR

Ramona Flightner is the author of the Banished Saga novels. *Resilient Love* is her seventh novel. She lives in Montana. When she isn't writing or conducting research, you can find her fly-fishing, hiking, or spending time with family and friends.

Follow or contact me at:
www.ramonaflightner.com
ramona@ramonaflightner.com

Made in the USA
Columbia, SC
18 February 2018